J. Courtney Sullivan
The Engagements

J. Courtney Sullivan is the *New York Times* bestselling author of the novels *Commencement*, *Maine*, and *The Engagements*. *Maine* was named a Best Book of the Year by *Time* magazine and a *Washington Post* Notable Book for 2011. *The Engagements* was one of *People* magazine's Top Ten Books of 2013 and an *Irish Times* Best Book of the Year. It will be translated into seventeen languages. Her writing has also appeared in *The New York Times Book Review*, the *Chicago Tribune*, *New York* magazine, *Elle*, *Glamour*, *Allure*, *Real Simple*, and *The New York Observer*, among many others. She lives in Brooklyn, New York.

www.jcourtneysullivan.com

www.facebook.com/jcourtneysullivan

ALSO BY J. COURTNEY SULLIVAN

Maine
Commencement

"An entertaining read of emotional maturity."
—*The Guardian* (London)

"Satisfying. . . . At each stage of the game, the engagement ring has a different meaning."
—Janet Maslin, *The New York Times*

"Sullivan has written an intricate, beautifully timed novel, so delicious in its gradual unfolding that readers will want to reread it immediately to enjoy the fully realized ties."
—*Library Journal*

"An honest interpretation of the American marriage along with the true story of how the diamond ring has become so deeply integrated into society." —*The Tampa Bay Times*

"[Sullivan] threads her story with the glitter of diamonds. . . . A tale that sweeps across varied emotional landscapes."
—*Daily News*

"Sullivan pulls off the difficult task of creating distinctive voices for characters spread across the past sixty years."
—*The Wall Street Journal*

"A generously populated, multi-generational tale."
—*Chicago Tribune*

"A modern update of *The Spoils of Poynton*; elegant, assured, often moving and with a gentle moral lesson to boot." —*Kirkus Reviews* (starred review)

"At the heart of each episode lies that sparkly symbol of romantic commitments. Given a sharp and crystalline coherence by virtue of Sullivan's sometimes bold, sometimes nuanced improvisation on the resonance of the diamond engagement ring." —*Booklist*

The Engagements

The Engagements

A NOVEL

J. Courtney Sullivan

VINTAGE CONTEMPORARIES
VINTAGE BOOKS
A DIVISION OF RANDOM HOUSE LLC
NEW YORK

FIRST VINTAGE CONTEMPORARIES EDITION, MAY 2014

Copyright © 2013 by J. Courtney Sullivan

The Library of Congress has cataloged the Knopf edition as follows:
Sullivan, J. Courtney.
The engagements : a novel / by J. Courtney Sullivan. — First edition.
pages cm.
1. Women in the advertising industry—Fiction. 2. Couples—Fiction.
3. Diamonds—Fiction.
I. Title.
PS3619.U43E54 2013
813'.6—dc23   2012043874

Vintage Trade Paperback ISBN: 978-0-307-94922-6
eBook ISBN: 978-0-307-95872-3

Book design by M. Kristen Bearse

www.vintagebooks.com

Printed in the United States of America
10 9 8 7 6 5 4 3 2 1

For Kevin

And what gives diamonds their hard and remorseless beauty, really? Whether they emerge from the death of a star or the life of plankton makes no difference, for these chips from the earth are nothing more than an empty cage for our dreams—blank surfaces upon which the shifting desires of the heart could be written.

—Tom Zoellner, *The Heartless Stone*

The Engagements

We spread the word of diamonds worn by stars of screen and stage, by wives and daughters of political leaders, by any woman who can make the grocer's wife and the mechanic's sweetheart say, "I wish I had what she has."

—1948 strategy paper, N. W. Ayer and Son

1947

Frances poured the last bitter remains of the coffeepot into her cup. The small kitchen table was covered in paper: layouts, copies of confidential reports, lousy ideas she had scrapped hours ago, and good ones, already published in *Look, Vogue, The Saturday Evening Post, Life,* and *Harper's Bazaar,* to remind her that she had done it before and could do it again.

For once, the apartment building was silent. Usually, from off in some distant corner she could hear a baby crying, a couple arguing, a toilet flushing. But it was past three a.m. The revelers had long been asleep, and the milkmen weren't yet awake.

Her roommate had gone to bed around ten—at the sight of her standing there in her nightgown and curlers, Frances was overcome with professional jealousy, even though Ann was only a secretary in a law office, who would spend tomorrow the same way she spent every day, fetching coffee and taking dictation.

Frances had just finished writing the newest De Beers copy, a honeymoon series with pictures of pretty places newlyweds might go—*the rocky coast of Maine! Arizona! Paris!* And something generic for people without much money, which she labeled *By the river.*

In a way, that one was the most important of them all, since they were trying to appeal to the average Joe. A decade earlier, when De Beers first came on as a client, the agency had done a lot of surveying to find out the strength—or really the weakness—of the diamond engagement ring tradition. In those days, not many women had wanted one. It was considered just absolutely money down the drain. They'd take a washing machine or a new car, anything but an expensive diamond ring. She had helped to change all that.

The honeymoon ads read, *May your happiness last as long as your diamond.* A pretty good line, she thought.

"Time for bed, Frank," she whispered to herself, the same words her mother had whispered to her every night when she was a child.

She was just about to switch off the light when she saw the blank signature line that the art director had drawn on the layouts, which she was meant to fill in by morning.

"Rats."

Frances sat back down, lit a cigarette, and picked up a pencil.

A day earlier, Gerry Lauck, head of the New York office, had called her.

"I think we should have something that identifies this as diamond advertising," he said. "A signature line. What do you think?"

When Gerry Lauck asked what you thought, it was wise to understand that he was not actually asking. In her opinion, the man was a genius. Unpredictable and a bit gloomy at times, but perhaps all geniuses were like that.

"Yes, perfect," she said.

Gerry looked like Winston Churchill, he acted like Winston Churchill, and sometimes Frances believed he thought he *was* Winston Churchill. He even had fits of depression. The first time she had to go to New York to show him her ideas, she was scared to death. Gerry looked them over, his face giving no indication of what he thought. After several torturous minutes, he smiled and said, "Frances, you write beautifully. More important, you know how to sell."

They had liked each other ever since. Half the employees of N. W. Ayer were afraid of Gerry Lauck, or couldn't stand him. The other half thought he hung the moon, and Frances was one of them.

"The line shouldn't say anything about De Beers, of course," Gerry continued over the phone.

"Of course."

For nine years, De Beers had spent millions on ads that barely mentioned the company itself. To even name it as a distributor would be breaking the law. So the advertisements were simply for diamonds, and they were beautiful. Ayer pulled out all the stops. They couldn't show pictures of diamond jewelry in the ads, which left the art department in a pickle. In theory, Gerry had nothing to do with creative. He was a straight-up businessman and just handed out the assignments. But as an art lover, he thought to commission a series of original paintings from Lucioni, Berman, Lamotte, and Dame Laura Knight. He purchased preexisting works from some of the finest galleries in Europe for the De Beers collection, by Dalí, Picasso, and Edzard.

The resulting four-color ads showed gorgeous landscapes, cities, cathedrals. Printed on the page, just below the artist's creation, would be a box displaying illustrations of stones, ranging from half a carat to three carats, along with approximate prices for each. Gerry was the first person to create an ad campaign featuring fine art. A year or two later, everyone in the business was doing it.

"I'll need the tagline by tomorrow," Gerry said. "I'll be in to Philadelphia in the morning and then on to South Africa by late afternoon."

"Sure thing," Frances said, and then promptly forgot all about it until now, the middle of the night.

She sighed. If she hadn't been bucking all her life for the title of World's Biggest Procrastinator, maybe she'd get some sleep one of these days. She knew she had to work tonight, but still she had stayed out with her pal Dorothy Dignam until Dorothy had to catch the nine o'clock train back to Penn Station.

Dorothy started as an Ayer copywriter in the Philadelphia office in 1930, but soon after Frances came to the agency four years back, Dorothy moved to the New York office at 30 Rockefeller Center to head up the public relations department. Like Frances, De Beers was her main priority. They had publicists in Miami, Hollywood, and Paris, too, just for this one client. Dorothy had even arranged for the creation of a short film with Columbia Pictures, *The Magic Stone: Diamonds Through the Centuries*. It started playing in theaters in September 1945 and by the time the run was over, it had been seen by more than fifteen million people.

Her friend would never tell her age, but Frances guessed that Dorothy was at least a decade and a half older than she was, probably about fifty. She had been in advertising in Chicago in the last year of the First World War. She was the *Chicago Herald*'s society reporter at seventeen years old and stayed until the day Mr. Hearst moved in and moved her out. She went from there to the offices of the Contented Cow milk company as a copywriter, and later to Ayer.

Dorothy was a real hot ticket. She was something of a model for Frances. She had traveled the world for Ayer in the thirties, working in London, Paris, and Geneva for Ford, sailing to Norway and Sweden to study household electrical progress. She even made frequent visits to Hollywood, where she went to the Trocadero for dinner and saw all the stars. She once ran into Joan Crawford in Bullocks Wilshire. Dorothy bought size 16 of the dress that Joan had purchased in size 14. *Just an inexpensive black daytime frock and very useful to both of us, I'm sure* was how she had described it in a postcard she sent.

Their dinner tonight had started off as a business meeting, but after two martinis each they were laughing uproariously at a table at Bookbinder's, eating oysters and telling jokes about the fellas at work. They were endlessly amused by the things they were expected to know as women in the office. A few years ago, Dorothy started keeping a sheet of paper in the vacant drawer under her typewriter, and every question that was asked of her, she typed down.

Tonight, she had read Frances a few of the latest: "How should a woman look when her son is seventeen? Could a winter hat have a bird's nest on it? Is Macy's singular or plural? Do women ever warble in the bathtub? What's the difference between suede and buck? Does Queen Mary have a nice complexion? How many times a day do you feed a baby? Is this thing an inverted pleat?"

They had had a ball, but now Frances would have to pay the price.

She glanced at a sheet of paper, a recent strategy plan, and read, *We are dealing primarily with a problem in mass psychology. We seek to maintain and strengthen the tradition of the diamond engagement ring—to make it a psychological necessity. Target audience: some seventy million people fifteen years and over whose opinion we hope to influence in support of our objectives.*

Well, that narrowed it down nicely.

In 1938, a representative of Sir Ernest Oppenheimer, president of De Beers Consolidated Mines, wrote to Ayer to inquire whether, as he put it, "the use of propaganda in various forms" might boost the sales of diamonds in America.

The Depression had caused diamond prices to plummet around the world. Consumer interest had all but vanished. There were only half as many diamonds sold in America as there had been before the war, and the few diamond engagement rings still being purchased were inexpensive and small. De Beers had reserve stocks they couldn't possibly sell. Oppenheimer was eager to bring the diamond engagement ring to prominence in the United States, and he had it on good authority that Ayer was the best in the business, the only agency for the job. He proposed a campaign at $500,000 annually for the first three years.

What Ayer had done for De Beers was a true testament to the power of advertising. By 1941, diamond sales had increased by 55 percent. After the Second World War, the number of weddings in America soared, and diamonds went right along with them. The price of diamonds went up, too: Today, a two-carat diamond could range in price from $1,500 to $3,300. In 1939, it would have been $900 to $1,750.

They had created a whole new sort of advertising for this campaign, and other agencies had been copying it ever since. In the absence of a direct sale to be made, or a brand name to be introduced, there was only an idea: the emotional currency attached to a diamond.

De Beers produced less than they could, to keep supply low and price high. Not only did their advertising approach boost sales, it also ensured that, once sold, a diamond would never return to the marketplace. After Frances got finished pulling their heartstrings, widows or even divorcées would not want to part with their rings.

On occasion over the years, she had imagined what the Oppenheimers must look like. The peculiar particulars of their relationship stoked her imagination, making her wonder what their faces did when they saw her newest ideas. Were there raised eyebrows? Slight smiles? Exclamations?

It was unusual for her not to have met a client, but De Beers was prohibited from coming to the United States because of the cartel. The company controlled the world supply of rough diamonds, a monopoly so strong that the mere presence of its representatives in America violated the law. They operated out of Johannesburg and London. Once a year, Gerry Lauck took the ads she wrote to South Africa in a thick leather-bound book for their approval. He kept a set of golf clubs there, since it was easier than lugging them back and forth from New York.

The first time Gerry went to Johannesburg to present market research to the Oppenheimers, the small seaplane he was traveling on made a crash landing off the Island of Mozambique. He used the large mounted maps and charts he had brought along as flotation devices to get to shore. Two others on board died, and *The New York Times* ran the headline AIRLINER IS WRECKED IN SOUTHEAST AFRICA: AMERICAN ESCAPES INJURY. Gerry felt that the presentation quite literally saved his life, and perhaps for that reason, he was willing to do whatever it took for De Beers.

Her roommate let out a great snore in the next room, interrupting Frances's thoughts.

Ann was waiting on a marriage proposal from a dull accountant she had been dating for a while now. After that, Frances would be back on the hunt for a new roommate, as had tended to happen every few months or so since the war ended. Rose, Myrtle, Hildy: one by one, she had lost them all to matrimony. But she was up for a promotion at the office, so perhaps when Ann left she could finally afford to live alone.

When Frances started working at Ayer four years ago, at the age of twenty-eight, she had convinced her parents that it was time for her to move away from home and into the city. But her paycheck demanded that she get a roommate to help with the rent. She wanted a house of her own on the Main Line. Then she'd never have to worry about getting enough hot water in the shower on winter mornings, or tolerating Ann's nasally soprano as she accompanied Dinah

Shore on the radio at night. She relished and dreamed about the prospect of living alone, the same way most single girls probably dreamed about married life.

Frances ran a finger over one of her new honeymoon ads. Other women never seemed to think about what came next. They were so eager to be paired up, as if marriage was known to be full of splendor. Frances was the opposite: she could never stop thinking about it. She might go to dinner or out dancing with someone new, and have a fine time. But when she got home and climbed into bed afterward, her heart would race with fear. If she went out with him again, then they might go out again after that. Eventually, she would have to take him home to be evaluated by her parents, and vice versa. Then he would propose. And she, like all the other working girls who had married before her, would simply disappear into a life of motherhood and isolation.

Dorothy had once told her that her beau George came home from the First World War and married a butcher's daughter. She said something clever, which Frances assumed she had said before: "The blow—as keen as that from any meat ax—was considerably softened by the thought that the Women's Advertising Club still loved me."

Frances couldn't picture Dorothy with a broken heart. She was too independent, too sharp, for all that. Say this George had returned and asked for her hand and hidden her away in a nice house somewhere. Wouldn't she have been bored out of her skull in a matter of weeks?

Dorothy's father was J. B. Dignam, an advertising pioneer and newspaperman who died when she was twenty. Ever since, she had supported herself and her dear mother, too. They lived in Swarthmore, Pennsylvania, for a time, and now resided at the Hotel Parkside, a rooming house in the Gramercy section of Manhattan. Frances wasn't sure how Dorothy managed.

After five years at Ayer, you got a medal bearing the company motto: KEEPING EVERLASTINGLY AT IT BRINGS SUCCESS. Whenever Frances saw one of the medals on someone's desk, she thought to herself, *Lovely sentiment. That and some money would be nice.*

Ayer employees had a saying: *It's a great place to work if your family can afford to send you.*

Frances had grown up mostly in Philadelphia, comfortable enough but without much extravagance. The family had one servant, a girl named Alberta, who taught her how to bake pies and braid her hair. Frances's father, the son of Irish immigrants, worked as a coal yard superintendent. Her mother's people hailed from Ireland as well, but they had settled in Canada, where they did an impressive business in construction, putting up skyscrapers all over Ontario. The Pigotts were well known there, but in the States no one had heard of them. Frances's mother liked to say that to Americans, Canada may as well be Zanzibar for all they knew about what went on across the border.

Her father lost his job at the start of the Depression. They had to let Alberta go. Eventually, they moved up north to Hamilton, her mother's hometown. Frances was fifteen when they arrived. She would stay until she turned twenty, when better times brought the three of them home. Back in Pennsylvania, her parents bought Longview Farm, a sprawling place in Media, where they now raised goats and horses.

As a teenager, it had been difficult to leave her friends behind and to try to fit in with her Pigott cousins, who were accustomed to all manner of luxury. But over time, Frances came to enjoy life in Canada.

There, she and her father grew closer than ever, the two outsiders. Frances was an only child, and if her father, like most men, had wanted a boy, he never let on. He treated her like neither male nor female, just as his one and only, his darling. Anything Frances wanted to do, he thought was swell. And if she didn't like something and wanted to give it a skip, that was fine by him too. Her father had saved her from the cotillions and socials and dance lessons that were the fate of all her female cousins.

As a girl, Frances had liked to write short stories. He read every one of them, giving her his critiques.

"You're not an editor," her mother once scolded him. "You're her father. You should just say the stories are grand."

But Frances thrilled to his criticisms. They made his praise all the sweeter. And they made her feel like she was a real writer.

At sixteen, while still in high school, she got a job at a community paper in Ontario, writing a shopping column. She went out and sold the advertising and wrote the ads, too, and made forty-five dollars a week in the middle of the Depression. That had lit a fire in her—she loved writing and selling. Most of all, she loved drawing her own paycheck. Her father was proud.

Frances thought that her time in Canada had prepared her well for working at Ayer. The company president, Harry Batten, was a self-made man who liked hiring wealthy Ivy League types, with a strong tendency toward Yale. They had plenty of clients like that, too. Men with names like du Pont and Rockefeller. Frances was the only person in the copy department without a college degree, but she carried herself with as much confidence as anyone else, and no one seemed to notice the difference.

Batten was fond of boasting that Ayer had an employee from every one of the forty-eight states.

A Nordic Protestant from every state! Frances thought. *Well done you!* The agency didn't look fondly on Catholics, and Jews were out of the question. But then, every agency was like that. She kept her Catholicism to herself. She only called in sick once a year, on Ash Wednesday.

Four years at the agency had gone by in a flash, her grandmother wondering each Christmas with greater urgency than the last when Frances planned to settle down and have a family of her own. Her parents had been older than usual when they married in 1911, after meeting by chance on holiday in the Thousand Islands. Her mother was twenty-eight, her father thirty. Another four years passed before Frances was born. Her mother could still remember all the questions and concerns her older relatives had thrown at her—she had married too late, they said. She was waiting too long for children. These complaints had hurt her deeply. So for a long time, she refused to bother Frances about such things. When the window for nudging opened, it was quite short, as Frances soon turned thirty-two, apparently the age at which everyone gave up hope. Just like that, she went from perhaps only a pitiable late bloomer to a full-blown maiden lady. It was a delight to have the pressure off, really.

She worked for the most powerful advertising agency in the world. She found her job far more exciting than any man she had met in the longest. Even this— staying up until all hours, jittery with the fear of not getting it right—even this thrilled her.

The irony of her situation wasn't lost on her: she was a bachelor girl whose greatest talent so far was for convincing couples to get engaged.

When Frances joined Ayer in '43, 103 employees were at war—10 percent of the agency. The only clients they took on during that time were the Boeing Airplane Company and the U.S. Army. Advertisements for luxury goods were seen as vulgar. From June 1942 until September 1943, De Beers advertising was confined to spreading the word of the company's contribution of industrial diamonds to the war effort. After that, jewelry advertising resumed, but they had to be sensitive about it. In 1945, Frances created a new campaign, unlike anything that had ever been seen in American magazines before. The ads celebrated the weddings of real American GIs who were returning home to civilian life, and the girls they had left behind. They featured illustrations of actual ceremonies and stories about the couples. At the same time, important information was given about diamonds.

During the war, Ayer made increasing use of women. Out of necessity, they were hiring girls on, and not just in clerical jobs and the steno pool, but in executive and semi-executive roles. There was Dolores in business production, and Sally in the media department. Two women in accounts, and Dorothy in public relations, of course.

In the copy department, there were now a total of thirteen men and three women. The women were meant to provide the feminine point of view when it came to creating campaigns for products that females would buy, or at least influence the purchase of.

For De Beers, Frances's own desires were no help. Instead, she studied her coworkers and her friends and her roommates. What did they want most? Well, that was easy—they wanted marriage. What did they fear? They feared being alone. The war had only heightened both sensations. She played off of that. She tried to say that the diamond itself could prevent a tragic outcome: *The engagement diamond on her finger is bright as a tear—but not with sadness. Like her eyes it holds a promise—of cool dawns together, of life grown rich and full and tranquil. Its lovely assurance shines through all the hours of waiting, to kindle with joy and precious meaning at the beginning of their new life to be.*

Much of the time, the ads appealed to men, since they

would be the ones buying the rings. They did a lot of rather fancy advertising about gentlemen—about good taste and accomplishment, and how both ideas could be conveyed through the ring you gave your beloved, even if you didn't actually have either one.

A friend had recalled one night during the war that her beau wrote to say he was worried about what might happen to her if he didn't come home. Mortality was on his mind, and, Frances reasoned, the minds of others like him. And so she wrote, *Few men can found a city, name a new star, shatter an atom. Few build for themselves a monument so tall that future generations may point to it from far off, saying, "Look, that was our father. There is his name. That was his lifework." Diamonds are the most imperishable record a man may leave of his personal life.*

It was all very dark and heavy-handed. Gerry Lauck thought it was brilliant.

Frances closed her eyes for a moment. She should sleep some, or else she'd look a fright at the morning meeting. But what to do about the signature line? She arranged a handful of magazines in the shape of a fan on the floor, all open to her ads.

In *Vogue: Your diamonds glow with loveliness at every wearing. Theirs is a timeless charm transcending every change in fashion.*

In *Collier's: Wear your diamonds as the night wears its stars, ever and always . . . for their beauty is as timeless.*

In *Life: In the engagement diamond on her finger, the memories will shine forever.*

She had clearly long been surfeited by this idea of permanence. She closed her eyes and said, "Dear God, send me a line."

Frances scribbled something on a scrap of paper, taking it to bed with her and placing it on the nightstand. She lay down fully dressed, without getting under the covers, and fell into a deep, dreamless sleep.

Three hours later, she woke to the alarm and looked first thing at the words she had written: *A Diamond Is Forever*.

She thought it would do just fine.

As her feet hit the cold hardwood, she heard Ann in the hallway making for the bathroom. In her roommate's case, the engagement couldn't come soon enough.

Frances quickly ate her breakfast and showered. She put on a long-sleeved brown dress, not bothering to check her reflection in the mirror. It was usually something of a disappointment to her anyway: her flat, wide cheeks, her goofy grin. She had been out on dates with men who called her pretty, but she knew the facts. She towered over half the boys at the office. She was all wrong for a woman in this day and age, when the gentler sex was supposed to be demure, quiet, and pocket-sized.

She rode the train downtown, clutching the slip of paper from the previous night. When she reached Washington Square, she hurried toward the Ayer building. She was dangerously close to being late.

In 1934, when the rest of the world was flat broke, N. W. Ayer and Son had enough cash to build their thirteen-story headquarters, directly across from the old statehouse. It was a magnificent structure, made of Indiana limestone, in the Art Moderne style.

She had been so proud the first time her father visited for lunch and whistled under his breath, "Wow, Mary Frances. That's really something." He only used her first name when he wanted to emphasize his point.

Now she opened the building's big brass door, so heavy that in the slightest breeze you could barely get it to budge an inch. The lobby walls were lined with marble. Classic, yet not at all fussy or ostentatious. Much like Ayer itself.

The middle-aged greeter sat behind an oak desk just inside the doors.

"Good morning, ma'am," she said.

"Good morning."

Frances waited for the elevator, willing it to come.

Finally, the doors opened, and there stood the blond elevator operator in her crisp uniform and white gloves.

"Tenth floor?" she asked, as she did every morning.

Frances nodded.

There was a strange sense of pride that came from a small moment like this—someone you didn't know anything at all about knew something particular about you. It still gave her a thrill that she could tell any taxi driver in Philadelphia to take her to the Ayer building and they would know exactly where to go.

She got off the elevator and stopped at the typing pool in the middle of the floor. The wooden box that the stenographer, Alice Fairweather, and her four underlings worked in gave the impression that they were barnyard animals who needed to be penned. Frances always felt a bit silly talking to them over the low wall.

"Morning, Miss Gerety," Alice said. "What have you got for us today?"

Frances handed over the honeymoon copy. "I'll need it before the meeting."

"Certainly."

It would be returned to her in perfect shape before it moved along to the art department downstairs. The copy chief, Mr. George Cecil, was an absolute stickler for proper English. A ten-year veteran of the department had once let an ad go out with a typo. Cecil fired him the next day.

Frances was at her desk by 9:05.

The morning meeting would start at ten. Mr. Cecil would look at new lines and hand out more assignments. He was old-fashioned, buttoned up, but the execs loved him. He was considered the greatest copywriter alive, having created the lines *Down from Canada Came Tales of a Wonderful Beverage* for Canada Dry and *They Laughed When I Sat Down at the Piano but When I Started to Play!*— for Steinway, and about a hundred others.

Nora Allen two offices down was yapping into her phone at top volume. The cubicles had doors and high brown walls, but no ceilings. You couldn't see anyone if you shut your door, but you could certainly hear them.

Frances tried to read over a memo on her desk. She was tired. Someday she'd have to start keeping normal hours, but she had always come awake at bedtime. She should have worked the night shift of a newspaper.

Some coffee would have hit the spot, but Harry Batten had forbidden them from drinking it in the building after an art director spilled a cup on an original finished photo that was ready to go to publication. The ban was particularly painful given that Hills Bros. was one of their biggest clients; there were cans and cans of coffee around, just waiting to be brewed. Mr. Cecil had even coined the term *coffee break* back in the twenties as part of the company's advertising. Ironic, as there would never be a coffee break in the Ayer building as long as Batten lived.

Frances heard two voices in the hall, one of them the undeniable sound of Mr. Cecil in a foul mood.

"Who is that?" he said, irritated.

"Nora Allen, I believe," his secretary replied.

"What in God's name is she doing?"

"I think she's talking to New York, sir."

He scoffed. "Why doesn't she use the telephone?"

Frances chuckled to herself. But in the meeting, she

found that Mr. Cecil's grumpiness had now made its way to her. When she presented her line, he rose from his chair and began pacing the floor, a sure sign that he was about to rip her idea up and down.

"Why did we go to school to learn grammar if you people are going to just disregard it?" he said. "You need an adjective here. If you said *A diamond is expensive,* or *A diamond is hard,* or *A diamond can cut stone,* that might work. But this?"

Frances was about to reply when he continued, "What do you think, Chuck?"

Her eyes met Chuck McCoy's. He was a solid writer, good at his job, but certainly not the most forceful of men.

Chuck cleared his throat. "Every love affair begins with 'I'll love you forever.' That's the intention of a marriage, that it will last forever, right? I think I like it."

Frances gave him a grateful nod, just as he turned to Mr. Cecil and spat out the words, "But it isn't correct grammar, sir, you're right."

She shook her head. *Stupid sycophant.*

Frances spoke up in defense of herself. "As far as I'm concerned, the word 'is' means it exists. It's a synonym for 'exists.' But change it if you like. I'm certainly not wedded to the idea."

"No pun intended," Chuck said.

Frances rolled her eyes. "If we talk about it, I'm sure we can find something similar that will do the trick."

She considered adding, *I only gave it about three minutes' thought in the dead of night,* but stopped herself.

"Yes, let's talk about it," Mr. Cecil said.

They tossed ideas around for the next three hours. The ashtray in the center of the table filled to the brim. Frances could feel her stomach rumbling. At this point, she'd accept anything Mr. Cecil wanted if it meant she could pop out to the Automat for a cheese sandwich.

Finally, Gerry Lauck poked his head in and said, "I've got to get to the airport now, George. What's the word on the De Beers line?"

Mr. Cecil said, "Frances has come up with *A Diamond Is Forever*," in a tone that almost made it sound like he was tattling on her.

Gerry looked up at the ceiling, thinking it over.

"Let's try it," he said. "We'll show it to the client and see what they think."

"But it's not proper English," Mr. Cecil said.

Gerry shrugged. "Don't worry, George. It's not that important. It's just a way to sign the advertising for now."

Part One

1972

On the table in the front hall there rested a pile of fifty envelopes, stamped, sealed, and addressed to a P.O. box in New
Jersey. Evelyn swept them up into her hand.

"Darling, I'm off!" she called to Gerald in his study at the
back of the house.

"Safe travels!" her husband returned.

"Mailing your entry forms!"

"You're a saint!"

As she pulled the door closed, he shouted something she
couldn't make out.

Evelyn sighed and went back in.

"What was that?" she said.

Nothing. She hadn't yet grown accustomed to having him
around at nine o'clock on a Tuesday. She walked toward his
study—past the parlor, and the living room, and the formal
dining room, where she had already set the table for three
with a linen tablecloth and her mother's good china. There
was a large crystal vase in the center, which she would fill
with tall flowers later this morning. She couldn't say why
she was going to such lengths for her son. After what he had
done, she ought to just feed him a tuna fish sandwich on a
paper plate and make him eat it out on the driveway. She had
always considered her inability to make a scene one of her
worst qualities.

In the study, Gerald sat at the desk, his typewriter in front
of him, a box of envelopes leaning against his coffee cup.

"More?" she asked with a frown.

"This is for a different contest. A weeklong bicycle tour

in Tuscany sponsored by Prince Spaghetti!" His eyes lit up. He looked like a portrait of himself as a child that had once hung in his mother's sitting room.

Her husband, at sixty-six, did not get a thrill from beautiful women or fast cars, but from sweepstakes and contests of all varieties. Evelyn had always felt sorry for the eager young secretaries assigned to him at the insurance company, who probably thought they would be helping with important deals but instead spent hours on end filling out self-addressed, stamped envelopes.

Since his retirement, the hobby had turned into something of an obsession. He usually didn't win, but on the rare occasion when he did, it made him go twice as hard the next time. Gerald argued that the odds were in his favor, since most people entered a contest only every now and then (*or never*, she thought), when something they really wanted was at stake. But Gerald entered them all. In the twenty-odd years he'd been doing it, he had won just a few things, none of them very exciting: a pair of Red Sox tickets, a kayak, a hideous brown icebox that now resided in the garage, motor oil, a painting of dogs riding on a sailboat, and a lifetime supply of Kaboom breakfast cereal, which neither of them ate.

"You May Already Be a Winner . . ." How many times had she seen those words splashed across a page? Most sweepstakes dropped out of sight a few years back, when the Federal Trade Commission issued a report revealing what she had long suspected to be true: the biggest prizes seldom got awarded. These days, the few games that remained were mostly run by grocery stores and service stations as a promotional device.

There was one called Let's Go to the Races in which you picked up a free preprinted betting slip at Stop & Shop and then watched a weekly horse race on TV. If the horse on your slip won, you got the grand prize. Her husband sat before the television each Friday, clutching his ticket, so hopeful. Evelyn couldn't bring herself to mention that the races had probably been filmed long ago, and whoever had created those tickets in the grocery store knew exactly how many winners there would be.

The whole situation embarrassed her. They didn't need anything, after all. But she had come to realize that needing and winning were two entirely different things.

"A bicycle tour?" she said now. "When was the last time you rode a bicycle?"

"I'm sure I was a tot in short pants, Evie, but that's exactly the point—I'm retired! Anything is possible."

"Yes. But on the other hand, now you have to fill out all your own entry forms."

"True enough," he said. "If only I could get my wife interested in the job."

She pointed a finger at him. "Not a chance. Anyway, what were you saying? I couldn't hear you."

"I was just asking if you needed me to do anything while you're out."

Evelyn smiled. Retirement had made a new man of Gerald, though perhaps more in thought than in deed. He had never before offered to help around the house. But the few times she had taken him up on it in recent weeks, everything went pear-shaped: the dishes were washed and put away with scum all over them, the hedges were clipped to the nubs like a pack of sad poodles.

"I don't think so, but you're a dear to ask," she said.

"All the beds upstairs are made?" he asked. "Where should we put him tonight?"

Evelyn's body tensed up.

"He's not staying," she said.

"No?"

"No."

She had told her son that they would have lunch, not dinner, for this very reason.

"We have six empty bedrooms," Gerald said.

Evelyn stared at him. She had conceded many points in this battle already, but on this one she intended to remain firm. It was a good sign that Teddy was coming. She hoped it meant that he had come to his senses. But when Evelyn thought about his wife and children in the house across town, and the fact that he had abandoned them for the past five months, it felt as if someone were twisting her heart like a dishrag.

Teddy hadn't mentioned whether or not he planned to sleep at his own house tonight. If not, let him stay in a hotel.

"I'm sorry. I shouldn't have—" Gerald started.

"No, no. It's all right."

Over the phone last week, Teddy had said he wanted to see them.

"There are some things we need to discuss," he said. "And we never got a chance to celebrate Dad's retirement."

It made her sad to see how much this last part pleased Gerald. Never mind that the firm had thrown a lavish retirement party for him two months earlier and Teddy didn't bother to come up from Florida for that. Her husband always thought the best of their son, despite any and all evidence to the contrary.

Gerald believed that Teddy was coming home to make things right in his marriage. Evelyn hoped it was true, but she had her doubts. Why had Teddy said that he wanted to come alone when she suggested inviting Julie and the girls to lunch? Gerald said he probably wanted to talk it all through with the two of them before he went to his wife.

"Maybe even apologize to us," Gerald remarked.

Evelyn just nodded when he said it. She cared a great deal

about keeping the peace, at home especially. She and Gerald rarely argued, and when they did she quickly nipped it in the bud, silently reciting an Ogden Nash poem entitled "A Word to Husbands," though she thought it applied just as well to wives:

> *To keep your marriage brimming,*
> *With love in the loving cup,*
> *Whenever you're wrong, admit it;*
> *Whenever you're right, shut up.*

But these past few months with Teddy had strained things between them. Gerald made it clear that they must stand by him, no matter what, and that if they did, he would realize what he had done wrong. Evelyn had never interfered with her son's dating life when he was a young man. She had bitten her tongue on several occasions. His first girlfriend was a drinker, and together they were thrown out of nearly every barroom in Boston, usually for having screaming arguments with each other. The next one was arrested after getting into a physical fight with her own mother. Teddy had to ask Gerald for the money to bail her out of jail. But then he married Julie, a wonderful girl, and they had two beautiful daughters.

Up until then, Evelyn's biggest regret in life had been that she was only able to have one child. She would have adopted five more if Gerald had let her. But when Julie came along, she felt that she at last had a daughter. They laughed together so much, and traded books and magazines. Julie asked for her recipes, and Evelyn copied them down by hand, giving her the whole collection one Christmas. The ten years since her son's marriage had been some of the happiest of her life. For the first time, the house felt full. They ate meals together as a family once or twice a week.

On Sundays after church, the children fed chunks of stale bread to the ducks that bobbed about at the shallow edges of the pond, as she and Julie sat on the patio drinking lemonade and chatting. Once a year, the four of them dressed up and went for tea at the Ritz. The girls brought their favorite baby dolls, and fed them sips of Earl Grey from delicate china cups.

Evelyn and Julie met as teachers at the same high school. In the beginning, she observed Julie from afar. Tall and slim, with pretty blond hair, she seemed so at ease with the students, so delighted by them. In the teachers' lounge, the male faculty members tripped all over themselves to sit next to her at lunch. Evelyn thought immediately of Teddy. This was the type of girl he should be with—someone who loved children, someone steady, with a good heart.

After a few weeks, Evelyn got up the courage to talk to her. Her stomach fluttered with nerves, as if she herself were the one with the crush. She learned that Julie had moved east from Oregon three months earlier and knew few people in the area. She was the oldest of four siblings. Her parents were academics who had settled on a working cherry farm sometime in the fifties.

Evelyn told her best friend about her plan. Ruth Dykema taught freshman algebra and always spoke her mind.

"Careful there," she said. "Matchmaking can sometimes backfire on a girl."

Evelyn tried not to feel hurt, or to wonder whether her friend's warning had to do with her son's unsuitability. But Ruthie was so close with her own devoted son that it stung all the more.

Truly, Evelyn was thinking of Julie's best interest too. In those days, if a woman wasn't married by her mid-twenties, she would probably never get married. Julie was twenty-three.

"You must come to a little party I'm throwing next week-end," Evelyn said to her at lunch the next day. She could introduce them there. She knew you couldn't force these things, but surely you could help them along a bit.

Evelyn was up all night before that party, thinking of the best way to get them talking. If Teddy could sense that the setup was premeditated, he wouldn't want anything to do with it. To her surprise and delight, they found their way to one another on the front porch the moment they both arrived. When Evelyn opened the door, there they stood, Teddy beaming in a way she hadn't seen in ages.

They began seeing each other, and six months later they got engaged. Sometimes she wondered if Teddy had told Julie about his past, or if she herself had some obligation to do so. But eventually she decided not to worry. Julie seemed to have rehabilitated him. Evelyn thought then that perhaps he was just slow to mature. She felt relief, imagining that Teddy would become the sort of man Gerald had with time. The girls were born, and she assumed that was the end of the story. No need to worry anymore. She should have been smart enough to remember that in life you could never predict what would come next.

Her older granddaughter, Melody, had first told Evelyn the news of his leaving them last spring.

"Daddy went to Naples on business and he fell in love," she said plainly, when Evelyn stopped by with tulips from the garden and found her daughter-in-law in tears at the kitchen table.

Evelyn smoothed Julie's hair, and fixed two glasses of brandy. She never drank during the day, but the situation seemed to demand it. She assured Julie that this was just a stupid mistake that Teddy would come to regret and for which he would inevitably repent.

"He called and said he's staying down in Florida for a

while," Julie said, stunned. "He said no one's ever made him feel the way this woman does. When I asked him what exactly that meant, he said she makes him feel like a man. She makes him feel free. He sounded so excited. Almost as if he thought I would be happy for him."

"He's lost his mind," Evelyn said.

She made them dinner that night, and stayed until the girls were in bed. "He'll call and apologize in the morning. I know it," she said. She wondered if he was drinking too much again. She felt like apologizing on his behalf, getting down on her knees and begging Julie to forgive him, though she knew there was no point to that.

When Evelyn got home and told Gerald the story, he only said, "What a mess."

"How could he, Gerald? What should we do about it? Should you fly down to Florida and talk some sense into him?"

She had expected him to be on her side, but Gerald shook his head with a sorrowful look. "We need to stay out of it, Evie. It's not right to be plotting with Julie. He's our son."

For a time, she ignored her husband's advice. She talked to Julie every evening, and strategized ways that they could get Teddy to come home. But eventually, Julie seemed to view her as only an extension of Teddy anyway. Now she saw her grandchildren less and less. Julie didn't even want to speak to her.

Evelyn looked at the clock on Gerald's desk. Teddy would arrive at one. That gave her just under four hours to pick up the roast, and the flowers, and the cake, to get lunch into the oven, and to change her clothes.

"I've got to go, sweetheart," she said. "I'll see you in a bit."

Gerald walked over to where she stood.

He placed his hands on her shoulders. "Whatever the day brings, we'll get through it."

She gave him a warm smile. "I know."

A few minutes later, she started the car up, feeling hopeful. She would try to focus on the positive. It wasn't her way to go borrowing trouble. A week ago, before Teddy called, she had believed that he might just never return. But soon he would be here. One day they might look back on this as a dark chapter; that was all. Men made mistakes and when they asked forgiveness, women forgave. It happened every day.

She took a moment to appreciate the crisp fall morning. The leaves were turning, and all over town the trees burst bright orange and red and gold. Evelyn had to be mindful not to stare too long when she was behind the wheel, lest she drive clear off the road.

They had been blessed with three wooded acres in Belmont Hill, a house set far back from the street, and a pond twinkling in the distance. Her entire property had welcomed autumn—the yellow leaves looked lovely set against the stately brick; the recent rainstorms had left the grass a robust shade of green, and the boys from O'Malley's Landscaping had been out to mow it two days earlier. The high lilac trees and rhododendron bushes were long past blossoming, but still green enough to show well. Years ago, she had planted perennials and a vegetable patch and her roses out back. She loved to garden. She volunteered at the Arnold Arboretum once a week, working as a school program guide and organizing an annual fund-raiser, for which she arranged tours of historic Massachusetts homes, including her own.

Evelyn placed Gerald's envelopes on the seat beside her, along with her to-do list and her purse, and then opened the windows to let in some air. A tune she recognized and quite liked played on the classical station—Dvořák's symphony *From the New World*. She turned the volume up as she drove down the long driveway and out into the street.

She stopped first at the post office, popping Gerald's envelopes into the box. These were going toward a record player. For what Gerald had spent on postage, he could practically have purchased his own, but never mind.

In the town center, she found a parking spot in front of the bookshop. She gathered up her belongings, crossed Leonard Street, and walked toward Sage's Market a few doors down. When she reached it, out stepped Bernadette Hopkins, holding the hand of a little girl in pigtails. It had been ten years. Bernadette had gained a few pounds around the middle, and she wore her hair high in a bouffant style, but her baby face had not changed a bit. Evelyn never forgot one of her students. So many of them were just marvelous about keeping in touch. Years after she'd taught them, they invited her to their weddings and sent Christmas cards by the dozens with photos of their own babies tucked inside, all of which she saved in a box up in the attic.

"Mrs. Pearsall!" Bernadette said. She turned to the girl. "Rosie, this is Mrs. Pearsall. She was my favorite teacher in high school."

"You can call me Evelyn now," she said with a smile.

"Oh no. Never. I couldn't."

Evelyn laughed. It was a common response.

"Just home for a visit?" she asked.

Bernadette nodded. "A cousin of mine in Newton had a baby."

"Where are you living these days?"

"We're in Connecticut. Darien. My husband's from there. We met in college—he was a Notre Dame guy. And I was at St. Mary's, of course." She turned again to the child. "Mrs. Pearsall wrote my letter of recommendation."

Evelyn pressed her lips together. It seemed unlikely that the girl could possibly care about a thing like that. Maybe

Bernadette had only wanted to let Evelyn know that she remembered.

"Oh, you were everyone's favorite," she continued. "Remember my friend Marjorie Price? She works in the editorial offices of *Ladies' Home Journal* in New York City now. She tells people that you're the reason she became a writer."

"I'm honored," Evelyn said. "Please give her my best. Are you in touch with many of the other girls from your class?"

She recalled Bernadette as a member of the student council, perhaps not the smartest girl in the room, but certainly one of the most enthusiastic. She had been popular, and kind to everyone, a rare combination.

"Oh sure," Bernadette said. "Wendy Rhodes and Joanne Moore are housewives like me. Each of us has a two-year-old and a four-year-old. Joyce Douglas is a dental hygienist, which is funny when you think about the fact that her brothers played hockey all those years. And I assume you heard what happened to poor Nancy Bird?"

Evelyn shook her head, though she had a hunch what was coming.

"A year and a half ago, her husband, Roy, was home on leave from Vietnam. He told her his commanding officer had assured them that all Americans would be out for good in six months. He went back, and a few weeks later he was killed."

Evelyn felt the weight of this. Poor Nancy, still so young.

"How is she?" she asked.

"She's a wreck. She has a baby boy now. She found out she was pregnant a week before Roy died."

Evelyn was startled for a moment, a function of age having turned her into a fuddy-duddy: when she was young, no one said the word *pregnant* out loud.

She made a mental note to write Nancy and see if there was anything she could do to help.

Bernadette's voice took on a breezy tone now. "When I heard you'd left Belmont High, I felt so sad for my nieces, who would never get a chance to have you in class," she said. "My sister's still living in town. Same block as my mom and dad."

For a moment, Evelyn thought to ask whether she might know Julie—they would be about the same age—but Bernadette rolled on without stopping for breath. "You look great, by the way. You always were so pretty. I remember all the boys had crushes on you, even though you were so—"

"Old?" Evelyn suggested.

"Older than us, is all," Bernadette said. "But truly, you look just the same."

They all said this, too, even though it wasn't true. Evelyn had worn the same long skirts with high-collared blouses since just after college, and she usually kept her hair up in a loose bun. It had been blond for most of her life, like Julie's and the girls', but it had recently turned a not unpleasant shade of silver. She was tall for a woman, five foot nine, and thin, but never skinny. She had been a swimmer all her life, and even competed when she was a student at Wellesley.

She had retired nine years ago, when her first grandchild was born, so that she'd be around to help Julie whenever she needed her. Evelyn was happy to do it, but she missed being a teacher. Her favorite day of the year was the first of September, the day she finished her summer vacation and returned to school to set up her classroom. She could still recall the sheer pleasure she took in the smell of unused chalk, the sight of the literary quotations written on construction paper, which she hung on the bulletin board each year, and the blank grade book with the names of every new student running down the edge of the page, full of promise.

She taught sophomore and junior English. Other teachers she knew would do anything to avoid children that age, but she adored them. Even the most troubled or vexing among them had something to offer if you just looked hard enough. Some teachers never wanted to get involved, but she had a passion for it.

The only child she could never reach was her own son. That was her greatest failing. It was expected that she would quit her job after marriage, as most women did, and she did quit, for a while, to be with Teddy, and to open up a job for someone else during the later years of the Depression. There was real bitterness aimed at working girls at that time, especially the ones with husbands. Most schools in the country wouldn't hire a woman anymore.

But she longed to be back in the classroom, and after Gerald returned from the war she started teaching again for the first time in more than a decade. It was uncommon for a man of her husband's station to have a working wife. But Gerald understood her better than anyone, and he knew what teaching meant to her.

The children changed as the years passed. It was strange and enlightening, being the human stopping place for all the fifteen- and sixteen-year-olds in town. The parents changed as well over time, and for the better. She understood that bad parenting came from having a bad childhood. It was just a vicious cycle. But still, she loathed the parents who were cruel, who sent their children into school with bruises on their arms and legs, without feeling so much as a hint of shame. She had never hit her son, or allowed Gerald to do so, even though everyone did it back then.

Her friend Ruthie was still teaching, and kept her abreast of all the latest changes. She had recently stopped by with a pamphlet the PTA had distributed called "How to Tell if Your Child Is a Potential Hippie and What You Can Do About It."

Evelyn thumbed through the pages of warning signs:

1. *A sudden interest in a cult, rather than an accepted religion.*
2. *The inability to sustain a personal love relationship— drawn more to "group" experiences.*
3. *A tendency to talk in vague philosophical terms, never to the point.*
4. *A demanding attitude about money but reluctance to work for it.*
5. *An intense, "far-out" interest in poetry and art.*
6. *Constant ridiculing of any form of organized government.*
7. *A righteous attitude, never admitting any personal faults.*
8. *An increasing absentee record at school.*
9. *A tendency to date only members of different races and creeds.*

The last page of the pamphlet contained a note from a psychiatrist, which Ruthie had read aloud in a bad fake accent: *"Naturally, some of these signs may be observed in perfectly normal adolescents. But it is when the majority of the traits are present that the child is on the way to becoming a 'hippie.' There are also the fairly obvious signs like shaggy hair and mod clothing. But those alone do not make a 'hippie.' Sometimes it's just a fad. There must be a great deal of dialogue— sometimes very painful dialogue—to establish a new position of belief for the young people. They will deny they're hostile until their last breath. Until that underlying hostility is brought out, the children will be keyed to rebel. Have a good understand-*

ing and be more tolerant. Adolescence is at best an extremely disturbing time."

Ruthie had laughed, but Evelyn thought of her older granddaughter, Melody, how in just a few years she would be confronted by all of it. She feared that this was the hardest time in history to be a teenager.

Bernadette's daughter was getting antsy, bouncing on the balls of her feet. "Let's go, Mama," she said.

Bernadette kept smiling, as wide and steady as a jack-o'-lantern. She ignored the child. "Are you keeping busy?" she asked.

"Oh yes," Evelyn said. "I've got two granddaughters."

In truth, she didn't have much to do these days. Before Teddy left, she picked the girls up from school twice a week, and usually watched them on Saturday nights so he and Julie could go out. She always had an activity planned—papier-mâché in the backyard, or cookie baking in the kitchen. She loved to read to them, from the same books she herself had read as a girl. She made up stories, too, and was pleased when they liked one well enough to ask for it again and again. But Julie hadn't asked her to watch them in two months. When Evelyn invited them over, Julie said they were busy and didn't have time to come.

Evelyn let the cleaning lady go, since it seemed absurd to ask someone else to scrub her bathroom and make the beds when she had all the time in the world to do it herself. Gerald's mother, God rest her soul, would have been appalled, but then she had always thought that Gerald and Evelyn acted far too common. Though they lived a certain way, Evelyn never had any interest in the Junior League or things like that, and while Gerald enjoyed the occasional round of golf, they both preferred the comforts of home to the tedium of social functions. She'd go out only if it was for one of her favorite charities, or with a select few couples from their circle whose company they enjoyed, and one Sunday a month, for lunch with Ruthie.

Since Julie had begun to keep the children away, Evelyn was alone much of the time, a sad sensation that reminded her of her own childhood in New York. She had been raised by governesses, more or less. The youngest of four children, separated from the second youngest by fifteen years. An afterthought, perhaps, or more likely just a mistake. Her father was always working. Evelyn saw him for half an hour each night while he drank his sherry; she would be whisked in by invitation and then whisked out just as quickly.

Her mother seemed slightly annoyed by her existence. She had hoped to be on to her own life by then. Evelyn could still see her now, tall and striking, ready for a suffrage lecture in a long, dark velvet dress and white gloves, a sable cape draped across her shoulders, and black boots on her feet. Atop her head, a black hat with a black ostrich plume. Perhaps her parents had been in love once, but the only time she ever saw them interact was when they were arguing.

As a child, Evelyn found comfort and friends in the pages of beloved books—mostly novels about plucky heroines who possessed great imaginations. Her favorite was *Little Women*. She must have read it fifty times. She pretended that the March sisters were her own.

These days she usually managed two books a week. She loved the Victorians, especially Dickens and Eliot. She adored Jane Austen. Her greatest indulgence was to spend an afternoon sitting by the pond, reading the poetry of W. B. Yeats or Elizabeth Barrett Browning.

When she was pregnant with Teddy, she feared that she'd give birth to a child who disliked reading. It would be like giving birth to a foreign species. Well, that was one of Teddy's strengths. He did like to read, at least as a boy. He had loved *The Secret Garden* most of all, a sign, she thought at the time, of his sweet sensitivity and empathetic nature. And he carried around that stuffed lamb, which he called Lambie Pie. He didn't understand when she wouldn't let him take it to school. He wept. He had those curls, those blond ringlets, which she could not bear to cut. When had he become so hardened?

Evelyn hadn't been listening to Bernadette.

"How old?" Bernadette asked, clearly for the second, or maybe even third, time.

"Pardon?" Evelyn asked.

"How old are the grandkids?"

"Nine and seven now. Two girls. They live here in town."

They chatted a while longer before bidding each other farewell. Evelyn stepped out of the sun, into the crowded market, and made her way to the butcher counter, where four young women stood in line. An older lady up front was taking her time, demanding to be shown each piece of meat.

"Undercut roast for eighty-nine cents a pound?" she was saying. "Well, is it any good?"

Evelyn gave a weak smile to the girl at the back of the line, and stood behind her. Gus, the butcher, waved, and she waved back. She checked her watch. Teddy's flight was supposed to have landed at Logan by now. Despite everything, she said a silent prayer that he had gotten in safe.

She began to twist her engagement ring back and forth on her finger, a nervous habit of hers. Evelyn had been wearing the ring for so long now that there was a permanent line of smooth white skin beneath the band, as if the ring provided a shield from age and dry weather, sun and wrinkles, and all.

She had never been much of a jewelry person, but her ring was the exception. She loved it. Even after four decades of marriage, she would sometimes find herself staring. It was a unique piece, with two large, round old European cut diamonds set in what was called a bypass style. The two sides of the band came up over the top of her finger, but instead of meeting to form a circle, they wrapped around the stones, like vines made up of tiny diamonds. There were three small marquise diamonds on either side, which to the careful eye resembled leaves. Most engagement rings contained one large diamond, or possibly three. But two were a rarity, and to her it made perfect sense—the two of them, herself and Gerald, set in stone for all eternity, their love strong and solid as a diamond.

Years ago, she left the ring to Julie in her will.

It was made by a jeweler in London in 1901, and came from Mrs. Pearsall's personal collection. She had wanted Evelyn to have it. The diamonds themselves went even further back than that, to at least Gerald's great-grandmother. Gerald told Evelyn she could choose a ring of her own at Tiffany's, but wanting to please her new mother-in-law, Evelyn had accepted the gift. The Pearsalls were the kind of people who believed in keeping jewels and art and furniture in the family, and she liked that about them.

"I think it suits you," Gerald said the day he gave it to her. "It's supposed to be a flower, isn't it? And look, this makes it truly yours."

He pointed to the inside of the platinum band. He had gotten it engraved with his nickname for her: EVIE.

At times, the ring had made her uncomfortable. It was beautiful, but so opulent that she was afraid to wear it to school, or in front of her students' parents. She didn't want to give the wrong impression. Of course, there was only one impression a ring like that *could* give: that she and Gerald were well-to-do. It was made for a much more delicate woman, the kind who had a staff and never made a bed or wrote on a blackboard. The stones sat so high on the band that she was forever snagging them on things, and getting fibers from her sweater or a strand of hair stuck beneath a prong.

For years after she married Gerald, the engagement ring from her first marriage hung on a chain around her neck. But on a trip to the Greek Isles when Teddy was a boy, she took the necklace off to go swimming. When she returned to her towel, it was gone. In that moment she felt as though her first husband, Nathaniel, had died all over again. People were funny about certain possessions. That ring was just a simple gold band with a tiny emerald—her birthstone—yet she had cherished it as if it were worth a million dollars.

Eventually, she reached the front of the line and paid for the six-pound rib roast she had ordered a few days earlier. Gus wrapped it in butcher paper, and placed it in a brown paper bag.

"That's usually a Sunday thing," he said, as he gave her the change. "Is it a special occasion?"

"We're retired now. Sunday, Tuesday, it makes no difference to us!" Evelyn was trying to sound jovial, but her own words struck her as depressing.

At the flower shop, she tried to cheer herself by buying dahlias, orchids, and roses, spraying forth in a bouquet almost too large for her to hold in one arm. She would have to drop off her loot at the car before heading to the bakery. She had ordered a coconut cake from Ohlin's. Usually, she would just make it herself, but she had been so conflicted about this lunch that every time she thought of it she decided something else was far more urgent—the summer clothes needed to be put away, and the winter ones taken out of storage. The windows needed a thorough cleaning.

She reached the car and placed the flowers and the roast on the backseat. On the floor, she spotted a shiny pink bow, one that she had seen her granddaughter June wear in her hair on countless occasions. Evelyn sighed and picked it up, running her fingers over the fabric, even lifting it to her nose to see if she could catch a trace of June's sweet scent. After a moment, she slipped the bow into her purse. Best not to think too much about it now.

She planned to make an avocado dip to have before lunch, since that's what all the young people seemed to like these days. And she would serve her usual cheese balls and stuffed celery, and a Waldorf salad. She was going over the ingredients in her head when she passed by the bookshop, turning her face toward the window for a glimpse at her reflection.

There, on the other side of the glass, stood Julie. Their eyes met. Evelyn smiled and went toward the door.

Julie turned away and walked to the back of the store.

Evelyn felt stung, but she pressed on, approaching Julie from behind and putting a hand on her shoulder.

"Hi."

"Evelyn, please go," she whispered.

"Julie. Darling."

Now Julie swiveled back to face her. Evelyn could see she had been crying.

"Do you know he's coming to town?" Julie demanded.

Evelyn nodded.

"And what he's asked of me?"

She cringed. "No."

"He wants a divorce."

Evelyn could feel her heart crack like a thin sheet of ice.

"There have to be grounds for it," Julie said. "Someone has to have committed adultery or desertion or be impotent or perpetually intoxicated or cruel and abusive."

Adultery, Evelyn thought, but Julie went on: "He hasn't seen his children in five months, or even called them, and when he finally does call, it's to say that his lawyer suggested the abuse approach. Apparently, it's the easiest to prove because whatever you pick, there has to have been a witness. He said they'd do me the courtesy of not making me say that I'd caught him in bed with someone. The courtesy! He wants me to get on the stand and say he gave me a black eye, punched me in the face, and threw me up against the wall. I'm supposed to have a friend or a neighbor testify that they saw the whole thing. He even suggested you might do it."

"That would be perjury," Evelyn said.

"He said people do it all the time."

She felt overcome with shame, as if she herself were to blame for what he had asked. How could her son want his own wife to lie about something so horrible? Had Evelyn really believed he was coming here to make amends? He had robbed her of her family. Robbed his children and his wife. Evelyn was aghast at his selfishness. Almost forty years old, and Teddy could not fathom that this decision was about all of them, not just him.

"Julie, this is absolutely crazy. Teddy has lost his mind."

"I'm taking the girls to Eugene to be near my parents," Julie said.

Evelyn nodded. "I think a visit would be wonderful for all of you. While we sort this out."

Her daughter-in-law looked her in the eye. She thought she could make out a faint hint of tenderness on Julie's face.

"We're leaving for good, Evelyn."

Evelyn felt like she had been struck.

"Don't leave," she said. "It's not too late. You can tell him you won't accept a divorce. He doesn't get to make all the rules."

"I know you mean well, but please. I am begging you. Go."

"But—"

"Please," Julie said again. "There are lawyers involved. I'm not supposed to talk to you."

Evelyn wanted to say that she would testify on Julie's behalf if it ever came to that. She wanted to say that later this afternoon she would convince her son to come home for good, through whatever means necessary.

Instead, she just nodded and made her way toward the door. She managed to pick up the cake at the bakery, and back the car out onto the road, but once she was driving and at a safe enough distance, she began to cry. Long, sorrowful gasps, the sound of which only made her cry more. She let herself keep going until she reached home.

1987

The thermometer by the back door read fourteen degrees.

It was five a.m. on Christmas Eve, and pitch black out in the yard. James had switched the porch light on, but he could barely see a thing. The darkness put a knot of fear in his chest, which he knew was childish, but that's how he was lately—anxious, hyper-alert. He locked the door behind him, something he hadn't bothered to do in the morning until recently. Upstairs, Sheila and the kids were still asleep.

The driveway was slicked over with a fresh sheet of ice. Two days earlier, he had thrown salt down here, and at his mother's place, but already he could tell they'd be needing more.

The dog pulled, and he choked up on the leash, since falling on his ass seemed like a less than ideal way to kick off the day.

"Slow down, buddy," he said. "Jesus, Rocky, take it easy."

The nine-year-old basset hound let out a groan, but he did as James said, slowly shuffling toward the curb. Once he got there, he took a giant piss on Sheila's holly bush at the edge of the property. The orange glow from the streetlamps brought the neighborhood into view.

They lived at the very end of a residential street, full of houses crowded in together like teeth. Their house stood on the corner lot, facing a busy intersection. Headlights shone through the downstairs windows after dark, the glare making it impossible to see the TV during the evening news and Johnny Carson. They watched in the bedroom instead, on a thirteen-inch black-and-white with a dial switch.

James turned his face up toward the sky, rolling his neck. His back ached. He rubbed the lower part of it with his fingers through his coat. He was getting too damn old to be lifting stretchers all day.

A week-old snow covered the front lawn. The weatherman predicted that another foot might fall by evening. It would probably make for a quiet workday, but when he got home tomorrow morning he'd have to shovel the steps and pathways. An old buddy of his, Dave Connelly, worked for the town and always plowed him out during a storm. Plowed his mother's driveway, too. James brought him a six-pack of Buds to repay the favor each time, leaving it on Dave's screened-in porch without a note.

Now, he watched as a guy in a van sped through a red light and into the drop-off lot of the North Quincy T station.

"Asshole," James muttered to the dog. They started walking.

There was a gas station a block away, and across from that a car dealership, a McDonald's, a Dunkin' Donuts. There was always trash on the ground, which he spent most Sunday mornings picking up while he raked the lawn, or mowed it. Chip bags and soda cans and candy bar wrappers and occasionally, to his disgust, a condom. They lived three blocks from North Quincy High School, and sometimes he thought of this as his penance for all the shit he must have dropped on the street or thrown out a car window as a teenager.

Sheila never let the kids play out front. She feared that one of them would get snatched or run over. Instead they played in the small backyard, which was surrounded by a chain-link fence and had just enough room for a painted metal swing set, a plastic sandbox in the shape of a turtle, and a blue and white statue of the Blessed Virgin Mother, which the baby referred to as "Mama's dolly."

In October, a toddler in Texas had fallen down a well. For two days, it was the only thing anyone could talk about. Patients in the back of his ambulance who were in much worse shape than Baby Jessica would express their concern for her, ask if he'd heard any updates on the radio. Now Sheila had added this to her long list of worries about the children. James tried to point out that both their boys had been born as big as Butterball turkeys, and wouldn't be able to fit even one leg inside a hole that size.

The house itself was small, half the size of the one across town that Sheila had grown up in. Gray vinyl siding. Two bedrooms and an outdated bathroom upstairs. Downstairs, a tiny kitchen, with dark maple-colored cabinets from the sixties that didn't quite close; a TV room; and a dining room where they never ate. The dining table mostly served as a halfway house for clean laundry, brought up from the basement but not yet folded and put away, stacks of mail, back issues of *TV Guide*, and a week's worth of the *Herald*, which he intended to get around to eventually.

The house didn't get much light. Even at noon, with the sun blazing outside, it was dark in every room. But Sheila was a great decorator and had her touches all over the place—stencils of rubber duckies on the bathroom walls, pirate ship wallpaper in the boys' room. He could do without her prized Cabbage Patch dolls. She had six, lined up on the sideboard in the dining room. Sheila desperately wanted a girl, but he felt strongly that two children were enough.

He was lucky he had talked her into getting Rocky when they did. She never would have let him get a dog after the kids were born. James walked Rocky every morning, and every night when he wasn't working. Even while freezing his nuts off, like now, he enjoyed this part of the day more than any other. In nice weather, on his days off, he took the dog to Wollaston Beach and let him run. But in winter, they were both content to walk a few blocks and get the fuck back inside.

They turned up Holmes Street. There were Christmas lights on some of the two-family houses—Sheila thought the white ones were the classiest, so that's what he hung. Their neighbors on one side had rainbow-colored lights, and their neighbors on the other had blue. Blue were the tackiest, according to Sheila. In fourteen years of marriage, he had never told her that as a kid he had dreamed of living in a house with blue Christmas lights.

He grew up about a mile away, on a slightly better block than this one, in a little bungalow where his mother still lived. His in-laws, Linda and Tom, still lived in Sheila's childhood home too, a big old house right on the ocean in Squantum. Linda and Tom helped out a lot with the kids. They were ten years older than his mother, but they seemed decades younger. They went out on their sailboat every Saturday in summertime, and had friends over for sunset cocktails on the patio. Sometimes, seeing them this way, James thought of his own mother cooped up alone in her house, smoking cigarettes in front of the television set, and had the urge to punch a wall.

He knew they thought Sheila could've done better. Maybe this would bother him more if he didn't happen to agree. Once, he had overheard Tom say to her, "Should've married the lawyer when you had the chance."

Joking! Just joking, of course, Sheila said later when he confronted her about it. Sure.

On the whole, they were good people. But Tom, who had his own contracting business, was always trying to tell him what to do—over the years, he'd offered James work, and money. A month ago, glancing up at a flaky patch on James's kitchen ceiling, he'd said, "That's not just cosmetic, Jimmy. What you've got there is a leak from the upstairs bathroom.

Best not to let it linger too long." As if James didn't know it was a goddamn leak. As if he'd just been waiting for some-one to tell him, so he could call the plumber right away and fork over a week's pay.

Last week Tom had asked, "Do you need some help with the kids' Christmas presents?" James got offended and quickly answered no, but in truth, he was strapped—they had had to put half the gifts on a credit card they'd probably never pay off, and the other half on layaway.

Sheila thought the boys could learn to do without some-times, but he said no, especially not at Christmas. James could still remember when he was eight and spotted a J. C. Hig-gins bike for sale at Sears when his mother took him shop-ping for back-to-school clothes. He wanted it bad, dreamed of it for months, but it cost $39.95 and he knew his mother didn't have the money, so he never once mentioned it. He told some department-store Santa in downtown Boston, just in case, but he knew the bike wouldn't be there on Christ-mas morning. Instead, he got a toy tractor that sparked, made for a much younger kid. James pretended to love the thing for his mother's sake, laying it on thick, even bringing the tractor to bed with him at night. When he thought about it now, it wasn't the fact of not getting the bike that upset him. It was his own awareness that he shouldn't even wish for a present like that. He wanted his boys to wish. It wasn't their fault that he was so lousy with money you'd think he was making a concerted effort to be broke.

They bought the house at the worst possible moment, right after Parker was born. A few years earlier, it might have cost half as much, but by the time they had the money for a down payment, inflation was at its worst, home prices had skyrocketed all over the country, and the best interest rate they could get was 14 percent. Their first year in the house, when money was so tight they were eating cereal for supper, they discovered mold all over the basement. James was an idiot kid about these things—they'd gotten the place inspected, done everything right, so it shocked him that it was his responsibility to fix it.

This was the dream: to have a house of your own, to fill it with furniture and paint the shutters whatever color you chose. But a fine-looking house could conceal so many horrors. It seemed they spent half their lives just trying to hold it together. Since the mold incident, there was some new problem every few months: The gutters needed to be fixed. The chimney got clogged. Parker cracked the porcelain sink in the kitchen and the whole counter had to be replaced. A tree fell through the garage roof during Hurricane Gloria.

Sheila's parents had loaned them the money for the mold removal. She said they probably didn't expect to be paid back, but James couldn't stand being indebted to his father-in-law. He saved enough cash to repay Tom by putting a lot of other things on a credit card—groceries and furniture and gasoline and clothing for the baby, everything he could. After a lifetime of scrimping, the way his mother had, it felt exhilarating to find this new approach to their expenses. They weren't totally out of control; they didn't go to Florida on the Visa, or buy a pool table for the basement, the way a lot of their friends did. They only used the card when they needed it. But increasingly that seemed to be all the time.

In '84, when he lost his job with the fire department in Lynn and was out of work for a year, they just kept spending like they normally would, putting everything on the plastic. They refinanced the house. He tried to make up for it by letting Dave Connelly talk him into betting what little cash he did have at the track, and on a few Pats games. Dave assured him it was easy money, and for a while they just kept coming out ahead. But in the end James lost it all. When his mother got sick, her savings vanished within six months. They had had to cover some of her medical bills. They still helped her out sometimes, even though they couldn't afford to. He knew it was his own fault, all the debt they'd racked up. Bad decisions combined with shitty luck. At first, they had only done it to survive, to help themselves out of a hole. He didn't understand that he was just digging them deeper until it was too late.

They had stopped answering the phone in the evenings. It was usually a creditor. Pressure hung in the air around them, knowing how much they still owed and how unlikely they'd be to pay it back anytime soon. Twice that fall the electricity had been shut off. They told the kids that they were playing a wilderness game—candles at the dinner table, bedtime stories read under a flashlight. Of course, after that Parker wanted them to live in darkness every night.

When they fought, it was usually about money. Sheila did all right; the nursing shortage meant that Boston hospitals were paying a fortune, recruiting women from as far away as Ireland. But his salary was a joke. He would have given anything for it to be the reverse, even though they would have ended up with the same amount of money.

They said horrible things to one another, unforgivable things, but they always forgave. He felt like he knew her completely, better than anyone else, but once in a while she'd say something that made him wonder if he had somehow misinterpreted his own life. She said he wasn't the man she had married anymore, that he was too sad, too angry. She called him violent, though he hadn't been in a fight for sixteen years. She said that didn't matter, that a person could be violent without ever throwing a punch.

He felt like shit after they argued, and so did she. But the smallest thing could get them started. His in-laws prided themselves on never going to bed angry—they had written this down under the heading "Golden Rule of Marriage!" in a card they gave Sheila on their wedding day. But how the hell could two people make that promise? It made James wonder if Tom and Linda had never faced any kind of hardship, or if they just didn't care that much about one another to begin with.

They tried not to argue in front of the boys. Everyone said that was the worst thing parents could do. But it wasn't exactly like they planned their fights in advance—*Every Wednesday at seven, let's rip each other's guts out while the kids are at Little League!* Their worst fights usually took him by surprise, often coming after a moment of calm: a great family dinner, or a trip to the movies.

She had been pissed for weeks that he agreed to work Christmas Eve, but he thought they both knew it was settled. His boss had offered to pay double, and he couldn't turn that down.

Then, a few days back, they were having a nice Sunday breakfast. She had made bacon and eggs and they were laughing about something or another, when all of a sudden, out of the clear blue, she brought it up again. She felt angry that he'd leave them on a holiday like that. He couldn't believe she didn't understand why he had to do it, or how little he wanted to.

"These are supposed to be the happy years," she said. "Why do they feel so shitty?"

"I don't know, honey, why don't you tell me? I'm sure it's all my fault."

"Oh yeah, go ahead and play the victim. You do it so well."

"I learned from the best."

James didn't realize they were screaming at each other until Parker put his hands over his ears and said, "Please, you guys. I don't know whose side I'm supposed to be on."

That had just about killed him.

If he had it to do over again, he would have put his foot down on naming the kid Parker. James had wanted to name him Bird, as in Larry, who scored the most points of any Celtic in 1980, the year his first son was born. Sheila said the mere suggestion of that would be grounds for divorce in some women's books. He let her have her way, since she had been through hell trying to get pregnant. Sheila miscarried six times before Parker came along. They had been married seven years by then, and everyone had started to look at them funny, as if there were no earthly reason to be married if you weren't going to have kids.

Now, inexplicably, in what seemed like a minute, Parker was seven years old. The baby, Danny, was already two.

James stopped outside Pat Flaherty's house while the dog sniffed at a patch of grass poking through the snow. There were no Christmas lights on the bushes, and no cars parked out front. Pat's wife had left him one Sunday after dinner, announcing her affair with the local parish priest as she served the apple pie. Dave Connelly said she had taken the poor bastard to the cleaners.

"She'd have to, if she'll be living off a priest's salary now," James had joked, but he was thinking of Sheila, of whether she might someday just up and go, too. At eighteen, he had gotten her name tattooed on his right arm. They got married when they were twenty-one. Sometimes, especially lately, he wondered if she'd make the same choice again today.

A new FOR SALE BY OWNER sign hung on Pat Flaherty's lawn. James didn't know where he had gone—was Pat staying at his mother's in Wollaston? Thirty-four years old and having to start from scratch? The thought of it was depressing as hell.

He'd hear all the details soon enough. His buddies from

high school were as gossipy as a bunch of old ladies. Connelly, O'Neil, and Big Boy were all married with kids. He watched Pats games with them at someone's house every few weeks, or sometimes at Dee Dee's bar while his mom sat with the boys. There were a few guys in town from the old days who he avoided: troublemakers, drunks, who still broke the law and got into fights like they were seventeen years old. And then there were the ones who had gone to college, who he saw only once a year, the night before Thanksgiving, when everyone from their North Quincy High days went to Dee Dee's and got shitfaced. He burned with embarrassment when he had to tell yet another one of them that yes, he still lived in town. He had always talked such a big game about his plans.

James heard a clanging sound behind him now and turned to see Doris Mulcahey dragging two metal trash cans to the curb.

"Lemme help you," he said, crossing the street toward her.

"I'm okay," she said cautiously. She squinted in the dim morning light. "Is that Jimmy McKeen?"

He hated the sound of his own name. In school, they called him Jimmy. When he started working, he tried to go by James. Some people respected this—his partner, Maurice, and Sheila, when she remembered to. But his mother and brother and old friends and everyone else all kept calling him Jimmy, and there was nothing he could do to stop them.

"Hi, Mrs. Mulcahey."

She had been on a bowling team with his mother for years. Hardly any of those bitches had visited her since she got sick, and this made him hate every last one of them.

"How's your mum feeling?" she said.

He nodded. "Pretty good."

"She's a tough cookie, God love her. Tell her I say Merry Christmas. I've been meaning to pay her a visit."

"Sure will."

"And your boys? Are they getting excited for tomorrow?"

"They've been counting down the days since Halloween," he said. He dug his toe into the sidewalk. He felt like a kid, eager to escape her.

But then she whispered, as if there were anyone there to hear it, "How's poor Sheila?"

So she knew. All of North Quincy probably did.

"She's fine," he said, making each word as small and tight as he could, as if to indicate that there would be no further conversation.

"You ready to turn back, bud?" he said to the dog. Rocky looked up at him with those big, brown eyes that could melt you. "Yeah, you want your breakfast. Me too. Take care, Mrs. Mulcahey."

"Merry Christmas, Jimmy."

They walked the five minutes home in silence. James could see his breath. Whenever he thought about what had happened, he felt as if he were wound so tight that he was just half an inch away from brutality—like if someone were to accidentally brush up against him or call him a name, he might rip the guy's head right off his body, then stand there and watch him die.

A month ago, Sheila got mugged coming back from the grocery store. Some cowardly fucker with a knife took everything she had: her watch, her wedding band and engagement ring, her pocketbook, even the goddamn diaper bag. When he got home an hour later, James found her sobbing at the kitchen table while the kids were in the other room with the TV turned up loud. He had heard the TV first, made a joke about it before he saw her face.

The baby saw it all. Two years old and he'd had to watch some piece of shit hold a knife to his mother's throat. The guy had choked her. Two days after it happened, dark bruises appeared all over her neck. Seeing them, James went into the bathroom and cried into his hands.

It was his fault. Her car was in the shop, and he was supposed to get home at eight a.m. sharp to drive to the market before she had to leave for work at nine. But he was late. His partner Maurice came down with something, so James sent him home, saying he'd take care of the cleanup for the day. It took twice as long as usual—there had been a construction accident in Kendall Square, and there was blood splatter all over the back of the ambulance. Leaving it there would mean a steep fine, which he couldn't afford. So he scrubbed as fast as he could, feeling the minutes tick by, knowing from experience that she'd be pissed.

Sheila had waited until eight-fifteen and then decided that she couldn't wait any longer. She needed to pack something for Parker's lunch and get milk for Danny. She took the baby out and left Parker home alone for the first time. Worried about him, she rushed through her shopping and took a shortcut back through an alley off of Hancock Street, and that's where the prick came up from behind and grabbed her so hard he knocked the wind out of her.

James called the brother of a buddy of his, who was with the police department. The guy sent a couple of officers over to the house to take a statement, but James could tell it was mostly just a formality, an attempt to make them feel as if they had some control over the situation. When the cops left, he went into a rage, telling Sheila exactly what he'd do to that kid once he found him—it wouldn't be enough to torture him. You had to hit the bastard where it hurt; tie him to a chair, and then stab his grandmother, his mother, his children, to death, right in front of him. Let him watch them suffer, let him know real fear. Then let him live with it for the rest of his life.

Sheila had looked up through tears. "Oh, what's the point of saying any of that shit? You weren't there."

Ever since, he hadn't been able to sleep. He wasn't a good sleeper to begin with, and now, even though he was usually bone tired when he got into bed, as soon as his head hit the pillow his heart began to pound, and he was suddenly wide awake. James would force himself to close his eyes. For the next few hours, he'd lie there, thrashing around, trying to get comfortable. By morning, it was impossible to know if he had slept at all. He never felt rested. All day, he dreamed of sleep. He was dizzy, unfocused. But then he'd finally reach his bed, and the cycle would begin again.

Sheila had been having nightmares. She insisted that he check the locks two or three times every night. She wanted them to move. She was worried about the kids, and about James's mother living on her own in what Sheila had now decided was a bad neighborhood. He felt defensive of the street he'd grown up on, even as he knew his wife was coming from a good place. His mother had moved in with them for a while after her stroke two years back. Sheila had a newborn to care for, but she nursed his mother back to life like it was nothing; she did reading exercises and physical therapy with her, practicing the right way to hold a hairbrush and walk down the stairs. She gave his mother sponge baths and painted her toenails, without so much as a single complaint.

James wished there were some way to start over. The mugging had broken something in him, some part that was already dangling, not firmly in place to begin with. Everything he had suspected about himself had proven true. He had failed to protect his own family. And now that it was clear, there was still nothing he could do. He couldn't afford to move them someplace safer, with a big backyard and a pool. He was stuck, and they were stuck with him.

In high school, people thought of him as one of the best-looking guys in their class, even though he was never tall like his brother. Sheila told him all the time how lucky she felt that someone as handsome as him had chosen her. He remembered this electricity in the way they'd move together at CYO dances, the nuns putting a ruler between them and commanding that they leave some room for the Holy Ghost or else their mothers would be notified. James felt now like he had tricked her. Her friends, who she had felt so superior to back then, had seen their average-looking husbands grow into men with money and power, the sort of guys who took them to the Bahamas for an anniversary, or out to dinner in town every Friday night. And what did Sheila have? The formerly handsome teenager who had failed to live up to his potential.

A few months ago, they had gone to Papa Gino's for pizza one night, a rare dinner out. As the boys fiddled with the table-top jukebox, James saw her slide a coupon across the counter to the girl at the register—two medium pies for the price of one. When the girl turned to answer the phone, Sheila quickly snatched the coupon back and put it in her purse. She glanced over at him and winked, as if they had just pulled off a bank heist. His wife was proud of herself, and it made him feel like the biggest asshole to ever walk the earth.

A blind man could see what a failure he was, but rather than try to make up for it by acting like a prince, sometimes he just lashed out at her. His Irish temper, his mother called it. He would never hurt Sheila or the kids, but out of frustration he had broken things—a cracked lamp, a shattered glass, a hole in the wall. He once punched himself in the face during a fight with Sheila, gave himself a black eye. She had mocked him for that one for ages. The simple truth was that she was everything to him. If he lost her, that would be it.

Inside the house, he unhooked the dog's leash and started the coffee. He went to the cabinet to the left of the sink and pulled out the big bottle of ibuprofen. He took three, and swallowed them down without water. As he leaned his head up to do this, he could see where the paint was cracking. The spot had started out the size of a pancake but was now as big as a hula hoop. Inside the dark brown ring the ceiling had started to sag, threatening him. James looked away. He vowed not to look again until after Christmas.

He felt dead tired, staring down the prospect of his third twenty-four-hour shift this week. He would give anything to go back to bed—just crawl in beside Sheila and wrap himself around her and sleep all day. They hadn't done that in ages, not since before the kids. Sheila worked in the OR at the Brigham, three eighteens every week, on his off days. They had set it up this way for the boys, but they hardly saw each other anymore, other than Sundays.

He had never wanted her to have to work after they had children. Her mother hadn't, and her sister Debbie didn't now. Sheila never mentioned this, but he could feel the weight of it every time her sister went on about spending a Tuesday at the Y with her kids, or the fact that Sheila really ought to get more involved in the PTA.

Debbie was the bane of his existence. She had married a sleazebag named Drew who went to college at UMass Amherst and now she lived the life of Riley in a nice house in Milton. In the seventies, Drew and Debbie were disco freaks. It was one thing for a woman to get into that shit, but what self-respecting man would? To this day, James referred to Drew almost exclusively as John Travolta. He was one of those shady lawyers who advertised on TV: *Your husband died of asbestos? Call now! Your kid ate lead paint? Call now! A pit bull chewed up your grandma? . . .*

James probably hated Drew most of all because of the

way he and Debbie had met: right after high school, when James and Sheila split up for close to a year, Sheila had dated some jackass who was in law school. Drew was the jackass's best friend.

Every time they went to Debbie and Drew's for supper, James could feel them holding it all over his head: they were doing better by a landslide, they might buy a summer place soon. Sheila and Debbie were close, so they unfortunately saw a lot of each other. In his opinion, Debbie took every chance she could to rank on Sheila, though his wife said that's just how sisters were.

Sheila had gained some weight with the boys, mainly right around her stomach, and she was self-conscious about it, even though she was still as beautiful as the day he first saw her. She bought exercise videos and made fun of herself, telling the kids, "Look at Mommy—I've got an extra butt in the front." Debbie, on the other hand, worked like a maniac to stay thin. It was a job to her—aerobics class every morning, a jog in the afternoon, something called Jazzercise twice a week, to which she wore hot pink leg warmers and a black leotard, and after which she lay in a tanning booth for half an hour. Yet she complained to Sheila about her weight, which only made Sheila feel worse. Last summer, Debbie had returned from a trip to Hyannis with a gift for Sheila: a wooden wall hanging printed with a picture of a hippo in a bathing suit, teetering above the words *I Don't Skinny Dip, I Chunky Dunk.*

"Isn't it funny?" Debbie said. "I got one for me, too!"

Seeing the injured look on his wife's face, he had wanted to smack her sister, or—since he'd never hit a woman— maybe John Travolta instead.

James waited for the water to boil, then poured himself a cup of black coffee. He pulled a clean towel from a stack on the dining room table and glanced into the living room, where the Christmas tree stood, slightly tilted, in the corner. Sheila was crazy about Christmas. She had been hanging garlands everywhere and singing carols for the past month. James went out and got the tree the first morning the local nursery had them in. It was small, and they had suffocated it with gold tinsel, strands of which he kept finding in the boys' hair, in his pockets, stuck to the bottom of his shoe. Last year, they had waited until Christmas Eve to buy one, when all the trees were half off, but this year he was determined to make things special for her, whatever the cost.

He made his way up the staircase toward the shower, stopping at the door to the boys' bedroom. He peeked in at them. Their chests rose and fell rhythmically with each breath; the smell of their sleep hung in the air. Parker had four Ninja Turtles arranged in a straight line beside his head. He always instructed James to wish each turtle good night.

"Sweet dreams, Raphael," James would say, holding the plastic figurine up to the lamp before tucking it beneath the sheet and picking up another.

"Michelangelo, I know you're a party dude, but it's time for bed."

Parker laughed hysterically every time. It was so easy to make him laugh.

On his nights home alone, James fed the boys frozen fish sticks or microwaved chicken nuggets with ketchup and put them to bed around seven. He read them stories and sang to them—"Blackbird," "Norwegian Wood," all sorts of sad, dark songs that were inappropriate for kids if you really thought about it, but they didn't seem to notice the words. Afterward, he'd watch them sleep, sometimes for half an hour.

Now, through the open door across the hall, he could see Sheila turning under the covers. He took a step and the floorboards creaked beneath his feet.

Sheila's head shot up.

"It's me," he said.

"Hi, hon. I didn't hear you come up."

He went to her, sat on the edge of the bed.

"Sorry. Didn't mean to scare you."

"You didn't scare me. What time is it?"

"Almost five-thirty."

"The pants from your uniform are in the dryer," she said. "And your shirt is hanging up down the basement."

"Thanks," he said. "Weather report says a foot of snow today."

She sighed. "Jesus."

"I know."

Parker padded across the hall and into their room, blinking several times, struggling to open his eyes.

"Only one more day until Christmas, Mom!" he said. "How many hours?"

"Twenty-four. Go back to bed, honey," Sheila said. "It's too early."

"It's not too early for me," Parker said, his voice booming.

"Well, it's too early for me," she said. "Inside voices, okay? You'll wake the baby."

"It's not too early for Dad. Will you read me the funnies before you leave, Dad? I know you've got to go, but just a couple?" Parker's tone was impossibly hopeful, as if he'd asked for the moon.

"You'll be late," Sheila warned. "Parker, back to bed."

She always said James turned her into the bad cop by putting himself in the role of the fun one. But how could you deny the kid a request so sweet and small?

"Just one?" Parker pleaded. "*Family Circus?* Or *Garfield?*"

"Just one," James said, though they both knew he'd read

them all. He walked to his son and took him by the hand, leading him out into the hall and back toward the stairs.

"Are you gonna do the voices, Dad?"

"I'd say it's a pretty safe bet."

Parker beamed. "Mom isn't good at getting the voices right."

Sheila's words sailed out from the bedroom: "I heard that!"

He could almost hear her smile.

"Of course she did," James whispered.

Parker stood up tall, like he did around his older cousins. He shook his head, and said knowingly, "Of course."

Then he asked, "Dad, do you think Santa's gonna bring me the Rolly Robot?"

The Rolly Robot was the hardest toy on earth to find. Every toy store in Massachusetts said they'd be getting in a new shipment on January third. A lot of good it was going to do parents then. James and Sheila had gotten obsessed somewhere around the middle of the month. Together and separately, they had driven as far as Worcester and stopped at every store along the way, even the hardware stores, which made no sense. He finally found one wedged behind a display of back massagers at the Radio Shack in the South Shore Plaza. Maybe somebody had hidden it there, or maybe God had finally decided to cut him a break. Whatever the case, he couldn't explain the sheer joy that came over him then. He felt like he was unstoppable. Like he had just invented penicillin or something.

Parker was in the room when he got home that night and told Sheila the news. "The thing came through," he said.

"Huh?"

"I got the thing." Had he said this twenty years earlier, she would have assumed he was referring to beer or maybe a joint, but she realized what he meant, and said, "Oh wow. You're my hero."

Now he turned to Parker and said, "It probably depends on whether or not you give your mom a hard time today while I'm at work."

"I won't," Parker said earnestly.

"Then I'm thinking it's a strong possibility."

"Woohoo!" Parker shouted, as loud as his lungs could manage.

Right on cue, Danny's wail broke out through the house. Rocky slumped up the stairs and began to howl in solidarity.

"And we're off!" Sheila said. She appeared in the hall a moment later, looking like an angel, pulling on her robe.

2003

The dress was an old shirtwaist of her mother's: dark blue, with tiny light blue flowers swirling across the skirt and bodice. It had a thin leather belt, the color of a cloudless sky. Delphine thought she could remember her mother wearing it, though as with all memories of her mother, this may just have been her imagination.

Earlier that morning, she folded the dress carefully and wrapped it in tissue paper before placing it in the suitcase with the rest of her things. But then she decided to slip it on. She had lost weight these past two weeks. Even when she pulled the belt to its tightest, it fell slack across her waist.

She added the vintage Chanel heels, which she had purchased in a boutique on the rue de Passy when she was at university twenty years earlier. She had had them resoled half a dozen times since.

She wore this exact ensemble on the night they first flew from Paris to New York, her hand squeezing P.J.'s from takeoff until landing. She remembered looking down at the buildings below, which twinkled like toys and seemed flimsy compared to the man by her side. The diamond ring he had given her glowed on her finger. It fit perfectly, as if it were made for her, even though it was probably a hundred years old.

When they stood up to leave the plane that night, the stewardess touched her shoulder, holding up a sweater and asking, "Does this belong to your husband?" Delphine had not corrected her to say that they were only engaged. She loved the sound of it. *Your husband.* Their lives were all before them. P.J. was helping an elderly woman pull an overstuffed shopping bag down from the compartment above—he was six foot one, with broad shoulders and a wide, muscular back. His dark hair did not yet contain a single strand of gray. The sight of him, every time, made her breath catch in her chest.

Delphine had never felt anything like it. For him, she had gladly left her life behind—her business, her home, her marriage to Henri.

Only a year had passed since that night. There was something about this fact that made the situation all the more painful; it was no time at all. She had followed her desire down a path that history had proven would lead to disaster. Yet she had been selfish enough to believe that in her case, things would be different.

On West Seventy-fourth Street, she stepped out of a taxicab and into the late August sun. She held her suitcase in one hand and balanced a brown paper grocery bag on the opposite hip. His apartment building loomed above her, casting a shadow over the sidewalk. The building had a name, the Wilfred, which put her in mind of an elderly man with thinning hair and a cigar. New York struck her as a masculine city, full of tall buildings and sharp edges, lacking any softness.

"Morning," the Russian doorman said as he opened the glass door. "Do you need help with the bundles?"

She eyed his white-gloved fingers on the brass handle.

"No thank you."

"P.J.'s already gone to work," he said.

The doormen all called him by his first name. P.J. insisted on it. The sound surprised her every time. It was too intimate; it seemed forced.

"I know." She smiled. "I have my key."

He gave her a suspicious look. She wondered if P.J. had

told him everything. She could just picture him swaggering home drunk from some bar, draping an arm around this man's shoulders. *Hey buddy, have I got a story for you.*

Or perhaps the doorman had only noticed her absence. He hadn't been on duty the night she left, two weeks earlier. It was the older fellow, the Irishman, who bowed his head as she made her way out in tears, lugging her things behind her. Then again, the doormen probably all talked and knew the business of every tenant. When she lived here, they had seen her fiancé come in and out with another woman—how many times?—yet they always smiled at Delphine, keeping his secret.

For the past few months, even before everything went wrong, she had missed her home in Paris, on the fourth floor of a typical Haussmannian apartment building in the seventh arrondissement. The building, which dated to 1894, sat on the rue de Grenelle, just off the rue Cler, a neighborhood she had always thought of as terribly *bourgeois*. Her husband had inherited the apartment when his parents retired to the country. It was large—four *chambres*, a parlor, a dining room, living room, and study. Delphine had never loved it. Even after she replaced much of his mother's Louis XVI furniture with clean, modern pieces in white and gray, and crammed her books onto the shelf alongside Henri's, part of her felt like a guest. But now she had the strangest desire to be back there. To slip into the claw-foot tub once again, to stand in the elevator, with its black metal grating that had to be forcibly pulled aside before you could get in.

It was odd how you could long for a place that you had never much cared about. She sometimes missed an intersection or a perfume shop, the old men playing afternoon *boules* on the esplanade des Invalides. At a random moment, she might crave the feeling of standing at the *comptoir* of a certain café, where she drank coffee some mornings in her twenties, or the sight of children eating ice cream cones carved into the shape of flowers, which had become popular just before she left.

Now she entered the Wilfred's marble lobby, which was too cold, as usual. After all this time, she still had not grown accustomed to the American obsession with air-conditioning. Every store and subway car had it—an ecological disaster, but an apparent necessity for American comfort. In apartments, people perched giant, unsightly metal cubes on the windowsills, which used up an incredible amount of electricity to force cold air into the room. The backs of these cubes hung out of thousands of windows around the city; all summer long, condensation dripped off them and straight onto your forehead as you made your way along the sidewalk below. She hadn't grown accustomed to that, either.

Nor had she gotten used to the portions they served you in the restaurants, enough food to feed a family but meant for a single person. *Doggie bags.* The way the waiters tried to clear your plate while you still held a fork aloft, or rushed you out as soon as you paid the bill, not caring whether you had finished your coffee.

Coffee was another thing! The ubiquity of Starbucks. The women in yoga pants ordering their lattes in the morning without a bit of makeup on their faces, their hair up in haphazard buns, as if they had been awakened from a deep sleep and forced to go outside at gunpoint. The men were even worse, with their haircuts like helmets, and their beer bellies, and their shoes. In France, men's shoes were made of the softest leather, with paper-thin, elegant soles and tapered toes. Here, they resembled boats.

There were small things and big ones: Water served with ice. Grains in the sugar bowl instead of cubes. The false familiarity of strangers here, the way someone who you might have had a nice chat with at a party would say the two of you must go out sometime, for shopping or dinner, she'd give you a call, and then you'd never hear from her again.

Of course, New York had its charms, like anyplace. She would not soon forget the beauty of the Chrysler Building. The way the sun gleamed off the glass skyscrapers at midday. How it felt to have your choice of Broadway shows on any given evening. She detested the American tendency to *go go go,* and yet she admired their idea that anyone could achieve his or her dreams, no matter the childhood they'd had. P.J. was proof of that. No, she mustn't hate New York.

But then again, even New Yorkers complained about it. They seemed to take pleasure in detailing all the worst parts of urban life: The stench of the garbage in summer, the impenetrable crowds in Times Square. The expense, the pace, the pressure, the small apartments, the anonymity. In Paris, they were proud of their city. *I love Paris every moment, every moment of the year,* went her father's favorite Cole Porter song.

At the elevators, she pressed the top button and watched it light up. A moment later, the silver doors to her right slid open and she stepped inside, letting them swallow her. The walls were mirrored—she couldn't look away. People in New York often told her that she resembled Jacqueline Kennedy. The highest compliment you could get in this country, P.J. had once told her proudly, and she had thought of how the French admired Jackie because she seemed like one of them, not like an American at all.

Now she noticed the dark, puffy circles beneath her eyes, the wrinkles at her lips. She was forty-one, and for the first time in her life she looked her age, perhaps older. Her father had told her when she was a girl that there were many things that made a woman beautiful, but none so much as being in love.

When she first discovered the truth, Delphine had felt despair that ran through her body like liquid, creeping into every crevice, filling her up, so that all she could do was lie in a hotel room bed with the shades drawn. She wailed pitifully. She did not sleep or eat. Instead, she replayed each moment of their love affair, searching for the instant that it all went wrong. Things had been strained for a few months, she realized that. But she had never expected a betrayal like this. She had almost no money left, no job, and no friends anymore. She saw in an instant that she had turned P.J. into her world.

After a week and a half at the hotel, Delphine woke one afternoon and went to the window. She pulled the heavy curtains back and looked out on the ugly city below. She was still heartbroken, but she felt stronger somehow, clearheaded, the way you feel on the first morning of recovery after an illness. She knew what she needed to do.

She would leave New York—she had no reason to be here without him—but she would not just slink off, the pathetic scorned woman. She would make him remember.

She had ignored P.J.'s calls, which led him to pout—he left voice mail after voice mail demanding that she let him know where she was, in a tone that made him sound like some stubborn brat who refused to eat his vegetables and vowed to hold his breath until his mother took his plate away.

P.J. was a child. She should have recognized it from the start. Maybe she *had* recognized it, but then she went mad. Yes, he was young. Only twenty-four years old, and no doubt that was part of it. But he was also an American, and an artist. No one had ever asked him to be a man in the true sense.

The fastest way to lose one's enthrallment with an artist was to live with him. Other people saw P.J. as a virtuoso, and treated him as if he were the leading expert on every thread of human existence. The truth was that he had only this one thing—he could play the violin better than almost anyone. But the ability did not hint at some greater genius. His focus had been on his music for so long that other parts of him were dead from disuse, or had simply never developed. He wasn't particularly bright or cultured, and he wasn't sensitive.

Even as she stood before him that night, sobbing, screaming that he had ruined her, he had taken her by the shoulders and said, "I can't live with you hating me. You have to say you'll find a way to be my friend."

It was these words, and not what he had done, that ran through her mind, keeping her awake.

He had destroyed their life together and now all he cared about was that she might dislike him. How could she have fallen so deeply in love with such a pathetic coward? How could she have risked so much?

The elevator deposited Delphine on the sixteenth floor. She took in the familiar scent of cleaning fluid and freshly vacuumed carpets as she made her way to the apartment, inserting her key into the lock. After their final argument, he had not asked her to give it back, and she had not thought to offer. The key and the ring. She had kept them both. But she would leave the key behind when she left today, and mail the ring back to his mother as soon as she reached her destination. She could have just sent it from New York, but she dreaded the American post office, with its surly employees who acted as if she were speaking Latin. "I can't understand you," they'd say roughly, and she would feel herself blushing with embarrassment in front of a line full of strangers.

Inside the apartment, all was still but for the sound of the dog, Charlie, shuffling out from the bathroom. He cocked his head inquisitively, and then went back to the cool tile floor. P.J. was obsessed with that animal. He said the dog reminded him of a simpler time, of running through the backyard of his parents' home in Ohio.

He let the dog sleep in the bed. Once, when he had a performance with the Los Angeles Philharmonic, they had driven there and back, staying in dreary motels along the way, because he refused to put Charlie in an airplane's cargo hold, and the only person he trusted to dog-sit was out of town. Delphine had never liked dogs, or, for that matter, people who were overly infatuated with them. Dogs were needy, making gods of their masters. Now she saw that P.J. was exactly the sort of person who would crave that kind of arrangement.

She walked through the foyer, putting her suitcase on the floor before she stepped into the living room. The Stradivarius had a place of honor, upright in its stand in the far corner. This morning he was teaching a master class at Juilliard. For that, he would have taken something less impressive, but still very good: the Guadagnini, perhaps.

Delphine remembered seeing the class written on the calendar in red ink, in the middle of an otherwise empty block of days. She had reveled in that emptiness, imagining all the things they would do with a rare week off. He was away so often, fifty shows a year. She dreamed of the time when their life would slow down some. In a few years, he might be offered an endowed chair at a prestigious conservatory, and then he would be on the road so much less.

These were the sorts of thoughts she had had only two weeks earlier. Amazing how quickly life could change, and with no warning. Or perhaps there had been a warning. Yes.

Delphine went to the violin. The Stradivarius had brought them together. She had known it much longer than she had known him. It was beautiful. The finest she had ever seen, made by the Master himself in 1712. When P.J. played it, a single instrument became a symphony orchestra.

The critics praised him for the uniqueness of his playing, which they said was technically perfect yet full of imagination. They called him "the Rogue," because no other living concert violinist was quite like him. He played with his entire body, moving to the rhythm, his hair falling into his eyes with every stroke of the bow. In particularly emotional moments, he had a tendency to press his cheek sideways in the chin rest and close his eyes, like a young boy snuggling into his pillow. He smiled when he played. Privately he might complain—about the travel, the pressures—but onstage, he seemed a world away from any cares. Delphine had once thought that this spoke to his true love of the craft, but now she saw that it had more to do with his powers to deceive.

She went to the kitchen and placed the brown bag on the counter. The room was tidy and clean, which surprised her. Then came a hard, mean punch in the stomach. Of course. He was keeping it nice for *her*.

When Delphine moved in, there were things she couldn't know about him; they hadn't spent enough time together yet. P.J. usually had the TV blaring when he was home, and even turned it on for the dog when he went out. He made a mess without noticing, and left the sink full of dishes.

The first time Delphine saw the apartment, she nearly cried—when he told her he owned a large one-bedroom in a nice Art Deco building on the Upper West Side, he failed to add that it was decorated like a college dorm room. There was a futon positioned a few feet away from the world's largest television set and flanked by milk crates on either side. In the bedroom, a mattress lay on the floor beside a splintering dresser and bookcase that he had pulled from a stranger's trash on moving day, and a set of bright orange van seats, which he had actually paid for when a favorite rock band came through town and decided to upgrade to a tour bus.

"I'm on the road a lot," he said then, pulling her close. "And it's just been me here. It needs a woman's touch."

This was not the sort of remark that would normally have moved her to action. But as if under some spell, Delphine had transformed the place. After years of vying with Henri's mother for the role of design expert, now she had carte blanche to do as she liked.

She spent the fall in a haze of love, strutting along Madison Avenue and spending untold sums of both their money on Oriental rugs, thousand-thread-count sheets and towels, nice china, a glass-topped dining table with white upholstered chairs, and a king-sized mattress and box spring with a white fabric headboard. The bedding too was all white, topped with a white down comforter, so plush that it felt like you might float away.

In a gallery downtown, she found blueprints of Lincoln Center, which she had framed and hung over the mantel. She didn't miss her work back home in Paris, or even wonder how the shop was doing without her. At night she would return home to him with her latest treasures, and he would praise her progress. They usually wound up making love, wrapped naked in one another's arms until morning.

Now Delphine reached into the paper bag, pulling out two bottles of cabernet and opening them both. She poured herself a big glass and took a sip, even though it was not yet ten o'clock. She lit a cigarette, taking a long drag before resting it against a tea saucer. He did not allow her to smoke in the apartment. When he was home, she had always dutifully gone downstairs and out to the sidewalk. If he went away, she still feared that he'd pick up the scent, so she smoked with her head sticking out of the open bedroom window like a teenager.

She would begin there, in the bedroom. She walked in

purposefully, a bottle of wine in each hand. Standing over the bed, she held them sideways, and shook them up and down as if dressing a salad. The first splashes of purple on the bedspread made her heart thump. But it got easier as she went along, and soon she was emptying the remains of one bottle onto the pale blue rug, and the other straight into his pillowcase. She stepped back, surveying her work.

Delphine had wondered if perhaps she would feel sorry, seeing the apartment destroyed. But she felt free, like the only benefit of watching her world come apart was the fact that she had nothing left to fear. She had made this place perfect for the two of them, not for him and someone else.

She dropped the bottles onto the bed. Next, the shirts.

Delphine had often urged him to dress better, more like a man. P.J. wore the expected formal wear when he was performing, but the rest of the time he looked like a sloppy adolescent. Outside of work, he insisted on wearing the soft, candy-colored t-shirts he had collected through the years, translucent and tinged gray from overuse. If you saw him in the street, you would never guess who he was. She bought him a refined black suit from Dior and a pair of gorgeous leather shoes, but he never wore them.

She left the suit alone; he wouldn't care about that. But she pulled the t-shirts from a drawer one by one, building an efficient pile on her right arm. She brought them back to the counter, and opened the utensil drawer, where she found the kitchen shears she had purchased at Williams-Sonoma for eighty dollars.

She started with the black shirt that read COLLEGE across the front, and then moved on to the dark orange one with the words TEXAS LAW, and next a green, sweat-stained shirt covered in dollar signs and the peeling statement BANK-ERS DO IT WITH INTEREST. The sound of the stainless steel blades slicing through cotton was cool and precise. It reminded her of autumn leaves being crunched underfoot. She breathed in, snipping and snipping two dozen or so shirts until there was nothing left but a confetti of fabric at her feet.

She looked at her watch. She had planned every step of this like a general going into battle. So far she was running a few minutes ahead of schedule. She opened the cupboard and pulled out a jar of peanut butter, unscrewed the lid, and placed the jar on the counter. Then she lifted out a stack of plates. Delphine threw the first one down, but without conviction. It just wobbled on the floor for a moment before landing flat and intact. Something in her held back. She remembered the two of them standing in the china department of Bloomingdale's, playfully arguing over which pattern they should choose. Afterward, they waited in line at Dean & DeLuca for steaming cups of cappuccino, his arm wrapped tight around her waist.

Delphine took a deep breath, feeling her rib cage fill up with air. She lifted the next plate from the pile, and this one she threw with great force, watching it break into pieces as it hit the ground. She repeated the motion with each of the plates below, feeling something vaguely sexual with the impact of every smash. At some point, as she knew he would, the dog came in to investigate. She grabbed him by the collar before he could get near the broken pieces, taking the peanut butter in her free hand and guiding him back to the bathroom, where he would spend the next thirty minutes gorging on the stuff straight from the jar with the fan whirring overhead. This was what P.J. had done whenever they had a fight, so that, as he put it, the dog would not be traumatized.

Back in the kitchen, she peeked into the refrigerator, which contained most of what had been there when she left:

Camembert and blue cheese from Zabar's, and pickles and eggs. On the counter next to the fridge there was one new addition; a green glass bottle of *pastis,* about a quarter of the way gone.

Delphine opened the refrigerator door wider now, and left it open. She opened the freezer as well, then unplugged the machine from the wall.

2012

Kate woke to the sound of her mother's alarmed stage whisper in the kitchen. *They have nothing but soy milk in the fridge. You'd think when company's coming—*

Then, her sister May jumping to the rescue: *I'll go find a convenience store and get some regular milk. Wait, do they even have convenience stores out here?*

Because her cousin Jeffrey had decided to get married in the Hudson River Valley in April, Kate had six relatives—including the three kids—staying under her roof for the weekend. Above her head, the bedroom skylight revealed a square of perfect blue, the first sunny Saturday of spring. She could think of so many things she'd love to do today: take her daughter for a hike, dig around in the back garden, spend all afternoon out on the deck with a book. But none of that would happen.

"I hate weddings," she said.

Dan lay beside her with the comforter pulled up under his chin like every morning. She could tell that he was awake, but instead of opening his eyes he closed them even tighter. "Why do we have to suffer just because they're in love?"

Kate groaned. "I know it."

She should have gotten up earlier, before everyone else. She should have been showered and dressed by the time they all came downstairs. She should have prepared a delicious breakfast. A strata or frittata or something like that. Usually, Ava was her alarm clock, but today someone must have swooped in and gotten her out of bed. Kate knew she ought to feel grateful, but it meant that now it was after eight, and her mother was already judging the contents of her refrigerator. As Jeffrey's aunt and godmother, she would give a reading at the ceremony this evening. No doubt, this had her even more on edge than usual.

May and her husband, Josh, had brought along their three children, ages ten, eight, and five, because, as May had put it over the phone when the save-the-dates arrived, "It doesn't exactly align with our beliefs, but a gay wedding is a teachable moment. It's a coup these days to get your kids invited to one."

They had driven out from New Jersey the night before, shattering the country quiet as soon as May's massive SUV pulled into the driveway. Kate went out to meet them, inhaling deeply, asking the God she wasn't sure she believed in to give her strength.

Right away, May's oldest, Leo, had produced a green tube of braided straw from his pocket and said, "Aunt Kate, stick your fingers in this."

"Don't!" his brother Max warned, coming up behind him. "It's a Chinese finger trap."

Kate remembered the toy from when she was a kid. They used to buy them by the bagful at the five-and-dime.

"Shut up, Max!" Leo said. "You just ruined it."

"Leo. Language," said Kate's mother, Mona, who was the next one out of the clown car, followed by May's youngest, Olivia, wearing a blue Cinderella dress.

"Hi sweetheart," Mona continued. "How are you?"

She kissed Kate on the cheek.

"A girl we saw at the mall had to get her hand cut off after it got stuck in a Chinese finger trap," Max said. "They're really dangerous."

"I made that up, you idiot," Leo snickered. "I don't know why she didn't have a hand, but it wasn't because of a Chinese finger trap. Come on, Aunt Kate. Try it!"

"Is that okay to say?" Mona frowned, looking to Kate. "Shouldn't it be Asian finger trap now?"

"All right, let me see that," Kate said, slipping her fingers into the holes at either end of the tube. She made a big show of being stuck.

"Let me try it on someone," Max said.

"No," Leo shot back.

"I have something better than that," Max said with a pout. "I have a Mongolian finger trap."

"No such thing," Leo said, dismissing him.

May climbed out of the car, and rolled her eyes at Kate. "Please don't encourage them."

As if Kate had given them the Chinese finger trap as a welcome gift. As if she herself were eight years old. *And so it begins,* she thought.

They made it through the rehearsal dinner without any fighting, though May's boys fidgeted and complained until they were allowed to play video games at the table, which Kate could tell her cousin Jeffrey hated. She had never respected May's parenting style. May always told her, *Just wait. When you have kids, you'll understand.* But Kate had been a parent for three years now, and she still objected to the strange cycle of bribing children to be good and scaring the shit out of them when they were bad.

Now she turned to Dan. "I guess I'd better go downstairs."

He pulled her close, his body warm beneath the sheets. "Let's just stay here for the day. We'll tell them we're sick."

She grinned. "Yeah, right. And deprive the flower girl of her parents' adoring gazes?"

"We can tell her we'll just check out the pictures on Facebook later. You know your sister will find a way to post them before the wedding has even started."

May had documented what seemed like every instant of her children's lives online, as if a birthday party or a t-ball game were somehow not quite real until she told 437 of her closest friends and acquaintances about it.

Kate and Dan were silent for a moment, which allowed them to overhear the following exchange:

The first voice belonged to her mother. "What is this? Orgasmic apple juice?"

"*What?*" May said. "Let me see that! Mom, it says organic."

Kate laughed.

"Wow, that must have been a letdown for her," Dan said.

"I'm going in," Kate said, getting to her feet. "Wish me luck."

In the kitchen, May's three sat around the table eating Pop-Tarts. May and Mona stood against the counter, coffee cups in hand. Kate couldn't remember the last time they'd all been together in the morning like this. Her mother and sister always wore makeup in public. They looked odd without it now, like some small but vital part of their faces was missing—an eyebrow, or an upper lip.

Ava, still in her footie pajamas, was strapped into her booster seat, a crumbling Pop-Tart in hand. At three years old, she was already fiercely opinionated.

"Mama," she said. "I like this. I want more."

Kate wanted to rip the thing away from her and shove it in the trash. She would need to decide quickly whether to fight this particular battle. She fed Ava all natural foods, nothing processed or full of sugar, even though she and Dan still ate greasy Chinese one night a week and scarfed down the occasional bag of Doritos. They did try to eat consciously, aware of the evils of factory farming. They had cut out meat almost entirely. But they still ate plenty of junk. In some ways, they were a lost cause, but Ava, beautiful Ava, was pure. Kate thought of asking her sister why she had felt the need to undermine her authority so early in the day.

"You brought your own Pop-Tarts?" was all she said.

May frowned. "Good morning to you too, Sunshine! Sorry. My kids won't eat anything else."

"They're made with real fruit," Leo pointed out, trying to be helpful.

Kate knew they thought she was foolish to care so much about what Ava ate. "You were raised on hot dogs and Kraft macaroni and cheese, and you turned out fine," her mother had said on various occasions when the subject came up.

Mona and May treated Kate and Dan like they were a couple of radicals, even though there was nothing particularly unconventional about their life. Any choice Kate made that contradicted what her mother had done was somehow seen as a slap in the face. Moving to the country, feeding her daughter organic food, deciding not to marry.

Kate had believed that Ava's birth would take some of the pressure off the idea of marriage, but that had been a total miscalculation on her part. In the flurry of Jeff's wedding preparations these past several months, it had all come back to her: the day after she announced that she was pregnant, her mother bought her a white dress. ("It just reminded me of you, that's all.") The week they found out they were having a girl, May made her husband take Dan out for beers and try to pressure him into proposing.

"Your child will be illegitimate. Don't you care about that?" her mother said when Kate was seven months along, and there was no longer time to even pretend at subtlety.

"In what way exactly will she be illegitimate?" Kate had asked.

"Her parents aren't married."

"Neither are mine," Kate said.

"Yes, well, that's different."

"Why?"

"Because we were married, once upon a time."

Kate's had been a relatively traditional suburban childhood. She grew up in Montclair, New Jersey. Her father was the letters editor for the Newark *Star-Ledger*, her mother the dean of students at a small nearby college.

She attended a good public school, played soccer and softball, though not particularly well, and was in the Girl Scouts until age eight. Her parents' house, a normal-sized Colonial, was always in a state of near messiness that could be cleaned up for guests in thirty-five minutes or less. She had her own bedroom, and so did May.

They were born four years apart. Far enough that they didn't really play with one another if there was any possible alternative. They each had their own friends, and the only times they socialized were during boring family parties or when they went away on vacation.

They bonded, sort of, during their parents' divorce. Kate was a freshman in high school and May was a senior. Neither of them saw it coming. Yes, their parents fought a lot, and from time to time her mother had made threats. While driving them to school one morning, she announced that she felt she was finally ready to leave their father, as if they might congratulate her on the news. May started to cry. Kate was silent, though she worried for months. But then two years passed, and nothing changed.

She wept when her parents told her for real. On some level she understood that they would both be happier apart. But screw their happiness: she didn't want to be the child of divorced parents. Couldn't they at least have waited until she went away to college? She considered high school the worst possible time for this to happen. She knew people whose parents had split before their first birthday, and she considered them lucky beyond belief. They had never known anything different.

When her parents divorced, the court granted them joint custody. They decided that she and May would spend Sunday through Wednesday with their father in the original house, and Thursday through Saturday with their mother, in a cheap rented condo she got through campus housing. This was how Kate spent her high school days, and she hated it.

After the divorce, May tried harder than ever to be perfect—pretty, polite, well dressed, popular, always with a boyfriend by her side. It seemed as if every choice she made was an attempt to erase the taint of the broken home. Kate went in the opposite direction. On Fridays, she stayed out late with a bunch of college kids she and her friend Brandy had met at a party and quickly latched onto. They claimed to be BU students themselves, and spent many nights in dorm rooms, drinking, smoking pot, listening to Radiohead and Ani DiFranco; discussing literature, feminism, and life with the women in the group, before making out for hours with the sleepy-eyed boys, who smelled of Tide and cigarettes.

The differences between the two sisters were only emphasized by the fact that they looked so much alike. May and Kate were both five foot five, with brown hair and olive skin. They had the same skinny legs and arms, the same flat chest, even the same tiny, hairless gap in their eyebrows, which May spent untold amounts of time and money getting waxed and plucked and lasered, so as to correct the imperfection, while Kate just left it alone. She could look at her sister and see exactly how she herself would look if she spent an hour applying makeup each morning and took great care with her outfits. But Kate's style, if she had one, could only be described as unintentional. She sometimes wore a bit of lip gloss, that was all. She never learned how to apply eyeliner; the few times she had tried, her lids clamped shut as soon as they came within three inches of a pencil, making her wonder if she'd been blinded by a stick in a previous life.

Their father remarried when Kate was a freshman in college. His wife, Jean, was a nice woman from the paper, also divorced with two kids. Kate was happy for him, and relieved—his lonesomeness was one thing she could cross off her long list of worries. But she found it odd that her father and Jean still lived in the house she grew up in. It was like he had just replaced one woman with another, keeping everything else the same. Even the sofa in the den was the same, and the brass poster bed in the master suite. Jean's kids from her first marriage had grown up with a deadbeat dad they never saw, so they looked to Kate's father as their own in a way, even though they were in their twenties. This could be hard to take. *You should call your brother and congratulate him on the new job,* her father might say over the phone, and it would take Kate a moment to figure out what the hell he was talking about. *Brother?* She didn't have a brother.

Her mother never remarried. Mona was married to her life—her work and her friends. She had once told Kate that after women got out of lousy marriages, they generally had the good sense to stay away from the institution altogether. While men just kept trying to get it right because they were incapable of being alone.

Despite this, Mona wanted her daughters to get married. She had obsessed over planning May's wedding like there was an award to be won. Like her sister, so many of Kate's friends had watched their parents languish in bad marriages or go through painful divorces, only to jump right into marriage themselves, as if they could fix the whole messy business of their elders' mistakes with a next-generation do-over.

Early on, even as far back as high school, Kate was distrustful of marriage. The popular perception was so sad and discouraging, so *Everybody Loves Raymond*. After the divorce, her father started reciting a Rita Rudner quote whenever the subject came up: "Men who have a pierced ear are better prepared for marriage—they've experienced pain and bought jewelry." Each time he said it and laughed, Kate felt slightly ill.

The fall of her sophomore year at UVM, she took a class called "The History of Marriage," in which she learned that, historically speaking, marriage wasn't about love at all. It was essentially a business transaction.

Through centuries and across cultures, women were intimidated and coerced into marriage through horrible means—kidnapping, physical violence, even gang rape. In eighteenth-century England, the doctrine of coverture dictated that a woman had no legal rights within a marriage, other than those afforded her by her husband. Early American laws replicated this idea, and did not change until the 1960s. Before then, most states had "head and master" laws, giving husbands the right to beat their wives and take full control of family decision making and finances, including the woman's own property.

Every bit of new information sickened her. This was marriage?

While home for Thanksgiving, Kate made her feelings known: she wanted to have a family someday, but she knew in her heart that she would never get married.

"Marriage is a construct," she said as she poured gravy over her turkey breast. "It's been sold as a way to keep women safe or make their lives better, but for the most part it's been used to keep them down. In Afghanistan today, a woman might be encouraged to marry her rapist."

"This isn't Afghanistan," her mother said, looking embarrassed.

"Well, here in America, a woman couldn't get a credit card or a bank loan without written permission from her husband until the seventies. And until then, a man could also force his wife to have sex with him. There was no such thing as marital rape."

"Please stop saying *rape* at the dinner table," her mother said. "Grandpa, would you pass the cranberry sauce?"

Everyone thought it was just a phase, including her college boyfriend, Todd. They were together for five years, moving to New York after graduation and breaking up the summer they both turned twenty-five. When he proposed to her on a weekend drive to Burlington, Kate was shocked. She had told him hundreds of times why she didn't want to get married, and he had seemed to agree. For a long time, he acted as if he had hit the jackpot by finding a woman who wasn't interested in all that. But a few months before his proposal, it was as if someone had flipped a switch in him—he started saying that it was childish not to get married, what would people think of them, of their future kids? Plus, the government made it impossible not to marry, he said. If you were married, you got benefits and tax breaks. She told him that wasn't exactly true: "Only for traditional, patriarchal setups, where the man makes all the money and the woman stays home. Our tax system punishes couples where both members are high earners."

He shook his head. "Whatever. I don't want to marry you for tax purposes, Kate. Way to suck all the romance out of it."

She said she wanted to be with him, but not marry him. He said that was bullshit, that every woman wanted to get married deep down. They broke up. Six months later, Todd was engaged to someone else.

Around this time, Kate's mother started to panic. "You know," she said, "a lot of us form grand ideas in college that we later abandon. There's no shame in it." She suggested that they go to therapy together, to sort out exactly how much the divorce had damaged Kate.

She tried to tell her mother that it wasn't about the divorce. It was about the fact that marriage was outdated and exclusionary, and worked only 50 percent of the time anyway. But none of this logic made a difference. In every other way, she was an ideal daughter: high achieving, devoted. But the fact that she wouldn't get married made her suspect in her mother's eyes.

The men she dated in her late twenties seemed similarly suspicious. When she told them that she did not want to get married, she was usually met with disbelief or some variation on the word *feminazi*. By the time she turned twenty-eight, Kate felt certain that she was never going to meet someone to be with for the long term. She made peace with the idea. She had a small rented studio apartment in Brooklyn Heights. She was self-sufficient and had fulfilling work and wonderful friends, and maybe that was enough.

Then she met Dan—ironically, at the wedding of their mutual friend Tabitha. He was from Wisconsin, a website designer, who before moving to New York had spent eight years working in Sweden. There, it was perfectly common not to get married. Plenty of his friends in Stockholm had purchased houses and had kids but never made it official. He probably would have gotten married if he'd ended up with anyone else, but he liked the idea of two people choosing each other every day, rather than feeling stuck with one another, as though they were a failure if they couldn't make forever happen. Dan had a slight suspicion of authority to begin with, and once he thought about it, he saw no reason why the government should be a part of their relationship. What had been a brick wall with every other man she had ever dated was suddenly just no big deal.

They were a good match, for this and a hundred other reasons. At the wedding where they met, a female minister in flowing white robes had said something that Kate never wanted to forget. *Outdo each other with kindness.* She and Dan tried to. If something between them irritated her, she attempted to work it out herself, or talk to him in a calm, compassionate way.

She remembered too many weekends when she was a kid that had been ruined by her parents' bickering. It usually started out with a nudge from her mother over breakfast, a slight twist of the screw: *Gary, I thought you said you were going to run the dishwasher last night. Now there are no clean mugs in the whole damn house.* Perhaps most men would apologize or make a joke out of it, but Kate's father would ignore his wife, turning his attention instead to the children, his human shields. *Well, what should we do today, huh? Do you want to go to the aquarium?*

The passivity drove her mother insane. Maybe that's why he did it. *Gary, I was talking to you,* she'd say. *Gary!*

I heard you, Mona. I can just think of a lot better ways to spend a Saturday than fighting with you about the stupid dishwasher.

Kate would sit between them, her body filling up with concrete, willing her mother to back down. But Mona didn't know her own strength. She'd usually take the conversation somewhere cutting and out of the blue, saying something like, *Maybe if you were able to take just the tiniest bit of constructive criticism, you might have gotten a promotion sometime in the last decade.* From there, it would start to snowball, and Kate knew that soon enough her father would be locked away in his woodworking shed out back, her mother shrugging her shoulders, asking what his problem was.

Kate had long feared that she possessed the same ability to harm that her mother did. When Dan came along, she saw him for what he was at once, and vowed not to mess it up. Dan was a straight-up good, midwestern guy, with the right politics and a big heart. The kind of guy who would turn a tails-side-up penny over on the sidewalk for the next person to find.

Her family grew hopeful when they met him.

"Do you think you'll get married?" May asked after they had been dating a few months.

"I think he'll be the father of my children," Kate said. It felt right, and enormous. She expected her sister to hug her.

But May responded hotly, "If you're not picturing yourself in a wedding gown, that's a bad sign."

Leaving marriage aside, there was the issue of weddings. These two wildly different concepts were forever entwined in her sister's brain—if you were in love, May reasoned, you would have thoughts of buttercream icing and swing bands and bridesmaid dresses skipping through your head at all times, and this was no different than thoughts of spending your entire life with someone. None of it appealed to Kate. She knew that a woman was supposed to want to be married, but everything about weddings made her skin crawl, nothing more so than the brides who wanted to be different somehow—"I'm not like other brides!" all her friends had declared, before promptly acting like every other bride in the history of brides. She had been to the six-figure Hamptons wedding, the Brooklyn food-truck wedding, the laid-back Kentucky hoedown wedding, the Irish castle wedding. They were all the same.

Kate went along to each of them with a smile. She brought a good gift, and danced and toasted the happy couple. She didn't mean to be a curmudgeon. She wished she could feel more live-and-let-live about it all. But deep down, she hated other people's wedding photos. She hated the way a bride would raise up her bouquet in victory after saying "I do," as if she had just accomplished something. She hated that even normal-sized women dieted for their weddings until they looked like bobble-head versions of themselves. She hated all the money thrown into some dark hole, when it could have been put to good use in a million other ways. Every one of her friends got so overwhelmed by the event, as if they were planning the Macy's Thanksgiving Day Parade. Now there were even blogs for the stressed-out bride, the reluctant bride, the indie bride. But no one she knew, other than her, had stepped back and asked themselves, *Why be a bride at all?*

The outside pressure to be married was intense. This had surprised her a decade ago, but now she thought she understood. People wanted you to validate their choices by doing the same thing they had done. She was blessed—or cursed, depending on how you looked at it—to be the kind of person who really didn't care what other people thought, as long as she believed it was right. She and Dan had never had a single conversation about whether they ought to get married just to please their parents or get everyone off their backs. But even so, Kate sometimes felt frustrated that her relationship wasn't taken as seriously because it wasn't a marriage. She had been with Dan longer than some of her married friends had even known their husbands.

Some women confided in her that they wished they had been brave enough to buck tradition the way she did, but then they'd gone ahead and done the expected thing to make everyone else happy. Others couldn't believe this was what she really wanted. When she and Dan had been together two years, they were out with a coworker of Dan's and his fiancée one night. "Are you two close to getting engaged?" the woman asked her. "No," Kate said. The woman patted her hand and whispered, "You probably just haven't cried enough yet."

Dan joked that they should tell everyone they were both divorced, since if you'd done it once, people usually left you alone. It explained something that was otherwise unfathomable: the reason why two people in love did not want to marry.

For a while, Dan had told anyone who asked that they were boycotting marriage until their gay friends could take part. It was mostly a lie, but it tended to shut people up. The real reasons were too complicated, and anyway, no one ever believed them. You could spend hours telling someone in great detail about how you didn't think the state had any business playing a role in your most intimate relationship, how you were wary of the Wedding Industrial Complex, and they'd still come away thinking, *So basically you're afraid of commitment.*

But now their gay friends could get married. Kate remembered the evening Jeff and Toby had told them they were engaged. They had come up from the city for the weekend, and they were all sitting on the deck, watching the sun set.

"Do you hate me?" Jeff asked after he broke the news.

"Yes," she said.

"I'm going to be a Bridezilla, you know that, right?"

She groaned. "This is gonna be even more painful than May's, isn't it?"

"More painful, but less tacky," he said. "The good news for you is we won't be doing a real bridal party—we're a bit old for all that, right? Though we want Ava to be the flower girl. If I can't wear a pouffy white dress, by God, she'll have to wear one for me. And we want to do it out here in the country. So you'll have to help me find a caterer and a florist and all that. We've already got the venue booked."

"Where?" Dan asked.

"The Fairmount," they said, and then joined hands.

"Oh God. They've gone over to the dark side. They're even speaking in unison now," Dan said. He got up from his chair. "I think we might have a bottle of champagne left over from New Year's. I'll be right back."

As Dan walked inside, Jeff went on, "We booked the garden for a sunset ceremony and cocktails. Three-hundred-and-sixty-degree views of the mountains and the Hudson."

Toby beamed. "It's stunning, Kate. As long as it doesn't rain, we'll be fine."

"Mother Nature best not be messing around that day, let me tell you," Jeff said. "I've waited ten years for this."

Kate smiled. "I'm sure she wouldn't dare cross you."

"Now the actual dinner will be in the Riverview Ballroom. Getting that room on a Saturday in April is nothing short of a miracle, but we did it," Jeff said. He sounded more proud than he had when he passed the bar exam, or won his first major case. "Picture this: Floor-to-ceiling windows. A neutral color palette of cream, mushroom, and sage that looks flawless with any wedding decor you choose."

Dan returned then with the champagne and four glasses. Kate grabbed hold of the edge of his shirt as if to keep herself from falling, even though she was sitting down.

"Honey, stop. We're scaring her," Toby said.

"No, no!" Kate said. "Go on. The views sound amazing. And whatever you said about mushrooms. That sounded good, too."

She wanted to be happy for them. They were her best friends. She and Jeffrey had always been close, the two black sheep of the family. He was gay and she was Kate, and that was all there was to it. But now he wanted to be just like the rest of them. He wanted to be married. Kate couldn't figure out why.

Late that night, she stood beside her cousin, looking out over the mountains in the distance.

"You're being a trouper," Jeff said. "Even though I know you don't get it."

Other than Dan, he was the one person she had always talked to about these things, the only one who ever seemed to understand why she never wanted to be married. And, though she knew it wasn't about her, the whole thing felt like a small betrayal.

"There are so many countries in the world where people don't even care about marriage anymore," she said.

"But not America," he said.

"No. Not America."

"Where'd you come from, anyway?"

"I don't know. I think May must have depleted our mother's womb of some nutrient that causes a child to be normal."

"That sounds about right. What was it Fran Lebowitz said?" Jeffrey asked. "Why do gay people want to get married and be in the military, which are the two worst things about being straight? Something like that. We just want our relationship to be accepted and acknowledged as much as anyone else's. It might sound dumb, but it's really that simple. We want to be the same."

"That's one of the reasons I *don't* want to be married," she said. "Because I don't feel that what I have with Dan is the same as what May and Josh have, or any of our friends, or, God forbid, my parents. I don't think any two relationships are really the same, so why rubber-stamp them all like that?"

"That's not what I mean when I say the same," he said. "I mean equal."

"I know."

"In my heart we've always been married. But now we'll

have the same basic rights as straight people. Insurance and inheritance and all that. You know we want to adopt someday. I've been afraid forever that if something happened to Toby and we weren't married, his crazy parents would try to take the kid away from me."

She put an arm around him, and as much as she could, Kate understood.

Since then, she had been a good sport. A few weeks later, the guys came upstate again one weekend. She prepared a feast: pumpkin bread and blueberry muffins, short ribs and potatoes au gratin, green beans and apple crisp, and buckets of red wine. For two days, they sat around her kitchen table, stacked high with wedding magazines and their laptops, and planned. Dan called it the War Room.

In the mix of magazines was a new publication called *Wedding Pride*. If Kate had assumed it would be harder for the wedding industry to monetize marriages between two men, she was mistaken: here were the ads for tooth whitening, Botox, laser eye surgery, because God forbid you should wear glasses to your wedding. Jeff got annoyed by an article entitled "My Big Fat Gay Honeymoon: Ten Gay-Friendly Locales Around the Globe."

"Please," he said. "I'll have my honeymoon where I damn well want to."

Toby glanced at the page. "It's a practical concern," he said. "There are a lot of places we wouldn't feel comfortable. Places where people would be hostile. You're an East Coaster, you have no idea."

"Hey! I studied abroad in Madrid," Jeff said, which prompted an eye roll from his fiancé.

Jeff held a book in his lap and made notes.

"What is that?" Kate asked after a while.

"It's my bride book," he said.

"Excuse me?"

"Emily Post's Wedding Planner."

She looked at Toby, who just shrugged.

"Give me that," she said. She flipped through the pastel pages, and with each new task her anxiety level doubled: There were flowers to think about, and a wedding website, a band for the reception and music for the ceremony, place cards, forks and linens. Invitations and favors for all your guests. Something called *tablescapes.*

"This thing makes me feel like I'm going to have a panic attack, and it's not even my wedding," she said. She pointed at a page: "You're supposed to have an emergency contact for each of your bridesmaids, and document their height and weight, and exactly when their dress fittings will take place?"

"But we're not having bridesmaids so we can ignore that," Jeffrey said.

"Okay." She flipped to another page. "You're supposed to create personalized gift bags for every guest's hotel room and tell them about fun things to do in the area?"

"Well, of course."

On Sunday, they drove around and checked out Jeffrey's top five favorite venues, just to make sure he was certain about the one he had already booked. They did a tasting with a caterer whose specialty seemed to be stuffing foods into other foods—tomatoes stuffed with shiso and wasabi, figs stuffed with gorgonzola, red pepper stuffed with chicken and rice. All the stuffing felt a little violent to Kate, but she didn't mention it to Jeff, only Toby, who said, "Maybe marriage makes her angry."

She knew that weddings had become big business: every time she turned on the television, there was another show about choosing the perfect dress, the perfect theme, the perfect cake. But still, she was flabbergasted by the expense: An empty barn strung up with fairy lights and nothing else cost six grand for the day. A country inn charged two hundred dollars a head for dinner.

When she worked at a nonprofit in New York, it had often been her job to create press releases that could express need in dollars and cents. People were more likely to donate if they could imagine exactly where their money might go. Now she had a bad habit of extrapolating this out in real life. For the price of two people's dinners at this wedding, they could buy a deep-well pump that would provide clean water to an entire community, or fund a year's education for sixty students at a refugee camp in Kenya. For the price of the flowers, they could buy a thousand mosquito bed nets that would protect five thousand Cambodian children from malaria. On a research trip, Kate had met a mother of nine who had already lost her husband and two oldest sons, ages fourteen and twelve, to the disease. The family had only one net, big enough to protect five bodies, so each night the woman had to choose two of her surviving children to sleep outside of it, in addition to herself. Five dollars was all it would take to save their lives. They weren't supposed to, but Kate had emptied her pockets to this woman and her neighbors. When she saw their joy at receiving such a small sum, she felt ashamed of American excess. Now she pictured the eighteen gorgeous centerpieces Jeff was planning—roses, peonies, hydrangeas, and scented geraniums, all of which would be in the trash by the next morning. She felt ill.

Kate realized people didn't think about money in this way. Jeffrey and Toby were generous; when asked to give, they gave. So no one would begrudge them for spending seventy thousand dollars on a wedding for two hundred. It was simply what one did.

They had wanted a more intimate affair, maybe eighty people. But the second her aunt and uncle heard about the engagement, they drew up a list of a hundred guests.

"Would you ever in a million years have thought that my parents would be clamoring to invite people to their son's gay wedding?" Jeff said. "My dad's already joined Weight Watchers. He wants to lose twenty-five pounds. And my mom is up in arms that we're not having our reception in New Jersey. She told me it's tradition to have the wedding in the bride's hometown and people will think it's strange that we're doing it here. I told her we don't exactly have a bride."

Toby raised an eyebrow. "Oh, don't we?"

After that weekend, a mania took Jeffrey over, as it did all of them, all the brides she had ever known. When she spoke to him about anything other than the wedding, she could tell that she didn't have his focus. He told her that he lay awake in the middle of the night thinking about whether to have the caterer serve scallops as an hors d'oeuvre during cocktail hour, or whether he ought to jump to the next price level and go with mini lobster rolls. Were they perfectly whimsical or just goofy, and out of place so far from the ocean? He could spend hours consulting old weather charts and the *Farmers' Almanac* online to try and deduce whether there would be rain. Once, in the middle of a phone call about their sick great-aunt, he had said, "Mason jars are huge right now. Have you noticed?"

"Excuse me?" she said.

"People use them for everything at weddings: candles, cocktails, centerpieces. I have to admit I like them. But are they overdone?"

He was stressed all the time. He told her his hair had started falling out, that he woke up some mornings covered in hives. He'd go to his office, but instead of doing any work, he'd find himself manically Googling the wedding photos of strangers, so that he could steal ideas about flowers and lighting. Entire days were lost to TheKnot.com. He became obsessed with Pinterest, which was basically online wedding porn: pictures of gorgeous tents and tables, golden retrievers in bow ties, freckled ring bearers out of a Norman Rockwell painting.

Jeff obsessively read a blog called Near Mrs., about women who had broken off their engagements. He showed her a site called WeddingWhine—he had started looking there for tips about vendors, but got sucked into a rabbit hole of postings between strangers. The would-be brides had their own language, full of acronyms: BM (Bridesmaid), FH (Future Husband), DOC (Day-of Coordinator), BSC (Batshit Crazy), STD (Save the Date).

They had profile names like *The Future Mrs. Johnson* and under this on the screen it might say something like "Only X days to go until I marry my love," the words floating over a line of dancing hearts. (Or worse, a pink tape measure, flowing like a ribbon, with pounds lost and left to lose before the big day.)

"It's so tragic when it says zero days. It reminds you that at some point the wedding will just be over and done," Jeff said, and she knew he was a goner.

Kate started looking at the sites herself. Mixed in with questions about the best officiants or calligraphers, they wrote about discovering that their fiancés were meeting other women online for sex, or admitted to feeling the spark go out of the marriage two weeks after the wedding. Once they started sharing, they couldn't stop—some had been married for years and now just chronicled their fertility issues, *The Future Mrs. Johnson* changing her name to *Layla's Mommy*.

There was something fascinating about the juxtaposition of their obsession with perfection—*Will it rain? Which dress should I pick?! How will the food taste?*—with their darkest concerns about love and life, and how easily it could all unravel. Kate wondered if this was the reason weddings had gotten so out of control. Were they meant to distract you from your fear and uncertainty?

"Be sweet to Jeff," her sister instructed over the phone one night. "This is one of the most stressful things a person goes through in life. They say it's on par with losing a parent."

Kate tried to be sympathetic, but it irritated her. How did one go from normal person to Zombie Bride just like that? What made otherwise sane human beings care so much about a five-hour party? Some small, dark, curious part of her—the same part that wondered what it might be like to try heroin or scream out in a crowded theater—wished she could experience the sensation just for a moment, so that she might understand.

Much of our market each year is made up of new people moving into the marriage age bracket. Future sales depend upon persuading millions of new individuals that an engagement diamond is essential. This is not practical as a short-term objective because it takes years for individual opinions to develop into a definite course of action—specifically in this instance into an insistent demand for an engagement diamond.

—N. W. Ayer and Son,
Annual Report to De Beers, 1952

Older people—parents, other relatives, and friends—exert a subtle but strong influence on the market. For their *expectation* that the engagement will be symbolized with a diamond ring is an important influence in the maintenance of the engagement diamond tradition.

To prevent young people from breaking away from the tradition, we need the support of these older people.

Our advertising objective is to leave the impression with young people that the diamond is the only meaningful symbol of the love inherent in the engagement promise. The advertising should be targeted at these young people, but in such a way that it will encourage appreciation of the diamond engagement ring tradition by the entire public.

—N. W. Ayer and Son,
Annual Report to De Beers, 1966–67

1955

Frances drove up to the gates of Haverford College at nine o'clock. A dazzling sun cut through the haze, promising a warm, dry morning. Of course. In the twelve years since she was hired, it had never once rained on the company outing, much to her chagrin. The event was held each year on the second Friday in June. The Haverford students had gone home for summer vacation, and the employees of N. W. Ayer and Son descended on the place for several hours of games and bonding. Frances usually woke the day of with a certain tightness in her chest. She'd prefer to be at work given the option, but Ayer prided itself on its family-friendly atmosphere, and this included mandatory attendance here today.

The company had a girls' basketball team, a dramatic society, a baseball team, and an interdepartmental games club, all under the auspices of the House Recreation Committee. There was a cafeteria in the basement of the Ayer building with windows and curtains painted straight onto the walls by the art department. To Frances, these elements made the place seem more like a junior high school than an advertising agency, but she kept the thought to herself.

She was fairly private around her coworkers, more conservative than most. Friendly, but from a safe, professional distance. She went to lunch if anyone asked her, and drank two martinis and told a few jokes. But besides Dorothy, none of them knew anything about her, really.

Up ahead, she could make out the large welcome banner hanging between two pine trees, and a cluster of tables covered in red-and-white-checked cloths. She made a right down the hill into the parking lot, where Howard Davis and his wife Hana were gathering up their little boys into a red wagon. They gave her a wave and she waved back.

Howard was handsome—tall and thin like Jimmy Stewart and a hopeless flirt, though he was still clearly smitten with his wife.

At the edge of the lot, Mitch Duncan and his wife stood before a cardboard sign nailed to a tree. He was pointing at an arrow for VOLLEYBALL, and she was shaking her head, bouncing a fat baby on her hip. Mitch was a senior copywriter with a temper. He never let one of his lines slip away if he thought it was good. But now he shrugged and followed his wife and children to the crafts tent, kicking the dirt in defeat.

Tom Williams stepped out of a Ford, squinting as he lit a cigarette against the wind. While he did this, his wife, Judy, came around the car, licked her palm, and smoothed his cowlick. Tom didn't even react.

Frances put a hand over her mouth. She was used to seeing these men in a restaurant at lunch, sipping scotch with their ties loosened, cracking crude jokes about the backsides of various members of the typing pool. To see how they behaved around their families was strange. Funny. Sobering. It was precisely the reason she had never wanted to be married in the first place. She had no desire to play the role of wifey-poo. She wanted to always be simply herself.

She parked and got out of the car, brushing the front of her slim black skirt and pulling straight the shoulders of her cape. It wasn't exactly picnic attire, but she and Dorothy had scheduled an afternoon meeting with an editor from *Motion Picture Magazine,* who, as luck would have it, was in town from California. They told Gerry Lauck that the meeting just couldn't happen on any other date, and that they were hoping to secure an article entitled "The Day I Got My Diamond: How Six Actresses Played Ring-Around-a-Romance." Shirley MacLaine and Jayne Mansfield had already agreed to take part. As a copywriter, it wasn't technically Frances's job to go to this sort of meeting, but thankfully Gerry didn't protest.

"Morning, Frances!" Tom shouted from across the lot.

"Hello!" she called back. "Hi Judy!"

His wife waved, but she wore a sour expression.

It was Judy, wasn't it? She felt quite certain it was Judy.

Each year at the outing, Frances tried to act merry around the wives of her colleagues, complimenting them on their dresses and their adorable, well-behaved children, cheering as the urchins gave the egg toss their all, and making light of the ensuing tantrum when someone inevitably came in last in the three-legged race.

Most of the wives were nice enough, though she knew some of them pitied her and she pitied them right back. Others treated her like an exotic pet—a woman of forty, who worked alongside their husbands, with no apparent interest in a husband or children of her own. They asked her silly questions, like who she telephoned when she came across a mouse or a very large spider in her basement, or whether the men she dated found a career girl intimidating. (She hadn't been out on a date in years, but she kept this fact to herself.) They offered to have her over for a home-cooked meal, as if a single woman were incapable of turning on a stove.

A few were downright awful to her.

"They think you want their husbands," Dorothy whispered last time around. "Or worse: that their husbands want you."

Frances found this laughable. She had overheard herself described by these men as a Plain Jane a hundred times. Once

Randolph Spears had called her "borderline pretty," and that was supposed to be a compliment. She didn't do anything to try to change their opinions, either. She dressed in dark, solid colors with high necks and wore no makeup. She could drink any one of them under the table, and they knew it. In the eyes of her coworkers, Frances was practically a man. A girl in this business had to be, or else she'd get eaten alive.

She shouldn't have thought she'd give any wife cause for worry, yet such women truly did exist. Janey Welch was one—a wispy little thing with white-blond hair and eyebrows, and four tiny towheads to match. She seemed to believe it was only a matter of time before Frances fell victim to the seductive powers of her husband Ralph, a roly-poly fellow on the business side who desperately clung to the four remaining strands of hair atop his head as if they were keeping him alive.

"It's not natural for a woman of a certain age to want to work in a stuffy office with men all day, if you ask me," Janey had said last June when she knew full well that Frances was within earshot. "There's something unsavory about it, am I right?"

Two months later, Frances was not particularly sorry to see Ralph Welch locked in an embrace with his secretary at a tucked-away table at Shoyer's.

The truth was, she had never wanted to marry or have children. As a girl she didn't see any way around it. Growing up, she had one childless great-aunt named Doreen. Everyone acted like Aunt Doreen was insane for choosing a spinsterhood full of novels and lapdogs over a life of domestic bliss. The only women in the family who were allowed to remain single without suspicion were nuns.

"Who will take Doreen for Christmas?" she had heard her mother ask once. And, more times than she could count: "Poor Doreen. What will become of her?"

For a long time, Frances had simply believed what they said, but as a teenager it dawned on her that Aunt Doreen was perfectly content. It was everyone else who couldn't understand how. The instant she realized this, Frances felt free.

When she and her parents moved back to Pennsylvania after she graduated high school, Frances found work at a local paper and went to night school at Charles Morris Price and to the University of Pennsylvania on Saturday mornings, where she took every English course they offered. Like everybody else, she was planning to write the Great American Novel. It was through Charles Morris Price that she got her first real job, as advertising manager of Steiger Walking Shoes. That gave out, and next she got a position with a small agency down in Wilmington that handled all sorts of retail accounts.

Her goal was to work in Philadelphia, but not at Ayer. It was too big and imposing a place. Frances intended to always work at a small agency where she would do everything. But in 1943, she went to one such office and the man was so impressed with her work he said, "Well, I don't think you belong here, but before I give you an answer I want you to go to Ayer." He told her to see George Cecil, head of the copy department, or else Harry Batten himself. And so she made a telephone call on the pay phone in Wilmington, and talked to a man by the name of Pierce Cummins, Cecil's second in command. He said Mr. Cecil was out ill but he would be glad to talk to her. But the man had told her to talk to Cecil or Batten, so she hung up, put another nickel in the phone, and called Mr. Batten. And he said, "Well, as a matter of fact, we just lost a woman copywriter. We might be very interested. Call Pierce Cummins."

She went to see Cummins on a Friday in July, but when she arrived he wasn't there. Cecil was. By this point, Frances had just about had it with all the foolish back-and-forth. She didn't have enough sense to be scared of these men. She wasn't afraid of anybody.

She marched into Cecil's office and said, "I'm your new copywriter." She had no intention of actually taking a job, but they were ecstatic about her samples and offered her a position on the spot at one hundred and forty dollars a week.

She worked under a white-haired lady named Betty Kidd. Frances liked Betty fine, but she was eager for the day when Betty would retire and all her accounts would be passed down. The day came after just a year, and Frances felt that her career had begun.

Since then, an entire world had bloomed around her. She had a lovely group of single girlfriends. Together, they had taken ski trips to Vermont and Quebec, and visited the beaches of Mexico. She had a busy work schedule: after twelve years at Ayer, she was a senior copywriter, the highest position a woman could hold on the creative side. She was active in her church. She lived alone, in an apartment in Drexel Hill. A year ago, she got a Great Dane named Charles, from a breeder friend of her mother's. On weekends, she took him to her parents' farm and let him run to his heart's content while she rode horses and did chores and helped her mother with the most recent litter of baby goats. Her parents were in their early seventies now. It pained her to see them growing old. But for the most part, Frances felt quite pleased with her life.

During the war, she sent gifts to everyone in her extended family back in Hamilton: ration items that cost a pretty penny in Philadelphia, and were impossible to find in Canada. Nylon stockings in the right size for her aunts, a hot water bottle for her pregnant cousin, and candy for all the children. She felt proud that she had spending money, and that she didn't need to ask anyone how she could or could not spend it.

Frances only remembered that others found her odd every now and again: At the holidays, visiting her cousins in Toronto, watching them fuss over their kids. Or here at the company outing, when she felt herself being quietly judged, observed, by other women.

But this year, she didn't care. For this year, the outing would not be merely several hours to endure, but rather the means to achieving an important goal. She had stayed up late the night before, rehearsing exactly what she would say to Ham Patterson once she got him alone.

Frances walked slowly up the hill now, breathing in the sweet, fragrant air, looking around for Ham. She made her way to the cluster of tables set up on the grass in front of a large stone dormitory. Boxes of doughnuts and thermoses of coffee were being passed around. In just a couple of hours, they'd be replaced by burgers and franks. The men would sneak out flasks of whiskey, and she'd wish she had remembered to bring one herself.

She took a paper cup of Hills Bros. French Roast from one of the wives doing the pouring. She sat down on a wooden bench. This was one of the few times each year when she felt how unusual her situation was. At work, they were all alone, each one an individual—yes, she knew they all went home to their families at the end of the day. But it never quite sank in until she was right in the thick of it. Was she lonesome? No, not exactly. There was an art to being alone, and she had mastered it. But sometimes it might be nice to be part of a team. She shook her head at her own thought: *Part of a team. How romantic, Frances!*

She watched as a girl of four or five worked diligently at the edge of the baseball diamond, wordlessly scooping sand into her baby brother's hair. Frances glanced around half-heartedly, in search of an adult to tell, but then just looked away and sipped her coffee.

She lit a cigarette and smoked it slowly to calm her nerves.

"Howdy there," someone said.

Frances glanced up to see Paul Darrow standing over her. He was a lovely man, widely considered the best art director in the country. He did the art for all the De Beers ads that she wrote, although they never interacted much at work. Paul was short of stature, and had a very severe tick—blinking that never stopped. Sometimes she found it hard to concentrate on what he was saying, between the blinking and the fact that he always smoked his cigar so far down to the nub that you'd swear he ate it.

"Nice day, huh?" he asked.

"Swell."

They chatted a few minutes, before he moseyed off to the tennis courts.

A while later, at last, Ham came up the path. His wife, Meg, followed close behind, carrying a casserole dish, wearing high-waisted Capri pants and a bandanna in her hair. Frances adored them both. Ham was a sweet fellow of twenty-nine, with a giant laugh. His wife was a lot of fun, and she liked Frances too. They had gotten to know each other at the company Christmas party and several long client dinners.

The two were clearly crazy for each other, but they had no children, which seemed unusual for a couple who'd been married a few years already.

Frances got to her feet. "I was looking for you!"

Meg kissed her on the cheek. "Wonderful to see you, Frances. You look lovely."

"You're a little overdressed for all this, aren't you?" Ham asked.

"Honestly," his wife said, hitting him with her glove. "Is that any way to talk to a lady?"

Frances smiled.

"I've got some business that I've got to deal with this afternoon. A meeting."

"On the day of the company outing?" Ham said. "You do realize that's sacrilege."

"Yes, the golf team will have to soldier on without me."

Ham's face lit up. "They have golf here this year?"

"Oh well, no, I suppose not. But speaking of—"

Here was her chance! But Ham interrupted, "Frances, I was just telling Meg about the time you got to meet Marilyn Monroe."

"Is it true?" Meg asked, beaming that pretty smile of hers.

"Yes," Frances said, though they hadn't really met. But they'd been in the same room, and that seemed close enough. "For our diamond client."

"De Beers," Ham said.

Frances nodded. "You know the tune from *Gentlemen Prefer Blondes*? 'Diamonds Are a Girl's Best Friend'?"

"Of course!" Meg said. "You wrote that?"

"No darling, I'm a copywriter, not a lyricist. We saw Carol Channing do it on Broadway a few years ago, that's all," Frances said. "Dorothy Dignam and I were there on opening night. From the start of the show's run, Dorothy began publicizing the idea of the song. When all the fashion editors came to New York that summer to see the new fall lines, we took them to an evening performance and entertained them afterward at a supper, where they got their pictures taken with Carol Channing. She wore the original diamond tiara of the Empress Josephine. The event was a huge success."

"What fun!"

"Yes. And when we heard a big Technicolor version of the play was coming, we persuaded the people at Fox to show Marilyn Monroe wearing gobs of real diamonds in the film. I shouldn't take any credit. It was really Dorothy who thought it up. Anyway, the two of us went out to California and had a ball."

"Oh! I didn't know you did things like that."

"We never had before."

Frances recalled sitting at a crowded table, full of men, with her at one end and Dorothy at the other, trying to explain why it made more sense than using just prop pieces. Smoke filled the room and martinis sloshed on the dark carpet as she wondered whether their plan would work.

Dorothy was still quite pretty, even in what Frances guessed were her late fifties. She dressed to the nines. She wore a wide-brimmed hat with a feather, even in the office. She gave all the new girls the same piece of advice: *Women in advertising need to keep a stiff upper lip with some lipstick on it*. She also liked to remind them that if Ayer wanted just a copywriter, they'd hire a man. They hired women to write copy for women. Because women knew what other women wanted, at least in theory.

"Now we do it all the time," Frances said. "We loan diamonds out for actresses to wear to the Academy Awards, the Kentucky Derby, you name it. Sometimes the client pays for them to pop up in a film, or around Elizabeth Taylor's neck."

"But how does it help the client if they don't get mentioned?" Meg asked. "I remember that part in the movie where Marilyn's singing and she says"—now she struck a pose, her voice turning smoky—"*Tiffany. Cartier. Talk to me, Harry Winston, tell me all about it.*' But she didn't say De Beers."

Ham laughed. "What was that? I must say I enjoyed it, whatever it was."

"De Beers owns all the world's diamonds, more or less," Frances said. "A vote for diamonds is a vote for them. They're the ones who get the stones to Tiffany or Harry Winston."

"Oh!" Meg said. "How clever."

She seemed genuinely interested. She was a smart girl. Frances wondered what she did at home alone all day while Ham was at work. Meg was a traditional woman, but before she got married she had worked as an air hostess. She had once told Frances that she would have liked to continue, at least until she had children, but the company had a strict policy against employing married women.

"I used to fly at thirty thousand feet, and now Ham won't even let me drive the car," she had said, but she laughed as she said it to show that it didn't really bother her.

"What was Marilyn like?" she asked now.

Frances thought it over. "Stunning, of course. Shy."

"Shy? Marilyn Monroe?"

"Yes. Jane Russell had to walk her out onto the set every morning. She was scared to death of the cameras."

"Poor thing."

They had been invited onto the set to watch the scene by a producer friend of Dorothy's. The two of them stood in the darkness with their clipboards, surrounded by crew members, everyone staring. It was such a thing to behold! Women dressed in clingy black hanging from the chandeliers. Pretty girls in pale pink ball gowns spinning around in the arms of handsome young men. And Marilyn Monroe at the center of it all in her hot pink silk gown and gloves, dripping with diamonds, ascending a red staircase, surrounded by boys in tuxedos, saying, *No, no, no, no* in her tiny baby voice, then switching to an operatic lilt, hitting a line of potential suitors with her fan one by one, until they all shot themselves in the head and dropped to the floor.

Later, between takes, Frances watched Monroe and Russell sit on those same stairs, Monroe drinking a bottle of Coke, Russell checking her powder. Their long legs seemed to grow straight out of their spangly showgirl skirts.

When Frances went to see the film the day it premiered, she stayed in her seat long after the lights came up. She had been there. She had seen this happen. How many people could say a thing like that?

"Frances wrote the company motto, '*A Diamond Is Forever,*'" Ham said now. "It's a good one. You wrote it, what, five years ago?"

"Eight."

"Eight! And they're still using it."

Meg looked impressed. "I bet that made you the star of the copy department."

"You'd be surprised."

Frances had gotten a small bonus for the line eventually and word that Sir Ernest was pleased, but that was all. No one ever made a fuss about it. It was just part of the job.

Watching Marilyn Monroe sing in the cinema that day, Frances had noticed a line in the song that sounded a lot like something she would write, only a hair more blatant: *Time rolls on and youth is gone and you can't straighten up when you bend. But stiff back or stiff knees, you stand straight at Tiffany's. . . . Diamonds are a girl's best friend.*

Yes, that was the idea—that the diamond would last even if the love did not. Even though youth would not.

Meg wore a large round diamond on her ring finger. Almost all the girls did nowadays. Eight out of ten American brides. When Frances caught sight of them—at the gro-

cery store, or in the pews at church—it gave her a tiny burst
of pride. They didn't know why they wanted diamonds, but
they wanted them all the same. There was no tradition, not
really. But she had convinced them otherwise.

There had been only two years on her watch when diamond sales did not increase over the last: marriage rates
peaked in 1946, but started decreasing in '48, and that paired
with a recession scare slowed sales for a bit. They had to get
creative. Realizing that the engagement market could only
ever be as big as the number of girls marrying in a single
year, they turned their attention to something more elastic,
which they called "Later in Life" diamonds. These fell into
two categories: jewelry for anniversaries and other occasions, and deferred engagement rings, for already-married
people who had never gotten a diamond or who might want
to replace a small stone with a bigger one.

In 1950, when boys started shipping out to Korea, engagement ring sales spiked, and they had gone up every year
since. A greater number of jewelry stores were selling rings
of two carats and larger—70 percent more than just a few
years earlier. And diamond wedding bands were popular
now, too. Thirty percent of brides in America today wore
one, in addition to the engagement ring, not instead of.

Ayer would soon start their first ever international campaign for De Beers, attempting to expand the diamond
engagement ring tradition around the world.

They continued to push the ideas of gift diamonds and
deferred engagement rings, since this market was made up
largely of couples in their forties and older, with greater
purchasing power than the average newlyweds. They added
magazines to their preexisting stable, publications read by
affluent people, like *Town & Country*, *The New Yorker*, *News-
week*, and *Time*.

Gerry Lauck was reading Thorstein Veblen's *Theory of the Leisure Class*, and he said it had given him plenty of ideas.

"It's called 'conspicuous consumption,'" he told her. "We ought to promote the diamond as the essential object through which a man can convey his success."

Gerry handed her a memo with the details. Frances glanced down and saw the description of the tone he wanted her to set: *Should have the aroma of tweed, old leather, and polished wood which is characteristic of a good club.*

And so they ran a series of photographs of well-to-do-looking men in nice suits, with copy like: *No other gift expresses you so well. Your discriminating taste . . . Your affectionate regard . . . Your discerning sense of values . . . Your place in the world.*

And: *A diamond, most valued of gems, steadfastly suggests the measure of your devotion.*

Frances wasn't sure a diamond was any more valuable than any other gem, but once she started writing it, it became a fact.

They wanted the average Joe and his girl to see diamonds everywhere worth looking. Dorothy was just terrific at getting diamonds into the press. At least once a month she sent a release to all newspapers with a circulation of over fifty thousand that used photos on their fashion pages. It contained pictures of diamonds incorporated into the newest fashion trends, often accompanied by a news article. She regularly sent interesting tidbits about movie stars and their diamonds to press syndicates. These were placed with publications around the country, and each week they actually ran her stories as if they were news.

Every year at Christmastime, she'd suddenly appear as a guest columnist in the Women's Pages, writing under the name "Diamond Dot Dignam." On the surface, these arti-

cles were about the basic fact that more diamond engagement rings sold in December than in any other month. But
Dorothy would soon segue into celebrity mentions: *Precious
goods come in small packages and sometimes in rather peculiar
ones. Frank Sinatra, in the blush of early romantic love, gave
Nancy a diamond wristwatch in a 10-cent bag of jelly beans.
Ellen Lehman McCluskey, New York society decorator, once
designed a tiny fir tree to come in on the Christmas morning
breakfast tray of the wife of a client. Just one ornament on the
tree—a diamond bowknot.*

Dorothy was willing to try anything, which made the
campaign a hell of a lot of fun. She was the person who had
decided to sell Fords to women through Parisian fashion
shows, in which the models draped themselves over auto-
mobiles. She now hosted diamond fashion shows in New
York and Paris each year, too. She got diamonds on the
covers of magazines, and live television news shows. She
convinced other high-end advertisers to feature diamonds
in their ads so they would become synonymous with luxury
goods.

Dorothy even approached the British royal family, since
they had a vested interest in promoting South Africa's biggest export. She wrote dozens of releases about their love
of diamonds. During the soon-to-be Queen Elizabeth II's
royal visit to America in 1952, Dorothy was the only person who had advance photographs of all the jewelry she
would bring, courtesy of De Beers. Dorothy got to travel
on the royal train and sent dispatches daily to the Associ-
ated Press. Not long after, she offered a story on the Coro-
nation, with a focus on the diamonds in the British Crown
Jewels. More than three hundred requests carried the tale to
millions of readers. Dorothy's snappy opening had made
Frances laugh: *The story is told that the first time baby Prince
Charlie saw his mother, the young Queen Elizabeth, posing for*

a photographer in her diamond tiara, he chuckled and pointed and asked, "What's that funny hat, Mummy?"

The boom of suburban living had created a trend toward more casual clothing and fewer opportunities for people to wear and see diamonds on a daily basis in real life. So it was their job to make sure that everyone saw diamonds on the women they aspired to be, or to be with. When it came to diamonds, Dorothy always said, "The big ones help sell the little ones."

Frances wrote an entire campaign around socialites, to date perhaps the biggest headache of her career. In-house they called them "the role models" for the middle class, but she could think of a few other choice names for them. They all had opinions on how they ought to dress and pose. Each advertisement in the series showed a portrait of a bride, show-casing the ring on her finger by having her hold a fan or a cigarette or something. And then her name, single and married, along the lines of: *Mrs. Washington Irving, the former Miss Frances Schmidlapp of New York, painted by Gerald Brockhurst.*

Brockhurst was an artist of some renown among society types. He had painted the likes of Marlene Dietrich and the Duchess of Windsor, so the girls clamored to have him paint them, too. After one ad was prepared and approved, Frances received a hysterical phone call from its subject, who reported that she had suffered a broken engagement.

"Please don't cancel the ad," she sniffled. "Please! I'll be engaged again by the time it appears."

Below each portrait would be Frances's hopeful, yet instructive words. *In the fair light of an engagement diamond, the joy and beauty of life's most important pledge are endlessly reflected. Because tradition does endow it with such special meaning just for you, your diamond, though it may be modest in cost, should be chosen with care. You will need the advice of a trusted jeweler.*

Every jewelry store in the country benefited from the De Beers ads, from Tiffany to some small family business in Arkansas. Ayer developed the Diamond Promotion Service, to keep them interested in selling diamonds, through all sorts of tricks.

The lecture series was an essential part of this. A woman named Gladys Hannaford had been giving talks to youth groups, high schools, colleges, and women's clubs since 1944. She could reach ten thousand students in a week. Along with Dorothy, she had written a series of classroom lectures for various courses: geology, gemology, business economics, geography, fashion, retailing, merchandising, and design. Whatever the label of the course, Gladys always focused the talk on the engagement diamond in the end.

With themes like *Who Sets the Fashion in Diamonds, Histories of Famous Diamonds, Secrets of the Diamond Experts,* and *Diamonds with a Past,* she brought along samples of the rock formation in which diamonds are found, rough gems, and, most important of all, a selection of modern engagement rings for the girls to try.

They expected a surge of marriages in the sixties because of the baby boom of the forties, and it was never too early to start targeting those future brides and grooms.

Meg Patterson touched her shoulder. "Will you join us for croquet?"

"Hmm? Oh sure, love to."

The three of them walked through the grass, and Frances began her pitch. "So Ham, Meg. You belong to Merion, right?"

But they were interrupted now by that snake Janey Welch and her awful children, who wanted to play too. Frances passed the next two hours smiling through gritted teeth.

Over lunch, Harry Batten addressed the assembled crowd and gave the usual speech.

"I couldn't be more proud to be the chairman of this great company. The inventor of the advertising business. Headquartered in the greatest city on earth: Philadelphia."

Most people whooped and cheered, but Frances saw a few of the boys from the New York office roll their eyes.

Batten became president in 1937, and had been promoted to chairman a few years ago. He started at the firm as a printer's devil, and worked his way up to head of the copy department. He was obsessed with Philadelphia. He spent all his time and money buying up town houses around Washington Square and throwing his support behind the most popular local politicians.

Batten didn't give a damn what was going on in New York. The advertising business had begun to shift, so that some believed being there was almost essential. But he saw no reason for Ayer to change. They were the best in the business and always had been.

He prided himself on not having a big-city attitude like some of the New York agencies. At Ayer, only the business side was based there. If you so much as said the word "Manhattan" in Batten's presence, he'd start in about all those bozos at J. Walter Thompson who were out of touch with America. *You've got to be inside the consumer's head! To want what he wants, and to know why he wants it. Why, do you think these New York admen on Madison Avenue have ever even been to Coney Island? They're not real Americans, that's all. How do you think we got the Bell System? Because we're the only non-socialists in the business!*

It seemed to Frances that they were forever trying to prove that somehow Philadelphia was closer to New York clients than the New York agencies were. She had worked on the Lever Brothers account last year. She would have to go up to New York in the morning and present advertising and listen to the product man, then return late, getting home after midnight. She'd be back in New York the next morning for coffee.

Batten continued now, "N. W. Ayer was founded in 1869 by Francis Wayland Ayer. He named the agency for his father, a country schoolteacher. In 1892, Ayer employed a full-time copywriter, and this was the start of the first-ever agency copy department. Some of you youngsters probably don't know that before the turn of the century, advertisers wrote their own ads and the agency's job was just to be the middleman between publisher and client. Ayer changed that. And our copy department was only the first in a long line of innovations. Ayer was the first agency to arrange a radio broadcast program on behalf of a client, in 1924. The first agency to work in television. Starting a decade ago, we began producing telecasts for Atlantic Gasoline, Goodyear Tire & Rubber Company, AT&T, United Air Lines, the Army and Air Force recruiting services, and others."

Frances sighed. They had all heard this before. She had to leave in half an hour, and she still hadn't gotten her chance to ask Ham.

"None of our success would mean anything if it weren't for our integrity," Batten went on. "We have always refrained from using celebrity appeals, or playing on people's insecurities. Others in the business might call us sticks in the mud, but in reality we have only tried to avoid the abuses of advertising and be truthful."

A large round of applause went up. Frances doubted that anyone was so moved by what he said; they just wanted him to shut up so they could enjoy their lunch. Though she thought it was true that they all felt a real sense of pride working at Ayer, knowing this was where it had all begun, the agency that stayed on top. Complaints were inevitable, the way you might complain about your own family. They didn't really mean it.

She felt someone touch her back, and turned to see Doro-thy, deviled egg in hand, wearing her trademark hat and a long swinging skirt that pulled in tight at her waist. "Sticks in the mud? These fellas? Never!"

She winked and popped the egg into her mouth.

Frances hugged her. "You're a sight for sore eyes, dar-ling."

"Likewise. Do you want to hear some of the latest ques-tions the boys around the New York office have asked me? Just to pass the time?"

"Of course."

Dorothy pulled a sheet of paper from her pocket and unfolded it dramatically, clearing her throat. "Do women ever make automobile slipcovers? What's the difference between a party call and a party line? Does a woman know when to change oil? What do you give a girl graduating from a convent? How high is a continental heel? Would men use a flesh-tinted body powder? Would you have any feelings about seeing a horse in a bed-sheet advertisement?"

They laughed. There was no one else who understood Frances's day-to-day life the way Dorothy did.

Dorothy had been the one to tell her about the pay. No one at Ayer ever talked about how much money they made, and Frances had never given it any thought. But over cock-tails in New York one evening a few weeks back, Dorothy had told her. "You know we make half of what the men do. And we're kept out of lots of the serious business. All of the most important meetings in this company happen on the golf course at Merion."

"Merion?"

"Well, yes. What defines you as a member of Main Line society is a membership to the Merion Golf Club, or else the Merion Cricket Club, and bully to the man who has both. Most of the senior Ayer men belong."

Frances thought about the pay issue that night. The general consensus in the business was that women came second to men. They were only there to handle the ladies' products that were beneath male sensibilities, and so they got paid less. She reasoned that there wasn't much she could do about that. But she kept thinking of what Dorothy had said about Merion.

The next day, she went straight to the country club.

It was a swanky place, to say the least. It had hosted the U.S. Open back in 1950. The grand building was marked PRIVATE. But Frances wasn't intimidated. She thought of her relatives in Canada—these people were no greater than any of them. She passed the main dining room, with its Oriental rug and plush chairs. There was a fireplace on one wall and a trophy case directly across from it.

In the office upstairs, she asked to speak with the manager. A skinny man in glasses stepped out from behind a door and greeted her warmly.

"I'd like to become a member," she said.

"All right. Are you new to the area?"

"No, sir. I've lived here most of my life."

"Splendid." He pulled a pen from a jar as if to take notes. "And what is your husband's name, ma'am?"

"I have no husband. Just me."

The man chuffed. "I'm sorry, ma'am, but all memberships here are for men."

"I know plenty of women members. Rose Jackson. Meg Patterson."

"Well, yes. But their husbands are members too. We've never had a woman on her own."

"As my father likes to say, there's a first time for everything."

He smiled warily. "Around here, things don't change very much. That's part of what our members cherish about it."

"Is that so?" She traced a white-gloved fingertip across the counter. "How would I proceed if I just wanted to give it a try?"

"You would need a sponsor, and I doubt you'll find anyone willing to take that on."

She thought immediately of Ham.

"We'll see," she said. "Thank you, Mister—"

"Adams," he said. "Floyd Adams."

"I'll be in touch, Mr. Adams."

As she turned to go, he stammered, "Even if you did find someone, the board would have to discuss it. It's never been done before. And even if they approved you, women absolutely cannot vote here. That's non-negotiable. It's against policy."

She felt a flutter of excitement. He was considering it!

"Very well."

"And you couldn't golf with the men, of course. Strictly against policy."

"Of course. Would I be permitted to breathe the same air, or is that also against policy?"

He smirked as she walked out.

She had decided that the company outing would be just the place to ask Ham and Meg to sponsor her. But now she was running out of time.

"Meet me at my car in ten minutes?" she said to Dorothy.

"You've got it. I can't wait to leave, Fran! I may go down to the lot right now and just putter around."

Frances found the Pattersons standing against a tree, eating burgers off of one paper plate.

"I've got a big favor to ask," she said.

Ham looked worried. "Oh?"

"Well, not so big. It's just that I was thinking. I love golf, as you know, and I'm an Ayer man through and through. Perhaps I ought to join Merion."

Ham laughed. Not the reaction she was hoping for. Frances plowed ahead.

"They say I'll need a sponsor, and I thought you might be it."

She could tell that poor Ham would rather be anyplace else on earth in this moment.

"Far as I know, there aren't any single ladies that belong there," he said.

"I know."

"Wouldn't you feel strange?"

"No, not really."

"And you spoke to Merion about this? They'd allow it?"

"They said they'd think about it. I need to get the sponsor first."

"Huh." He frowned, and she saw what a large thing it was to ask—the men of Merion wouldn't want her around, and he wouldn't want to be responsible for her presence.

"Can I give it some thought?" he said.

"Of course."

Frances kissed Meg on the cheek and started in the direction of her car. She hadn't cried in ages. Years, probably. But now she felt tears in her eyes, and quickly tried to blink them away.

She knew a woman had to choose one path or another, and she had chosen hers long ago. But on occasion, it hurt to see what she had given up. Not children, not even love, but just the normal things that every coupled woman took for granted.

As Frances walked, she heard quick footsteps behind her. She turned to see Meg.

"Wait!" she said. She touched Frances's arm and dropped her voice to a whisper. "I shouldn't be telling you this. But there's a good chance Ham and I will be moving to New York."

"What?" Frances said. "When?"

"He's gotten an offer from Young & Rubicam. It's a lot of money. The man said his talents could be put to better use in New York. He said they're doing much more sophisticated stuff up there, and the pay is better, and he said—oh, never mind. I've already said too much."

"No. Tell me," Frances said. "What did he say?"

"He said that Ayer is dying. But of course he'd say that, right? He works for Ayer's competitor!"

It wasn't the first time Frances had heard it. A few years ago, they started saying that Doyle Dane Bernbach had turned the business upside down.

But Frances agreed with Harry Batten on this one: she just didn't believe it. And anyway, it didn't impact her even if it was true. She would never leave Philadelphia. She didn't have the kind of personality it took to move around every six months, or whatever they did in New York. They might pay you a hell of a lot of money, and then you'd have to figure out the hard way that as soon as they felt like it, you'd be out on your neck. She had heard that in New York, it was the rage now to make every potential employee go through a full psychological evaluation. They'd take you to lunch, and if you so much as used the saltshaker, they wouldn't hire you.

It was a zoo up there. Cocktails at breakfast, staying in the restaurant all afternoon. In Philadelphia, you had two drinks at lunch and went back to your desk. It was just a more respectable place. She only ever wanted to have one job and grow in it. Ayer was the perfect agency for her— old-fashioned and conservative, maybe, but solid and dependable.

"The reason I'm telling you all this, is just to say that I don't care what anyone at Merion thinks, and neither should Ham," Meg went on. "We won't belong there much longer anyway. Don't you worry, Frances. I'll get him to sponsor you."

She felt unbearably grateful. "Really?"

"Sure! It will be fun to shake things up at stiff old Merion for a change. We're some of the youngest members, you know. They probably expect these sorts of shenanigans from us."

"Aww Meg, you're a peach."

Frances could see Dorothy in the distance, leaning against the passenger-side door of her car, smoking a cigarette. After the meeting, they would probably go out for a couple of cocktails. Then Frances would go home and fix dinner for herself, and watch television with the dog at her feet.

Just like that, she was happy again to be free. Right as rain.

Part Two

1972

Evelyn stood at the kitchen sink, arranging the flowers in a crystal vase. The roast was in the oven, and the aroma had just begun to fill the room when Gerald walked in.

"Smells delicious!" he said.

Since returning home from her errands, she had left him alone in his study. They called hello to one another when she arrived, and that was all. But now, as he wedged in beside her to fill a glass of water, she said, "I saw Julie."

"Where?"

"Downtown. At the bookshop."

"What did she say?"

Evelyn could feel a lump rising in her throat.

"She said Teddy's asked her for a divorce. So that's why he's come, then."

Gerald rubbed his temples. "I was afraid of that."

"But you said you thought he had realized his mistake."

"That's what I hoped."

"He wants her to say in court that he abused her. And I'm supposed to say I witnessed the whole thing."

"Christ. Has he lost his mind?"

"Yes!" she shouted, so loudly that they were both caught off guard by the sound.

"Oh now, come on," he said, hugging her. "It will be all right."

"How can you say that? You want our son to be divorced?"

"Of course not. I'm sick about it. But there's nothing we can do."

When she was Teddy's age, divorce was something people

only whispered about. A scandal. An absolute last resort. An escape from horrible drunkenness or insanity. But in the last few years, divorce seemed to be everywhere. There was even a new law in some states, declaring "no fault," to help avoid the exact situation poor Julie was in. Maybe it made sense in a court of law, but practically speaking a marriage didn't get destroyed for no reason. It had to be someone's fault.

Is this how America would be now? Anytime the wind blew you might leave behind your entire life and start another? What would it do to her granddaughters, and all the other children like them? Evelyn had been lucky with Gerald; he was a wonderful man, and theirs was a happy marriage. But she thought of others who were less fortunate—her parents, for instance, had never gotten along. Even so, they had kept their vows until the end.

Since she and Gerald were young, what it meant to be an American had changed. There was so much emphasis on the self now—self over country, self over family, self over all else. Her son was a shining example of the consequences.

"I don't want to see him today," she said. "I've changed my mind."

"Well, we can't exactly turn him away."

"Why not?"

Of course she knew why not, and that was why she was standing here arranging flowers when she'd rather be crying into her pillow.

"Evie! They haven't gone to court yet. Nothing is carved in stone. Maybe when he gets to town, sees his girls, sees us, he'll have a change of heart."

"Do you really think so?"

"I don't know what to think anymore."

"Julie was so cold to me," she said. "Like I was a stranger. Or no, something even worse than that. Gerald, she's taking the girls away. All the way back out west."

"She said that?"

"Yes."

He took a deep breath. "You have to remember that it's not you she's angry with."

"I know, but the thought of her leaving for good—I miss her already and she's just across town. I haven't missed anyone quite so much since Nathaniel."

Gerald ran a hand up and down her back. "I know."

"And maybe it's even harder, since she's still here. I can see her, but she won't let me in."

Gerald shook his head. "Imagine what Nathaniel would say about all this."

"He'd say our son needs a swift kick in the you-know-where."

Her husband let out a laugh. "That is exactly what he would say."

Over the years, they had often asked one another what Nathaniel might make of a new trend or a story in the news or some bit of drama in their lives. It was a small way of keeping him alive, even though he had been dead now for far longer than he had lived.

Gerald was Nathaniel's roommate at Harvard, and he had been one of only ten guests at Evelyn's first wedding. Outsiders might think it odd, but she and Gerald had a perfect understanding about Nathaniel. They had both loved him dearly, and they would each continue to love him that way until the end. This didn't threaten either of them. They saw no point in pretending he had never existed. In fact, she would go a step further and say that they both believed pretending he never existed would be strange and quite impossible.

Evelyn met the pair of them at a college swim meet in 1927, when she was a senior at Wellesley. Gerald's cousin was on the Radcliffe team, and they had come to cheer her on. It was Gerald who spoke to Evelyn first, right after she won the freestyle competition.

"That's quite a sidestroke you've got there," he said, catching her eye as she dried off by the edge of the pool.

"Thanks."

"You look good doing it, too."

Then Nathaniel swooped in behind him in his raccoon coat, as dashing as any man she had ever laid eyes on. "Please don't mind my friend. He doesn't get out much."

Evelyn laughed.

"I'm Nathaniel Davis," he said.

"Evelyn Green."

By the time she got to the locker room, she had secured a date for Saturday night.

Until college, she had been painfully shy. But at Wellesley, surrounded by lively, outgoing girls, she began to come into her own.

She had a roommate named Midge, who bought *Liberty* magazine every week, and from its pages they learned all the latest dance steps, which they practiced unabashedly in the bathroom mirror, shuffling and tapping across the wide tile floors. In bed at night, they read Dorothy Dix's advice column aloud to one another. DD, as they called her.

Midge introduced Evelyn to shorter skirts and crepe dresses and felt cloche hats, to which they secured jeweled brooches their mothers had given them back home for an entirely different purpose. They wore Mary Janes with high heels and buckles. Midge taught her about rouge, powder, lipstick, eye shadow, and nail polish, though Evelyn never wore as much as the other girls. She knew her father would be mortified to discover that she had ever been seen in public with makeup on her face. Midge made her own shift dresses, with dropped waists, and tassels fluttering at the hemline.

Her entire life, Evelyn had known adult women to wear corsets, pulled as tightly as possible, so as to make the waist look tiny, the breasts high and full. But Midge insisted that they go free, other than the bust bodices they used to flatten their chests and create a more streamlined look.

Midge helped her get ready for her first date with Nathaniel.

"What's he like?" she asked as she ran shadow over Evelyn's eyelids, and Evelyn replied, "Handsome." Truly, she didn't know much more than that.

At dinner, she learned that he was also well mannered, smart, funny, and kind. He had grown up in Pittsburgh with three sisters, the only son of a steelworker. He read Hemingway and Faulkner, and liked poetry. He was studying literature, and hoped to become a lawyer someday, and then later, maybe a politician. After dinner, they went to a jazz club and danced until closing.

On their second date, they came in third place at a dance marathon, lasting fourteen hours on their feet. Her heels bled the next day, but she could not remember having had a better time in all her life.

On their fifth date, he told her he was worried about his roommate. They were getting to the point where they should be looking for the girls they would marry (this he said with a knowing nod in her direction, which thrilled her), and still Gerald never dated serious women, or even appropriate ones—just a string of chorus girls and waitresses. They tried to fix him up with Midge, but Midge said he was too silly, not intellectual like Nathaniel, or handsome enough, either. Gerald did tell terrible jokes, and he would flirt with a hat stand; a reasonable woman could hardly take him seriously. At twenty, his hairline had already begun to recede, and he was shorter than Evelyn, though admittedly she was tall for a girl. Next to Nathaniel, he looked slight.

Gerald came from a tremendously wealthy family. One got the impression that he didn't have to try very hard at anything, so he didn't. For Nathaniel, affording a Harvard education was a struggle. He cleaned toilets for his tuition, and had worked for this opportunity all his life. For Gerald, Harvard was a given, simply what a Pearsall man must do.

"He'll find a proper woman who will help him spend his inheritance," Evelyn told Nathaniel. She herself had grown up around them—the wives of rich and powerful men, who entertained and kept the house running. No doubt, her father had wanted her mother to be that sort of wife.

"But that's just the trouble," Nathaniel said. "I want him to find someone who will love him despite all that, not because of it. He'd be miserable with some stuffy socialite."

Evelyn was touched by how much he cared for his friend. It was the mark of a good man. She thought to herself that they ought to make a point of including Gerald when they went out. In the months that followed, the group of them—Gerald, Nathaniel, Evelyn, Midge, and anyone else who cared to join—spent their nights roaring through the streets of Boston in Gerald's car, with the girls in the rumble seat in back. They ate cheap suppers and went dancing and drank at hidden speakeasies that the boys somehow knew how to find. Gerald always tried to pay the bill. When the rest of them resisted, he'd say, "It's not my money, it's my old man's." He always left a huge tip, 30 percent at least. It made Evelyn wonder if he was very generous or just awful at math. Nathaniel said it was the former.

They graduated in 1928, the year Herbert Hoover was elected president on the slogan "A chicken in every pot, a car in every garage." She remembered Gerald merrily saying, *As long as there's not a chicken in every garage—that could get strange*. At which they had all rolled their eyes.

Their merry band split up then: Midge accepted a proposal from a medical student she met at a Boston University mixer, and followed him back to his tiny hometown in Indiana. She sent Evelyn letters, saying she had never felt so cold. The New England chill was nothing, she said, compared to this. Indiana cold crawled inside of you, under your skin and into your ears and nose. A coat and hat were no match for it.

Gerald went to Chicago to head up a new division of his father's company. Nathaniel reported that Gerald found his coworkers to be a bunch of wet blankets; they never wanted to go out after work, perhaps because he was the boss's son. *I'm lonesome. I miss our days of getting spifficated in Cambridge*, Gerald wrote. Evelyn laughed when Nathaniel read this aloud. She missed them too.

She herself had decided to stay on in Boston, mostly to be near Nathaniel. Just before graduation, she heard someone in her dormitory talking about job openings for teachers at a public school. It was in a dangerous neighborhood, and no one wanted to work there, the girl said. Evelyn applied the next day. It gave her something to do, something meaningful enough that her mother might approve and not question her decision to stay.

She lived with a roommate in a rented apartment on Beacon Hill and began teaching third grade. Evelyn loved her pupils; they were bright and boisterous and they made her laugh. They made her want children of her own with an intensity she had never experienced. She and Nathaniel intended to marry, though he told her he couldn't propose until he was worthy of her: "If I went to New York now and asked your father's permission, he'd shout me all the way back to Massachusetts."

Despite the fact that her mother said teaching was a noble vocation, her parents were alarmed. They thought she ought to come home and move back into their house until she found someone suitable to marry. And they thought that while Boston girls might try to make their way in Manhattan, there was no earthly reason for a New Yorker to settle in Boston. Her decision to attend Wellesley instead of Barnard or Sarah Lawrence had been acceptable only because two of her cousins were already in attendance, and it was assumed that they would keep an eye on her.

Her father sent her money each month, concerned about the way she was living. But Evelyn put the money in a drawer, determined never to spend it. She would survive on her own, as Nathaniel did.

The first year after college was strange and sometimes scary, but she was pleased to remain away from home and close to him. With Nathaniel drawing a salary, they were able to go out two or three times a week. Not usually anything fancy—maybe a movie or coffee during the week, and dinner and dancing on Saturdays. He told her once that he worried he'd never be able to give her the kind of life she had grown up with: servants and chauffeurs and all that. She told him she didn't want that life anyway. She liked to cook him dinner: roast beef with carrots and potatoes, a pound cake for dessert. When she did this, it felt almost illicit: as far as she knew, her own mother had never cooked a meal. Her parents would say such things were beneath her. But Evelyn liked the idea of living a simpler life, being a teacher, a mother, a wife. She saw in Nathaniel all the things she could ever ask for in a man.

He brought her little presents whenever they met: a single daisy, or a tiny box of chocolates from the sweet shop near his office in Faneuil Hall. He read to her at night before he went home, as she dozed on the sofa after dinner.

In the fall, Nathaniel started Harvard Law School. She imagined a proposal might come any day.

But then the stock market crashed, and all around them

people they knew were suddenly out of work. They heard of old college pals who were barely making ends meet, and read in the newspaper about former businessmen selling apples in the streets of New York. The children Evelyn taught were poor even in the best of times. Now, half her class vanished, their parents needing every last family member at home, earning money any way they could. Those who remained were struggling. Their school was lucky enough to be under the supervision of the Boston School Committee, which received hot lunches from the Women's Educational and Industrial Union. In most schools in the country there was no free lunch, and hungry children fought to pay attention and stay awake in class. But as Evelyn watched her pupils, she saw that hardly any of them ate the food provided. Instead, they wrapped it up and placed it in their book satchels. When she asked why, one of the more outspoken boys said, "It's dinner for our families, miss."

She told the principal what she had learned. He just shrugged and said, "They all do it, it's sad."

After that, she used the money her father sent each week to make sure her children were fed during the day. She mostly bought items that she could stretch a bit—peanut butter and bologna and apples and bread. But once in a while, she'd roast a chicken, something with a bit more sustenance.

All through the fall, she and Nathaniel thanked God that the troubles hadn't come to their doorstep. At Thanksgiving, Gerald came to Boston to visit his parents, and she cooked at her apartment on the Saturday night. The three of them laughed and gabbed, like old times. But one evening the following week, Nathaniel's father didn't return home after work. Days later, they learned that he had been fired after thirty years in the steel mills. Hearing the news, he threw himself off a bridge, into the icy waters below.

Nathaniel decided to leave law school until he could get

his mother and sisters back on their feet. Gerald loaned him what Nathaniel called an embarrassing sum of money, without his having to ask, but Nathaniel was too proud to take it, and sent it directly back.

He went home to Pennsylvania for two months. Evelyn accompanied him to his father's funeral and then returned to Boston alone. It was the saddest period she had ever spent, and she understood with great clarity that she never wished to spend a day apart from him again. He sent her love letters, and she fell asleep at night clutching them in her hand. The months that followed were grim. To get through them, they often reminded one another that this was the most difficult thing they would ever have to endure.

They were finally engaged at Christmas, 1931, with plans to marry in front of one hundred people at her parents' home in New York the following May. Evelyn was elated at the thought of being Mrs. Nathaniel Davis at last. She knew all girls must feel this way about their engagements, but she wondered if perhaps it was more pronounced for her, since they had been through so much darkness together these past few years. Now, finally, there would be joy.

To celebrate, they met Gerald at the Winter Olympics in Lake Placid the first week of February. He looked ten years older, even though it had only been two since Evelyn had seen him last. He brought along a chippie he was going with named Fran, with short red hair and tight clothing. Evelyn asked Nathaniel if he thought Gerald was serious about her, and Nathaniel replied, "When has Gerald ever been serious about anything?"

Indeed, on the very first night, he made a toast. "To my dear friends, Nat and Evie. Embarking on marriage at last! I read recently that John Watson predicts that in fifty years' time there will be no such thing as marriage."

"Who's John Watson?" the chippie asked.

"He's a renowned child psychologist, and apparently an expert on the topic of matrimony to boot. Now me personally, I'm with him. Let's do away with the whole messy business. It's usually such a disappointment when all is said and done."

Evelyn felt uncomfortable, shifting in her chair, until Gerald concluded, "But if anyone can be the exception to the rule, it's you two."

They stayed in a beautiful lodge with a fireplace in every room, which Gerald called a camp. It looked like a hotel, but was a private residence owned by his aunt and uncle. Evelyn loved it there. She could have spent the entire week reading on the window seat in the parlor, looking out at the pine trees in the distance. But the boys wouldn't stand for that— these were the first Winter Olympics ever held in America, and they wanted to be sure to see every last bit of them.

Gerald seemed to be perpetually drinking from a flask of bourbon he kept strapped to his boot. In college, they had all enjoyed their cocktails, but not like this. Gerald appeared to be drunk from the first moment she saw him each morning until the second they all parted ways for bed. He wanted the rest of them to be just as bad as he was—he tipped his flask into poor Fran's drink every time she opened a bottle of pop or poured a cup of coffee. *"Come on, have some giggle water. It's more fun this way, baby."*

Nathaniel said he was concerned, but he didn't want to put a damper on their trip. He would write Gerald about it after they returned home.

The weather was unseasonably warm that week, which threatened the chances of the bobsled event, and also the skating. But on the last day, they saw Sonja Henie glide across the ice with such grace that you could almost convince yourself it was easy. Though women's skating was a noncompetitive event, the arena was packed to the gills, and standing-room-only tickets went for five dollars apiece. Gerald had gotten them seats in the very first row.

"The better to see Sonja's gams," he said, and then, looking at Fran, who seemed genuinely annoyed, "Aww baby, you know yours are the only gams for me."

Evelyn had read in the paper that morning that the Organization of American Housewives had urged the female figure skaters to wear the old-fashioned long skirts, *to avoid unnecessary wear and tear on the morals of the males who will witness the figure skating exhibitions.* But the female skaters declared that they would not do this unless the sprinters of the summer program agreed to run in Oregon boots and the swimmers to swim in Mother Hubbards.

The article concluded, *However, for the benefit of any husbands of any of the ladies of the Organization of American Housewives who may happen to attend the winter games, it should be noted that there are still some harness shops in the Adirondack villages where they can obtain horse blinkers.*

She laughed, and pointed the page out to Fran. "Maybe we should invest in some of these for Mr. Wonderful."

Before they parted ways at the end of the trip, as the boys were packing up the cars, she overheard Nathaniel ask, "So, do you see any potential with her?"

"Nah," Gerald said. "It's just a bit of fun."

"Haven't you had enough fun? You're an old man now. I want you to find someone who'll take care of you. I want to see you settled down."

"That's easy to say when you've got a girl like Evie," Gerald said. "I don't think you realize how rare she is."

Soon after they got back to Boston, Nathaniel headed home to Pennsylvania for a short visit. He wanted Evelyn to go along, but she didn't think she should leave her students.

"We'll go during my summer vacation, and we'll stay a whole month," she said. "It will be our honeymoon."

He smiled. "By then, we'll be man and wife."

"Your mother can teach me how to make all your favorite meals."

"Anything you make is my favorite," he said, and kissed her.

He was gone for less than a week, but like a lovesick teenager Evelyn counted the days until his return. She busied herself with buying a new dress for their reunion and getting her hair styled at the beauty shop. He was due back Tuesday evening, and that day after school she bought steaks and all the ingredients for a gingerbread cake. As she stood in her narrow kitchen preparing dinner, Ozzie Nelson and his orchestra played "Dream a Little Dream of Me" on the record player, and she thought about everything that lay ahead—their wedding, at which she would wear her mother's satin gown; the house they'd buy in Pennsylvania, with half a dozen children chasing butterflies on the lawn. She was almost twenty-five. Most of her friends already had a baby or two. They would have to start trying right away, once they were married. Her heart was so full that it almost ached. She could hardly wait for Nathaniel to walk through the door so she could throw her arms around his neck.

When he hadn't turned up by seven, she started to feel nervous. She had never known Nathaniel to be late. But she reminded herself that there might be congestion on the road. A year earlier, her father had spent nearly an hour at Christmas dinner complaining about the fact that New York City had installed traffic signals at busy intersections—they slowed everything down, he said, and made it impossible to get anywhere on time. She said a silent prayer that Nathaniel hadn't gotten a flat tire or had trouble with the engine.

By eight-thirty, she was pacing the kitchen in a panic. When the telephone rang just after eleven o'clock, she was sitting at the table shivering, as if she already knew what was to come.

It was Nathaniel's oldest sister at the other end of the line. The accident had happened in Framingham, less than an hour from home. A drunkard had crossed the median and driven head-on into his car. An ambulance had taken Nathaniel to Boston City Hospital. He was unconscious, and bleeding internally. No one could say if he would make it through the night.

After she hung up, Evelyn sat very still and cried for a bit. But when she was done, she stood straight, wiping the tears from her eyes. She knew exactly what she must do. Her fiancé was in danger, but she would bring him through it. She went out into the frigid night air and hailed a taxi, forgetting her coat.

Though she had prepared herself, the sight of Nathaniel lying in a hospital bed still came as a shock—it felt physical, an electric jolt that shot through her body. His eyes were closed, and his face was bloodied and broken, the lower half of it wrapped in gauze like a mummy. In the next bed, an elderly man with paper-thin skin was moaning. She tried to say hello to the man, but he stared past her, out the window, which faced nothing but a plain brick wall.

Evelyn pulled a chair to Nathaniel's side and spoke to him gaily, as if they were out on a marvelous dinner date. She told him about the cake she had baked, and demanded that he wake up to have a slice, or else her feelings would be hurt. She gently stroked his hand. It was the only visible part of him that was not altered, and she stared at its familiar parts—the long, elegant fingers, the dry spots around the knuckles, the crescents of dirt beneath the nails—until the rest of the room vanished.

First thing in the morning, she called Gerald. He told her he would come right away, and though the propriety in her rose up to say no, she pushed it down, knowing that his presence would be a balm to her and Nathaniel both. As soon as he arrived, Nathaniel was moved to a spacious single room with a view of the tree-lined street below. Evelyn didn't know what Gerald had said, or how much he had paid, but she was grateful.

It wasn't until two days later that she thought to call her own parents and tell them the news. Neither of them was home when she rang, and Evelyn was just as content to leave word with the housekeeper as she would have been to hear what they had to say. They had never brought her much comfort. She had learned to make it for herself, and of course to find solace in Nathaniel. She could not dream of a world without him in it.

When Nathaniel's mother and sisters came, Gerald insisted that they stay at his parents' house in Wellesley. Every morning, he drove them to the hospital, and just before dinner he brought them home. He'd often return later, to be with Evelyn, who rarely went back to her apartment. He brought her warm food from his parents' cook, and novels that his mother recommended. He told her to go home and rest for an afternoon, but she could not bring herself to leave Nathaniel. She wanted to be there the moment he woke up. Gerald sometimes stayed through the night with her. They played checkers and did jigsaw puzzles at three a.m., both of them making a point of including Nathaniel in the game, even though he remained unconscious: "Your lady here's about to get creamed," Gerald would say, and she'd reply, "Oh honey, don't listen to him, he's full of hot air."

She was happy he had come. The doctors wouldn't say much to her or to Nathaniel's mother, fearing that they were too fragile to hear the worst. But they would tell Gerald, and he passed the facts along to her without hesitation.

Gerald read to Nathaniel from all the newspapers, telling him about Roosevelt's campaign stops and Howard Hughes's new gangster movie. He seemed to think he might entice Nathaniel back to life by letting him know all he was missing. Sometimes Evelyn thought that it just might work.

It was through Gerald's daily news updates that she learned that the infant son of Charles Lindbergh had been kidnapped from his crib at the family's secluded mountaintop home in New Jersey, while Lindbergh and his wife were downstairs eating dinner. Lucky Lindy was the most famous man in the world. On the occasion of his first child's birth two years back, newspapers all over the globe had printed stories—never had an infant gotten such attention. It was reported that the Lindberghs received more toys from well-wishers than they could manage to fit into their massive house. The child was now twenty months old, a cherub with chubby cheeks and blond curls, a deep dimple in the center of his chin.

The baby's nurse had discovered him missing. Right away, there were troubling clues: A window in the nursery left open. A makeshift ladder found below, and muddy footprints that went on for half a mile. At the edge of a wood, these were joined by a smaller set of prints, belonging to a woman. Where the footprints ended, it was believed that the pair had gotten into a car. Highways were brought to a standstill as police searched every automobile. President Hoover met with the attorney general, and federal agencies were called in, as well as the entire police forces of New York and New Jersey. There was a demand for ransom left in the baby's room, and the next day a penny postcard arrived, written in the same handwriting: "Baby safe. Instructions later. Act accordingly."

The newspapers ran photos of the beautiful boy lying in his bassinet, and cradled in the lap of his mother when he was only a month old. Anne Morrow Lindbergh, slight and pretty, wearing a short dress, her hair cropped up over her ears, staring adoringly at her only son. Evelyn became obsessed with every news item, every update, every rumor passed on by one of the nurses at the hospital, who knew someone who knew someone who had heard something interesting. Mrs. Lindbergh revealed to the hordes of motion-picture cameramen and newspapermen who had gathered outside her home that the baby had a cold. She told them what precisely he ate, in the hopes that the kidnappers would take good care. Colonel Lindbergh said he was willing to pay any ransom that was asked.

It was reported that, like Evelyn, they did not sleep. Sitting in a chair by Nathaniel's bed at dawn, she would imagine Anne Morrow, a girl about her age, pregnant with her second child, pacing the floors of her house, praying for her baby's safe return. Somehow the two tragedies got linked in her head so that Evelyn was convinced if they could just find that child happy and bouncing in some old grandmother's lap, then perhaps Nathaniel could get well, too.

In May, she walked out of the hospital for air one bright morning to hear the newsboys hollering, "Baby dead!" Their voices were almost gleeful, for they knew the story would mean a good day's pay. Evelyn had half a mind to buy up every last paper in Boston, just to silence them. Instead, she bought only one, and read it with shaking hands. The child had been found by a truck driver, facedown in a pile of leaves, five miles from home. He had a fractured skull, due to either blunt trauma or being thrown from a moving vehicle. The police speculated that the kidnappers probably had intended to return him, but that the baby's loud cries had made them panic, and so they quickly decided to kill him instead. He had been dead for several weeks, even as they had continued to claim he was alive, still seeking their ransom and raising his poor family's hopes. By the time the child was discovered, much of his face and body had been destroyed by wild animals.

Evelyn pictured that innocent baby, lying helpless and alone as his father flew planes overhead, searching, searching. Her whole body started to shake. She felt as though she couldn't breathe. She became so hysterical that she had to go back inside the hospital, where she was sedated and placed in a bed for several hours.

Three weeks later, Nathaniel woke up. The doctor warned them that nothing was certain yet, and they shouldn't let themselves feel too excited. But after everything they'd been through, Evelyn couldn't see why not.

They were married in the hospital chapel the following afternoon. She wore a white skirt suit and tan pumps from her closet, her hair pulled back and topped with a little birdcage veil. Nathaniel sat beside her in a wheelchair, looking groggy but happy, as his family and Gerald and a group of nurses looked on. The nurses had taken a real interest in their story, and they liked Nathaniel, mostly because Gerald brought them candy and told them how marvelous they looked at the end of a long shift. One of the nurses baked a cake, and they pooled their money to buy Evelyn flowers and candlesticks and a pretty porcelain dish.

After they were married, she slept beside him in the narrow hospital bed at night, her body pressed to his. For a brief while, she thought they had been spared. But a few days passed, and on a Thursday morning the doctors discovered an infection that had spread to Nathaniel's blood. By the weekend, he was gone.

Despite everything they had known about his chances, his death stunned her. Most of the time, she felt tremendously grateful that he had woken up: they had had those final days together; they were married now. But she could easily get herself worked into a rage wondering why God would give her such a gift, only to take it away.

Evelyn took her time choosing the clothes he would be buried in. With each decision, she knew she would have to close one more door on him, until finally it was done. She stood alone in his tiny apartment in Cambridge, and though she wept, she didn't want to leave. The place still smelled like Nathaniel. She picked the navy-blue suit he had worn when he proposed to her outside the restaurant where they'd had their first date. Aside from in the hospital they had never spent the night together, and now she wished desperately that they had. She slept alone in his bed that night, imagining that the sheets were his arms, wrapped tight around her.

At the funeral, she busied herself with whatever tasks needed doing. She didn't want to stand still. She was Nathaniel's wife, but many people there did not know it. It was strange to think of these other parts of his life: the people who remembered him only as a son, or a brother, or a small boy from the old neighborhood. Rightly so, their sympathy was for his mother and sisters, who had endured one tragedy already, enough for any lifetime.

Afterward, she felt a constant ache. She often looked at strangers who didn't seem altogether terrific—a mother shouting at her son in front of school, a man spitting in the street—and she wondered why they should be able to live and not Nathaniel. Evelyn would stare, nearly believing that there was some way to exchange one of them for him.

In bed at night, she lay awake and thought of the hour his car had been hit. He was all alone out on the highway. Nathaniel had wanted her along on that trip. She should have said yes, she should have been there when those foreign headlights came through the windshield. Then maybe she'd still be with him now, on one side or the other.

1987

James banged a u-ey out of the lot.

They had clocked in only ten minutes earlier, and Maurice was already off and running with one of his stories. While James had done the usual check, making sure that the last guys had left the ambulance fully stocked and everything was working properly—defibrillator, EKG, suction, IV, burn kit, stretcher—Maurice had started in. Now he couldn't stop.

"So I say to the guy, there's nothing wrong with your tire alignment. Your parking brake is probably stuck," Maurice said. "And big surprise, I was right. Now I just saved him ninety bucks and half a day at the mechanic's. And that's another thing. This mechanic he uses is crooked as hell. A Mexican."

Maurice didn't trust Mexicans. James thought it was kind of funny, seeing as Maurice himself was black. When James told him this, Maurice had said, "What? You think black people aren't allowed to be just as prejudiced as everyone else?"

Now, he went on, "Cindy says I sounded like a know-it-all. Like he thought I was judging him for not knowing how to fix his own car. And I swear, at this neighborhood Christmas party, it was like he was looking right through me. So now I kinda want to confront him about it. I mean, we're two grown-ass men. I'm not gonna be standing in my driveway waving at him across the street if meanwhile he's thinking I disrespected him. I should have just let him go on making skid marks on the road and not knowing why."

James pulled up to the regular spot. Two other ambulances idled at the curb. "I hate to interrupt this riveting monologue, but—coffee?"

Maurice nodded.

"I'll go," James said. "You want anything to eat? An egg and cheese?"

"I'll have a sandwich," Maurice said. "A Turkey Delight. Nah, make it a cheeseburger."

"You gotta be shitting me."

"What?"

"Whaddaya mean, what? It's eight in the morning."

"And?"

"Never mind, you savage. Do the reports."

Maurice held up the binder. "I'm doing them. Wasn't kidding about the burger."

"I know you weren't. That's what scares me."

James got out. It was freezing. He could smell snow in the air. He pulled his leather jacket tight across his chest.

Inside Elsie's, he saw the usual suspects sitting at the counter and waved.

"Morning, gentlemen."

Ron Shanahan nodded his head. "Top of the morning, Mr. McKeen," he said, the same thing he said every day.

The job was equal parts adrenaline rush and routine. While on duty, they traveled the same streets over and over. The city of Cambridge was 6.25 square miles, and James knew every inch of it by heart. In a single hour, he was likely to pass through Harvard Square three or four times. He saw the same cops, nurses, and firefighters every day. He got along with most of them. The single people in the mix went out drinking most nights at the Ground Round or the Ding Ho in Inman Square, and were either in love or not speaking, depending on the day.

The younger guys thought they were cowboys—they

were only eighteen, nineteen years old. To initiate a rookie, they might handcuff him to a telephone pole and beat him to a pulp, or hold a loaded shotgun to his head in broad daylight, while onlookers screamed, knowing that when the cops arrived they would just laugh and keep driving. James stayed out of all the drama.

The work itself was always different. There were slow days and crazy ones. On average, they probably went out on about a call an hour. Today it was supposed to snow. Snowstorms were usually quiet, but it just depended. You could be eating breakfast one minute and crawling through a flipped-over car on Memorial Drive the next.

Cathy stood at the counter, pulling her hair up into a ponytail. Her Christmas ornament earrings bobbed up and down. She was in her mid-thirties, pretty, though she wore too much makeup. Her jeans always looked like they were painted straight onto her ass.

"Hey James. Two coffees?"

"Yeah, and a cheeseburger."

"This early?"

He shrugged. "Talk to the guy with the tapeworm out in the truck. You closing up early today?"

"Around four, so I can go over my aunt's house for dinner and then take my mother to midnight Mass."

"Sounds nice."

"Clearly, you haven't met my mother."

She turned away and called the order out to Phil, the owner, who manned the grill.

James's eyes were sore. He closed them tight, rubbed them with his fingers. He didn't know how he was going to get through his shift. Hopefully they'd have some downtime so he could try to sleep. Caffeine wasn't going to cut it today.

It was typical for a medic to work two twenty-fours

a week, but for the past six months, he had been working three. The economy was in the shitter, so he was banking time now, just in case.

When the stock market had crashed a couple months back, James didn't care at first, since he personally had no stake in the stock market. If anything, he was a little bit glad to see rich people feeling scared about money for once. His new favorite joke, which he'd heard from a patient and repeated back home a hundred times, was, "What's the difference between a pigeon and an investment banker? The pigeon can still make a deposit on a Mercedes."

Maurice said he didn't care about the stock market crash either, but he didn't like how much of it had to do with computers. "Do you know they're using them now to figure out trading?" he said to anyone who would listen. "It feels like we're in the hands of a robot and nobody cares."

But now James was starting to worry some. Not about robots, but about money. Last month, the General Motors plant in Framingham shut down, and his buddy Big Boy was out of a job. What had seemed like just a rich person's problem started to feel like more.

His supervisor liked to tell new hires that their field was recession proof: "As long as there's drugs, alcohol, old people, and cars, we'll be busy."

It was true to a point—in hard economic times, they tended to be busier than ever. Unemployment made for more drug and alcohol abuse, depression, suicides, things like that. You'd see a lot of people down on their luck, people with chronic illnesses that they'd ignored for months because they lost their health insurance and couldn't afford to go to the doctor.

So yeah, there was more work, but less of it got paid. The companies would bill, but patients wouldn't respond, and eventually that started to affect staffing.

After he got fired in Lynn, it had taken him a year to find another job. James was lucky to be hired by anyone, given what had happened, and he was determined not to lose this gig.

He felt glad that he'd be out with Maurice today, and not that dumb shit, Andrews. He and Maurice had worked two shifts a week together for the past year and a half. They got along; they had a nice rhythm down. A year and a half was longer than James had ever worked with anyone—the turnover rate was high, especially in a private company like theirs. Not many guys were willing to work such crazy shifts for ten bucks an hour for long. He knew Maurice would leave soon. This was just a stepping-stone for him. Most of the guys eventually became supervisors or operations directors or physician's assistants. One had even quit to become a garbage man—a waste management specialist, he had called it—because the pay was better. A lot of them were waiting for something to open up with the fire department. Through it, a medic had better hours and a higher pay grade. He could retire at fifty-five with 80 percent of his pension.

James was the only guy he knew who had already been with a fire department. He had blown his chances as far as that went, so it was hard to imagine how he could ever move up from here. He deeply regretted what happened, even now, after three years had passed.

For a year, he had tried to get a job with another department, but his reputation preceded him everywhere he went. A buddy from his Lynn days had been the one to tell him that he should try to find work with a private company and never mention what had happened. So that's what he did. He got hired on in Cambridge as an EMT, and went even further into debt to get his paramedic certificate at Northeastern last year. He knew this meant he was more valuable to the company than a basic EMT, and that was worth the money.

Most of his classmates at Northeastern were former Army medics who knew a hell of a lot more about what they were doing than he did. The workload was intense, with time divided between the classroom, the ambulance, and the ER. The written tests reminded him too much of high school. His eyes would fog over when he tried to study. The first time he got a test back, his grade was so low that the instructor stapled a Burger King job application to the booklet. But in the truck, or at the hospital, James felt fired up.

They were the first class of paramedics in the state, and there was a certain cachet to that—they could do more than anyone else. They called them the God Squad. If a patient was in diabetic shock, your basic EMT couldn't do anything but shove sugar packets down his throat. But a paramedic could give a D50 injection and start an IV. A basic EMT would find a guy not breathing from a heroin overdose, and the only thing he could do would be to flop him onto a stretcher and drive to the hospital. James gave the same guy Narcan, and a minute later he'd be sitting up on the sidewalk saying, "I don't know what you're talking about. I've never touched drugs."

The paramedics wore a badge, and it really meant something. But even so, a few of the guys in the company somehow seemed to know about his past. It hung over him, no matter what he did. He could tell they thought he was a reject, a loser. It was damn near impossible to get fired from a civil service job, but leave it to him to find a way.

One night, late, while their trucks were parked outside 7-Eleven and Maurice had gone inside for a Double Gulp and a hot dog off the roller, James stood out front with a prick named Tommy Benson. Tommy had actually had the balls to just say it: "I heard you got booted from the fire department in Lynn. So what is it with you, McKeen? Are you a druggie? An alkie? Or a thief? Or all three?"

James had the urge to hit him, but he thought of Sheila and the boys and just got back in the ambulance.

Maurice was the only one in the company who knew the truth. James feared what might happen if his boss ever found out. He would be fired in a second. The paramedic's license might offer some protection, but not enough.

The new guy, Andrews, who he had to work with one day a week, was ex-military. He had arrived in Boston five months back from somewhere out west. In July, when Andrews started, it was miserably hot inside the truck. They drove around all summer with the back doors flung open, taking turns standing on the back step, where you could breathe, and watch the girls go by in their miniskirts. On their first morning together, James found Andrews already positioned on the step, ready to go.

"Hey kid," James said, pointing his thumb toward the driver's seat. "Screw."

But that didn't last long, because whenever Andrews drove, James got nervous: the kid didn't know his way around, and that was dangerous. He was forever turning the wrong way down one-way streets. Driving to the Beth Israel once, he said, "So just go toward that neon triangle thing, right?" He didn't even recognize the CITGO sign. James had smacked him in the back of the head. "Are you an idiot? Have you never seen a Red Sox game on TV?"

He could tell from experience that Andrews wouldn't last long, maybe a couple months more. He prayed for the day when the kid just didn't show up.

Some guys couldn't take the worst of it. Even if they'd spent time patching up soldiers on the battlefield, there was something different about going into people's homes. In

October, they had found a teenage punk, strangled to death
and probably raped, her body shoved into a broom closet
in some crummy apartment. James had seen her hanging
around the Pit in the weeks before she died. She didn't look
like one of the true homeless kids, more like the suburban
type who was just experimenting before going off to college
and a lifetime of cashmere sweaters. She couldn't have been
older than seventeen. She had a tiny silver hoop through her
nose and blue hair hanging down to her shoulders. Andrews
wept when they left the scene. His legs gave out for a second.

A month later, a woman called 911 complaining of back
pain. When James and Maurice got to her apartment, she
seemed all right, if slightly deranged—she was walking
around the place, oozing a strange energy. James's first
thought was that she was addicted to pain meds and looking
for a fix.

"Did you really need an ambulance, ma'am?" Maurice
asked.

"Yes. My kids are going to ride along with me. Now
where are their jackets?"

"Sorry, ma'am, we can't bring kids," Maurice said. "Can
you leave them with a neighbor?"

"Oh no," she said.

James had a sickening feeling. The apartment was so still.
"Where are your kids, ma'am?"

"In the bathroom," she said brightly, pointing at a
cracked wooden door. He went toward it, bracing himself
as he turned the knob. There were two small bodies floating
in the tub. Water and blood all over the place. A struggle.
She had slit their throats. When he went to touch them, their
skin was cold.

He and Maurice both knew those kids were already gone.
But still, they rushed them to Children's Hospital as if every
second might mean a miracle.

"OSDF! OSDF!" James was screaming from the back of the truck. *Oh shit, drive fast.*

Afterward, he was covered in blood. Even after he washed his hands, it settled in the lines in his palms and the space beneath his fingernails. It clumped in his hair and seeped into the legs of his pants.

James told the new guys at work to do what they could for the patient and then move on. You couldn't let yourself get too caught up. But that one had just about done him in. At home the next morning, before he went inside, he kicked his car in the driveway. It felt good, a tiny release, so he kicked it again, and then again, and again, until there was a huge dent in the driver's-side door and his big toe was broken. Inside the house, he woke Parker up, pressing his son against his chest until Parker whispered, "Daddy, I can't breathe."

James had been raised Catholic, and if he had never exactly believed in God, he had never had a reason not to believe, either. He still remembered the Tuesday after JFK was killed. As the president's funeral processed in D.C., Boston mourned. His mother in her veiled hat sat in a crowded pew at Sacred Heart, with James to her left and his brother to her right, squeezing both their hands. She kept a picture of JFK on her mantel, alongside her wedding portrait and her sons' school photographs. Now she cried softly, as did all the parishioners around her. The place was packed to the gills. When the priest began to speak, James took note of the looks on people's faces—they wanted so badly to be comforted, to have someone else make sense of the madness. The priest said that God had called the president to heaven, and though we might never know why, we must remember that it was part of His divine plan. All the heads bobbed up and down in agreement. James was only ten years old, and for some time he carried that memory with him, believing that faith was essential, that God brought solace to soothe unimaginable pain.

But now that he had watched so many strangers take their final breaths, he felt certain that they did not go anywhere at all. The heart stopped and the brain stopped, and that was the life. Gone. His mother believed that there was this brief period of time after someone died but before they got to heaven, when the person's spirit filled the familiar air. When her own mother passed, she took James to her childhood home and asked, "Do you feel her, Jimmy? Nanny's still here." At the time, he thought that maybe he did, and told her so. His mother seemed pleased.

Cathy returned and handed him the coffees. "Another couple minutes on the burger."

James stared up at the TV in the corner while he waited. The highlight reel from last night's Celtics game flashed across the screen. The Celts had beat the Bullets, 122 to 102. Larry Bird had scored twenty-seven points.

"Good game," he said, to no one in particular.

He had stayed up watching until the end. Even though he was exhausted, he knew he wouldn't be able to sleep, so what was the point of lying there, turning and tossing? He drank five beers during the game. This was a new habit of his, to buy a six-pack and drink five. It was kind of like the way Sheila devoured her dessert but left the last bite of cake on the plate to show restraint.

He felt like shit now, but it was worth it. The only times he really felt alive anymore were when he was watching basketball, or listening to his records from high school, or taking his old Ford Coupe out of his mother's garage for the first time each spring. Pathetic maybe, but true.

He still loved all the music he had loved back when he was playing with his band—the Beatles, the Stones, the Doors, Aretha Franklin, and the Supremes. When he heard those songs, he was transported to a time when it felt like anything was possible. Every one took him back to a moment. The first time he and Sheila spent the night together, when her parents went out of town, was "Today" by Jefferson Airplane: *I'm so full of love I could burst apart and start to cry.*

Junior year, when she said they were through, was Diana Ross singing "Reflections" over and over for three days straight until Sheila changed her mind.

James had a junky bass guitar that had been handed down to him by his cousin. He used to get stoned in his bedroom playing along with the Velvet Underground on the record player and then, high and inspired, he'd write songs of his own, and tape them to the walls. Days later, making out with Sheila in his bed, or jerking off to one of his older brother's *Playboy*s under the plaid bedspread, he'd look up at his creations and feel powerful.

James glanced at his watch. His mother would be up by now, waiting for him to call, like he did every morning around this time. He walked over to the pay phone.

She answered on the first ring. "Jimmy?"

"Ma?"

She paused, he wasn't sure why. She had made an almost full recovery after her stroke, other than her peripheral vision, which was shot. But sometimes she couldn't manage to get her words out.

"Merry Christmas Eve," he said.

"How's your day?"

"Can't complain. I saw your friend Doris when I was out walking the dog this morning."

"I hope you said hello."

"Nah, I just shoved her aside and kept walking."

"Jimmy. Don't be fresh."

"Did you sleep okay?" he asked. She had told him that she was waking up short of breath lately, her heart racing.

The thought of it made him want to move her into his house so he could keep an eye on her at all times. That was probably where they were heading eventually, though James had no idea where they'd put her.

He knew in his bones that she wouldn't live much longer. Whenever he said so to Sheila, she replied, "Every morning when your mother wakes up, she has six months to live. It's been that way for ten years, Jimmy." But he was certain, and the knowledge broke his heart. Standing in the small, dim rooms of her house, James sometimes felt sick thinking that someday soon, all he would have of her would be objects— musty tea towels and eyeglasses on skinny gold cords and plaid furniture that reeked of cigarettes.

"I slept fine," she said.

"Good. Whatcha up to now?"

"Just listening to the cardinal say Mass on the radio, and cooking some eggs for breakfast."

"You know it's gonna snow, right? Don't be planning any long road trips, okay?"

She laughed. She couldn't drive anymore. She never went anywhere on her own. They took her for her weekly outings to the doctor's office and the church and the beauty parlor, where she still got her hair set every Friday, though he couldn't figure out why or who for.

"I'll be by tomorrow morning to say hi. And then I'll be back for you around noon for Mass. Then we'll go to Tom and Linda's for dinner, okay?"

"I'll be ready."

"Maybe we can take the kids into Boston to see the Christmas lights on the Common this weekend. We can have lunch at Brigham's. Would you like that?"

"Oh yes," she said. "I haven't gone in town for ages."

His mother was a saint: a sweet, patient woman who had done her best raising two wild boys alone. He had this memory of one of the few times she had tried to take them on vacation. They went to a motel in Hampton Beach. First his brother got in trouble for finding a stray dog and bringing it into the pool. Then James got into a fight with a kid on the boardwalk over an arcade game and ended up with a black eye. Their mother had brought along her electric frying pan so they wouldn't have to spend money eating out. That night, she tried to make spaghetti in their room, but when she plugged in the pan it blew a fuse, and the entire place lost power. They got thrown out. He could recall her laughing and crying at the same time, all the way back to Massachusetts.

"We really are a motley crew, aren't we?" she said through her tears, and oddly enough, James had felt proud.

The radio was always on in their house growing up—Nat King Cole, Frank Sinatra, *The Irish Hour*, and Mass every morning at seven. "To keep me company," his mother had often said, and it was only now that he realized how young she had been. Eighteen when his brother was born, twenty-two when James came along. A widow by twenty-three. He could still see her pretty young face, frowning whenever he lied. *Jimmy McKeen, you fess up this instant. It's obvious you're fibbing, you have a face like a Russian flag.*

She used to sit out on the front porch before work, chain-smoking in her pink bathrobe and rollers. Now she was fifty-six and looked seventy. Until the stroke, she had worked every day of her life. First as a receptionist in a dental office, and later as a lunch lady at his high school, which had mortified him at the time. Some days James ignored her when he saw her in the cafeteria, pretending she was a stranger. Thinking back on it now made him burn with shame. She waited tables at night some years to make ends meet. Yet she had almost nothing to show for it.

As a young woman, she had probably never imagined

that she'd have to work once she got married. Her husband would provide and she would look after the kids, and that would be that.

James's father drank himself to death. That's how everyone had always put it. Now James knew that drinking yourself to death was just a sanitized way of saying that his father was such a bad alcoholic that he managed to destroy all the cells in his liver, which were gradually replaced with a fatty buildup that turned his skin yellow and made his fluid-filled belly swell so that in the only remaining pictures, he resembled a skinny guy who was eight months pregnant. But he just kept drinking, and eventually ended up with full-blown liver failure, which then led his kidneys to fail, too. It was a slow death that killed him at just twenty-eight. A real overachiever, that guy.

People seemed to want to comfort James over the loss of his father, but how could you mourn someone you couldn't even remember? He figured it was harder for his older brother, Bobby, who actually knew the man, and maybe that accounted for the fact that Bobby had always been an ass, taking every opportunity to beat on James and make him feel small.

Sheila said he buried his feelings. Once, she had even suggested that he might think about talking to a shrink. But really, he had nothing to say. He wished his mother didn't have to be alone, but then he wished a lot of things. Truth be told, he felt sadder about the time when he was in high school and his fifteen-year-old basset hound died. In Sheila's opinion, this was significant, since his father had loved the breed and kept a collection of basset hound mugs and statuettes and spoons and things, all of which got left to James and Bobby.

She said James loved that red '49 Ford Coupe so much because it had once been his old man's. His mother had let the car sit rusting in the driveway, and that year after high school, when he had nothing better to do, James fixed it up to perfection. He put in a Hurst floor shifter and the leather seats from a wrecked Mustang that he found in a junkyard. But he did not think of his father when he drove it. The car felt like his and no one else's.

If anything, James was defined by the man's absence more than the man himself. Growing up in the fifties, they really did believe that most families were Ozzie and Harriet. His friends all had two parents—a father who went to the office, and a mother who stayed home. James used to dream that maybe some kind man would come along and rescue them. But his mother never went on a single date after his father died. She still went by Mrs. McKeen to this day, though her husband had been dead since 1954. It wasn't that she pined for him. She never spoke about the guy. It seemed to James that his mother's behavior had less to do with devotion, and more to do with some old-fashioned belief that when it came to marriage you got one shot, and that was it.

"So I'll be by right after my shift tomorrow to shovel," he said now. "Just stay inside until then, okay? Don't even go out to get the mail."

"Jimmy, don't worry about me," she said. "I'm worried about you. You're working too much. You need a break."

"Sheila will probably go grocery shopping after lunch," he said. "So get your list together."

They took complete care of his mother. Bobby was no help. He had come back from Vietnam with his head a little scrambled. Sheila thought it was unfair, the way he shirked his family obligations, but James was willing to cut him some slack, considering. When they were kids, American children absorbed patriotism without even seeing it, like his own boys got fluoride from the drinking water. Vietnam had

killed this in so many of them. No one knew what they were
fighting for.

Bobby drifted around for a while after the war. He got
involved with something called *est*, which he described as
a personal improvement course, though it seemed like a
straight-up cult to James. He married a maniac he met there.
They moved to Arizona, so James didn't see his brother
much anymore. Whenever his wife's name came up, Sheila
said, "The woman sells Mary Kay cosmetics door-to-door.
Her greatest desire in life is to sell enough lipstick to win
a pink convertible. Your brother's a nut job for marrying
her."

James heard the jingling of the bell that hung above the
door to Elsie's. A rush of cold air. Then Maurice's voice
saying, "McKeen, let's go."

"I'm getting called out on a job," he said into the phone.
"I'll see you tomorrow, all right?"

"Love you, Jimmy," she said.

"Love you too, Ma. And Ma—don't skimp on your heat.
Promise me."

There had been a rash of cases lately, old people who
couldn't or didn't want to spend the money on heating their
homes, so instead they froze to death in their rocking chairs.
A week ago, they had responded to a call from a woman
who hadn't seen her elderly neighbor for a few days. James
knew it was a rent-controlled building, and the heat was
the first thing he thought of. But when they got inside, the
apartment was warm. Maurice checked the thermostat. "It's
off," he said.

In the kitchen, the oven was set to 400 degrees. Its door
hung open. Three feet away, a tiny white-haired lady in a
pink sweat suit lay slumped on the kitchen floor, dead of
carbon monoxide poisoning. The neighbors were lucky
they hadn't all died along with her.

He hung up the phone and turned around. "Hey Cathy——"

"I know," she said with a smile. "You have to go."

"Hold on to that burger for me, will ya?" Maurice said, though they all knew she would make him a fresh one when they returned. All the EMTs came here, so Cathy was used to it, and she was a good sport——sometimes after closing, she brought the day's unclaimed sandwiches to their break room at Cambridge Hospital for whoever might be hungry, free of charge. They, in turn, tipped her like crazy.

James put a five in the jar on the counter before heading out.

He got into the driver's seat. He and Maurice switched off every few hours, and he always took the first leg.

"Two-forty Albany," Maurice told him, buckling his seat belt.

It was a spot they went to at least once a day, the only wet shelter in the city. Every other shelter required sobriety, but at 240 Albany a person could get a bed no matter how drunk he was, as long as he behaved. There were those who wanted to see the place closed, along with the nearby Salvation Army. There was a real chicken/egg debate about the homeless population in and around Central Square——were they there, causing trouble, because that's where all the services were? Or had the services popped up there, because that's where the homeless people lived? Could you get rid of them just by moving the shelters?

It all came down to the fact that while Cambridge types liked to think they worshipped diversity, at heart they didn't want it in their neighborhoods. The city had changed these past few years. MIT was buying up all the old candy factories and turning them into offices and condos: Superior Nut, Tootsie Roll, the chocolate factory, all of them repurposed. There were high-rises going up in Kendall Square to house Biogen and other new tech companies——it made it so that the area was bustling with activity during the day and then dead at night, besides the Marriott. The mass exodus of middle-class white people back in the seventies was over, and now the yuppies were moving back, gutting old Victorians, and complaining endlessly about the homeless drunks and drug addicts in Central Square, who had never left, and so to James's mind were the rightful owners of the place.

The drunks were the worst. Those guys depressed the shit out of him. They usually ended up dead, and it was sad, because you'd run into them sober every once in a while, and it was like meeting an entirely different person: a glimpse of who they could have become had they just been able to kick the booze.

There was traffic on the road. There was always traffic. In Milwaukee two years earlier, they had started putting paramedics on Harley-Davidsons. James thought it was a good idea, while also thanking God that he didn't have to do it himself. If they tried to put him on a Harley, he'd be the one who would end up needing an ambulance.

He switched on the siren. Most of the cars in front of him pulled gently to the right, but a mom in a station wagon just sat there in the middle of the road, as if he should drive through her.

"Move the hell over, lady!" Maurice yelled.

Eventually she did. James hit an open patch of road and pressed down on the gas.

"We're heading for a psych," Maurice said. "He was acting weird and someone called on his behalf. He's bleeding. Possibly violent."

"Sounds like a blast," James said.

"Yup. Merry Christmas to us."

By the time they got there, the guys from the fire department had already arrived. They stood a few feet away from the patient, though they weren't interacting with him.

"Thanks for the care stare, guys," Maurice said under his breath.

The private companies and the fire departments were always at war. Their company held the 911 contract for all of Cambridge, which meant they saw action every day. Without the contract, they would just be doing hospital transfers, leaving the real work to the fire department. But an engine company still came to every call. The fire department was eager to hold on to the funding that emergency services provided, but most firefighters had no interest in helping out in a case like this. They only wanted to save people when it required hazmat suits or a dive team. Anything basic they thought was beneath them. James knew the drill. He had been one of them once. He remembered when blood pressure cuffs had come in to the Lynn rescue squad. The guys had pitched a fit. *What do you think we are, a bunch of fucking nurses?* they all said. But when they got a cuff with a digital readout, they shut up. They'd take any excuse to use the thing. They were like Parker with his Nintendo.

James and Maurice left the lights on, and got out. The guy was probably in his late forties, dressed in a flannel work shirt and stained dungarees. He looked drunk or high, or both, bobbing from side to side, his head lolling backward. There was a deep cut on his right cheek, blood trickling down to his collar. He had recently been in the hospital—he was still wearing the plastic bracelet.

There were certain druggies and homeless guys they knew by name—frequent fliers, they called them. They knew these guys' complete medical histories, their Social Security numbers, by heart, that's how often they saw them. But James didn't recognize this one.

He smelled like booze and piss and rotting flesh. It didn't take much persuading to get him into the ambulance and onto the stretcher. Maurice climbed in back and James returned to the driver's seat.

The stench of the guy was so foul that he had to breathe into his sleeve.

James rolled down the windows and kept it in park for now. He radioed to the doctor on call to request permission for an IV, just in case Maurice wanted to use one. You always had to ask the doctor's permission, every time, even though they never said no.

Afterward, he picked up the binder off the passenger seat and started in on the reports. But he was listening with one ear, making sure Maurice was safe.

"Do you drink regularly?" Maurice asked.

"Yes."

"When was the last time you had a drink?" He paused, and then answered his own question. "Today, obviously. Do you do drugs? Pills? Cocaine?"

"No, none of that stuff. I'm through with that shit."

"Uhh-huh. When was the last time you did it?"

"I'm trying to think of it."

"All right."

"There's something different going on today," the guy said. "Like an itching inside my head."

"Okay. We're going to try to figure that out." Maurice's voice was calm and soothing, as if he were talking to one of his own children. "So. What have you been in the hospital for?"

Silence.

"I need to know when the last time you did drugs was." Maurice's tone grew a little more forceful now, a dad scolding a first-time offender for coming home after curfew.

The guy's tone was defiant. "I never did drugs. Actually."

Maurice nodded. "Did you ever do Valium? Did you ever do rock cocaine?"

"Sure."

Maurice started to unbutton the guy's shirt, talking all the while. He pulled a stethoscope from his pants pocket, checked the heartbeat, and, as if he were just making friendly conversation, asked, "When was the last time? Did you take any drugs today?"

"No." The guy raised his voice, and James turned his head to look. "I fucking hate drugs. And I hate fucking Ronald Reagan."

He gripped Maurice's wrist, but Maurice shook out of the hold. "Try not to grab me."

His partner was as calm as ever, but James felt full of anger.

"You were just about to hit me, weren't you?" the guy accused.

"No, I don't think so."

"Yeah you were, dude. You were gonna hit me. It's okay."

"I wasn't going to hit you," Maurice said.

The guy's words took on a mocking rhythm. "How does it feel being the Afro-American All-American?"

Maurice had grown up down south. His wife was a Yankee, as he put it, a black girl from Roxbury. He liked to say that Boston was far more racist than Georgia had ever been.

"Fantastic," he said now, not letting his emotions show. "When were you in the hospital?"

The patient raised his voice, threatening: "How does it feel being the Afro-American All-American?"

"It feels great. Now you answer my question. Do you have any psychological problems?"

"Do you?"

"Sometimes," Maurice said. "What do you have, man? Do you have schizophrenia, depression, anxiety?"

"Everything, Georgetown."

"Looks like you had an IV in your hand."

"You ever been to Georgetown University?"

Maurice sighed. "No, I haven't."

"I went there. I want to go to the Cambridge Hospital psych ward."

"All right, but we're gonna stop off at the emergency room first," Maurice said. "Now, this cuff is just going to take your blood pressure."

"You know what the truth is, dude, I love you, buddy."

"I know you do."

The guy lifted his head. "How's your penis?"

"It's fantastic."

"See? I know you. That's the motherfucking truth. You're Rick."

"I'm Rick. Are you gonna let me do this IV? Do you shoot up?"

"No, I never shot up."

"You've got a bunch of scars all over your veins. New ones? Don't move, okay?"

Maurice gently inserted the IV. It couldn't have hurt, especially for a junkie who was probably used to needles, but the guy shouted, violent, "If you bend my motherfucking hand, I'll bend your motherfucking hand!"

James took a deep breath, feeling his own hands curl into fists. He could tell now that the idiot was probably going to try to throw a punch. He pictured having to jump over the seat, pummeling him. He was afraid that once he started, he wouldn't stop.

"You're okay, nothing's going on. I'm just lifting your hand," Maurice said softly. "I'm just putting your seat belt on, so relax."

The guy allowed this, and Maurice gave James the nod to get going. James put the truck in drive, with the siren in phaser mode.

"What's your name again?" Maurice asked. He was just trying to keep things light.

"What's your name, Rick?" the guy said.

"Rick. What's yours?"

Now he went back to screaming. "If you fucking ask me one more time, I'm gonna punch you."

"Take it easy. What's your name?"

"Give me a handshake."

James eyed them in the rearview mirror. For some reason, Maurice was dumb or kind enough to extend his hand. James could see the guy reach out, take hold, and start to squeeze down, lifting his other fist to try and deck him.

"McKeen, pull over," Maurice shouted, ducking out of the way.

"Yeah, pull over, McKeen," the guy said snidely, but he dropped his fist.

James pulled over, took a sip of coffee.

Maurice regarded the guy. "Are we okay? Do I need to restrain you?"

"We're okay, Africa. Give me a handshake."

There were medics who would have pulled the truck down a dark alley and beaten the shit out of this asshole. But Maurice wasn't like that. A few months ago, a guy in the middle of a fit spat blood in his face and said, "There. Now you've got AIDS too." Maurice just wiped the blood away with his sleeve and kept going, like nothing had happened.

Now he said, "We're through shaking hands. Am I gonna have to call the police?"

"All right, Rick, you're a tough guy, you win. The doctors don't help me. I've had all these seizures and they won't help me."

"Well, we're gonna take you in and try to get that taken care of."

"Yeah, but they probably won't."

Maurice nodded at James again, and he signaled back out into traffic. He radioed ahead to let the ER know that the patient was combative. A small part of him felt bad for the guy. He was clearly nuts, and he was alone at Christmas. James knew they would joke about it later. They made dark jokes all the time, especially when they saw the worst— murders, or anything to do with kids. At least once a month, they'd pick up a child who'd been running with some object in his mouth that went straight through the back of his throat when he tripped—a knitting needle, a Cross pen, they had seen it all. Last month, there was a six-year-old boy who choked on a hot dog and was now in a coma. They even joked about that: *How do you turn an all-beef frank into a vegetable?*

As a kid, he had never worried about danger. How many afternoons had he spent out back, chucking beer bottles at the shed for no reason, and later pulling tiny slivers of glass from his arms and legs? How many times had he and his buddies hitchhiked for a ride into Boston, or jumped off the roof of Big Boy's garage, cannonballing into the above-ground pool? Now he thought of all the things that could have gone wrong. His own kids wouldn't be like that, so unsupervised, so careless.

From the back of the truck, he heard the homeless guy starting up again.

"Where in Africa you from, buddy?"

"Atlanta."

Five minutes later, they arrived at the hospital. James was all too happy to drop this particular piece of shit off to the nurses. He could tell Maurice was wound up.

Once they got back in, he asked, "Do you want to hang out here, or—"

"Nah man, I want that burger."

James nodded, and started to drive toward Elsie's.

"Racist motherfucker, huh?" Maurice said.

James shrugged. "We've seen worse."

Big Boy and O'Neil liked to bust his chops about Cambridge turning him into some touchy-feely type, hanging out with a bunch of homos and black guys, his patients. James would just tell them, "Homophobic hardline redneck Irishmen like you people couldn't handle what I do for a day. You guys are a walking hate crime."

His boss called it cultural competency. Basically that meant that you had to know every patient's way of being— one minute you'd be asking some street addict, "What did you do, an eight ball?" The next, you were at some rich guy's mansion and he was complaining of stomach pain, and you were all, "Have you experienced any flatulence today, sir?" Like you were in some goddamn Grey Poupon commercial. You had to be comfortable with rich, poor, gay, straight, white, black, whatever.

It was a black kid who had mugged his wife. James tried not to mention it around Maurice, for fear that he might say something he'd regret.

He was grateful at least that she just let the scumbag have what he wanted. Sheila said if the baby hadn't been there, she would have fought back, and James didn't doubt it. He remembered a night in high school at a dive bar in Charlestown. They were there with one of his older cousins, and didn't even need to use their fake IDs. Three members of the Honey Bees had come in, and the place emptied right out. Even guys were scared shitless of the Honey Bees, because those girls were crazy. They had once stabbed a frat boy to death for a case of beer. But Sheila insisted on staying put and finishing her drink.

She hadn't made much of the fact that the mugger was black, but her parents kept saying that on their side of town you just didn't run into that kind of element. It would probably sound racist as all hell if he were to say something to Maurice, but James sometimes wondered if Maurice didn't quite get it.

He had been in his twenties, still a fireman, when the forced busing started in South Boston. All you heard of when people talked about it now was that the white-trash Irish in Southie were racist, that they threw rocks at the black kids. But a cousin of his, a Boston cop, was called to the scene when an innocent white guy was pulled from his car and beaten into an irreversible coma, with a bunch of black people standing around, yelling, "Let him die."

It wasn't something James liked to think about much, but given the right set of circumstances absolutely anyone could become a savage.

"Did I ever tell you about my anniversary dinner at Jimmy's Harborside?" Maurice said now.

He had told James the story a hundred times, but once he started in, there was no use trying to shut him up. And anyway, it was a good one.

After dinner, Maurice's wife had gotten the car from the valet while he was in the john. As he walked out of the restaurant and saw her idling at the curb twenty feet away, a white guy in a suit approached him.

"He didn't even make eye contact," Maurice said now. "He just shoved his keys at me and said, 'Blue BMW.' Assumed since I was black, I had to be the valet."

"What did you say?" James asked, happy enough to set him up for the punch line.

"I said, 'Just a moment, sir.' Then I walked a block and threw his keys into the harbor."

They laughed as James stopped at a red light.

His eyelids felt heavy; keeping them up required actual effort. James knew from experience that the light would take forever to change, so he let his eyes close, just for a minute, relief setting in.

Next thing he knew, Maurice was shaking him by the shoulder. "McKeen, you okay? Did you fall asleep?"

"What? Nah."

"You want me to drive?"

"No. I'm fine."

They arrived back at Elsie's, and he pulled over to let Maurice out.

"You want a sub?" Maurice asked.

James looked at the clock. "It's still not even nine, man. I'll have a Diet Pepsi."

He drank a crazy amount of the stuff, maybe eight or nine cans a day. He let Parker have some with his pizza on Friday nights, which Sheila hated.

James had taught him to say, "But Mom, it's the choice of a new generation."

She always replied, "It's poison."

Eventually, James would probably give in and stop drinking it. Over the years, Sheila had changed so many of his habits. She had gotten him to quit smoking pot before Parker was born, and cigarettes when she was pregnant with Danny. And every time he drank more than a couple beers in front of her, she liked to remind him about his father.

2003

Delphine lit a fire in the gas fireplace.

It was as simple as flipping a switch, an act that seemed unnatural. To make a fire ought to be a challenge, involving sticky sap-covered wood and balls of newspaper that left black stains all over the palms of your hands. In their weekend house in the backcountry, she had often watched her husband, Henri, struggling with lighter fluid and logs that were too damp to be of use. When a flame finally appeared, they would both cheer and shout, *Hourra!*

A gas fire seemed like cheating, though P.J. had once said that he bought the apartment in part because of this feature. He had warned her not to put anything in it. "Even just a sheet of paper could mess up the system, make it overheat and break the glass," he said.

All around her, the place was in a state of disarray: His t-shirts in shreds on the kitchen floor, alongside broken chunks of china. The paintings pulled from the walls. The rugs sliced into strips of fabric, and the dog in the bathroom, stuffing himself full of peanut butter.

She held a stack of important papers, the type that everyone keeps in a safe or file cabinet somewhere, the story of a life told in signatures and numbers. In P.J.'s case, the crucial folder lived in a plastic storage bin under the bed, crammed in with old phone bills and love letters and programs from concerts he had played with the English Chamber Orchestra, the Pasadena Symphony, the Warsaw Philharmonic.

Into the fire she tossed his birth certificate, his bank documents, and a blue sheet of notebook paper covered in letters and numbers. He never memorized any of his account numbers or passwords, choosing instead to just consult this list whenever he needed to.

The ring on her finger glistened in the firelight: two large round diamonds that formed a tilted figure eight, with diamond accents all around. The ring had such a unique look, almost like a flower. People were forever asking her about it—when it was made and where. But Delphine had no idea about its provenance. She always meant to take it to a jeweler who might know more. There was a word etched into the metal band. EVIE. She had asked P.J. what it meant once, but he said he didn't know.

Delphine let her imagination roam. Was it someone's name, or did it stand for some secret message between two lovers? What had happened to make them sell it? Or had they simply lost the ring, or given it away? Whatever the case, it was no longer theirs. After today, she too would be just a former owner.

She closed the glass door, watching the flames lick up gently over the paper.

The process took longer than she had imagined. A gas fire could only ever grow so big. It was meant to represent something wild and untamable, but was in fact only a meek, pale imitation of the real thing.

"*Hourra,*" she said, and thought of home.

Delphine Moreau met Henri Petit one week after her thirty-third birthday, at a small shop on the rue Constance in Montmartre. The shop sold rare and antique musical instruments, some dating back to the fifteenth century. It had stood there on the ground floor of a four-story apartment building for forty-one years, right in the middle of a narrow, sleepy block paved with cobblestones, a hidden gem, beloved by collectors all over Europe for its unique inventory, as well as for its lively owner, François Dubray. He was a portly yet handsome man, with a full, dark beard and a laugh that could make a statue turn and smile. Dubray had an almost encyclopedic knowledge of music, and he was a renowned *luthier*. In his workshop in the back of the store, which hardly anyone was allowed to enter, he had repaired and tuned violins for the world's most celebrated performers. They came to him once a year, and he slipped a tool into the f-hole, moving it just a hair to the left or right, altering the sound according to the specific way in which each violinist played.

Two months earlier, Dubray had died of a heart attack while taking out the trash, and now his three children were looking for someone to buy the shop, someone who would vow to preserve it for its original purpose.

As a girl, Delphine had spent countless hours with her father, gazing at the collage of instruments displayed behind Monsieur Dubray's dusty window. At the center, an array of violins hung from the thinnest of floss over a piano, seeming to float like magic. These were flanked by dozens of flutes and clarinets, and a harp that was taller than she was. There were instruments that the average person would never recognize, and her father knew the names for all of them: the virginal, which resembled a shrunken harpsichord; an African lamellophone, its sound box made of an intact tortoise shell.

Dubray's children, all in their early twenties, were building their lives elsewhere, the oldest two in London and the youngest at a university in Montreal. They had returned to Paris for the funeral, and to hold an open house from two o'clock until five that Saturday, at which they intended to thoroughly vet each and every prospective buyer for the shop.

Only Delphine and Henri showed up.

She sat in a chair by the door as the children questioned Henri at a desk a few feet away. Delphine could remember them running around the neighborhood when she was a teenager and they were just babies. It was clear that none of them had inherited their father's passion for music. Their questions were simplistic, having more to do with feelings than facts—*What sorts of songs are your favorites?* they asked, and *Why would owning this store make you a happier man?* It was clear too that Henri was immensely qualified for the job. He had learned restoration from Dubray himself, and as such believed he was the rightful heir to the place. He seemed almost offended that Dubray had chosen to will the shop to his own children rather than to him. Henri told them that he worked as a consultant at the Musée de la Musique, one of the largest instrument collections in the world. When he was a much younger man, just out of university, he had managed a small shop off the Place des Vosges that specialized in seventeenth-century stringed instruments.

Delphine felt herself sinking deeper into the chair with each confident word he uttered. She rehearsed what she had planned to say: She had a background in sales after spending the last few years as a realtor, and she had walked by this shop hundreds of times, thousands maybe, in awe of the place. She had wanted to own it for as long as she could remember. This had been her father's dream, and he had passed it along to her as clearly as he had passed along his long, lean legs and sharp nose. He called her many things: *ma tourterelle, mon petit canard,* choosing the names of birds to describe her. But in the end, it was he who flew away.

When her turn came, Delphine forgot about whatever meager credentials she might have, and instead told them that she too had lost her father, only a year ago.

"Oh no!" the children cried out, for they could remember the handsome and good Ludovic Moreau, who had lived just around the corner in the ivy-covered house on the rue Cauchois. You could see the house from the front door of the shop if you craned your neck to the right.

"Do you still live there?" the girl asked.

"*Oui,*" she said. "Your father was such a good man. I know I could love this store every bit as much as he did. It is my favorite place in all of Paris. When I was a child, my father used to bring me here on Saturday mornings. He was a pianist, you know, and this shop was his house of worship. It meant more to him than any cathedral in France. When he died, I came here. I wasn't expecting to, but I started to cry. Your father was so kind to me. He told me my father was a good man, one of his favorite customers, and that I should come in anytime."

Afterward, the children went into the workshop. Even they had never been allowed inside when their father was alive, and she wondered what it felt like to them now. They did not say goodbye, nor did they promise to return. Delphine couldn't be certain if they would come back momentarily and announce their decision, or call her later with the verdict.

"Are we supposed to wait?" she asked Henri, and he shrugged as if he didn't particularly care, but then he went outside and she watched him pace on the sidewalk in front of the cobbler's shop for ten minutes. He was a compact man, about her height. Slim, with waves in his silver hair. He looked to be around fifty. He wore sophisticated black-rimmed eyeglasses and a nice suit, but he seemed uncomfortable. She imagined that he was the academic type most of the time, the type who lived in oversized sweaters at home.

Eventually, Dubray's children returned. The girl waved Henri inside the shop with a smile, and Delphine felt disappointed, but also somewhat relieved. The whole thing might have been a dreadful idea, really. She knew little about historic instruments, and even less about restoration. Perhaps this was just the fates saving her from herself. But then again she needed something new, a challenge that could fill up all the holes in her. She no longer had any interest in romance, not now, although it had been her favorite distraction in the past.

The oldest boy, probably twenty-five or so, said, "Monsieur Petit. Mademoiselle Moreau. Please, sit down."

They all sat around the desk this time.

"We have talked it over, and we've decided that there is a perfect solution," he said, sounding more like a child than a man. He had his father's kind eyes, and Delphine smiled at him, knowing how these sorts of decisions could weigh on a person. The children's mother had been much younger than their father, but she too was gone, having died of cancer a few years back. They were orphans now, like Delphine herself.

The boy went on. "The perfect owner for the shop is—"

"Both of you!" his sister interrupted.

The boy's entire body drooped. She had robbed him of his moment, and he could not hide his dismay.

"Pardon?" Henri said.

"Monsieur Petit, you know this business well. You studied with our father," the oldest boy said. "And Mademoiselle Moreau, she is full of light and excitement. She is of the neighborhood. She understands the sentimental value of the place. You will work well together."

"So you want me to buy the shop and hire her?" Henri asked.

"We want you to buy it together," the girl said.

"This is not how these things happen," Henri stammered. "You don't just buy property with a stranger. It could go so horribly wrong. You must let us each make an offer and accept the best one. Be sensible."

Delphine bit her lower lip. She could not afford to get into a bidding war with this man. She had only enough to buy the shop for the low listed price, and hardly even that.

The older boy shook his head. "We don't care so much about the money. We just want to do as Papa would have wished. If we could, we would keep the shop in the family, but it's not practical."

Henri scoffed. "Oh, and this idea is practical? You'll regret this later, I promise you."

"No," the girl said. "We will only regret coming back in five years' time and finding that the store is gone. Our father gave us strictest orders to find the best possible person—or people—to buy it if anything ever happened to him."

"And Papa was a romantic, so . . ." the younger boy added, trailing off and nodding in their direction. Delphine had no idea what he meant, not until she thought about it weeks later, at which point she let out a great peal of laughter.

"I cannot accept this," Henri said.

"Just think it over," the older boy said, and that was all.

Afterward, she and Henri walked out. Delphine assumed he would turn right, toward the Metro Blanche, and so even though her apartment was in that direction, she went left. But then so did he. She could feel his presence weighing on her back. She stopped abruptly to turn around, and they collided on the sidewalk.

"Do you agree that it's absurd?" he asked, as if just noticing her for the first time.

Maybe so, but plenty of things were absurd. It was absurd that she had not had a boyfriend to speak of since university, and that boyfriend was now married with two children, and living in a vineyard in Bordeaux, while she still managed to get her heart broken every year or so; a hopeless romantic with a taste for unkind men. It was absurd that she was thirty-three and yet still unsure about what to do with her life. It was absurd that her father, the best and strongest man who had ever lived, was now dead and buried in the Cimetière de Montmartre, where cats and American tourists regularly walked over his grave. In a way, Delphine blamed him for her restlessness. He had treated her as if she were the most special girl on earth, and she had assumed that the world would agree. Yet she had lived her life so far with no clear plan, blown about by circumstance.

"It's a strange proposition, yes," she said. She wondered how long Henri would fight for the store, and whether he would win.

They turned onto the rue Lepic, where cafés and shops and pâtisseries lined the street. They followed the road up the hill until they got stuck behind a guide, speaking English to her group in chipper tones: "Vincent van Gogh had little professional success in his lifetime. It was here in his brother Theo's house that he lived in the years before he fatally shot himself. His last words, according to Theo, were *La tristesse durera toujours*. Does anyone know what that means? No guesses? It means, 'The sadness will last forever.' "

The Americans began snapping pictures of one another in front of the house.

Henri raised an eyebrow. "And what do you suppose they will do with those photos? Turn them into Christmas cards?"

" 'Peace and joy to you this holiday season. Here is where van Gogh lived just before his horrific suicide!' "

He nodded. " 'P.S. The sadness will last forever.' "

She smiled.

"I detest Montmartre," he said. "Nothing but tourists and pretentious artists and *bobos*. Where do you live?"

"Montmartre," she said. "I grew up here."

The fact had already been established at Dubray's. Was he mocking her?

"Ahh!" he closed his eyes, slapped his forehead. "I'm an idiot."

She saw now that he had somehow missed it. He seemed genuinely embarrassed.

"No, no. It's all right. Montmartre is not for everyone," she said, although in truth she couldn't imagine anyone wandering these streets without falling in love.

The area had changed some since she was a child. Back then, there was a *boulangerie* on every corner, and now most of them were gone. Two of her father's favorites retained the old signs, but had been converted—one into a pre-school, the other a law office. Many of the old *tabacs* were now late-night grocery stores run by North African immigrants. There was even a frozen-foods shop around the block from her house.

But these changes pleased her. Paris was always evolving—the original and the bold right on top of what had been there for thousands of years, old and new peace-fully intertwined. In recent years, she had gone with her father to see the Red Hot Chili Peppers, David Bowie, and Iggy Pop perform at La Cigale in Pigalle, in the same theater where her grandparents had once seen Maurice Chevalier.

In some ways, arriving in Montmartre still felt like enter-ing another time. You could go to Au Lapin Agile for per-formances and sit in chairs that had once been occupied by Modigliani, Picasso, Renoir. Every October as a child, she stomped grapes like a good country girl at the Clos Mont-martre, where nuns and monks had produced three hundred liters of wine each year since the twelfth century. Her father didn't care for the tourists who flocked to the cathedral and the carousel at the foot of the steps, asking, *Where is the Moulin Rouge, the entrance to the funicular, the statue of the bra of Dalida*—Dalida, who had brought so much joy through her disco music and her bouncing breasts, only to meet a tragic end. But Delphine felt proud that outsiders wanted to peek at their world. And anyway, she thought the best parts were the ones that the tourists never noticed—the astonishing view of Paris from the outdoor tables at Chez Pommette, toward the top of the hill. The artist studios built high up in the garrets of old houses.

The tourists disappeared at the bottom of the hill, where rent was cheap and, in years past, anyway, bohemians congregated by the dozens. She had lived there, on the fourth floor above a café on the rue des Martyrs, for most of her childhood. She grew up knowing the names of the butcher and the cheese monger, the old woman who ran the pâtisserie and snuck her a *moelleux chocolat* every day after school, and the couple from Auvergne who ran the *tabac,* all of them comprising the only big and boisterous family that she, the lone child of a widower, would ever have.

When she was ten, they moved a ways up the hill, into the brick house on rue Cauchois. Delphine had always thought it the most beautiful house in Paris, its walls climbing with ivy, the bright red geraniums in the window boxes set against tall white shutters that her father flung open each morning with a song for the birds. It didn't look like other houses in the city—it was not Haussmannian or even Art Nouveau— and this made it special. The owner, Madame Delecourt, lived on the first floor. There were two apartments on the second level, and three on the third. Delphine and her father lived in one of these. He stayed there until just a few years ago, when he moved in with his horrible girlfriend, at which point Delphine moved back in on her own. Madame Delecourt had since died. Her nephew now owned the building. Delphine sensed that he was eager for her to go—as soon as she vacated, he could rent the place out for five times what she paid. But she had no intention of leaving.

"Would you like to get a coffee?" Henri asked her now.

She said she would, though in truth she wasn't sure. They went to the café on the corner. He ordered café au lait, and she had a *citron pressé*, not wanting the effects of caffeine in her already nervous state. They each lit a cigarette, and talked about music, which seemed likely to be their only common ground. They agreed about the great masters, of course: Bach, Beethoven, Chopin, Mahler. He said his favorites were Ravel and Debussy.

Delphine smiled. Her father had preferred the French composers too, taking such pride in them. She could hear him playing "Clair de Lune" at the piano in Madame Delecourt's parlor when she came home from school for the lunch hour.

"Lately I've been listening to a lot of Arvo Pärt," she said. "I just love his music. There's such soul to it. It's deceptively simple, I think. But it seems the simplest can sometimes be the hardest to carry off."

"Ridiculous!" Henri snapped.

She was surprised by his intensity, and she knew her expression made it clear.

"I'm sorry," he said. "I don't know what's wrong with me today. It's all very odd." She supposed he meant the arrangement with the store, but now he returned to his point.

"I don't care for contemporary composers," he said. "Pärt, when set against Schubert or Brahms or Bruckner, shows himself to be nothing of consequence."

Her father had always said to beware a Bruckner fan.

Henri went on about how tragic it was that the best of music was long past. He had little respect for anyone presently composing. "The new generation," he called them dismissively, as if Pärt, Takemitsu, and Philip Glass were a gang of young hoodlums.

"How did you come to know so much about classical music?" he asked. "Dubray's children mentioned your father. Was he a musician?"

"A pianist," she said. "He studied at the Paris Conservatory."

She left out the fact that he made his money playing Gershwin and Cole Porter in a hotel bar, and saved on the rent by giving lessons and impromptu performances for the landlady and her friends. Henri struck her as *coincé*, uptight, and overly serious. She could only imagine what he'd say about that.

He told her that his own father had studied violin as a child and had pushed him in the same direction.

"I love music more than anything," he said. "But I have no talent for it."

She nodded. "I am just the same."

"My father was a collector, and I followed him in that," Henri said. "As a boy of seven, eight, nine, I visited flea markets, estate sales, and public auctions all over Europe to assemble the collection I have today. It runs from the fifteenth through the nineteenth centuries."

"Do you have a favorite piece?" she asked.

"I have a perfect François-Xavier Tourte bow," he said.

"Ahh."

Her father had taught her about Tourte, who destroyed any bow that wasn't flawless, who enhanced the very sound of the violin in the late eighteenth and early nineteenth centuries, and whose bows now sold for roughly the price of a new Ferrari.

"It's not my favorite, though," Henri said, bragging a bit, she thought.

"No?"

"No."

"What then?"

"The year I was born, my father bought a Stradivarius violin for almost nothing. He gave it to me on my tenth birthday. Another made in the same year just sold for two million dollars in America. That one belonged to a general in Napoleon's army. After the sale, I got many inquiries. I won't part easily with mine, though."

She pulled back in surprise.

"Where do you keep it?" she asked.

"At home in my study, in a glass case."

It seemed tragic that the violin never got a chance to be played. Such a perfect specimen, wasted. A caged bird. And it was bad for the instrument. He was a *luthier*, he must know that.

"Do you ever loan it out?"

"On occasion."

Henri took the last sip of coffee in his cup, then nibbled on the piece of chocolate that had come with it.

"Twenty years ago, knowing how much the violin was worth, I might have sold it. And then I surely would have had regrets."

She nodded. She could tell he was trying to make a point, but she couldn't say what it was.

"Dubray's children are being hasty. They see that there is money to be made; they want to make it."

"Maybe it's more than that," she said. "Maybe they love the place, but they just can't bear it."

She remembered how she had felt cleaning out her father's closets, wanting at once to hold on to every dirty handkerchief and musty page of sheet music, and yet wishing she were anywhere else on earth, free of it all.

"I worry that you may not understand what you're getting into," he said.

"Oh?"

"I ran a shop something like Dubray's once, and these businesses fluctuate. There are years when you're all right, and then without warning it gets very quiet. Dubray had debts. Whoever buys the store will have to absorb them. Are you aware of that?"

She could sense that he was not a bad man, though he could be slightly arrogant. He just wanted the shop, probably much more than she did. And anyway, he was right. She didn't know about debts or how to safeguard against a fall. She was outmatched.

Delphine was about to say as much when Henri said, "What if Dubray's children were to hold on to the store for one year, while the two of us attempt to run it together? A trial period."

She was surprised, but then the place was sacred to him, just as it was to her. Perhaps he didn't want the burden of keeping it alive all on his own.

Delphine agreed to try it.

Once they got started, she realized that she could never have done it without him. The children, who had seemed to be acting on a foolish emotional whim, had been right. Henri knew every important dealer and symphony conductor in the world, and he had an understanding of fine instruments that rivaled Dubray's. He could repair a violin, assess its value, recognize a find when anyone else might have missed it. He was calm, so calm that you might think him dull at first. He lived inside his head.

Henri had no interest in chatting with customers all day. This was where Delphine thrived. Her father had had to be fluent in English for work, so he could communicate with the drunk American patrons who wanted to chat, leaning on the piano as they asked him about Paris and requested something from *West Side Story*. He taught her everything he learned, all the phrases she wouldn't have known otherwise. How to make the tourists feel at ease, when they expected the French to be stuffy, unkind.

Now she put his teachings to use. She found that she could convince an American couple on vacation to pay eighteen thousand francs for a harp, when neither of them had ever thought of owning a harp in their lives. She could see an instrument and understand the power of its beauty, its capacity to bring someone joy, even when she didn't know a thing about the maker or the quality of the wood. Dubray, like Henri, had never bothered much with tourists; Delphine made them her focus. When a film director from Los Angeles came in to browse one day with his wife, a long conversation led to a new relationship with movie companies in America who were searching for instruments to use in historical dramas.

With the pair of them in charge, the shop did a better business than ever before. On the one-year anniversary of their first meeting, they bought it.

For that first year and half of the next, Delphine referred to Henri as her business partner. He was also a friend, she sometimes thought, but the bulk of their interactions happened at work. Of course, they were always working. She saw more of Henri than anyone. Their business brought mutual acquaintances into their lives, and together they entertained them; most were collectors and experts like Henri, who picked apart the elements of music in a fashion that she found maddening. Delphine enjoyed talk of performances to a point, but she also thought you could talk all the beauty out of it. It irritated her when Henri would ask, "So? What did you think?" immediately after a recital, wanting to examine it before the lights had even gone up.

When she was a girl, a few times a year her father would take her to hear a concert in the Église de Saint-Germaindes-Prés. He would tell her in advance to be quiet and still, to let the music fill her. Afterward, they might have mussels on the square at Café Central or just wander through narrow streets and out to the river, without dissecting what they had seen, without discussing it at all.

Some nights she made Henri dinner at her apartment after work, just the two of them, and they spoke about their families, their childhoods, their shared love of music. They both worshipped classical musicians like other people worshipped rock stars.

Henri was a formal man, and scandalizing him brought her a strange pleasure. She loved secretly replacing his Bach CDs with the Beastie Boys in the shop. He was fifteen years older than she, and looked even older than that—Delphine teased him about his age, making him blush. She saw him as a kind uncle, or perhaps a much older brother.

Once, after too much wine, she told him about how much she missed her father, and confessed that she had never wanted children of her own because of everything that had happened with her mother. She hadn't told anyone that before. Henri had wanted them once, he said, but now it seemed too late. She couldn't picture him bouncing a baby on his knee, or tossing a ball with an older child. When she tried, she laughed out loud. But then again, she had once watched him teach a young boy from the neighborhood how to restore a fiddle the child had found in his grandmother's attic, adding a neck and scroll, and polishing it up until it glowed. "The purfling here is very good. There's a great difference between spruce and maple," he told the boy, who nodded quite seriously as if he were an auctioneer at Christie's.

Henri first kissed her on a quiet Tuesday when the shop had been empty for hours. She could not have been more shocked if he had walked right up and slapped her in the face. He pulled away, and before she could even speak, he said, "I've got a meeting to get to. See you tomorrow."

The next day, he asked her out for a proper dinner. They ate *entrecôte frites* and drank a bottle of wine. Henri's brow was dewy with sweat. He talked almost exclusively about the store—rambling on about the need to boost sales at Christmastime, and asking whether she thought it was wise to run a few ads in the local papers.

Delphine felt incredibly uncomfortable, and confused. She had assumed that this was a date, but now she wondered if it was merely an apology for the kiss. Henri paid the check, but he always paid the check when they went out. He walked her home to her apartment, but he always walked her home if it got late.

Outside her door, she said, "Well, thanks for the meal. I'll see you tomorrow, yes?"

At which point he grabbed her around the waist and kissed her urgently. She kissed back; it seemed rude not to. But she kept her eyes open, and could feel them growing wide.

She did not invite him upstairs.

The following morning, she entered the store through the back door, knowing he'd be in front. On her desk in the workshop, he had left a vase of roses with a card. Her stomach turned. The card read, *As you probably know by now, I'm madly in love with you.*

Delphine nearly jumped. *Madly in love?* It was hard to imagine Henri worked into a state even vaguely resembling madness. She thought for a moment of running away, but then he stepped into the room, his arms full of papers. When he saw her there, his cheeks went red.

"I didn't hear you come in," he said.

She could tell he was nervous. She pointed at the flowers. "They're beautiful."

He smiled. "Good, good. I had a wonderful time last night."

You did? she thought. But she answered, "Me too."

He paused. "I better get back out front."

For a moment, she wondered if the florist had simply attached the wrong card. Maybe somewhere in Montmartre, a newly engaged woman had just received a bouquet with a note that said, *Good work on setting a record for our most flutes ever sold in a single month.*

That night in bed, Delphine thought it over. Henri loved her. Or at least he thought he did. How had the idea never even occurred to her? She knew he wasn't going to sweep her off her feet, but that never led anywhere good anyway. Henri was kind and smart, and they had the shop, which was the closest either of them would ever come to having a child.

They went out for more dinners, which got better over time. They laughed with ease. The sex between them was nice, if not overflowing with passion. She learned more about Henri as they went along—he ate very little of his own accord, as if his brain were far too occupied to think of anything as pedestrian as food. Though he often appeared to be the most confident man in France, he was prone to dark moods, like her father had been; he sometimes took to his bed for a day or two or three.

And, like her father, Henri became her self-appointed caretaker, constantly worried about her safety, her health, her happiness. When a thief ripped her purse from her shoulder one night as they were locking up the shop, Henri chased him to the top of the hill, and though he never had a chance of catching up with the boy, the attempt had touched her deeply.

Henri had inherited his massive apartment in the seventh arrondissement, while she just rented her place. For this reason, after five months of dating he suggested that she move in with him, even though it was far from the shop and the neighborhood in which she'd grown up—all the way across the river.

"I can't leave Montmartre," she said. "My apartment. I'll lose it forever."

"It wouldn't be big enough for both of us anyway," he said, forgetting momentarily that she had lived there with her father for ten years.

"How can I go from Montmartre to this wealthy neighborhood that is not at all bohemian? That is entirely *bourgeois*?"

"Surely you won't miss the crowds. The *bobos*," he said. When he saw that she wasn't smiling, he took her chin in his hand and said, "We will still be there all the time for work. Eventually, we can move back if it's what you really want."

She knew it was a lie—he hated Montmartre, would never choose to live there. But she allowed herself to take some comfort in his words anyway.

Henri hadn't changed one piece of furniture after his parents gave him the apartment. The pieces were oppressively *vieille France*, Louis XVI and Empire style. All straight, harsh lines, with laurel wreaths carved into the oak and gilded fluted columns everywhere, as if they were living in ancient Greece. Heavy velvet drapes blocked out the sun. Delphine insisted on taking them down, but on his parents' first visit after she did so Henri's mother yelled, *"Ferme les volets!"* as soon as she entered the parlor. She ran to the window and grasped the air as if the old curtains might materialize. Seeing that this was hopeless, she settled for pulling the shutters closed.

In Henri's world, it seemed, sunlight was the enemy, its only mission to fade centuries-old upholsteries and rugs. Delphine thought of the artists of Montmartre, sweating in their studios five stories up, built in tiny maids' quarters for the sole purpose of welcoming the northern light.

In her new life on the rue de Grenelle, she sometimes did not recognize herself. It wasn't until she arrived in her precious Montmartre each morning that she felt like she could breathe.

A few months after she moved in, they were engaged. She hadn't seen a need for marriage. Lots of people went without it these days. They said half the children in France were born to unwed parents now. But it mattered to Henri. As a girl, she had dreamed of a man who would propose to her in some romantic way—going to her father for permission, coming up with an elaborate surprise. But her father was gone, and Henri only asked her over dinner one Friday at Le Florimond.

At their wedding at his parents' house in the country, everyone danced until six a.m., and then the guests drank *soupe à l'oignon* while she and Henri hid in a broom closet, waiting to be found. His mother had insisted that they play the game, in keeping with tradition. Delphine thought it was amusing, especially after several glasses of champagne. She assumed that most couples took the opportunity to be physically close for the first time in their married lives, maybe even sneaking in some illicit act. But Henri was a grump about the whole thing. "This is ridiculous," he said. "I can barely breathe."

He wore a stiff black suit and an old-fashioned *chapeau haut-de-forme*.

She imagined what her father would say to her if he were there to see it. She somehow couldn't picture him in the scene. Henri was too brittle a man for his tastes, too serious. But he was also kinder than any man she had ever loved before him.

Shortly after the wedding, a city magazine that focused

on music sent a reporter to cover the story of how François Dubray's death had led to their meeting. Delphine told her, "I married my best friend." It sounded so lovely, and it was true, after all. But she knew that other people heard it as *I married my soul mate*, when what she really meant was *I married a kind and stable man who will never treat me poorly, nor set my heart aflame.*

Six years passed. Six years of waking together at seven to the sound of Henri's alarm clock. He skipped *Good morning* in favor of asking *Quelles nouvelles?* as soon as she opened her eyes. As if there could be any news between two people who spent every moment of their day and night together. They ate *tartines* after rising, and he read the newspaper aloud. Then they drove to work together, discussing the store, spending all day together at work, going home or out to dinner together at day's end.

They bought a weekend house in Normandy, in a village called Muids. They hired a woman to mind the shop on Saturdays and went to the country most Fridays on the six o'clock train from Paris Saint-Lazare. The house sat right on the banks of the Seine. She often watched young couples zipping past on bicycles, laughing, a picnic basket draped over someone's arm. It looked like fun, but Henri would never want to spend a Saturday like that. He preferred to stay on the porch and read, though he would agree to a game of tennis or a walk along the water if she wanted. Sometimes in the evenings they played Vivaldi through the open kitchen window as they sat in the grass, gazing up at the stars.

It was a fortunate life, a pleasant life, but after six years, Delphine had begun to feel restless. There was a constant buzzing at the base of her skull as she thought about the fact that this was all there was or would ever be. She and Henri were friends, or, more precisely, family. There was such ease between them, but even that disturbed her. When he touched her arm or took her hand, she felt numb.

She began to wonder if people had children in part to ward off this quiet, uneasy sensation—at least parents had something to look forward to, to worry about, to plan for. Sometimes she wondered if she ought to try to find another job. Perhaps less time together would help. But she couldn't imagine leaving the shop, and she knew that one of the reasons they did such a good business was because people liked the idea of a husband-and-wife team. In her lowest moments, she wondered if this was why he had wanted to marry her in the first place. Most of the time she thought that Henri had picked her simply because she was the woman right under his nose. Marriage for him was like a Sunday lunch—he would never seek it out or even think of it, until someone presented it to him on a silver tray.

Her husband could be stuffy, boring, in social situations. She sometimes feared that people saw a married couple as just one person, so that his awkwardness and need to be right at all times reflected poorly on her. But eventually she realized that people saw them as two distinct parts of the whole; she softened their impression of him, and he gave her some heft. What could either of them ever be without the other?

They were kind to one another. They didn't ever fight. Delphine sometimes wished he would have an affair, arouse at least her anger and her suspicion if nothing else. Even jealousy had to be better than indifference. But she knew Henri was incapable of such a thing. And for a long time, she believed that she herself was, too.

2012

Sometime in winter, Jeff and Toby bought matching diamond rings, handmade by a jeweler in Stockbridge. One of Kate's many duties was to pick them up a few days before the wedding. All along, as she had helped order the flowers and considered menu options, and taken Ava to two separate dress shops in Manhattan, Kate had tried to pretend that they were planning an elaborate birthday party. But when she went to get the rings, she could not deny that this was, indeed, a wedding. She was surprised that her cousin would ask her to do it, when he knew how disgusted she was by diamonds, but she reminded herself that he was no longer the Jeff she had always known, and he wouldn't be for at least seventy-two more hours.

The jeweler had set two velvet boxes side by side on the glass counter, open to reveal identical rings, each with a diamond that lay flush against a thick, flat platinum band.

"I was sorry to hear that Toby and Jeff weren't coming themselves, but I know how crazy things get, especially with them living all the way in New York," he said. "It's been such an honor this year, getting to make these rings for gay couples like your friends. And I love what we designed together. Aren't they stunning?"

It seemed like he expected her to do something, though she wasn't sure what—applaud perhaps, or faint, or cry.

"They're great," she said, flipping the tops of the boxes closed with two quick snaps. "Do you have a bag?"

He placed the boxes in a glossy red bag with a gold rope handle, then gave it to her and smiled wide.

She briefly imagined shaking the bag in front of him and saying, *You realize these stupid things have fueled entire brutal regimes in Africa, right? They're shiny little death pellets, let's be honest.*

Instead, she just said, "Thanks."

Kate was often preoccupied with how to do good in a corrupt world, where just by eating dinner or turning on a laptop each of us was complicit in someone else's suffering. She struggled with how to speak the truth when it put others on the defensive or made her seem like a downer.

The things she worried about on a daily basis included but were not limited to: Children starving in Africa. Chemicals in her daughter's food and drinking water. Corruption in Washington, everywhere you looked. The poor, who no one even talked about anymore. Rape in the Congo, which didn't seem to be going away, despite so much talk. Rape at elite American colleges, which wasn't going away either. Plastic. Oil in the Gulf. Beer commercials, in which men were always portrayed as dolts who thought exclusively about football, and women as insufferable nags who only cared about shopping. The evils of the Internet. Sweatshops, and, in the same vein, where exactly everything in their life came from—their meat, their clothes, their shoes, their cell phones. The polar bears. The Kardashians. China. The poisonous effects of Howard Stern and Rush Limbaugh and Glenn Beck and the seemingly limitless pornography online. The gun-control laws that would likely never come, despite the five minutes everyone spent demanding them whenever a child or a politician got shot. The cancer various members of her family would eventually get, from smoking, microwaves, sunlight, deodorant, and all the other vices that made life that much more convenient and/or bearable.

Throughout each day, the world's ills ran through her head, sprinkled in with thoughts about what she should make for dinner, and when she was due for a cleaning at the dentist, and whether they should have another baby sometime soon. She wondered if everyone was like this, or if most people were able to tune it all out, the way her sister seemed to. Even Dan didn't care all that much about the parts of the world that were invisible to him. But Kate couldn't forget.

She had always been this way, and the feeling had only intensified when she went to work at Human Rights Now after college. HRN was a nonprofit organization with field offices in forty-two countries. They compiled reports on atrocities involving war crimes, violence against women and homosexuals, access to water, and other issues. Kate started out as the assistant to the executive director, Ellen Cary, and was promoted four times in ten years. She traveled to Africa and Asia. She got to meet with policy makers, donors, and journalists to reveal findings and suggest strategies. She loved her job, but she found it hard to shut the door on it after hours, something that Ellen often warned her about.

The last report she ever helped to write for HRN was about diamonds. She was three months pregnant with Ava when their research team went to the Central African Republic and the Congo. Kate had planned to accompany them, but her doctor advised against it, and Dan flat-out refused to let her go. She could tell it was the start of a new phase in her life, one she wasn't entirely sure she felt ready for.

A decade earlier, people in the West had begun to hear about blood diamonds. It was estimated that as many as 14 percent of the diamonds sold in America came from brutal wars in Africa that had left millions dead.

Even though it had long been this way, Westerners were suddenly horrified. They didn't want to think of child soldiers with their hands hacked off in connection with their precious diamond rings. So forty-five nations got together and signed on to the Kimberley Process. Kimberley diamonds came complete with a certificate that guaranteed they were not mined in a country at war. On the surface, it seemed like a good solution. But HRN and other groups like them had their doubts.

The head researcher on the trip was a guy named Albert Foster. He had a weathered, lined face that made him look much older than his fifty-three years. He was the type of person who could handle things like this, and one day after he returned to New York he gave Kate the gruesome facts without so much as a grimace: he spoke of the children in the streets, dying from AIDS, grabbing their crotches when he walked by, as they learned to do—an indication that they would trade sex for food, for anything.

Kate wrote down everything he said, feeling useless. She should have been there herself. She thought of her own child, not yet born, yet already guaranteed so much more from life.

"Is Kimberley working at all?" she asked.

He shook his head. "Put it this way: The Central African Republic has mines that could only ever possibly produce five hundred thousand carats each year. But annually, almost a million carats claiming to be from the CAR are certified. They just get them in the Congo, where they're considered dirty. Take them over the border, and they're magically clean."

"And people buy them, knowing this is the case?"

"Absolutely. Once the stones get to wherever they're going to be cut and polished, De Beers is quick to mix them in with diamonds from everywhere else."

"So no one will ever know if they're buying a blood diamond."

"Exactly. And most people like to tell themselves they're not. Sometimes I think Kimberley's really just a marketing tool to help assuage everyone's guilt."

Kate knew from other reports they had done that the minerals used to make laptops and cell phones were just as bad, but they somehow seemed less corrupt to her—at least they weren't meant to symbolize love. She found it harder than ever to let go after that meeting. She read everything she could on the topic. When she saw a woman wearing diamonds on the street or at the movies, she wanted to pull her aside and start reciting all the awful statistics.

A few months later, HRN did a press briefing on the resulting report, and her boss Ellen and the other women from the office looked sheepish for once, instead of self-righteous. Ellen turned her engagement ring around so that the stone was hidden in her palm.

The morning of the wedding, May drank two cups of black coffee to protest the fact that Kate only had soy milk, then went upstairs to take a shower, leaving Kate in the kitchen with their mother and the four kids.

Kate ran her hand through Ava's hair.

"Are you excited for the wedding tonight, lovey?" she asked.

"Yes! How late can I stay up?"

They had discussed it a hundred times already, but it was Ava's favorite part: "As late as you can keep your eyes open."

Her mother glanced up from her newspaper. "You're going to regret that."

"It's a special occasion."

"When do I get to put on my dress?" Ava said.

206 *J. Courtney Sullivan*

"I'm going to pick it up from Uncle Jeff and Uncle Toby in a while," Kate said. "And I've got to bring them their rings."

"Ooh, let me see," her mother said. "Are they gorgeous? I'm sure they are. Jeff has such great taste."

Kate shrugged.

"You know," Mona said, dragging out the syllables so that it almost sounded as if she were singing, "there are a lot of awful jobs out there, far worse than digging in a mine. Without diamonds, those people in Africa would have absolutely no industry at all."

Kate shook her head in disbelief. "First off, mining is one of the most dangerous professions of all time, with some of the most horrible health risks. Second, do you realize that the policies in the South African diamond mines basically created apartheid there? Black miners were locked up at night. Made to get naked and have every inch of their bodies searched after work, because it was just assumed they would steal. None of that happened to white workers. A black person had to carry all sorts of identification. Any old white person could ask to see it anytime, and if a worker didn't have it on him then and there, he got put in prison. Any white person!"

Her mother sighed. "I just wanted to see your cousin's rings, Kate, not get a history lesson." She turned back to her paper.

"Sorry."

The red bag was on the windowsill over the sink, where Kate often stood, peeling vegetables as she watched Ava play out in the yard. She pushed the lace curtain aside now and took hold of the bag. It felt lighter than she remembered.

She glanced inside: only one velvet box where before there had been two. Her heart thumped.

Without a word, she slipped outside and checked the

car—nothing. She went to the hall closet and slid her hand into the pocket of every coat, even the ones she hadn't worn in years. She was almost positive that she had seen two rings before leaving the jewelry store. But then, she had closed the boxes so fast. Could it have been an optical illusion? No, no, she was sure there were two.

Returning to the kitchen, she wondered how long it would be before her mother left the room. She wanted to ask the children about it, out of earshot of the other adults. After fifteen minutes, no one had budged. May's three were playing their handheld video games at the table; her mother hadn't made it past the Arts & Leisure section; and Ava in her booster seat was basking in the presence of her family, who to her mind were all there to watch her walk down the aisle in a pink party dress.

Kate was bursting with curiosity. Finally, as calmly as she could muster, she asked, "Kids, did any of you touch this bag?"

All four of them shook their heads.

"Are you sure? You're not in trouble if you did. I'm just looking for something. Ava, are you sure?"

"I'm sure, Mama."

"Crap," Kate said. She went to the window, squeezed her eyes shut, and lifted the curtain once more. *Dear Universe: If you'll just let the ring be there when I open my eyes, I'll be forever grateful. Really, no questions asked. The fact that it wasn't there twenty minutes ago will be totally irrelevant.*

She opened her eyes. The only thing on the sill was a wrinkled tomato that she should have thrown out two days earlier.

"What? What is it?" her mother said.

"Toby's and Jeff's rings were both in this bag," Kate said. "Now there's only one of them in here."

Her mother put a hand over her heart.

"You look like you're about to say the Pledge of Allegiance," Kate said.

"You lost one of their rings?"

"No. I misplaced it, that's all. Help me look. I'm supposed to meet them in half an hour."

"Kate! You did this on purpose."

"Okay, how is that helping?"

"You were just saying how much you hate diamonds. Plus, everyone knows you don't want Jeffrey to get married."

"Be that as it may, Mother, I would not purposely lose his wedding ring to stop him."

"Oh, just like how you didn't purposely dye your hair blue the night before your admissions interview at Lanebrook Academy?"

"I was fourteen. Aren't you ever going to let that go?"

"I happen to think it's relevant."

Kate felt panicked now, her whole body rattling with nervous energy.

"Dan!" she shouted. "Dan! I need you!"

Just the sound of his socks on the staircase was a comfort. He appeared in the kitchen a moment later in his pajama pants and plain white undershirt. At thirty-five, with shaggy brown hair and dimples, Dan could still pass for a college kid. Sometimes she wondered if he'd ever stop looking like a baby, or if he'd have the same sweet face even when they were ninety years old.

"What's wrong?" he asked.

"I can't find one of Toby's and Jeff's rings."

"Shit. Whose is it?"

"They're both the same."

"Oh. Right."

"Uncle Dan said the s-word!" Max shouted, suddenly coming to life. "That's a five-dollar word!"

"Put it on my tab, bud," Dan said. "So. If I were a wedding ring, where would I be? Did you check your coat pocket?"

"Yup."

"I don't want a wedding ring, I want a wedding tiara," said May's only daughter, Olivia. She was five years old, and obsessed with all things princess.

"You have to have a ring, dummy," said Max. "Everyone gets a ring."

Forty minutes later, Kate got into the driver's seat and buckled up, plugging the address of the Birchland Inn into her GPS. She was terrible with directions. Until they moved upstate, she had driven maybe twice a year, but now it was a daily occurrence. She still wasn't totally comfortable, especially when Ava was in the backseat, asking her why you needed a key to start the engine, why the car was blue, why fish lived in the sea, why the sky got dark at night.

The radio was switched to NPR. Kate turned it off, grateful for the silence. They had searched the entire house and all the cars—even her sister's—but they still hadn't found the ring. She pictured it everywhere, like a mirage in the desert; she could see it in the dish on the nightstand where Dan kept his pocket change, and on the edge of the bathroom sink, where she sometimes left her watch. But when she checked each spot, she found nothing out of the ordinary there.

She had moved now from panic to acceptance. It was what it was. If they never found the ring, she'd just take a couple thousand dollars out of Ava's college fund and buy Jeff a new one. She laughed out loud at the absurdity of this—were there even a couple thousand extra dollars in the bank?

They had put nearly every penny they had into the house. She mostly thought it was worth it, though sometimes she suspected that homeownership was just another way in which a capitalist society took hold of your life and refused to let go. What did it mean to own the house? They could plant flowers and tear down cabinets without consulting a landlord. So what? They could take pride in owning something. Why?

They lived in Brooklyn until Ava was one, on the fourth floor of an apartment building that had once been full of crackheads and squatters, two blocks from the Gowanus Canal. In the evenings, they strolled along Union Street, past the Hess station and the diner and the mural dedicated to a boy named Raul Vasquez, who had been gunned down on that spot in the mid-nineties. Every year on his birthday, someone placed flowers against the wall.

The neighborhood was safer by the time they arrived, though it still felt gritty. The block between Third and Nevins consisted of nothing but casket warehouses. The men who worked there couldn't be nicer or more friendly, a fact that amused Kate somehow. Perhaps it was the constant reminder that life is precious that made them so jolly; whatever the case, they always waved or made a joke when she and Dan said hello.

Dan had once seen them carrying a plain wooden casket from a truck, not yet adorned with any fabric or cushioning. The word HEAD was stamped at one end.

"So that's what it all comes down to," he said glumly when he arrived home.

Kate's mother had taken one look at the area and told her they needed to move. But the rent was cheap and Kate liked the families who gathered on the sidewalks on summer nights—several generations, eating grilled meat, drinking beer and Mexican Coke, setting off homemade firecrackers that fizzled into golden blossoms outside their bedroom window.

There was a cast of odd characters on their block, who gave her a warm feeling—a giant of a man with only one eye who greeted her each morning outside the bodega on the corner. An old Italian woman with deep wrinkles who walked six tiny white dogs and spoke only three words of English, which she used constantly: "God bless you." A Puerto Rican grandmother who didn't look very old at all, but couldn't talk. Kate assumed she'd had a stroke. The woman spoke only in grunts, but with such enthusiasm that it seemed she didn't realize that no one could understand her. And in fact, it seemed like some of the neighbors could.

Dan said he wanted Ava to have a yard to run around in. They both agreed that being in the suburbs felt like waiting to die, so they moved two hours up the Hudson to a hamlet called Stone Ridge, which somehow seemed more real, just as the city had before it.

She occasionally wondered if subconsciously he had wanted to leave Brooklyn in part so that she'd have to give up her job. Her position at Human Rights Now was one of the few things they had ever argued about. Kate was proud of the work she did; it had always been a part of her identity, perhaps the biggest part. But after Ava was born, she found that it took too much from her. There were nights when she'd be up nursing her baby and thinking only about the children who were suffering elsewhere at that moment. In meetings, she'd become so upset that she would have to squeeze the underside of her chair with both hands to stop herself from leaving the room.

She had never seen the people they served as an abstraction, the way some of her coworkers seemed to. But now they were almost too real to her. She had lost all professional distance. She could not reasonably discuss five-year-old girls in an Indian brothel, or eight-year-olds forced to be child brides in Yemen, without thinking of them as she did her own daughter.

She knew she couldn't save them. Change came so slow, if it ever came. That was one of the hardest lessons she had learned.

Sometimes she felt like she was losing her mind. Even when the baby slept, she couldn't. Dan said he hated seeing her this way, that she ought to find another job that wouldn't rob her, or their family, of so much happiness. Kate agreed to some extent, but she thought that maybe she just needed time—when the baby was older, maybe her feelings wouldn't be so unbearable. Her doctor prescribed a low dose of Zoloft to help with her anxiety, but she couldn't feel it working.

Ava's first birthday arrived, and Dan put together a lovely little party with a few friends and family members. He hung crepe paper around the apartment and bought rainbow-striped pointy hats with cheap elastic bands that pinched their chins. The kids ate pizza and the adults drank wine.

Everyone brought presents. Not picture books and pop-up toys, but exquisitely wrapped boxes that filled their living room. May brought a set of hand-painted wooden sushi and chopsticks, and Mona brought a wooden kitchen set with an oven and fridge. Their downstairs neighbor had purchased a tiny purple tutu. She left the price tag on—lifting the tutu from the tissue paper, Kate saw that it had cost two hundred dollars. There were miniature UGG boots and sequined Mary Janes, a ridiculous fur vest that she would never put on Ava, and even, improbably, a t-shirt bearing a portrait of Frida Kahlo.

As Kate watched her daughter's chubby fingers dig into the wrapping paper of one more gift, she felt a tightening sensation in her chest. She couldn't breathe. "I'll be right back," she said with a smile, not wanting to ruin the moment. Dan gave her a concerned look, but she shook her head as if to say there was nothing to worry about.

It was Toby who found her sitting on the edge of the bed a few minutes later, staring out the window.

"The world is just so unfair," she said, knowing that she sounded like an angsty teenager. "All those over-the-top presents for a one-year-old who doesn't even want them. I don't mean to sound ungrateful. I just feel powerless. I don't understand how we can have so much when other people have nothing."

"Oh, I don't know. Compared to everyone on the Upper East Side, we have nothing," Toby said, trying to make her smile. "If they saw this place, they'd throw a fundraiser for you."

Until that day she was just like anyone; she knew precisely what was wrong with her life and what she might do to fix it eventually, but she never did those things. After the guests left, Kate took a walk and thought about what should have been a sweet and hopeful year. She realized that Dan was probably right.

Moving provided a reasonable excuse to quit. Ellen had said maybe they could figure something out; Kate could telecommute, or come in twice a week. But she turned the offer down. When they arrived upstate two years ago, she started doing press and fundraising for a local food pantry Monday through Thursday, which was still important, Dan pointed out, just more manageable. In the city, she had worked full-time, and though Dan had worked from home, they still had had a babysitter three days a week. Now they were trying to handle the child care themselves; she worked from home two of the four days, he was home all the time, and somehow they made it work.

Kate enjoyed the warmth and safety of the cocoon they

had created, but she sometimes felt smothered by it, too. Their closest neighbors lived half a mile away. She hadn't made any friends; all the women she worked with were in their sixties. They would occasionally have dinner with the parents of one of Ava's playmates, but if they were being honest, all they had in common were their kids.

She missed New York, and her work. She missed the bustling crowds of strangers that for years she had wanted to escape, each one of them thinking his or her own intentions were the most urgent and essential. She still went to protests in the city, and signed every online petition, and donated as much money as they could afford—more than that, sometimes—though it wasn't the same as having her hands in it the way she once did.

She was even more upset, more unsatisfied, more troubled about the state of the world than she had been before, perhaps because now she played no substantial role in changing it. Life in the country was peaceful, but there were too many stretches of time to think. At night, she dreamed of the people whose causes she had abandoned. It was one thing not to know about the evil in the world. But it was something altogether worse to know full well, and do nothing.

She tried to remind herself that she adored the country in some ways. The pace of life was different here; there were things she had intended to do in Brooklyn that now she actually did. She cooked dinners and wrote thank-you notes and gardened. She read a lot and did simple home-improvement projects that in the past she would have asked the super to handle.

The stone house was built in 1793, and it still had its original ceiling beams. There were three bedrooms and a bathroom with a copper tub upstairs, and downstairs, a cozy reading room, a living room where they watched TV at night, and an updated kitchen with a fireplace. They had four and a half acres, bordered by a creek in the back, with an actual chicken coop and a stone smokehouse that Dan used as his studio. He was happier here than she had ever seen him.

May called the place "more like a vacation retreat than someone's actual home," which Kate knew was not intended as a compliment.

Her sister lived in the suburbs. She had been a stay-at-home mom since her second son was born. May had resented their mother for working. It seemed she wanted to do the total opposite of what they had grown up with, in an attempt to end up with the opposite result of their parents' life. Kate wasn't sure it worked that way. Now, all May ever talked about were things—her SUV, the kids' toys, her new kitchen appliances.

In recent years, she had started watching a lot of Fox News. At one family dinner, she drank too many glasses of pinot noir and went on a thirty-minute tirade about how suspicious it was that President Obama refused to make his long-form birth certificate public. The worst part of it was that May hadn't even developed her hateful views on her own. She had just adopted her husband's politics along with his interest in skiing and his love of the Miami Dolphins.

Kate pulled into the parking lot of the Birchland Inn, where Jeff and Toby were staying in a suite with a fireplace and, Jeff had reported by text message earlier that morning, the biggest bed they had ever seen. They had chosen to stay here because it was the first place they had been on vacation together, ten years earlier.

Jeffrey had brought Ava's dress from the city. Kate told him she'd pick it up before ten. She was twenty minutes late, but Toby and Jeff didn't seem bothered.

They were sitting in white wicker chairs on the inn's expansive porch when she arrived, drinking coffee and looking out over the wide front lawn. Jeff was thirty-five and six foot two, with movie-star good looks and a full head of salt-and-pepper hair. Toby was several inches shorter, eight years older, and completely bald, but also handsome in his way. They dressed alike, in crisp, expensive sweaters and button-down shirts. She thought that they must share some designer moisturizer, since they both had the same perfect skin. Today, they were almost glowing. There was an excited, joyful energy around them.

"You two are the calmest about-to-be-married people I've ever seen," she said, hugging them hello.

"We had apple-smoked sausage and blueberry pancakes for breakfast," Jeff said. "And this granola parfait with clotted cream. We're in heaven."

"Plus, we have two more hours until my mother gets here," Toby said. "At which point we'll just start mainlining vodka."

She laughed. Her aunt Abigail and uncle Dennis had been caught off guard when Jeffrey came out of the closet his junior year at Vanderbilt. He had written Kate a letter telling her the news. *They're so upset,* he wrote. *They feel I've betrayed them. I hope this won't change things between us, too. I hope you won't feel as though I've kept a secret from you all these years. Or maybe, knowing you, you already had a hunch . . .*

Kate had known her cousin was gay since she knew there was such a thing as homosexuality. She sent him back a post-card, on which she wrote, *I love you, Jeff. I'm proud of you. And yes, I had a hunch.*

Abigail (her mother's sister) and Dennis took a long time to come around. Jeff had played baseball in high school. He took the homecoming queen to the prom. They couldn't understand how their All-American Boy would now be something entirely different.

"I'm not prejudiced, I just worry that this will make his life so much harder than it needs to be," Abigail said, more or less the same thing Kate's own mother had said when she went on two dates with a black guy at UVM.

For the longest time, Jeff never introduced them to anyone he was dating. But then Toby came along. Now Dennis called Toby to talk about sports, and Abigail referred to them both as her sons. It amazed Kate that the human heart could be unlocked in this way, that tolerance and even love could sprout up where both had seemed impossible.

Toby's parents were evangelical Christians. He had never told them he was gay. They had met Jeff plenty of times, but they referred to him as Toby's roommate.

"Why they think a forty-two-year-old film development executive would need a roommate is beyond me, but people believe what they want to believe," Jeffrey had said once.

The wedding announcement shocked them. Kate thought that on some level they must have realized their son was gay. But maybe there was a difference between knowing it, and having to acknowledge it. Toby's mother had cried. His father refused to come up from Alabama for the wedding, so she was coming alone.

"Gay or straight, the wedding becomes about everyone else, not just the people getting married," Jeff said now.

"Is that the word on the message boards?" Kate teased him, though she knew he was right. At May's wedding, her parents had been seated side by side in the front row, as if this blessed event might temporarily nullify all bad things— their mutual hatred, their bitter divorce. The sight of it was unbelievably odd. She wondered how her stepmother felt, separated from her husband's first wife by only the man himself.

"So? Where are the rings?" Jeff said. "I can't wait to see the finished product."

"Oh, did you want me to bring them here?"

She was a terrible liar. She could feel her heartbeat speed up. "I thought you wanted me to bring them straight to the Fairmount tonight."

To her great surprise, Jeff just shrugged. "That's fine."

"Do you want some coffee?" Toby asked.

"No thanks, I'll let you two be," she said. "But first: I came to see a man about a dress."

Toby got to his feet. "I'll get it. You guys chat for a minute. Sit."

Kate sat.

"So, how are the rings?" Jeff said.

"They're nice."

"Not too mob boss?"

"Nah."

"Good. I got kind of carried away. I know that's probably hard to believe."

"What did they cost, out of curiosity? Sorry, is that a rude question?"

"Yes, it is," he said. "Fourteen thousand."

"Fourteen thousand dollars for two rings?" she spat out. She couldn't help it.

"No," Jeff said. He took a sip of coffee. "Fourteen thousand apiece. Those stones are over a carat each. The rings were handmade."

Kate thought she might throw up. Why had Jeff involved her in this in the first place, when he knew she was entirely inept?

"It's a beautiful day for a wedding," she said.

"Yes, thank God. According to Weather.com, we'll have a low of sixty-one and zero chance of precipitation."

"Impressive. So. Are you nervous?"

He smiled. "I've been bridal bipolar for months, as you know. When I found out we got our dream photographer, I seriously felt like I was high on Ecstasy."

"I remember."

"But then sometimes I'd think about the expense, and about how fast it will all go by, and then I'd be so down. Today I'm just excited. I guess that's the upside of getting married later in life. On the day of, you don't sweat the small stuff."

"You make it sound like you're sixty."

"We've been waiting a long time, that's all," he said. "I'm glad we waited to do it in our own state. Getting married anyplace but New York would just feel weird."

Ten months earlier, Governor Cuomo had finally made same-sex marriage legal in New York. Hearing the news at home on the couch, Toby and Jeff had proposed to one another. One month later, on July 24, the marriages began. Clerk's offices all over the state opened to issue licenses, even though it was a Sunday. At Borough Hall, free cake and champagne were served. Outside the city clerk's office downtown, every time a newly married couple emerged from the building a huge crowd would applaud, blow bubbles, and toss confetti in the air.

People wanted to marry as soon as possible because the opportunity might suddenly disappear as it had in so many other states. Seven years earlier, several of their close friends had been issued marriage licenses in San Francisco, only to have the state supreme court rule their marriages void five months later.

Kate had stood by her cousin at a dozen demonstrations over the years, fighting to get him a right that she wasn't sure was even worth having. She wished people would protest in the opposite direction—fight to do away with marriage altogether—but she knew that was too much to expect.

Toby wanted to get married on the first day possible, but Jeff wanted a real wedding, the sort that took months to plan.

Toby returned with the dress now, a pale pink powder puff of a thing, with layer upon layer of taffeta in the skirt and tiny white silk rosebuds around the waist.

"The kid better not have had a growth spurt," Jeff said. "Otherwise I'm going down to the country store and snatching the first beautiful toddler who will fit into this."

Kate turned to Toby. "Are you sure you want to marry this guy?"

Toby had a huge, ridiculous grin on his face.

"It's so beautiful out here," he said. "So peaceful."

"The night before last there was a big kerfuffle outside our bedroom window when some kid beat up a tourist," Jeff said. "We didn't get any sleep at all."

"In Chelsea?" she said.

"It was nothing. And for that, they sent four fire engines. Can you imagine?"

"You could move out here," she said, though she knew they never would. The country wasn't for everyone. She wasn't even sure it was for her.

"I love it here, but not to live," Jeff said. "It's too quiet. At night, I start to think that every creaking floorboard is Dick and Perry coming to murder me."

Toby took his hand. "You know us. Rooftop cocktails are about as outdoorsy as we get."

A blue station wagon pulled slowly up the street, and turned into the driveway of the inn.

"That's the minister," Jeff said. "He's stopping by to run through our vows with us."

Kate almost made a comment about the fact that she had never heard the word *minister*, or any other remotely religious term, come out of her cousin's mouth in all the years she'd known him. But she resisted, knowing that this was just another part of the marriage carnival.

May had a minister at her wedding, too. Their mother was raised Protestant, their father Jewish, but they didn't have any religion growing up. Kate had been raised without any talk whatsoever of God. In middle school, when she asked her mother if she believed, Mona had cocked her head to the side and said, "I don't really know. Sometimes. Sort of." Her father had simply answered, "No."

Dan believed in God. She liked that about him. Hopefully Ava would inherit his good manners and his good nature and his faith that things generally made sense, even if you weren't sure how. Dan grew up in Kansas City. She thought his midwestern roots had a lot to do with his outlook on life, though he hated it when anyone spoke in generalizations about people from the Midwest, which they did all the time in New York. When he said Kansas City, they either asked if he'd grown up on a farm or made some reference to *The Wizard of Oz*.

Kate stood up. "I'll let you lovebirds be," she said. "Call me if you need anything."

Jeff rose to hug her goodbye. "Thanks for coming over. See you in eight hours. At my wedding."

He raised his eyebrows twice in glee.

He deserved a better friend here, someone who would squeal and jump up and down. But Kate was doing the best she could. They both knew it.

On the ride home, she thought about lasting love, the sort that Jeff and Toby surely had. For many years after her parents' divorce, she didn't have a grasp on what normal was—even after she met Dan, any little argument terrified her, making her wonder if it might be enough to ruin them.

The world seemed so full of warnings about the fact that love could never endure—time flying by, relationships turning sour—but the warnings were like a DANGER: FALLING ROCKS sign on a dark highway at night. You were already there in the middle of it. What were you going to do now, stop driving?

Kate had once asked her happily married boss the secret to a good marriage. Ellen and her husband seemed to genuinely enjoy each other after twenty years together.

"Men are happy if you serve them dinner. It can be Chinese takeout six nights a week, as long as you put it on a plate and hand it to him," Ellen said. "The cooking is really beside the point."

"That's it?"

"Mmm, yeah, pretty much. I pour the ketchup or soy sauce or whatever. I use a lot of ramekins. Do you know what those are?"

"No."

"I recommend finding out."

Diamonds are a traditional and conspicuous signal of achievement, status, and success . . . A woman can easily feel that diamonds are "vulgar" and still be highly enthusiastic about receiving diamond jewelry.

—1970s study commissioned by De Beers

There are many reasons why men decide to give their wives diamond jewelry. When a man is truly motivated by warm sentiment, he likes to feel reassured and encouraged. When his reasons are less than lofty, he likes to give himself a lofty rationale.

—N. W. Ayer,
Annual Report to De Beers, 1966–67

1968

On the morning of her fifty-third birthday, Frances picked up the telephone in her office on the tenth floor of the Ayer building.

"Frances," he said when she answered. "It's Paul Darrow."

"Paul? You're calling from downstairs?"

"I didn't want to come up there and see anyone. I just need to speak to you."

"All right."

She wondered for a moment if he had found out it was her birthday and was calling with good tidings. Dorothy Dignam had a tradition of sending her yellow roses each year, but since Dorothy's retirement in 1960, Frances never expected anyone at work to remember.

She lit a cigarette and took a drag.

"Have you seen the new diamond ads that Warner Shelly's taking to South Africa?" Paul whispered.

"There are no new ads," she said.

"Yes there are. They're phasing us out, Frances."

"What on earth are you talking about?"

"Come to my office," he said, and hung up.

"Honestly," she muttered, but she rose from her seat and took the elevator down one floor to see what the fuss was about.

The two of them had always been partners on the De Beers ads. He created the art and she wrote all the copy. Yet they rarely interacted. She had been in his office only a handful of times.

Paul sat at his desk, puffing away on a cigar, his eyes blinking even faster than usual.

He held a piece of paper aloft between thumb and finger, gingerly, as if it were garbage.

"I found this."

Frances took it from him.

It was a finished advertisement. A photograph of a diamond in a box of Cracker Jack. Casual, whimsical, impermanent. The antithesis of everything she had created.

Prize surprise, she read. *Diamonds sculpted to fit a finger and look anything but dowager. Because diamonds aren't any one period, style, or fashion anymore. Diamonds aren't even off-limits to those with a not-so-big budget. They're for any lady. To wear any time she wants to feel special. A diamond is for now.*

"What the hell is it?" she said.

"Don't ask me."

She felt uneasy.

So much had changed in the past few years. She now reported to a twenty-nine-year-old woman. A youngster named Jeremy Pudney who had married an Oppenheimer was now in charge of the internal marketing team at De Beers, and he was always after something new and fresh and young. Frances had taken each development in stride, tried to be cheerful, and still this was the result.

She turned to leave.

"Where are you going?" Paul asked.

"To get Gerry Lauck on the phone."

Gerry Lauck Senior had retired a year earlier and been replaced by his son of the same name. The son was a carbon copy of his dad in some ways—he had played on the golf team at Yale, and had the same sad smile. He was only a few years younger than Frances, but after having worked with his father for so long she saw him as practically a child. Just then, she longed for the original.

Back in her office, she dialed and asked the secretary to put her through. When he came on the line, she said bluntly, "It's Frances Gerety. Would you care to tell me what's going on with De Beers?"

"Frances, that's right," he stammered. "I have some good news. I guess I forgot to mention it."

There hadn't been anything resembling good news at Ayer in ages. They were losing clients left and right, and they both knew it.

"Oh?" she said.

"You know Deanne Leety, right?"

"Of course I do, Gerry. What's going on?"

Deanne Leety was a young and gorgeous thing who had been working in the copy department for three or four years now. They all made a fuss over her—so smart, so vibrant, so creative. *She's like the new Frances Gerety!* Gerry Senior had once said, and Frances had responded, *Oh? Whatever happened to the old one?*

A year ago, Deanne had gotten divorced. She went off to work in the New York office. Frances had never thought to wonder what she was working on.

"Right," Junior said now. "Well. She's giving you a hand on De Beers since you've been so busy."

"No I haven't," she said. "Not any busier than usual."

"Right. Well."

She suddenly felt overheated. The Ayer building might have been the last one in Philadelphia without air-conditioning. Frances stretched the phone cord to its absolute limit and pushed the window open. A cool breeze swept in, causing the papers on her desk to fly about the room.

"When you say she'll give me a hand, do you mean she's taking over my account?"

He paused. She could tell he was nervous.

Frances sat down.

"Are you dropping the motto?" she asked quietly.

"No! We still love *A Diamond Is Forever*. It's not as drastic as it sounds. Your retirement is coming up, that's all. It seems like a good time to begin the transition."

"My retirement is over a year away," she said.

"That's not so long, Frances."

"I don't know how closely you watch this account, but the diamond engagement ring tradition has been at an all-time peak these past few years. Somewhere between six hundred thousand and seven hundred thousand carats are being sold annually in the marriage market now. An average of half a carat per ring."

"Yes, but a lot of that is down to marriage rates that have already started to decline. And you know as well as I do that times are changing. These days, everybody under twenty-five seems to pooh-pooh everything everybody over twenty-six believes in. We need to find a way to sell the same old product to a whole new generation. The client wanted some exploration to that end."

It was true that many leading magazines wouldn't cover diamonds in their editorial every year anymore, or even every other year. The publicity department had done their job almost too well, and the novelty of diamonds had worn off a bit. But that was publicity. As far as her job went, Frances had kept it as fresh as she could.

"I've done that a hundred times before," she said. "I can do it again in my sleep."

She had been the only person to write for De Beers for the past twenty-four years. She had worked on other accounts: Yardley of London, Sealtest, Canon, Crane stationery. They had even given her a bonus for some silly thing she wrote about a princess telephone. *(It's little! It's lovely! It lights!)* But De Beers was the focus of her entire career.

"How long has this girl been writing my account?" she

asked. She felt like a wife asking her husband how long he'd been sleeping with his bookkeeper.

"She and Jerry Siano in the art department have been working together on some ideas for a few months," he said sheepishly.

"Months!"

They were both silent. She assumed he was waiting for her to make a scene. Lord knew she had never been afraid to do so in the past. Four years earlier, his father and Ayer's president, Warner Shelly, had gone to Johannesburg to celebrate the twenty-fifth anniversary of Ayer and De Beers. She felt stung for an instant upon realizing she wasn't invited. Nobody had thought of her. Frances said nothing, but when they came back all smiles, telling everyone that they'd never been wined and dined like that in their lives, that they had each been given a gold watch, she began to see red. She was the one who had done all the work!

Poor Gerry waltzed into her office to show her the watch, and Frances snapped, "Where's my gold watch?"

Well, his mouth flew open and his eyes nearly popped out of his head. No one dared to talk to him like that. No one but her. She had often thought it again since: *Where's my gold watch? Or better still, my diamond watch?*

But just now she felt too stunned to raise a fuss.

"Why don't I have Deanne come down on the train tomorrow morning and show you what she's done," he said.

Frances didn't respond. That sounded like absolute torture, but she didn't have much of a choice.

"There's something else," he said.

"Dear God, what?"

"We're moving some of creative to New York. Including De Beers."

Everyone had been expecting it ever since Harry Batten died two years back. Each time they lost another account, the reason the client gave was the same—they weren't in Manhattan, therefore they were out of touch. It was the exact opposite of the way it had been when she first got hired, when their outsider status made them seem more fully American than everyone else.

But they had been falling behind for a long while. They were the last of the big agencies to get 50 percent of their business in broadcast.

"AT&T threatened to leave, and that was the last straw," Gerry said now. "Warner wants art and copy in New York by next month."

"I can't just up and move to New York."

"I know," he said. "That's all right. Plenty of people will stay in Philly. Just some big accounts will go. You'll stay on where you are until you retire. You can take it easy."

"I don't want to take it easy," she said.

She knew De Beers didn't have to move anywhere. The Oppenheimers never even came to America. They wouldn't know the difference between ads written in New York City and Timbuktu.

She couldn't breathe.

Finally he said, "It's nothing personal. It's just the cycle these things take."

He was right. It was a ruthless business. Out with the old, in with the new. She had always known this, she had just never been *the old* before. For the first time in her life, Frances imagined how Betty Kidd must have felt when she came along, all eager and ready to take over. Poor Betty.

They hung up, and Frances sat with her chin in her hands, just staring at the wall. This shouldn't cause such a sting. She'd still have her other accounts. And yet.

At noon, she gathered up her purse and hat, and strolled to the elevator. If anyone asked, she would say she had gone to a meeting.

She drove out to the Main Line, where the city skyscrapers were replaced by grand old houses and lush trees. Once she got to Merion, she went down into the wood-paneled lunchroom, not bothering to lift her head as she walked past the ladies playing bridge in the parlor. She had never been here on a weekday before.

The waitress was a college girl named Victoria.

"Hello, Miss Gerety," she said. "A martini, two olives?"

"Yes please, dear. And the chicken salad."

"Right away."

When the drink came, she gulped half of it down in one sip.

"Happy Birthday, Mary Frances," she said out loud.

She felt utterly alone, ready for a pity party, though a couple of her girlfriends were taking her to dinner later. She wasn't alone, not really.

She wished she had a recording of the entire exchange from this morning, so that she might play it back and hear every word with fresh ears. Gerry had said that times were changing and they needed a new approach. The idea that she couldn't handle the job was ludicrous. It had been only a few years since she had last saved De Beers. Had everyone forgotten already?

In 1960, the De Beers folks decided to be in cahoots with the Soviets rather than compete with them, when they discovered massive diamond deposits in Siberia. The diamonds were small, mostly between .2 and .4 carats, and there were millions of them. There was no use for stones like that in the market Ayer had created, in which bigger was clearly better, but De Beers intended to control all the world's diamonds, wherever they were found and whatever the size.

Gerry went into a tailspin. "We've spent all this time telling people that a real marriage proposal can only be expressed by the largest stone possible. They want us to cut that off and say, 'Sorry, folks, now it's all about small diamonds'? We'll lack any and all credibility."

"All right," Frances said, her wheels already turning. "What is there to make a diamond special, other than its size?"

He waited only half a second before answering. "I can't think of a damn thing."

"I'll work on it," she said. "Not to worry."

At home that night, she poured herself a drink and wrote down fifty ideas or more, all of them awful. She feared that Gerry was right—you couldn't spend three decades telling women to want something and then all of a sudden demand that they desire its opposite.

In the morning meeting the next day, for the first time she could recall, Frances had to admit that she had nothing. They threw around more bad ideas—maybe women could get a large diamond *and* a small one now. Absurd things like that.

Afterward, she went to her office and pulled out a book she kept of all the ads she had ever written. She felt a bit emotional flipping through those pages. She was looking for something to spark her imagination, though she couldn't say what.

Eventually, she landed on a page from the fifties, covered in white daisies. They had tried for a brief time then to be a bit more scientific about rings. In that ad, she wrote about color, clarity, cutting, and carats. The idea wasn't a huge hit, so they dropped it and went back to lovey-doveyness.

She went to the creative director to tell him about it.

"The 4 Cs," she said. "What if we turn that into an official term? Something a woman would go to her jeweler and ask about. That way, you could buy a teeny stone, but feel confident that it's far more perfect than a gem three times as big."

"I like the idea, but I can't imagine women caring about how clear a stone is under a microscope, can you?"

She shrugged. "If the ads are convincing enough, why not? And if the jewelers will get behind it, which they ought to."

"But it didn't work last time," he said.

"Well, maybe we just didn't push hard enough."

They added a box called "How to Buy a Diamond" to all the ads. *Ask about color, clarity, and cutting—for these determine a diamond's quality, contribute to its beauty and value. Choose a fine stone, and you'll always be proud of it, no matter what its size.*

Frances wrote lots on the topic—for four years in a row they ran a full-page ad that was nothing but a chart dedicated to defining the 4 Cs. The publicity department worked the idea into stories for newspapers and men's magazines about how to acquire the best diamond. And now television hosts and Tiffany and every bride in America talked about the 4 Cs as if they were a concept as old as time.

More recently, Frances had begun to work on the idea of developing a diamond engagement ring tradition in countries where it didn't previously exist—countries like Sweden and Germany, where the custom of giving a plain gold band was firmly entrenched—to help get rid of the surplus of small stones.

Meanwhile, De Beers came up with a new ring. They called it the eternity band, meant as an anniversary gift, and made of twenty or more little Siberian diamonds, running in a line around the entire finger. In 1964, Frances focused her attention on this, and came up with the slogan *Diamonds bespeak an ever-growing love*. The campaign was a huge success.

Yet here she was, just four years later, getting the brush-off from the same men who had been praising her for a quarter century.

Gerry Junior had said it wasn't personal. Maybe that was true in theory. But Frances had made her work her life. Who was she without it?

She had never once thought about retirement, though she knew it was coming. Oh, maybe in some vague sense she had pictured herself moving out to the suburbs, waking up at ten and playing golf on a Tuesday. She had thought about what she might do besides work. But she hadn't thought of not working, the void that would leave.

Her parents died in 1959, six months apart. Her mother went first, and after that it was like her father couldn't find a single reason to stay alive. Frances kept in touch with her cousins, but her true family had been gone for years. What did she have, then? Other people could sink into their grandchildren, or rediscover their spouses, or whatever it was they did. Her longest relationship in life had not been with a man, but with a company.

Gerry Lauck Senior once showed her a letter written by Cecil Rhodes, who founded De Beers in the 1880s. Rhodes had never married either. In that letter, he wrote to a friend, "I hope you will not get married. I hate people getting married. They simply become machines and have no ideas beyond their respective spouses and their offspring."

And yet the two of them, he and Frances, were more responsible than anyone for the diamond engagement ring tradition.

"Excuse me? Fran?" came a voice from behind her. For a second she thought it was the waitress noticing her empty glass, but of course the waitress wouldn't call her that. She turned to see Meg Patterson standing there.

"I thought that was you. I was upstairs playing bridge

when you came in. We just finished for the day. Mind if I sit?"

Frances smiled. "No, please do."

She owed Ham and Meg for the fact that she even got to be here. They had had a whale of a time trying to get her her membership, with various old geezers on the board threatening to leave the club if a single woman was admitted. But now there were a few other maiden ladies who belonged, too. Of course, they still couldn't vote and probably never would be allowed to. But Frances didn't care about that. She didn't want to vote. She wanted to golf and drink martinis on the terrace at sunset.

Meg pulled a pack of Parliaments from her purse and offered one to Frances before lighting her own.

"Do you have a meeting here today?"

"No. I took the afternoon off. It's my birthday."

"Ahh! I'm so sorry I didn't know."

"How could you?"

The waitress brought the salad and offered to refresh her drink.

"Yes please," Frances said. "And what will you have, darling?"

"A White Russian would be great," Meg said. "Thanks, Victoria. Please charge everything to Ham's account."

"No!" Frances protested, but Meg raised a hand to say that she would not argue. "It's your birthday."

"Thank you."

"So what do you think about the big news?" Meg asked. "Ayer in New York."

Frances wondered if everyone on earth had known longer than she had. It seemed that in a single day she had become obsolete. She remembered now how thirteen years ago, just before she joined Merion, Meg had told her they were moving to New York. But they never had. Ayer was their family, and Ham was loyal, like Frances herself.

"I'll stay here," Frances said. "I'll go back and forth, as I do now. Nothing's going to change for me."

Meg nodded. "Ham's going to try commuting from here, too. I don't want to give up our house, I love it too much. Our neighbors are such lovely people. Ten years ago, I might have been up for a New York adventure, but now I'm stuck in my ways."

Frances patted her hand. "Me too."

"After Ham retires, I'd like to travel, though," she said. "I've never seen Europe."

"That sounds nice."

"I've always envied you a little, Frances."

She laughed. "Good heavens, why?"

"You've just always seemed so in control of your own destiny. I've ended up someplace I didn't expect to be. I pictured myself as a mother, ever since I was a young girl. But children weren't in the cards for us, I'm afraid. And that makes me, what? A housewife?"

"A damn fine one, I'm sure," Frances said.

Meg shrugged. "Sometimes it just feels like we can't tell what we've given up until it's too late."

Frances was still awake at two a.m. She should have called Dorothy to talk about what happened, or else her cousin Margaret, but now it was far too late. She knew she wouldn't sleep.

She tried to soothe herself. This was how things went. She had had other accounts taken away from her before, and she'd gotten accounts that had been taken from someone else. *Nothing personal.*

Morning came, and she put on her smartest dress, but she

still looked like a disheveled schoolmarm. Her hair hung
limp in a gray bob, and she had no choice but to wear the
thick glasses she'd been sporting for several years now. She
couldn't see a thing without them.

When Deanne Leety stepped into her office in stacked
heels and a tailored pantsuit, Frances had the strongest
urge to crawl under the desk and die. She had never seen
a woman in a pantsuit, other than on the cover of *Women's
Wear Daily*.

"Hi Frances," Deanne said. "Is this still a good time?"

"Of course. Sit down."

Deanne held a fat file under her impossibly thin arm. "I
brought along my ideas."

Frances nodded.

"Good. Let's see what you've got."

Deanne opened the folder. She was an entirely feminine
creature, pretty and fashionable, but somehow more confident than any other woman Frances had ever seen in this or
any office building. This was how the modern working girl
behaved. She didn't hide her femininity or apologize for it,
as they did in the old days. She flaunted it and, having been
given more than any woman before her, demanded even
more than that.

"First, let me say how much I admire your work," Deanne
said. "I like how many of your ads tell a story."

Frances forced a grin. "Thank you."

"I've just done some updating, really. Trying to appeal to
the hippies and the dreamers. Like this—"

Deanne slid a piece of paper across the table. The illus-
tration was a psychedelic blast of bright orange and blue: a
woman with long flowing hair, a crown of flowers resting
on her head, and her bare arms wrapped around the waist of
the man in front of her. There was a cartoon lion crouching
behind the pair.

Good Lord, she needed a cocktail.

The copy read, *A man who is his own man is my love. Strong and proud and sure. And now he's going to share his life with me. A diamond is forever.*

"I should probably warn you that De Beers is a conservative client," Frances said. "They have strict rules. No religion in the advertising. Men and women can never be— That is, nothing at all can suggest—touching."

"I know," Deanne said. "Although Jerry Siano says we can push the envelope, just a bit."

"Does he?"

"Yes. These have already been approved."

"I see." She tried not to show her surprise. "Still, it's important to remember your objective. In this case, it's to maintain the DER tradition while convincing consumers that a more unique, higher-priced DER is the most expressive way to acknowledge their love and commitment. DER stands for 'diamond engagement ring,' by the way."

"I know. Well, here, have a look at this one. It's for *Seventeen, Vogue,* and *Life.*"

Frances lifted the page up to the lamp.

The Prince or the Cowboy or the somebody you never told anybody about is suddenly real. And he wants to marry you. A diamond is forever.

It wasn't half bad.

"You're talented," she said, even as it pained her to do so.

"Thanks. Now, this is my favorite. It's a photo of Lucy Saroyan as a child, meshed with a photo of her as an adult. Both were taken by Richard Avedon. I'm still tweaking the copy, but I'm thinking of something along the lines of *A part of every woman is the little girl who dreamed about the day someone would find her and love her and give her a ring. A diamond is forever.*"

"Who is Lucy Saroyan?" Frances asked.

"The actress," Deanne said, as if it should be obvious. "Her father won the Pulitzer Prize. Her mother is married to Walter Matthau. And her brother is a poet. He writes those one-word poems."

Frances frowned. "My dear, there is no such thing as a one-word poem."

"The last thing I wanted to show you is a slight twist on your line. Something for that ever-growing group of women who don't want to get engaged. But maybe they'll buy diamonds for themselves. *A Diamond Is For Now.* What do you think?"

"I've already seen that one."

"Oh. All right then."

"You should be very proud of yourself," Frances said, not sure why she was saying it. "How are you getting on here? So many changes coming up."

"I'm thrilled to be back in New York," Deanne said. "When I first came to Ayer Philadelphia, I felt I'd been transported to the Middle Ages."

"What do you mean?"

"The boutique agency I used to work for was based out of the penthouse at the Plaza Hotel," she said. "Then I come to Ayer. It's just so antiquated. The fact that there's no conversation or collaboration between art and copy, for example. The two departments aren't even on the same floor. This business where you get a memorandum from some account executive explaining what an ad calls for: *This is your authority, to create an ad that conveys blah blah blah, to run in such-and-such publications.* It's so stiff. No one does it like that anymore. Dunning says this company is run like a fine clock, which is anathema to the creative process."

Frances raised an eyebrow. "Dunning?"

"Robert Dunning. The head of creative in New York."

"Yes. I know who he is."

She called him Dunning. Frances wondered if they were an item, or if this was just the way people talked nowadays.

"And don't even get me started on the way they treat women around here," Deanne went on. "They're making me a vice president. I'm not supposed to tell anyone yet, but they'll announce it soon. Nineteen sixty-eight, and they're just getting around to their first female VP on the creative side."

Frances felt shaken. In her day, not only were there no women in positions like that, she had never even dreamed that there ought to be.

This girl was entirely unapologetic. Of course, Frances herself might have been the same way, had she ever been given the chance.

"I don't know how you survived it the way it was back then," Deanne said. "I would have lost my mind."

Part Three

1972

The grandfather clock struck twelve-thirty.

Teddy would arrive for lunch soon, and Evelyn still had plenty to do.

Gerald had left the TV on in the den when he went upstairs to shower. Through the open kitchen door, Evelyn could hear strains of game-show applause, followed by the more somber tones of the midday news. As she chopped the celery, she made out the words *Saigon, Capitol building, cold front coming, annual Halloween parade.*

She went toward the set to turn it off, pausing for a moment while a reporter announced that after weeks of tip-toeing around the idea, George McGovern had now come right out and said that he believed President Nixon was per-sonally involved in the Watergate affair.

"But," the newsman said, "the Watergate scandal is a ho-hum for most of the people. Politics as usual, they say."

"Quite right," Evelyn said. There were far more serious things to worry about.

She twisted the knob until it gave a satisfying click, and the picture melted into itself.

In just the last few years, there had been so much unrest, so many attempts to alter the status quo: civil rights, women's rights, even homosexuals' rights. It was a different world, and it made an old person feel older. She was pleased when the schools desegregated. That was an important step. But now it was legal everywhere in America for blacks and whites to intermarry. Evelyn wasn't sure what to make of that.

There was even a black woman running for president. Gerald said she wasn't serious, but Evelyn thought perhaps she was. Her friend Ruthie had invited her to a consciousness-raising meeting, where they talked about campaigning for Shirley Chisholm. The women there also discussed a new bestselling book called *Open Marriage*, with a chapter all about how couples might choose to accept affairs as part of a healthy relationship. They had created words, like *chairperson* and *Ms.*, which to Evelyn's mind signaled a whole new order.

Ruthie took it all lightly—she was just keeping up with the young people. She didn't know what she really thought about half of what they preached.

"At least it's something to talk about besides that awful war," she said.

Evelyn supposed some of the changes were very good news. But she never went to another one of those meetings. Something about it frightened her.

It was probably the book that upset her most.

"Open marriage," she said to Gerald that night. "No wonder our son has no morals, when this is the world we're living in."

She thought of it again now, even as she knew she shouldn't let herself get this way. If she focused on Teddy's bad traits, she'd be boiling by the time he arrived. She tried to imagine him as a baby, wrapped in a blue blanket, coming home from the hospital. But it was no use. She was angrier than she had ever been. She thought of what Julie said: he had actually asked her for a divorce.

Evelyn imagined turning him away when he came to the door later today, but she knew she'd never go through with it.

She reminded herself that she hadn't always done what her parents wanted either, and things had turned out all right. But of course that had been different. After Nathaniel died, her mother and father insisted that she come home to New York, but Evelyn refused. All she had left of him was Boston. The restaurants where they had eaten dinner, the dance halls where they had laughed and perspired on summer nights. Eventually, she returned to work, where her students called her Mrs. Davis. Each time, the sound of the words made her heart seize up with a mixture of happiness and sorrow. The children's presence brought her pleasure, yet served to remind her that she would never have children of her own.

Gerald went back to Chicago. She missed their talks, and the way he could make her laugh on even the dreariest of days. When she spoke to normal people, it was as if she were on a time delay—she couldn't keep up with a simple conversation, couldn't remember what they had said a minute earlier. There was a group of single girls who taught at the same school she did, most of them a bit younger than her. They went out bowling on Friday nights and always invited Evelyn along. She never accepted their invitations. She was a married woman, after all. And it was easier to be alone.

A few months after the funeral, Gerald wrote to say that he was moving back to Boston. It was his hometown, so Evelyn didn't think much of the news, other than that she was pleased. His father's company was run out of Park Square, and she assumed that Gerald would work there. But when they met for supper on his first night in town, he told her that he had given his father notice. His dad was furious, but Gerald said that he couldn't get Nathaniel out of his head, talking about the importance of being a self-made man. And so, rather than continuing to follow in his father's footsteps in the banking world, Gerald had taken a job with an insurance company. He'd have to start from the bottom, which thrilled him, in a way. He hoped that now he might make friends at work. Of course, his inheritance meant that he wasn't self-made, and he knew it, but still it seemed a noble pursuit to at least try to walk his own path. Evelyn knew Nathaniel would have been proud to know he had made such an impact.

She thought perhaps Gerald was trying to improve himself in other ways, too. He looked a bit healthier, and he only drank one gin and tonic all night.

Like Evelyn, he worried about how Nathaniel's mother would get on. He had sent her enough money, he said, to keep her going for a year. (He continued to do so every year until she died.) Evelyn tried to visit her mother-in-law once a month in Pittsburgh, though she dreaded those weekends. The house felt heavy and dark, and no one ever mentioned Nathaniel by name. She couldn't tell if they welcomed her presence or if she was nothing but a painful reminder.

With Gerald, it was different. They cried, but they also spoke of Nathaniel with happiness and laughter, telling one another their favorite stories, even when they both knew the endings. She learned things about Nathaniel she had never known. There were private moments that existed between close friends, things a man wouldn't even tell his best girl. But now Gerald told her. It delighted her to find that there were still parts of Nathaniel she had yet to discover. It was like realizing that your favorite novel had four extra chapters you'd somehow never noticed before. Gerald understood this, and Evelyn could not imagine a more precious gift.

She had never spent any time alone with Gerald in the past. Away from Nathaniel he seemed softer, more earnest. He told her that he'd been shy as a boy, and when she dismissed this with a laugh, he said, "My hand to God, it's true. I overcompensated by becoming the class clown."

Despite his pedigree, he preferred simple pleasures. He

loved unfussy food, and baseball games. He hated the ballet. He didn't see the point in novels. He read only newspapers, which he said were stranger and sadder and funnier than fiction anyway.

On Sunday nights, he sometimes invited her along to dinner at his parents' stately home in Wellesley. Evelyn's own parents were relatively wealthy, but they were paupers compared to Gerald's. She felt a bit intimidated, but tried not to show it. She liked the way that Gerald was fully himself, making corny jokes, even as his mother furrowed her brow as if he were speaking a foreign language and a butler stood stiffly by his side, offering dessert wine.

No one else could cheer her like he could. It was almost embarrassing how many times Gerald had caught her in the middle of a pity party: sobbing into a handkerchief at home, listening to "Someone to Watch Over Me" on the record player.

"Let's go out, kid," he'd say, and they would.

They spent almost all of their free time together. It was different, spending evenings with a man who never had to think about money. Gerald suggested Locke-Ober for dinner, while Nathaniel would have taken her to the Wursthaus. Evelyn felt it was almost a betrayal of Nathaniel, and so she'd tell Gerald that she much preferred a hamburger to filet mignon.

One winter afternoon, they walked through the Public Garden in the snow, and talked about how excited Nathaniel would have been to see Franklin Roosevelt elected president. Gerald mentioned that he had seen Roosevelt give a speech in New York, back when he was dating Fran. It made Evelyn think of something that had crossed her mind now and then; since Nathaniel died, she hadn't known Gerald to go on a single date. She wondered if perhaps she was to blame.

"I don't think I would have made it this far without your friendship," she said. "Thank you, Gerald. It's just that I hope I'm not monopolizing too much of your time."

"Impossible."

"But truly. You came to Boston to start a new career and make friends and meet someone wonderful. Aren't I keeping you from all that?"

He looked surprised. "I came back here for you."

"What do you mean?" she asked.

"Just what I said."

"I thought you came back for a job."

"There were plenty of jobs in Chicago," he said with a shrug. "But I promised Nathaniel I'd take care of you."

"Oh."

"Plus, I like you, kid."

She smiled weakly, unsure what to say next.

"Do you want to stop on Newbury Street for a hot chocolate?" he asked, saving her from having to say anything at all.

It was a few months later, springtime, on the night they went to the Parker House for dinner. Nathaniel had been dead for one year, one week, and two days—she still kept count every morning when she woke. While they ate, she cried into her lobster thermidor. She told Gerald she could no longer remember the way Nathaniel smelled, or the exact tone of his voice when he laughed. Gerald was understanding, telling her that he knew just what she meant. Sometimes he'd forget the name of a song or a restaurant they had liked in college, and his first inclination would be to call Nathaniel up to see if he remembered.

When the waiter asked if they wanted dessert, Gerald suggested that they share something. She nodded.

"The sundae," Gerald told the waiter, just as Evelyn said, "The Boston cream pie."

They laughed.

"Well?" Gerald asked the man. "Care to be the tie-breaker?"

"I'm afraid I'll have to go with your wife's pick," the waiter said. "The pie is our specialty."

After he walked away, they sat in silence for a moment.

"Oh jeez," Gerald said.

"It was an honest mistake." She lifted her left hand, where her little emerald glistened. "I'm still wearing this. I suppose I always will. Do you think you're still considered a spinster if your husband is dead?"

"I think it would be impossible for anyone to mistake you for a spinster, whatever the circumstances."

She smiled. "I feel selfish saying this, but I'm jealous of other women. The ones who get to go on dates, the ones who get to have babies, and weddings. I feel half alive, Gerald. I'm not a part of it anymore."

"You will be," he said. "You'll see."

A month or two earlier, she would have hated him for saying so, but he likely wouldn't have said it then. As usual, she felt grateful for his presence in her life.

After dessert, they went out to the street. It was a warm evening, and Evelyn thought she might like to go somewhere for a nightcap. She started to ask Gerald if he felt like it, but stopped when she saw him staring at her with a strange expression on his face.

"What is it?" she asked.

"That waiter. He thought we were married."

"Oh Gerald, don't worry about that."

"I'm not worried. I liked him thinking it."

"What do you mean?"

He spoke in a rush. "Isn't it obvious, Evelyn? I'm crazy about you."

"Don't say that."

"But I thought—"

"You thought what? Just because I said I'm lonely, you've got to swoop in? You told Nathaniel you'd take care of me, and that means taking pity on me?"

He frowned. "Pity? Evie, I have carried a torch for you since the day we met."

"Stop that," she said.

"You were wearing a red bathing suit, and you had a big wet strand of hair stuck to your cheek."

"I did?"

"You were the most beautiful girl I'd ever seen. I wanted to ask you to dinner, but Nathaniel got to it first. I was mad about that in the beginning, to tell you the truth. But once I got to know you, I realized you weren't made for the likes of me anyway. You were out of my league, and squarely in his."

"Don't be so defeatist."

"But it's true, isn't it?"

Evelyn didn't know what to say.

"I think that's why he was always so worried about me finding the right girl," Gerald said. "He felt guilty, because he knew I had my heart set on you, even though I knew you'd never be mine."

"I've got to go," she said, just as a taxi pulled to the curb.

For a week, they didn't meet or speak. She missed Gerald. She'd laugh, thinking of a joke he had told. She would read something interesting and want to tell him straightaway.

When she came home from church the following Sunday, he was sitting on her stoop. She felt instantly full of joy.

"Feel like a walk?" he asked.

She smiled. "Sure."

They strolled along the cobblestone streets, trading stories about their weeks. Neither of them mentioned what he had said, and she found with some surprise that she wished he would. They went on this way for a couple months longer. Every time Evelyn thought of their situation, she felt perplexed. She wanted Gerald to kiss her, but she couldn't say why.

Finally, on a sweltering night in July, she kissed him. There was a spark there, which she never would have believed if you'd told her five years prior, or even five months.

"Are you sure?" Gerald asked.

"Yes."

They were married four months later, in the backyard of her parents' summer home in the Berkshires. When Gerald proposed, he gave her a slim gold chain along with the ring. Without a word, he slid Nathaniel's ring off her finger and threaded the chain through it, then draped the necklace around her neck and clasped it shut.

They never discussed whether Nathaniel would have approved, because they both knew the answer. They realized other people viewed their situation as the scandal of the season. At school one morning, as she stepped into the front hall of the building, Evelyn heard one of the other teachers say, "And the groom is the first husband's best friend! It's not right, if you ask me." When Evelyn rounded the corner, the woman turned red.

But she didn't care what anyone said. She and Gerald had fallen in love, as unusual as the circumstances were. And if Nathaniel was like an invisible third person in their marriage, it was only in the best sense—the thought of him and the briefness of life smoothed over any dispute or disagreement.

She got pregnant on their honeymoon, as she had hoped. They named their son Theodore Nathaniel, and at first it seemed almost like he had Nathaniel's heart and soul in him—Teddy was such a happy baby, so full of laughter and wonder at the smallest things. When he was born, Evelyn had loved those first few moments alone with him. It was the first time in her life that a stranger felt so utterly familiar. Later, when Gerald was allowed to come into the room, she thought of how the last time they'd been together in a hospital was the worst moment of their lives, but now there would finally be happiness.

She could still see Teddy as a child, sitting under the willow tree in the backyard, reading his Superman comics, X-ray glasses strapped over his eyes. She had tried to lavish attention and affection on him, nurturing his interests and his hopes. Since he had no brothers or sisters, she and Gerald made a point of playing games with him—Clue or Chutes and Ladders in the parlor after dinner, so different from the almost businesslike way in which her own parents had treated her.

But as Teddy got older, Evelyn lost him. He had a bad temper, and often got into fights at school. At Harvard, he was constantly being disciplined for fighting, drinking, vandalism. Finally, he was dismissed altogether for cheating on a history exam. He responded with anger, as though someone had wronged him. After that, there were gambling debts in the thousands, and more fights. Far too much alcohol, and God knew what else. He never had a real job, instead bouncing from one harebrained idea to the next, often with Gerald footing the bill. He had once stolen a blank check from Gerald's desk, making it out to himself for ten thousand dollars. Later, he apologized and said he'd pay them back. He never did, but they forgave him even so. Her sweet little boy grew into a man she didn't recognize, and she could never quite figure out why.

Gerald said there was no rhyme or reason to it, but she believed that a mother's love was paramount when it came to shaping a child. So what had she done to ruin Teddy?

A pediatrician had once told her that perhaps she held him

too much as a baby. As soon as he was born, she wanted to hold on to him for dear life, forever. When Teddy reached sixth grade, Gerald's family was adamant that he should be sent away to prep school, but Evelyn refused to let him go. Maybe it was because she had lost so much already, or simply that he was her first and only.

She sometimes wondered if Teddy had come to resent her because she started teaching again when he was twelve. Was he angry with her for giving other children her love? There were some students, especially, whom she had taken into her heart. A boy with a drunk for a father, whose mother was dead, was caring for three younger brothers on his own. His name was Adam, and one summer Evelyn took in the lot of them until their grandmother arrived from Memphis to care for them. There was a girl, Sabrina, who could not read much. Evelyn worked with her after school three times a week. She did it at the house, because sweet Sabrina was so worried about the other children at school discovering her secret. When a child was at risk, Evelyn made sure to keep an eye on him long after he was out of her class, even beyond graduation. She wrote letters. She had them over to dinner. But did Teddy not realize that she loved him more than all the rest combined?

Whatever the reason, things had gotten muddled, and now here they were, with Teddy thinking he wanted a divorce, when his wife was the best thing that had ever happened to him. Evelyn loved her son, but there was something she had never said aloud, not even to Gerald: though she was grateful for it, she had often wondered what had made Julie fall in love with him. Teddy wasn't a kind man, not chivalrous, or even particularly charming. She had long worried that someone would come along with dollar signs in her eyes and marry him just for his inheritance. But Julie had seen something in him.

Maybe what Julie saw wasn't real and never had been; maybe every good quality she imagined in Teddy was simply part of herself reflected back.

When the doorbell rang at quarter past one, Evelyn walked slowly down the front hall as if approaching the guillotine, her hands balled up into fists at her sides.

She didn't want to hear his explanation. She never should have allowed this visit in the first place.

Just as her hand touched the doorknob, it turned on its own, and Teddy pushed it open from the other side. He looked much the same as he had the last time she saw him, five months earlier, not a hint of shame on his face. He held a bunch of browning pink carnations wrapped in dripping paper.

"Mom," he said, and kissed her on the cheek. "I'd like you to meet my girlfriend, Nicole Standish."

Evelyn froze.

He had brought the other woman.

1987

While Maurice waited inside for his burger, James went around to the back of the truck, opening the doors. He could still smell the stench of the homeless guy. The smells were one of the worst parts of the job, worst of all in summer.

He pulled the sheet off the stretcher with just the tips of his fingers, the same way he might when one of his kids wet the bed. Twice in the past year he had gotten head lice from the same bum in Central Square. He opened a bottle of alcohol and poured a quarter of it onto a thick towel. As he scrubbed the seat, he thought of his wife, the way she liked to tease him when he washed the dishes, saying, "How about some more elbow grease there, McKeen?"

They dated for three years in high school. Afterward, Sheila thought he should go to college, for a deferment if nothing else, but as soon as he had that diploma in hand, James only wanted to get his band off the ground in a serious way. They were called Ulterior Motive. James played bass guitar and wrote all the songs. For eighteen months their junior and senior years, they tried to squeeze in practices wherever they could. James worked at the Stop & Shop deli counter four days a week after school and on Saturdays, which left only Friday nights and Sundays free. It was a point of contention between him and the lead singer, Chip McIntyre. Chip couldn't understand what it was like to have a single mom who needed help paying for groceries. His father was a doctor who owned a big house on Hospital Hill, and only lived in Quincy in the first place because he had grown up there and felt nostalgic about it or some shit. James thought Chip was a dick, but he'd been brought in after the other three got together by the drummer, Frank Rogers, and he liked the sound of the thing. They were playing covers when James joined, but now they did almost all their own stuff. It felt real. Important.

James knew college wasn't for him. Even if he could have somehow afforded it, he had always hated school. How many hours had he wasted watching the hands on a clock move so slowly that they seemed to defy the laws of space and time? How many algebra and chemistry classes had he sat through, writing songs in his notebook, pretending to pay attention? He had gotten caught once, and Mrs. Pierce (American history) had called his mother about it. She looked disappointed and tired when she got home from work that night. "Jimmy, why are you fooling around when you're supposed to be studying, huh?"

He wanted to tell her how he knew in his gut that music was the thing that would save him. The only thing he was any good at. That it was impossible to imagine himself growing old and fat behind a desk. But he just said, "Sorry, Ma, I'll quit it."

Some spark in his mother had fizzled when Bobby got sent to Vietnam. James knew he was all she had left, at least for now. He thought she would come around when the band started to make it. When he bought her a big house and a new car, and took her on vacation to Ireland.

School came to an end, and they were able to practice more often, though James now worked full-time at the store. They recorded a demo with money borrowed from Chip's dad, and they dropped their tapes off everywhere they could think of. They started getting gigs. They played actual clubs in town. They were written up in the *Phoenix* as "rising stars on the local rock scene." They drank and got stoned some too, but that was part of it.

Sheila enrolled in nursing school. They hung on for a couple months past graduation, but eventually she dumped him, saying he wasn't serious enough about his future. She didn't understand what James was trying to do. She thought it was silly, a pie-in-the-sky kind of thing. He thought those were her father's fears, not hers, but he couldn't seem to change her mind. James hated being apart from her. He knew he had to get her back, even if it took a record deal, a song about her landing at number one on the Billboard charts.

He never went out with anyone else. He fucked some girl in the bathroom at Dee Dee's, the only girl he'd ever had sex with other than Sheila. Later that night, after five shots of whiskey and who the hell knew how many beers, he wept in Dave Connelly's dad's Cutlass and punched out the passenger-side window, ending up with fourteen stitches in his hand and an order to stay away from the Connelly house that lasted until his first kid was born.

Sheila started dating a guy from her class—a male nurse, of all things. Connelly tried to cheer James up by calling him the Murse. That had hurt, but not so bad as the next guy, a law student at BC.

Debbie, Sheila's sister, had told him when she came to the deli counter one afternoon.

"How's it going, Jimmy? Pound of ham, and a half pound of American. You still living with your mom? Did you hear Sheila's dating a lawyer now?"

The August after graduation, Ulterior Motive was approached at a gig by a guy named Marty Klein. He had managed the Snowmen and Negative Attention, local bands who had ended up with recording contracts and national tours. He said he wanted to work with them, to get their demo some real airtime.

James quit his job and finally got the balls to go to Sheila's apartment and make a plea: she had to come back to him or he'd die. He was about to hit it big. But he couldn't do any of it if she didn't believe in him. He had never felt so high in his life as he did when he stood there, delivering that speech. Especially when Sheila wrapped her arms around him and said yes, she'd take the leap, she still loved him.

She dumped the lawyer, and they moved in together a month later, a fact that they somehow managed to keep from their parents.

But the demo never got any play, other than on a couple college stations. The guitar player went to jail for knocking a guy unconscious in a bar fight. Frank Rogers got drafted. Fearing his number would get called too, Chip McIntryre's parents forced him to go to school. And James was alone. The whole thing had seemed right on the brink of *happening*, but somehow it never did.

He moped around for almost a year, smoking joints in their apartment, keeping the place neat and fixing Sheila's lunch so she wouldn't get sick of him and throw him out. Then one day she told him that the boyfriend of a friend of hers worked for the Lynn fire department and they were hiring. She mentioned that these positions were sought after, that the pay was great, the job security fantastic. All you had to do was take a multiple-choice test.

Lynn was a shithole, and it was at least a forty-minute drive.

"You really want me working in that place?" he said. "You know what they say. *Lynn, Lynn, city of sin; you never come out the way you went in.* Sorry, I'm not interested."

Sheila told him if he didn't go to the station and apply, they were through.

So James became a firefighter.

The guys he worked with were former high school athletes, built like Mack Trucks. He was scrawny in comparison. A weakling. He started lifting weights in the firehouse between calls. He put on ten pounds.

Some guys in the station had been to Vietnam and back. They all knew someone who had died. At home, they hardly ever talked about the war, even though his brother had been, and lots of their old friends from high school. James was terrified by the thought of being drafted. The only way he knew how to deal with that was just to ignore it. There was an apartment complex on Storrow Drive in Boston that advertised with a billboard that read, *If you lived here, you'd be home now.* In August of '72, someone had altered it to say *If you lived in Vietnam, you'd be dead now.* James would go ten miles out of his way not to have to drive by the thing.

But in October, Sheila's cousin Fred was killed by a bomb in Quang Ngai. James came home from work that night to find her curled up crying on the sofa, an empty wine bottle on the table.

"That could have been you," she said. "That still could be you."

"No," he said. "This whole stupid war is almost over. The government won't draft any more than they already have."

"That's what Nixon said four years ago, and look where we are now."

"It's awful about Fred, but worrying about what-ifs won't help. There's nothing we can do."

"Let's get married," she said.

"You can still get drafted if you're married."

There was a day seven years earlier when, without notice, Lyndon Johnson changed the policy that kept married men safe from the draft. He decreed that only men who were married by midnight that night, or men with children, would be exempt. Moving forward, all men who were married without children would be treated like single guys. Johnson announced his plan at five o'clock Eastern time, too late for anyone on their side of the country. The only place on the West Coast you could marry without a waiting period or a blood test was Las Vegas. Thousands of men and their girls streamed there that night. James had an older cousin in California who made the drive and married someone he had known for six weeks. The marriage had since been annulled, but she probably saved his life.

"My parents lied about their age so they could get married before my father shipped off to World War II," Sheila said. "Now I understand why. This whole thing has made me realize it."

He shook his head. "You want to get married?"

"Why not? We would have eventually anyway, right? What's the difference if we do it now, instead of two or three years from now?"

He'd be lying if he said he had thought much about it before then. But his heart was pounding from happiness. She wanted to marry him.

"You're drunk," he said, reminding himself as much as her.

"I know I am, James. But that doesn't mean I don't mean it." She pulled him down on top of her. "What do you say?"

He kissed her in response, wondering if he could take her seriously, hoping that he could. In the morning, she said it again: "I want to get married. If anything ever happened to you, I'd want to know I was your wife. Just think about it, okay?"

James was sweating when he went to talk to her father three weeks later. He sat at Tom and Linda's kitchen table. The stained-glass light fixture overhead might as well have been an interrogation lamp. He drank three beers before he got there, but still his hands shook in his lap.

"Are you sure you two are ready?" Tom asked. "I mean, maturity-wise, not to mention financially."

"Yes sir," James said, though he knew he sounded like a kid. He was only twenty years old.

"My mother used to say, 'Marry in haste, repent at leisure,'" Linda added from her spot at the sink, where she was pretending to wash the dishes. "Why don't you wait a while, Jimmy?"

He just nodded. Their blessing would have been nice, but he didn't actually give a shit what they thought. He already had the ring.

James spent the absolute max that he could afford, but still, what he gave Sheila was puny; the diamond was only a quarter carat. Even so, the act of buying it made him feel like an adult for the first time in his life. He asked the jeweler to lay the stone flat inside the band, since she was a nurse and he figured anything that stuck out would just rip through her rubber gloves and get in the way.

James could still remember how he had felt, holding that ring in his pocket. He was afraid he'd bungle the proposal somehow—Sheila would only get this once in her life, and they said that it was the most important moment a woman ever had. But no matter how piss poor his delivery, he knew the diamond would communicate something that words couldn't. A woman wanted a diamond. It meant you were serious, committed for life. He proposed on the seawall at Wollaston Beach, and Sheila cried out in surprise as he got down on one knee, as if the whole thing hadn't been her idea.

They had been engaged for just one month on the Saturday in January when the war finally ended. They sat in silence in the den, watching the signing of the cease-fire agreement on TV. The phone rang. Outside the apartment, church bells tolled. The fire station two blocks away sounded its alarms.

"Wow," Sheila said. "It's really over."

James dug his fingers into the arm of the couch. He knew he should be happy, but he felt tense. He tapped his sneaker rapid-fire against the floor.

He looked at Sheila, trying to decipher whether there was something more in her expression than relief that the war had ended. She had wanted to get married in case the worst happened, but there was no longer any danger of that. He knew he should ask her if she still wanted to go through with it, at least give her the chance to back out. But he couldn't.

"What?" she said.

"Nothing," he said. "It's great news, that's all."

Sheila, her sister, and their mother spent the next seven months talking nonstop about the wedding. He hadn't known there were so many things to talk about—the food, the color scheme, whether to ask this friend or that one to be a bridesmaid. He stayed the hell out of it, and whenever she asked his opinion on some detail or another, James just answered, "Whatever you think is best," which pissed her off, but really, what enlightening thought could he add about centerpieces?

His grandmother liked to tell the story of how she and his grandfather got married for ten bucks. They had met at Castle Island three months earlier, and he proposed on their fifth date. After the ceremony, they went to a cousin's house for sandwiches and beer and ice cream, and that was it, the only reception his grandmother ever got. For as long as he could remember, she had worn just a plain gold band on her ring finger.

But James's wedding was to be an event. Sheila's parents were giving them a big party at Florian Hall complete with dinner, a band, and a two-hour open bar that would switch over to cash at four o'clock.

Every Saturday for two months beforehand, they went to the rectory at Mary Star of the Sea for Pre-Cana classes, where the monsignor talked about forgiveness and conflict resolution and how to negotiate which spouse did what around the house. You had to take the classes if you wanted to have your wedding in the church.

Who better to teach us about marriage than a celibate priest? James said on the way into class one afternoon. Sheila shooshed him, but she laughed.

Rain was predicted for their wedding day. The night before, his mother hung rosary beads from all the trees on Willet Street to ward it off. When they woke the next morning, the sky was a cloudless blue. He remembered it now as a happy blur of familiar faces and champagne and music. Sheila and her father danced to "Daddy's Little Girl," and Big Boy gave a speech for which James had still not completely forgiven him.

That night, in a hotel room bed that their wedding party had strewn with rose petals and rubbers, they sat on top of the covers still dressed in their wedding clothes and ripped open the stack of envelopes they had received, one by one. She did the opening, and he counted the money, placing the checks and crisp hundred-dollar bills in two neat piles. They made six grand all together. They went to sleep that night feeling as rich as a couple of kings. But the money was gone by their first anniversary.

Sheila had always said she loved her ring, and the fact that he was thoughtful enough to consider the way she would wear it. But over the years, whenever he saw the rings on other women's fingers—her sister Debbie's, all of her friends'—James felt a deep sense of shame. He should have gotten her something wildly beautiful, something that would prove to everyone that she was loved by a worthy man.

After the robbery, she said the only thing she really missed was her diamond. It had been on her finger for a decade and a half, and like all objects that once seemed incredibly important, it had faded into the background of their lives. But for the past month, he had looked at her bare hand with actual grief. He couldn't remember exactly when he'd made up his mind to buy her a new one, no matter what, but that's what he had done.

Two years after they got married, his chief came to him with a proposal: they needed a few guys to shift into medic positions, and he thought James would be good at it. Up until Vietnam, it had been the job of police departments and funeral homes to take emergency cases to the hospital, the latter with the understanding that when you died, they'd cart your corpse away, which was why those creepy old ambulances looked like hearses—they *were* hearses. Hearses were the only vehicles in which a person could lie down. But people had begun to realize that the quicker you got someone to the hospital, and the better care they got along the way, the better their chances of survival. So now the fire department had taken over, and there was a school specifically designed for this new line of work. James took a ten-week class in life support, and went from being a Lynn firefighter to a Lynn EMT.

He liked being part of the rescue unit at first. Sheila said he was made for the job—she had heard from some of the nurses she knew in the area about how good he was with his patients, how many close calls he had determined for the better. When it was going well, he got to feel like a hero. But there had been so many unhappy endings, too. They said those weren't your fault. If that was true, then how could you take credit for the good ones? Over time, he came to think that probably 90 percent of it had nothing to do with him. It had to do with what happened and how quickly someone discovered it, and at which precise moment they decided to call 911. Traffic flow, phone-line congestion, rickety old elevators that took an hour to go three flights. All of it mattered as much as what he did or didn't do.

Twelve years had passed since he first worked in an ambulance, and now when he thought about it, James realized that he had never made an independent choice in his life: Sheila told him to become a firefighter, so he did. She told him to propose. His chief had been the one to decide that he would be a medic. None of it had been his plan.

The only thing he was responsible for was losing the first and only good job he'd ever have. Back when he worked with the fire department, his partner had been a guy named Mac Kelly. Mac had charisma. The guy could talk a dog off a meat wagon. They were buddies, almost like brothers, though in the way that people imagined brothers would be, not in the way brothers actually were in James's experience. They even looked alike: short, pasty Irish guys with dark hair.

Mac drank a little too much. He had a temper. His wife was always threatening to leave, and once, she actually did. She came back a month later, but it seemed like that split had destroyed something in Mac. He had a nine-year-old son with Down's syndrome and he talked about the kid constantly—not about the fact that anything was wrong with him, just *My son loves this show*, and *My son said the funniest thing*. In James's book, this made him a quality guy. He felt lucky in comparison. Parker was four and healthy, and despite what people said about the strain that kids put on a marriage, he and Sheila were more in love than ever. James was making good money, and he finally felt like maybe things were coming together.

He tried to help Mac. He covered for him on a couple of occasions when he came into work piss drunk. Mac was always on probation within the department for some violation or another. It was a running joke, since no one ever got fired from the fire department.

A few months before the end, they were sitting at a red light when a homeless guy knocked on the driver's-side window. Mac rolled it down. "What's up, buddy?"

The guy shoved a gun in his face and Mac peeled out of there faster than James would've ever thought that truck could go. The asshole shot at them; you could hear the bullets hitting the back doors. In Mac's position, James was sure he would have blown it—frozen, or taken a wrong turn. But Mac kept calm, and just drove straight to the police station. He saved both their lives. The cops found the guy pretty fast, a lunatic looking for drugs, which they weren't even allowed to carry.

Crazy shit like that came in waves. A week later, a huge drunk guy in the back of the truck punched James in the face with no warning. James fell backward, and by the time he got up, the guy had a fresh gash in the center of his forehead—Mac had hit him dead-on with a clipboard. Blood dripped down his nose and into his eyes.

There was a cop in the truck who had witnessed the whole thing.

"That injury was there when we got here, right, man?" Mac said.

The cop nodded. "Yup."

"Gonna need stitches, I'd say," Mac said. "Now lie back and shut the fuck up."

The thing, as James and Sheila would come to call it, happened not long after that. Late one night, he and Mac were sent to a park on the edge of town, where crackheads had started congregating a few months back. Someone had called in a suicide attempt.

"How did they even notice? Aren't they all busy killing themselves over there?" Mac said. He was from Lynn, a working-class kid made good, at least compared to a lot of the guys he grew up with. His tolerance for druggies was nonexistent.

Crackheads were unpredictable. If one of them resisted, you'd usually end up in a brawl. The guy on crack would get you every time—you'd need two or three other guys to subdue him. The crackhead had no fear.

James took his time driving, not even bothering to run the siren.

When they arrived, the park was so dark that they had to go back out to the truck and get the wheat lamps, which they strapped onto their heads before finding the path, like a couple of miners. Crack vials crunched under their feet as they walked. All you could hear, from some far corner, was a girl moaning. They moved toward the sound, looking out for stray needles, even though the people here probably couldn't afford heroin. A couple years back, a guy on their squad had gotten pricked and contracted hep C. He died from it ten months later.

When they found the girl, she was lying over her boy-friend, both of them covered in his blood and high out of their minds. The kid—skinny and white, about six foot two—had slit his wrists. He refused to come with them at first. Finally, Mac got him onto his feet. He had the kid laughing.

James got in the front seat as Mac strapped the patient onto the stretcher. Everything was fine, and then suddenly it wasn't. When Mac went to wrap his wrists up, the kid started thrashing around, his blood landing on every surface.

"Calm down!" Mac yelled at him. "Come on, man."

The kid obeyed. But then he said, "I know you."

"Oh yeah?"

"Yeah. My cousin fucked your wife last year. You've got that retarded kid, right?"

Mac's response was instantaneous. One knockout punch to the head, which left the kid unconscious for three minutes. And a second punch, straight after the first, just because. James understood exactly why Mac had done it. He himself had never hit a patient, but he had come close. He wondered if what the kid had said was true, but other than that he didn't give the incident much thought.

A few days later, when they were called into the chief's office, they thought maybe he was going to tell them they were getting a raise.

Instead he said, "Which one of you jackasses do I have to thank for these?"

He slid a slim stack of photographs across the table. In the light from the wheat lamp, you could see the kid flinching, the fist raised to his face. And then the punch landing, his head thrust back at a sick angle. James noticed their plate number, plainly displayed beneath the images.

You could see him only from behind, but still the chief said, "Kelly, I presume."

James saw a drop of sweat run down the side of Mac's face.

Mac stammered, "Who took them?"

"There have been surveillance cameras in that park for weeks."

James did a quick mental calculation: his partner was already on thin ice, but he himself had never had a single infraction. And first-time offenders always got off with a warning.

"It was me," he said. "Sorry, Chief."

The chief raised his eyebrows. "You? Really?"

"Let me explain—"

"Don't bother. You're fired, McKeen."

"What?"

"You're fired. That kid you hit? He has a little rich girl-friend. Her father's threatening to send these to the *Globe* and take legal action unless someone loses his job over this. It sure as hell ain't gonna be me. You shouldn't have done it with the door open, buddy. That was just plain stupid."

James sat there, stunned. Mac didn't step in to save him. He just let him hang.

When he told Sheila what had happened, she got furious.

"I was trying to help a friend," he said.

"Oh. What a prince you are. And did you ever stop to think about your own kid? What are we supposed to do now, Jimmy?"

For two days, she wouldn't even speak to him, except to say once, in the middle of the night, while they were both lying wide awake in bed, "I might have some respect for you if you had actually hit the guy. But this is just sick."

In the year he was unemployed, James thought constantly about the band. He dreamed of his guitar, and woke up in a panic, thinking of how he had let it all slip away.

He hadn't played music outside the house in ages, but deep down he still dreamed of making it big. He knew every guy he had grown up with fantasized about becoming either Ted Williams or Paul McCartney, but in his case he felt that he really had the goods. Was there any way to get that time back?

He had a good ear, and he tried to keep up with what was going on in the music world, even though he was now essentially an old fogy. He watched MTV sometimes. He went to Tower Records and tried to converse with the pierced and dyed kids who worked there. They saw him as a kind of elder statesman. When they asked about Woodstock, James told them Monterey Pop could wipe the floor with it.

"Monterey was the best," he said. "Pre-corporatization. All about the music, man. Otis Redding. Hendrix just killing it. Grace Slick in her prime, when she was still so gorgeous. We used to call her 'The face that launched a thousand trips.'"

"Were you there?" one of them asked.

"Nah, man, I was only fourteen. My brother went, though."

James had begged Bobby to take him. He saw the documentary at the Cleveland Circle Theater a year later, the day it came out.

Back in '81, one of the Tower kids had slipped him an import called "Boy" from the band U2. James loved the sound of it: the guitar repetitions, the voice of the young and angry Irishman called Bono Vox. Earlier this year, U2 had done a new, more polished (less impressive, but still great, in James's opinion) record with Brian Eno, and now they were on their way to becoming the biggest rock stars in the world.

"They've gotta be careful, though," he said to the kid behind the counter when he bought his copy of *The Joshua Tree* last spring. "Too much attention too soon can fuck you. I mean, take the Clash. They fell apart pretty damn fast in '82 when they went on tour with the Who and suddenly everyone was saying that the torch of rock music had been passed. The timing has to be just so."

He thought it was a smart observation. He could tell the kid thought so too. When he got home, he repeated what he had said to Sheila, who just replied, "You know you're middle aged, right?"

"P-four," the dispatcher said over the radio now. That was them.

Nona had been working in Cambridge forever. James would recognize her voice even if he went fifty years without hearing it—a smoker's gravelly throat, a thick Boston accent.

He was just pulling a fresh sheet across the stretcher. He raced around to the front, picked up the radio, and pressed the button on the side.

"P-four."

"Patient fainted at Whitson Hall. Campus police en route."

"Don't you have any shootings or suicides you can send me to?" he said. "Please, Nona. Anyplace but Harvard."

"Sorry."

He groaned as he got out of the truck. Cambridge was a strange place, full of extremes. On a single street, you might have millionaires living at one end and nothing but cops and Teamsters at the other. Working in this city, you dealt with all varieties of people, from bums lying in their own feces to the most entitled Ivy Leaguers.

Personally, he'd take the bums. Harvard kids were just a bunch of rich spoiled brats who didn't know how to drink. It was a job requirement that they treat each patient kindly, and with respect. Most of the time, you wanted to do that anyway, since you were coming upon people at their worst, their weakest. James always said the only thing his patients had in common was that they weren't expecting to see him that day. But he really had to try with the Harvard types. It usually took some effort not to smack them. Sheila sometimes said she wanted Parker to go to Harvard one day, and James would think to himself, *Over my dead body.*

On weekend nights, he'd be on campus six, seven times. When normal college kids got drunk, maybe their roommate gave them an aspirin and a glass of water, and then they went to bed and slept it off. Harvard kids called 911 and then puked all over the ambulance, saying they'd sue you if you tried to pump their stomachs or if this somehow ended up on their permanent record.

In the neighborhood James grew up in, adults were constantly threatening you by making mention of your permanent record. The only things on his were a drunk and disorderly from a bar fight he was in the summer he was seventeen, and a petty theft charge from around that same time for stealing liquor from a place in Dorchester. A few of his buddies were still involved in some bad shit, and it was sometimes a temptation—they could make his annual salary in two months, just moving drugs around or messing with old ladies' Social Security checks. But he knew he couldn't do it and live with himself. He couldn't look his mother in the eye.

He went into the sandwich shop, nodded in Maurice's direction.

His partner was leaning against the counter, chatting with Phil, the owner. "Now? But I still don't have my burger."

"Sorry, man."

Phil shook his head. "It'll be ready when you get back."

When they reached the edge of campus, James looked out at the odd, slanted heating grates the university had installed on the sidewalks at the start of winter. They tore up the old flat ones so the homeless couldn't sleep there anymore.

They passed through the gates of Harvard Yard. Everything was incredibly still.

"Why is this kid even here?" Maurice asked. "Isn't it Christmas break?"

James shrugged.

In front of a dorm that vaguely resembled the White House, they pulled the stretcher out. James felt a crunch in his back, followed by a sharp, shooting pain. He grimaced.

"You okay?" Maurice asked.

"Yeah, I'm fine."

A campus cop waited by the entrance to the dorm. James had seen him a few times before, though he couldn't recall his name.

"How ya doing?" he said. "I regret to inform you, she's five flights up."

"Of course she is."

They started their climb. By the time they reached the fourth floor, James felt like his lungs might collapse. When they got to the door, there were three pieces of pink construction paper taped to it—one said SARA, one said JENNIFER, the other ADHIRA.

The cop knocked.

"Come in," she said.

The girl was Indian or something like that. She was sitting on a sofa in a cramped common room that smelled like incense. A red tapestry hung on the wall, and books were piled high on every surface. She was dressed in sweatpants and a t-shirt. Her black hair hung wet over her shoulders. She looked about twelve years old.

"I think I'm fine now," she said. She spoke with an English accent. "I shouldn't have called 911."

"What happened?" James asked.

"I was in the shower and I suddenly felt dizzy, like I was going to faint."

"Did you?"

"No. I got out and sat here on the couch and put my head between my legs, and I felt better."

"Good," James said. "Has this ever happened before?"

"No, sir."

Sir? Jesus, how old did he look?

"Have you eaten anything today?" he asked.

"No."

"Was the shower very hot?"

"Yes!" she said, like he was MacGyver over here. "As hot as it would get."

James tapped his foot on the hardwood floor. He looked around him at the warm, plumped-up sofa and the leather chair in the corner. This dorm room was nicer than his house.

"Do you think you need to go to the hospital?" he asked.

She shook her head. "I'm fine now."

They gave her a waiver to sign. James told her to lie down, relax, have a glass of water and some food.

"When will your roommates be back?" he asked.

"They're gone for the holidays," she said.

He wondered why neither of them had invited her, when she was clearly so far from home. It was irrational, but for an instant he thought of inviting her over to his house. And though it was really none of his business, he asked, "Do you have plans for Christmas?"

She nodded. "I'll be with friends tomorrow."

Maurice, James, and the cop made their way back outside. A light snow had started to fall. It was already sticking to the grass and the windshield.

"So basically she took a hundred-degree shower when she had low blood sugar and was surprised when she felt dizzy," the cop said. "These Harvard kids kill me."

James thought that maybe she had just felt lonely. They met enough people like that on the job, though most of them were either elderly or nuts.

"Last Friday a girl in this same dorm had to be intubated because she drank so much her airways stopped working," the cop said.

Maurice nodded. "Otherwise known as your average Friday night."

"Man, I hate those kids," the guy went on. "Do you know

what they chant at basketball games against UMass? 'Safety school.' That's their idea of an insult. Faggots." He shook his head. "Anyway. Have a good one."

Back in the truck, James leaned over and opened the glove compartment. He took out the bottle of Advil and shook three pills into his hand, making a mental note: that made six so far today. He swallowed them down, and then turned toward Elsie's.

A minute later, they heard the familiar sound of Nona calling: "P-four."

"Shit," Maurice said.

James reached for the radio. Before he picked it up, he said, "By the time you get that cheeseburger, it may actually be a time of day when it's no longer totally fucking disgusting to eat a cheeseburger."

Maurice's expression was deadly serious. "God, I hope you're wrong."

2003

Delphine stood in the middle of the living room, surveying her work. She had turned the coffee table on its side, just because, and scratched its surface with the sharp points of the scissors in a wild pattern.

She smashed a gorgeous lamp that she had found in an antiques shop in Brooklyn. She and P.J. had fought about that lamp. He said it wasn't *him*, as if he had ever had any sense of style or beauty. They were fighting about everything by that point.

In the course of six years of marriage, Delphine and her husband had disagreed on only two things. First, soon after the wedding, Henri decided that he wanted a child. He dreamed of a daughter named Josephine. It was the name of his older sister, who drowned when she was just three. It seemed strange to think of an older sibling who had never made it to her fourth birthday. Delphine doubted that Henri's parents would want to be reminded of the girl's name this long after her death, even if she were willing to have a baby, which she wasn't. She was forty, too old for all that. And though she never said so, she believed her husband was far too old to be a father. At fifty-five, he had no business asking her for a baby.

The other thing they fought over was the Stradivarius.

That violin was her husband's greatest pride. Whenever they had anyone over for dinner, he brought it to the table even before she served the cheese course. It lit him up in a way that nothing else could. Given a new audience, Henri could talk about Stradivari all night. He would tell their guests that there were many theories for what made a Strad sound so perfect, but in his opinion the most convincing had to do with a strange weather pattern known as the Maunder Minimum, a period lasting from around 1645 to 1715, during Europe's Little Ice Age. A lack of sunlight during that time made for low temperatures, which slowed tree growth, leading to the existence of abnormally dense wood. If you looked at the growth rings in the wood of any Stradivarius, you'd see it.

"The thickness is perfect at every spot," Henri would say, holding the violin up, turning it this way and that. "If Stradivari had shaved off even one extra millimeter of wood, the sound would be out of balance."

Their guests would usually be interested, but her dear husband never knew when to stop. "This is the original varnish. Imagine that. And it's not just for beauty. No, it impacts the sound. There is the slightest water damage on the lower bout, but it adds character. The 1721 Lady Blunt is probably the best-preserved Strad. It still has gut strings and no bridge. But of course that's because it's only ever been in the hands of collectors, hardly even played, which is a crime."

Delphine was always impressed by the extent of his knowledge on the subject, if slightly amused. Henri knew the whereabouts of nearly every one of the five hundred and forty Strads on earth, and he loved sharing this useless information with others: there were four at the Metropolitan Museum of Art in Manhattan, eight at the Royal Academy of Music, over a dozen with the Nippon Music Foundation, three at the Smithsonian Institution, two owned by Itzhak Perlman, and so on.

Fearing that everyone might fall asleep before he was

done, Delphine encouraged him to tell only the more colorful stories, the ones that involved some scandal or tragedy. In the mid-nineties, the 1727 Davidoff Stradivarius was stolen from the apartment of the virtuoso Erica Morini just days before her death at the age of ninety-one. She was in the hospital at the time, and her family never let on that the violin had vanished, wanting to protect her from such pain.

In 1936, during a fifteen-minute break from his weekly gig at the Russian Bear Restaurant in New York, a small-time violinist named Julian Altman snuck across the street to Carnegie Hall, where the Polish soloist Bronislaw Huberman was performing. Huberman traveled with a double violin case, containing two of the world's finest instruments: a Guarneri, and the Gibson Stradivarius. Having read as much in the newspaper, Altman's mother had suggested that he might steal whichever one Huberman wasn't using that night.

And so, Altman bribed a guard at the stage door with a fine cigar and snuck into Huberman's dressing room. He snatched the Stradivarius and hid it under his coat as Huberman stood onstage unaware, playing a flawless Franck sonata.

Altman concealed the violin's identity by covering it in shoe polish. He played it at weddings and pubs for nearly fifty years, only telling the truth on his deathbed. Huberman was awarded thirty thousand dollars for the loss in the thirties. When Altman's widow brought the violin to Lloyd's of London in 1987, it was valued at over a million.

Henri's Strad was called the Salisbury. Occasionally, he would lend it out to be played for six months or a year, but he always asked for it back after a period of time. He could barely stand to be apart from it, and when it returned he'd put it straight into its glass case and stare.

Plenty of collectors and musicians had tried to buy it

from him over the years. He turned them all down. Delphine had seen him entertain the idea only once, at a dinner party when an old curator friend of his from Moscow, Peter Yefimov, said, "You know the Rogue is interested."

Just briefly, her husband's eyes glowed, like a child beholding the candles on his birthday cake. The Rogue was one of Henri's favorite performers. A young virtuoso from New York. In general, her husband didn't care for American soloists, the showy types who recorded albums with Sting and mixed Simon and Garfunkel in with Bach. But though he was young and stylish, the Rogue was essentially a traditionalist, like Henri. They had once seen him perform Beethoven's Violin Concerto with the Berlin Philharmonic, and afterward Henri had pronounced him a genius.

"He's most unusual," Yefimov said that night at dinner. "A white, corn-fed midwestern American boy with skills like that!"

"What does the white or the midwestern matter?" asked another guest at the table, a young American woman who was in town on a buying trip for Paramount Pictures. Delphine held her breath. Americans were so touchy about any talk whatsoever of race, and she needed this account.

"These abilities run in certain groups and not in others," Yefimov said. "In the first half of the twentieth century, the greatest soloists in the world were Jews from Russia and eastern Europe. Jascha Heifetz, Nathan Milstein, Efrem Zimbalist, Mischa Elman. The talent is the main thing, but what is it that makes a talented child into a prodigy? Practice. That's all. And what child would choose that path for himself? It comes from some need in the parents. When Jews didn't even have the right to live in capital cities in some cases, the parents saw these children as their ticket to the West."

The girl from Paramount seemed satisfied with this

answer, since Yefimov himself was a Russian Jew, and Americans believed that you could say anything you liked about your own people.

But then he continued, "You will notice that today, a majority of the gifted young violinists come from Asia. Again, the parents crave this Western acceptance. We all know Asians are the hardest workers alive, and so, from a purely technical standpoint, they excel. But I feel that the musicality is missing. I think it's because the violin is not ingrained in their bodies and blood the way it is in ours. You listen to a Chinese man play his primitive folk instrument, and there you hear such real beauty, such meaningful sound. But on the violin? Heartless."

And now the American looked appalled. Delphine decided to bring in the *mille-feuille* a bit earlier than she had planned.

A week after the dinner, a formal letter arrived, from the Rogue himself. He wanted to make his interest known officially. He was willing to pay two million American dollars. Delphine did the math in her head—it was more than they had paid for the entire shop five years earlier, more than their home was worth. But she knew her husband would never sell.

"You could loan him the Strad," she said. "It might please you just to hear him play it."

"Yes," Henri said, but he didn't mention it again for more than a year. He had only just gotten it back from a young French soloist and he wasn't ready to be separated from it yet.

On a Thursday in the spring of 2001, Delphine was helping the only customer in the store, a collector in from London. He was there to see an eighteenth-century Tononi cello.

Delphine had looked him up on the Internet; he was vice president of a major advertising agency and earned a million pounds a year. In his spare time, as a hobby, he collected instruments.

"And you'll want to consider a bow we've just gotten in," she was saying in English when a woman in a dark suit stepped into the shop.

Delphine pulled the bow from its case and placed it in his hands. "Tourte *père*," she said, breathing in deeply as if it were covered in fine perfume. "Whoever played it last cracked the tip just slightly. You can barely see it, but of course it hurts the value some. Still, though, a beautiful piece."

The woman lingered in the doorway. She stared at Delphine.

"*Un moment, s'il vous plaît,*" she said to the customer. She felt excited. If they sold both pieces, it would be their best week in months. Henri would be so pleased.

Delphine approached the woman and asked, "May I help you?"

"I'm Helena Kaufman," she said, as if the name should mean something. "From the International Jewish Congress."

Perhaps she could tell that Delphine did not understand her meaning, because she continued, "I'd like to speak to the owner, please."

"I'm the owner," she said.

Helena Kaufman looked puzzled. "Is Henri Petit no longer the owner?"

"He is my husband. He's in Berlin appraising pieces at the moment. What is this about?"

The woman sighed. "I'm sorry. I don't mean to be rude. It's just that I've come all the way from Brussels on the Eurostar to speak with him."

"Was he expecting you?"

"No. But he never answered my letters, so I had to take matters into my own hands," she said. "You will have gotten my letters, I presume."

Delphine didn't know what she was talking about. "Not me," she said finally. "But perhaps Henri did."

"Could we talk for a bit?" the woman asked in a hushed tone, glancing toward the English buyer. "I know this might be uncomfortable."

"What is this regarding?" Delphine asked.

"We're speaking to as many owners as we can," the woman said.

"Owners of?"

"Oh, then you really didn't see the letters. Owners of violins," she said. "In particular, certain Stradivari, Guarneri, and Amati violins. All the best. You may not know this, Madame Petit, but thousands of the world's finest instruments once belonged to Jews who perished or fled during the war. The Nazis targeted these instruments for use in a planned university in Hitler's hometown. We believe they killed many people just to get exactly the type of violin you have here."

Delphine had never heard anything about this. She wondered why Henri hadn't mentioned the letters.

She led the woman to a pair of plush chairs by the door. She gestured to her to sit where she herself had sat years earlier, listening to François Dubray's children interview the man who would become her husband.

"Please wait," she said. "I'll just be a few minutes."

She returned now to the Englishman, who said, "You have a Stradivarius here in the store?"

He sounded disappointed, as if, had he known, he would have walked out with it half an hour ago.

"No," she said. "It's part of my husband's collection."

She felt uneasy. She wanted him to leave, didn't care what he took.

He bought the cello and said he would think about the bow. As soon as he was gone, Delphine went to the woman by the door, and sat down in the chair facing hers.

"You said the Nazis stole Strads," she said. "What does this have to do with my husband?"

"At the time they were stolen," the woman started, "the instruments weren't worth much, other than sentimental value. Most had been in families for generations. Those who made it out of concentration camps had lost so much. They weren't thinking about something as small as a violin. But these pieces are now worth millions. We are making efforts to get them back to the families of their rightful owners."

With that, Delphine understood why Henri had ignored the letters—he wouldn't have any interest in giving the Stradivarius back.

"I understand the predicament," Delphine said. "But my husband inherited that violin from his father. It's precious to him."

"And when did his father first own it?" the woman asked.

"It would have been the 1950s."

Helena Kaufman nodded knowingly, and sent her a look that said she ought to be ashamed.

"The Salisbury is among the violins that we suspect may have been stolen," she said. "You might be aware that its documentation prior to the purchase your father-in-law made has never been verified."

Delphine's own father had once taken her to the Mémorial des Martyrs de la Déportation, a monument to the 200,000 French victims of Nazi concentration camps. Of the 78,000 Jews deported from France—11,000 of them children—only 2,500 came back alive. She was haunted by the dark hallway lighted with a crystal for each victim, a carving on the plaque in the floor: *They went to the end of the earth and did not return.*

Afterward, she had nightmares for months. She cried to her father late one night, asking why he had brought her there. He told her for the first time what it had been like to live in Paris under the Nazis. He would never forget the start of the occupation, he said, the sight of people and animals streaming out of the city, boarding trains with no destination in mind. Then came the daily march of German soldiers up the Champs-Élysées. The swastika flag flying outside the Hôtel Le Meurice. There were gas rations that kept all but a few hundred cars off the road. Most everyone rode bicycles. There wasn't enough heat or food. They all went hungry, bones pushing through skin wherever you turned. Delphine's grandparents and their neighbors took to keeping chickens in their apartments. If they got news that a butcher had meat, people would line up at four a.m. even though it was illegal.

An older cousin of her father's was arrested and shot dead for being out past the nine p.m. curfew. Normally, such a minor offense wouldn't end so tragically, but the Resistance had killed one German soldier that day, and whenever that happened it was the German policy to kill twenty Frenchmen in retaliation, no matter what their crimes.

So many people just vanished, her father said, the things they left behind the only proof that they had ever been there at all. His Jewish next-door neighbors in the Marais were taken from their house one night. Later he learned that they had died at Auschwitz, the thin and quiet father who was always reading a book, the exuberant mother who sang as she hung her laundry, and the twin boys, just eight years old.

She thought about all this now, but only said, "It would be impossible for us to give it away. And how could you ever be sure that this was one of the violins in question?"

Delphine knew that the world of rare instruments was notoriously secretive. Unlike paintings or sculpture, some instruments came with little documentation, so you couldn't always be sure where they had lived before they came to you.

"In the past, we have been very successful at recovering things that the Nazis took from our people—bank accounts and paintings and such. Those were easier to trace. These will be harder, but we believe it's an essential task. Perhaps our most important. A painting would have just hung on a wall. But a violin tells the story of the ancestor who played it."

Delphine told her she would speak with her husband. After the woman left, she felt rattled. She couldn't sleep that night, thinking about it. Sometime after three a.m., she went into Henri's study and unlocked the glass case. She stared at the violin for a long while, as if she might be able to coax its story from the wood.

Her father was only twelve years old in 1940. He had not been part of the Resistance. But he worshipped those who were, even in some small way.

If you dared to align yourself with the movement, you were generally arrested and killed within six months. They estimated that maybe thirty thousand had died that way. But even normal people made their statements. Each morning, all the passengers would stand up when the Metro pulled into the George V station and then sit again when the train pulled away, a salute to the king.

Her father liked to tell the story of Hitler's trip to the Eiffel Tower. Hitler admired Paris. He wanted it to be the second city of the Reich, although he visited only once. Her father's uncle had employment at the Eiffel Tower, and when word arrived that Hitler wished to go to the top, he and his fellow workers quickly disabled the elevator.

He often spoke of the great heroes: Jean Moulin. Lucie Aubrac. And his favorite, Rose Valland. He once told Delphine that he had wanted to name her Rose, but her mother said no.

Valland was the overseer of the Galerie nationale du Jeu de Paume during the occupation. The Germans had said in advance that they would leave art collections and museums alone, but the French didn't trust them. By the time troops arrived in 1940, the Louvre was half empty. The French people had been hiding artwork for two years—in the crypt at Saint-Sulpice, out in the countryside, wherever they thought it would be safe. The *Mona Lisa* was taken to Toulouse by ambulance.

The French had been wise to do this, because whatever art remained was stolen. The Nazis used the Jeu de Paume to sort and store all the artwork that they plundered from the great museums and private collections of Paris, distributing it to German VIPs and high-ranking officers. What the Nazis did not know was that Rose Valland spoke German, and was recording where each piece of art came from, and where it went. After the liberation of Paris, she was personally responsible for recovering forty-five thousand works of art. Delphine wondered why she had chosen to make a hero of herself. What qualities did such a person have?

When Henri returned, she told him about their visitor.

"I think we need to do something about this," she said.

He waved her away. "Don't be silly."

"Suppose it's true. Suppose the Nazis stole the Salisbury from its rightful owner. Now we're part of that."

Henri sighed. "It's an absurd assumption that just because the Nazis may have done this terrible thing, we ought to make reparations now—we who weren't even alive during the war. And besides, you cannot own a Stradivarius. You can only protect it for a time, then pass it along to its next protector."

She thought there was a tinge of desperation to his words, as if perhaps he was trying to convince himself of their truth.

Henri continued, "We don't know the story of any of the instruments we sell or collect, really. They may have had the happiest of pasts, or something tragic behind them. But how can that matter now?"

She supposed he was correct, but from then on, each time Delphine caught sight of the violin, she felt a slight chill. When Henri traveled, she put a sheet over the glass case. Anytime anyone mentioned a prospective buyer, be it the Rogue or someone else, she grew animated, writing down all the information, and reminding Henri of the possibility for days and days.

Only five months after Helena Kaufman's visit, terrorists flew planes into the World Trade Center in New York. Watching it on television was horrible, something Delphine had never imagined she would see in her lifetime. She cried, thinking of all the families torn apart in an instant.

"This will be terrible for us," Henri said.

She was embarrassed by how selfish he sounded, even though no one else was listening. "Don't be ridiculous," she said.

But he was right. Their business fell apart. Americans wouldn't fly, and no one cared about buying instruments. The worst year they had ever had followed.

Henri was severely depressed. He grew quiet, going entire days sometimes without saying a word.

The shop stood empty much of the time. Their debts climbed. They had seen dips like this before for a month or two, always leading to relief at the last possible moment, but this dip had lasted ten months and showed no signs of stopping. In June, he told her with tears in his eyes that he would part with the Salisbury to save the shop. The Rogue was scheduled to record Bach's Double Concerto with the principal violinist of the Paris Opera in late July, and so it was decided that he would come in person to get it then.

Leading up to his arrival, Henri sat alone with the Stradivarius nearly every night after dinner. He stroked its side gently with the palm of his hand, as if petting a beloved old dog that was about to be put down. Delphine imagined that he might like to bring it to bed at night if she'd let him.

She was relieved to be rid of the thing, and yet she ached for her husband. On the last night, they both sat up late, gazing into the glass case. She squeezed Henri's hand. He was so sensitive, so easily bruised. She wondered how long it would be before he recovered.

"When we start doing a better business, we'll buy it back from him," she said, though they both knew it would not happen.

The next day, they waited at home, leaving the shop closed. Their apartment seemed funereal to her, but she tried to make it feel festive. She put out bowls of salted peanuts and olives, and a tray of canapés.

Twenty minutes after the appointed meeting time, the Rogue had still not appeared.

"*M'a posé un lapin,*" Henri said.

"No, he'll be here."

He arrived half an hour late, dressed in dark jeans, an untucked button-down shirt, and Converse sneakers. He was as handsome as she remembered. In every way, a large man—his deep booming laugh, his voice, his broad shoulders and swath of thick black hair. His largeness hadn't seemed so pronounced when they saw him perform in Berlin, but here in their apartment, so close up, he seemed to almost fill the room.

He insisted they call him P.J., a name that to her sounded slightly whimsical, and distinctly American. They all spoke English, not a single word of French.

She had worried about how Henri would behave, but as soon as he was in the Rogue's presence, he seemed happy. Henri brought out the Strad and asked him to play. She wasn't sure if this was asking too much; she had read in a newspaper article that the Rogue sometimes got paid a thousand dollars a minute for his performances. But of course, it was important that he try it, and he didn't seem to mind if they watched.

Over the years, there had been several blind tests in which the listeners could not discern any difference whatsoever between the sound of a Stradivarius and that of a child's violin. But when P.J. sat on her sofa and played Albinoni's Adagio, she could tell this was an extraordinary pairing. Delphine heard color in his music. Deep sapphire blues and bursting reds. The sound was so sweet and beautiful, yet there was something mournful in it, too. When he played it, all the sadness of her life returned and gathered in her throat, spilling over into tears.

They took him to dinner that night at Le Florimond.

This time, he was fifteen minutes late.

"Bonjour!" he said, pronouncing the *r,* when he walked in the door of the restaurant. "I got lost. All the streets around here look the same."

Throughout dinner, Henri behaved as if he were conducting an official interview.

"So you are from the state of Ohio."

"Right."

"You made your professional debut at age sixteen with the Cleveland Orchestra, am I correct? Your first album fol-

lowed the next year. You completed your studies at Juilliard
and then received an Avery Fisher Career Grant for promising American classical performers."

Delphine frowned. Henri sounded like he was trying to
educate P.J. on his own life.

"That's right. I won the grant when I was twenty-one.
That was a thrill," he said, although the way he said it made
it sound far from thrilling.

"Formidable," Henri said. "Now tell us about this recording you're working on while you're here. We are both Bach
enthusiasts."

P.J. opened his mouth to respond, but her husband kept
going. "It's exceptionally difficult, given that Bach didn't
put in any dynamic markings. How to be true to his intentions when none of the original scores survive."

"Except for the harpsichord concertos," Delphine
pointed out.

"Well, yes, but what would Bach have made of hearing
those played on a piano?" Henri said.

She laughed. "Next you'll be telling P.J. that the concerto
must only be played with gut strings."

"It's amazing to think that his music has lived almost
three hundred years," P.J. said. "Sometimes I wonder what
Bach would make of that. I've spent more hours than I can
say studying the dynamics, the ornamentation. It may be
my favorite piece."

"And what of the new composers?" Henri asked. "You
don't play much of them, am I right?"

"No, I'm embarrassed to say I don't. I'm still learning
one concerto a year, and I feel I've barely scratched the surface of the classics. But I do enjoy them," P.J. said. "I'm a
fan of Arvo Pärt. I'd love to perform his *Spiegel im Spiegel*
someday. But it seems like the audiences want more traditional works. They want Brahms. It's all so predictable."

Delphine was pleased with his assessment. "I agree completely," she said.

"And what do you make of our French composers? Ravel?" Henri asked.

"Oh, I love his music, of course."

"I think it's interesting that you've chosen to record the Double Concerto with a Frenchman," Henri said. "Are there any differences between the way we play versus the Americans, in your opinion?"

Delphine sighed, shaking her head. The only answer that would do would be for him to say that the French were superior in every way.

P.J. shrugged. "I've noticed that the French keep the bow high off the string, with the right arm being higher up. It makes for a slightly glassier sound."

She laughed; it was such a small thing, so insignificant, really. Neither of them seemed to notice.

"I've decided to play the Salisbury for the actual recording tomorrow," he said. "I didn't think I'd be able to get used to it so fast, but I feel we've been together forever. I brought my old Guarneri, just in case, though I'll be selling it when I get home to New York. I've already got a buyer lined up."

"How long have you been playing the Guarneri?" she asked.

"Three years. I got it when I was twenty. My teacher, the late great George Sennett, left it to me in his will."

"What type of case do you use?" Henri asked.

"A Bam backpack."

Henri smiled, satisfied. It was a good company, and, most important, a French one. But what a dull question!

"What made you want the Salisbury so much?" she asked.

"I've always dreamed of owning a Stradivarius. The depth of the sound is unreal," P.J. said.

"A musician of your caliber should be playing an instrument as good as that one," Henri said.

"Until I was twenty, I played a Strad, but it was just a loaner."

Henri sighed. "A hundred years ago, any serious musician could have gotten his hands on a Guarneri or a Stradivarius. Now, most have to borrow their instruments from some foundation or sponsor, and there are all these limitations on how they can play them. It's ridiculous."

P.J. nodded, but she tensed up. She wished Henri would stop acting like such an authority.

"It can be really frustrating being at the beck and call of a patron," P.J. said. "You have to go and play for them whenever they ask."

Something about him reminded her of her father. Though it was ludicrous to compare them, she thought of how her father had been at the whim of Madame Delecourt downstairs. She would ask him to come in and play Chopin while she wrote letters in the afternoon, or perform Mendelssohn's *Songs Without Words* during the cocktail hour of one of her dinner parties. Delphine's father acted cheerful about it. He loved playing her beautiful piano, he said, and it gave him a chance to practice the classics again.

"It breaks your heart when you have to give those loaners back," P.J. said. "It just isn't right. Outside of the strings, musicians can afford their own instruments. But a good violin and bow can cost more than the roof over your head."

"Now when you sign a management contract, is that part of the arrangement?" Henri asked. "You were what, sixteen, when you first did that?"

"Right," P.J. said. "My teacher arranged for me to play on *The Tonight Show* with Johnny Carson when I was only twelve, the year I got to the Cleveland Institute. Carson was the greatest. I can't imagine any of today's talk-show hosts allowing kids to come on and play complete movements of Vivaldi. Anyway, management interest flowed out of that, but I didn't sign for a few more years. And I was lucky because so many young people today have to enter competition after competition. For me it was much easier. I owe it all to George Sennett, really. I was so lucky to get to study with him."

They were both annoying her now. It was clear that P.J. was accustomed to being the star. He hadn't asked them a single question about themselves all night. He was gushing about a man they'd never met, whose prized violin he was about to sell to the highest bidder.

As they parted ways afterward, Henri quickly said, "Let us take you out again tomorrow after your recording is finished. There's a place we love in the Marais. Nine o'clock?"

P.J. looked surprised, but he said yes. She wondered if perhaps Henri was trying to hold on to his beloved Strad by holding on to the American. She half expected him to ask her if they could adopt him.

"I may just let the two of you go tomorrow," she said as they walked home.

He nodded. "Fine, fine."

But in the morning, when Henri woke, he gripped his stomach and said he felt ill. She wondered for a moment if he was depressed. Sometimes that started as a stomachache. The episodes often came on without warning: they might have tickets to the symphony, or plans to go to Brittany for the weekend, and everything would have to be canceled. When her husband got that way, there was hardly anything she could do to pull him out. She would try jokes and stories, his favorite CDs on the stereo, lingerie and home-cooked dinners. But he would slink around for days in despair, returning to her only when it chose to release him. Delphine feared that someday he might go to that dark place and never come back.

But in this instance, it seemed Henri really was sick. She watched him run to the bathroom, and could hear him vomiting from behind the closed door.

"I'm absolutely fine!" he said as he came back into the room. He promptly collapsed onto the bed. "*Merde!* How can this be happening when we have the dinner tonight?"

Delphine raised an eyebrow. In all their years, she had rarely heard him swear.

"I'm sure the Rogue will find something better to do than have dinner with us," she said.

"No!" Henri said. "We can't be rude and leave him alone. You'll go."

"Me? Why?"

"I don't think he brought a cell phone. We have no way of reaching him to say we can't make it."

"We could leave a message at his hotel."

"Just show him a nice time, darling. I know you didn't care much for him, but be polite. This is business."

She knew it was much more than that, but she did not contradict him.

Delphine arrived at the restaurant right at nine. She wore a red knee-length skirt, a sleeveless white silk blouse, a scarf tied around her neck, and nude heels, the same thing she had worn to work. Her hair was up in a loose knot.

He arrived fifteen minutes late, just as he had the night before. "Wow, you look nice," he said. "Where's Henri?"

She felt flattered, even as she took note of the fact that he hadn't apologized for keeping her waiting. As they sat down, she told him that her husband was home in bed with the flu.

"Oh, I'm sorry to hear that," he said. "You didn't have to meet me. You should have stayed home and taken care of him."

"He can take care of himself," she said.

"Okay then. If you're sure." He scanned the menu. "What's good here?"

The couple beside them glanced over. The place was small, with only ten tables clustered together. P.J.'s voice was louder than the rest, but he didn't seem to notice. She lowered her own to almost a whisper, hoping he might do the same.

"Everything's good," she said. She lit a cigarette and offered him one. He shook his head no.

"So. How did the recording go?"

"It was good! And afterward I did all the touristy stuff that you'd probably think of as a snooze."

"A snooze?"

"Boring."

"Ahh."

"I went to the top of the Eiffel Tower," he said. "It was a crazy wait, but it's beautiful up there. Do you ever go?"

"Not since I was a child."

He nodded. "I guess I've never been to the top of the Empire State Building and I live forty blocks away from it. Anyway, I did that and then I walked along the Seine and tried to go to the Louvre—well, I did go, but my God it's huge. I got this for my mother." He reached into a small paper bag and pulled out a plastic snow globe, with a tiny Notre Dame inside. "She collects them," he said. "And I sat outside at a café, since I read in a travel guide on the plane ride here about how that's the thing to do."

She laughed, thinking of how American it sounded: sitting outside enjoying the day because you read in a guidebook that you ought to. "And how did you find it?"

"Fine. Not much different than drinking coffee in New York, just more people smoking. The women are so beautiful here—I know that's a stereotype, but it's true. The language part is hard. That's half my life these days, being somewhere where I don't know how to say anything except hello. But here I feel like ten Parisians are judging me every time I open my mouth. It's a little awkward."

Delphine smiled. Not so awkward that he'd bothered to learn anything of the French language besides *bonjour* and *merci*. But perhaps that wasn't fair.

"What else should I do before I go?" he asked. "There's so much to see. It's overwhelming. A friend of a friend said to check out the Canal St.-Martin."

She nodded. It was a very young, bohemian neighborhood that Henri would never dream of visiting. She didn't know much about it.

"How long are you staying?" she asked.

"Another two weeks."

"Oh. Henri didn't mention that."

"I don't know if I told him. I probably didn't. I never stay anywhere longer than a night or two, but I decided that this time I'd take a real vacation. My schedule is pretty empty until September, which is rare. Please don't take this the wrong way. You've both been so kind. But I don't tend to socialize much with the music crowd if I can help it."

She didn't take his comment any particular way—she felt the same much of the time. But he seemed to think he had offended her.

"It's just that I'm sort of uncomfortable with all the business talk," he said. "I grew up in a family of five kids where the most serious topic we ever debated was whether we should watch *Family Ties* or *Hollywood Squares* on TV. My parents were good people, smart people, but not fancy at all. I miss that sometimes."

Delphine was unexpectedly touched by this. Most of the young talents in their world wanted to attend every concert and important social gathering in Paris. They spoke of their high-class families as if they had earned their membership.

She thought it was quite something that this life hadn't changed him. And she saw now that he was only being polite the night before.

"I hope my husband didn't overwhelm you. He gets so excited," she said. "My family wasn't fancy either. We loved music, but not everything that seems to go along with that for others. My mind sometimes wanders when Henri starts talking about theory. My father only ever cared about the sound."

He nodded. "Same here. I'd rather play than talk about playing. I give about fifty concerts a year now. Almost one a week. It's hard to make room in my life for anything besides the violin. I switched to a big management company a couple of years ago. Their roster is major. They've got Yo-Yo Ma, for Christ's sake. But it's mostly just a parking lot, you know? So impersonal, so fake. I have this manager named Marcy. She's great, but it's like every move I make is calculated. I play a free concert for charity every so often—her idea—but only because of the good press it gives me. Oh God, that makes me sound like a jerk."

"No."

"What I meant was, she really tries to capitalize on this story line of the poor, small-town kid made good. So when I donate a concert or something, it's supposed to be like I'm giving back to my own community. It just feels forced. Poor kids don't want violin solos, they want iPods."

She thought back to that night with Yefimov, how surprising he had found it that this white, midwestern boy could play so well. She wondered if that's what P.J. meant.

"Do you enjoy all the traveling?" she asked.

"Not really. I never get to see anyplace. Just a lot of hotel rooms. Usually I play at eight p.m., and I can hear my stomach growling onstage. But I have to go to a reception, thank the donors, give a talk. By that point, I'm starved. Restaurants are closed. A lot of times I have to remind myself what city I'm in before I go to sleep so I won't have a panic attack when I wake up. And I'm always mixing up names. Ever since I was a kid, I've felt like everybody knows my name, but I don't know anyone else's."

Again, she thought of her father, who had once told her that the only hard part of being a hotel piano player was coming to terms with anonymity—no one would ever care to know his name.

"You're a celebrity," she said.

He laughed. "Hardly. Nine-point-nine out of ten people on the street have no idea who I am. I don't mean to sound ungrateful. I don't usually talk like this to anyone. But I've been at it for five years now. It's lonely. I miss my dog."

She laughed.

"But really! When you're a soloist, everyone thinks you have all this freedom," he said. "But what that amounts to is showing up, not knowing anyone in the orchestra, playing one rehearsal and then maybe once for the conductor, and that's it."

She nodded. She had often thought to herself that it wasn't quite fair that in the world of elite musicians, you had to decide your own future before you knew anything at all about life.

"You should go to the steps of Sacré-Coeur with a thermos of wine at sunset," she said. "The Centre Pompidou, if you like modern art."

He wrinkled his nose.

"Then the Musée d'Orsay," she said. She had always loved Degas, his pretty ballerinas when she was a girl, and later, *L'absinthe.*

"Go to the Rodin Museum," she continued. "It's magnificent. All of his work displayed in his own home. And some of Camille Claudel's sculptures, as well. Such beautiful pieces. So full of feeling."

"Claudel," he said. "Now who was he?"

"She," Delphine said, "was Rodin's mistress."

"What is it with Frenchmen and their mistresses?" he said.

"This is different than any other kind of man, in your opinion?"

"Yes. Americans, for example."

"Bill Clinton?" she said.

"Oh, don't start in on him. I'm talking about real Americans. Rock stars and politicians don't count."

"But artists do?" she teased. "I've never understood why Americans care so much about the private lives of their public figures. As if a man's sexual proclivities had anything to do with his ability to govern."

"Don't they?" he asked. "A blow job in the Oval Office during business hours, for example."

"Well, would you fault the man for taking an afternoon walk as stress relief?"

His eyes widened. "You're equating an afternoon walk with oral sex from an intern? You're my kind of woman."

"Take our Mitterrand," she said. "He was married with sons, and he also had one daughter with his mistress. The mistress and daughter stood right beside the rest of the family at his state funeral. No one minded. The French simply don't believe in the public's right to know the way you do in your country. And we're more sensible about these things. Not that we do them any more than you do, but there's not so much outrage when they happen. Even the Élysée Palace, where all French presidents live, was built as a residence for Louis Quinze's mistress, Madame Pompadour. In America, you'd probably burn it to the ground."

When the waiter came, P.J. watched Delphine give the order.

They drank a bottle of wine with dinner, and each had a glass of champagne with dessert. Without Henri, the feeling between them was entirely different. They hardly spoke about work. He made for a better conversation than she had imagined, talking about films they had both seen or wanted to see, the movie stars who were causing a stir in America, and the way his country had changed after the terrorist attacks. When the meal was over, he insisted on paying the check.

"I'm so glad you met me here tonight," he said. "Thank you."

She could sense him saying goodbye, and she felt disappointed. She imagined arriving home to her apartment, the soft hum of the television news drifting out from the living room.

"Another place you should visit while you're here is Versailles," she said. "The palace and the gardens are so beautiful. It's a nice train ride out there. You'll go right past lots of sweet little towns."

"Okay," he said. "Thanks. Hey, would it be rude to ask if you want to have one more drink?"

Her heart tripped in her chest. "Not at all. I know a good place."

A few minutes later, she was directing a taxi driver to the Hôtel de Crillon. In the dark backseat, P.J. reached for his seat belt and his hand brushed hers.

"I'd better let Henri know what we're up to," she said.

The words sounded strange to her, but he was busy looking out the window at the buildings whizzing by.

"It's a beautiful city, isn't it?" she said. "There's nowhere else quite like it."

On her cell phone, she typed out a text message to her

husband: *The American wants another drink. Home soon, I hope.*

Henri wrote her back: *Poor you. I'm sorry! Thanks for doing it.*

"What's that?" P.J. asked her, pointing.

She looked up at the glowing neon Ferris wheel looming over the Tuileries Gardens.

"It's just a summer carnival," she said.

"Should we go?" P.J. asked.

"Now?"

"Sure."

He grinned. She told the driver to pull over at the gate. Inside, a Gypsy band shook tambourines and families sat at picnic tables, drinking wine, eating crêpes and cotton candy. Children jumped on trampolines, their lithe bodies seeming to float in the air. They walked along the path, past a haunted house on a track and twenty or so different games. A man was hosing off a ride that spun you all around.

"Looks like someone lost his dinner," P.J. said.

The city was so alive at this hour. She couldn't remember the last time she'd been anywhere but a concert hall or a restaurant after nine p.m.

When they reached the end of the fair, they passed through the gate and crossed the Place de la Concorde. She nodded at the doorman outside the Crillon before they went through the revolving doors, half expecting him to know her, even though they had never met.

When they entered the lobby with its checkerboard marble floors and white columns, its gilded crystal chandeliers, P.J. looked down at his clothes.

"Am I dressed up enough for this place?" he asked.

She nodded. "You're fine."

She led him past the closed door of the boutique, the glass light boxes showing the best of Dior, Prada, Lancel.

The lobby widened and then narrowed again as they passed large silver pots overflowing with fresh white roses, and then turned left into the bar with its red velvet chairs, dark wood-paneled walls, and frosted windows. It was totally different than it had been when she was a girl—in those days, the bar was in the basement, and far less fancy. They called it the American Bar.

"Come over here," she said, gesturing toward a table by the piano player. "This is my favorite spot."

It was still early, only eleven, and the room had yet to fill in. There were eight small tables, and twenty-four seats, plus eight more at the bar. Far fewer than in her father's time.

She lit a cigarette, inhaling deeply and then watching the smoke escape her lips. It had been ten years since she was here, at least.

"You don't smoke," she said.

"Nah. Just a few times in high school. Then my mother caught me and made me eat a cigarette as punishment."

"Eat?" she asked, thinking that perhaps she didn't understand his meaning.

"Eat," he said. He looked around. "Nice place."

"My father used to be the piano player here when I was a child," she said.

"Oh yeah?"

She nodded. "I used to sit at a corner table all night, watching him play. The bartender would fix me Shirley Temples and the waiters would play jacks with me when it was quiet. I'd be falling asleep in school the next day."

"That sounds—unusual," he said. "Not that practicing violin three to five hours a day when you're nine qualifies as usual."

Delphine smiled. "Did you ever wish for a more normal childhood?"

"Yes. Did you?"

She shrugged. "I never knew any different."

"Where was your mother?" he asked.

"She died when I was four."

This was what her father had told her for most of her life. When she turned twenty-five he revealed that in truth her mother had left them when Delphine was four, vanishing one night without warning. He never heard from or of her for fourteen years, until a coroner's office in Saint-Mandé sent a letter saying that she had died and he as next of kin should come get the body.

Delphine had sat with the information for weeks, allowing it to flatten her. But eventually she decided to un-know it; whether her mother had died when she was four or eighteen made no difference now. She was gone either way, and always had been.

She had only ever told Henri the truth.

"Oh man," P.J. said. "That's rough. I'm sorry."

"It was a long time ago."

"You must have been lonely," he said.

She had often painted a pretty picture of her youth for her husband and their business associates, all of whom loved her stories of sitting up late at Le Crillon with American actors, or wealthy Parisian businessmen and their whores. If you told a story enough times, it became almost true. But now, sitting here with P.J., she remembered. There had been too many nights when her father drank himself into a stupor; she had had to drag him home, afraid, always afraid. When she was only eleven, one of the businessmen followed her into the bathroom one night. After that, she convinced her father that she was old enough to stay home alone. But she hated the quiet apartment, and watched the clock, waiting for his return.

She told P.J. some of this now, leaving out the businessman in the *toilette*.

"My old man's a drinker too," he said. "From him I learned a hundred words for being drunk. Hammered, loaded, shit-canned, shattered, bombed . . ."

She felt guilty as she imagined what he might be picturing. She added, "But my father would have done anything for me. He was so talented. Until my mother was gone, he toured with a very well-known trio. He only took this job so he wouldn't have to travel. He worked days giving piano lessons so he could be there when I came home. He sent me to a good Catholic school, even though he couldn't afford it. All of this, for me."

The girls at Saint Agatha's had been cruel to her. She wasn't invited to their birthday parties or playdates. At fourteen, someone started a rumor that Delphine had seduced a young priest, and from then on no one would speak to her. She counted the moments each morning until it was time to run home for lunch. She didn't tell her father any of this. Delphine wanted him to believe that she was the happiest girl in the world. Sometimes she'd pretend to be gossiping on the telephone when he entered the kitchen, even though there was no one at the other end of the line.

"When I think of the sacrifices he made, it breaks my heart," she said.

Through the open door into the lobby, she saw a maid scurry across in a black dress and a white apron.

"My father was the same," P.J. said. "He gave up everything for us kids. You have to respect that, although sometimes I look at him and just wonder what his life's been for. I wonder if he resents us. Did your father go back to more serious music after you were grown?"

"No. He ended up in real estate. His girlfriend got him into the business, and me too for a while. I don't think he ever enjoyed it. And neither did I. I was just—lost. He made a lot of money at it, though."

She had used that money to buy the shop, which her father would have loved. Delphine had always thought that she was doing it for him, but perhaps the choice had been more selfish than that. Perhaps she was only trying to keep him alive on that day when she first met Henri. Her father had died at sixty, still so full of life.

The waiter came by—a skinny old man with white hair in a crisp black suit. Delphine didn't recognize him.

They ordered two glasses of champagne.

"This hotel is the best in Paris," she said. "They add such nice touches to everything they do. If a woman travels here alone, they put fresh flowers in her room each morning, and women's magazines, and a special diet menu and a guide to all the best shopping."

He smirked. "If a hotel in America tried that, they'd probably get sued."

"Why?" she asked.

"Feminism."

"So," she said. "Do you have a girlfriend in New York?"

"No ma'am. Plenty of girls and plenty of friends, but no girlfriend."

"And why is that?"

"Unlucky in love, I guess. There was one girl, Shannon. A long time ago."

"What is a long time in the life of a twenty-three-year-old?" she asked. "You're practically an infant."

He laughed. "We broke up a year ago."

"What happened?"

"Well, first off, I have no time. We hardly ever saw each other. She was special, though. Smart, but from a family like mine. My mother adored her. I thought we'd get married for a while there. But all we ever did was fight. Fight, then make up, then fight again. The usual."

"Let me guess," she said. "You fall madly in love with a

lot of women as soon as you meet them. But then you go out once or twice, you talk all night long, you get them into bed, and you lose interest. It is no one's fault, perhaps, but these women, they mourn for you, they beg you to take them back, and you feel nothing."

He cocked his head to the side. "Maybe."

"You are a man in a big city, and there are so many options you can't help but gorge yourself like a boy in a chocolate shop."

"You sound like an expert," he said.

"Perhaps. You are *un cavaleur*. A pickup artist."

"I prefer to think of myself as a romantic," he said.

She laughed.

"You're not very impressed by me, are you?" he asked. He sounded delighted by the idea.

"You're young," she said. "You can't help it."

She could not stop mentioning his youth, as if to prove to herself that she was not flirting, merely educating the boy. She often enjoyed the safety of flirtation when it happened in front of Henri. Men were different to her now that she was married. But this felt more dangerous than the rest.

"Well, what about Henri? How old is he, sixty?" P.J. said. "He must be thirty years older than you, am I right?"

"Stop trying to flatter me."

"I'm serious," he said. "What is it with gorgeous women and older men? You should give a young guy a chance for a change."

His words floated there for a moment, until the waiter came by with the champagne. Delphine felt as though they were two schoolchildren who had narrowly escaped being caught cheating on a test. She took a tiny sip of her drink to steady herself. This conversation must end. It wasn't fair to poor Henri.

"Henri is only fifty-five," she whispered. "We are fif-

teen years apart." Her age was something she wouldn't
share with just anyone, but this American, this whole night,
seemed not quite real.

"Neither of you looks your age," he said. "You're gorgeous. People must tell you all the time, don't they? They
must come up and stop you in the street."

Delphine laughed. "The drinks have gone to your head."

"No offense to old Henri, but he must get down on his
knees every day and thank God he landed a woman as hot
as you."

In fact, though she had spent a lifetime being told by men
that she was beautiful, Henri had rarely commented on her
appearance one way or the other.

"My husband is more concerned with the beauty of
instruments than the beauty of women," she said.

Once the words were out of her mouth, she realized that
she too was very drunk. She should go home. She would
finish just this one drink and leave. Meanwhile, she would
change the subject to something neutral.

"Do you like the music?" she asked. The piano player
was halfway through a perfect rendition of "Night and
Day," a favorite of hers.

"Very much. I'm a sucker for Cole Porter."

"Ahh, me too," she said. "There's an interesting history
in this place when it comes to pianos. Marie Antoinette took
her lessons here, back when this was the private home of the
Duke de Crillon. And there's a suite upstairs where Leonard Bernstein used to stay, with one of his beautiful wooden
pianos in the sitting room. I've never seen it, but it's supposed to be spectacular."

"Why don't we go up and have a look?" he said.

Then she felt it—his warm hand on her thigh. Delphine
was surprised by how unsurprising she found the sensation.
He leaned forward and kissed her.

"I think you're the most fantastic woman I've ever met."

"And how many times have you thought that before?" she asked, but she wanted it to be true more than he could imagine.

"If I were to go to the front desk and rent a room, would you come upstairs with me?" he whispered.

She could feel her nipples grow hard, her legs tingling.

"I think I ought to slap you for suggesting something like that."

He kissed her again, his hand in her hair, and then rose from the table. "Give me two minutes."

Delphine waved to the waiter and calmly paid the check, as if she did this sort of thing all the time. The drinks were twenty euros apiece. She knew that the rooms were somewhere in the range of nine hundred a night. For all the time she had spent in this hotel, she had never once been upstairs.

When P.J. returned, he did not mention the price, or the fact that he already had a perfectly good room reserved somewhere in the Latin Quarter. He just extended a hand and said, "Follow me."

In the elevator, they pressed together, her back to the wall, his hands all over her body. His kisses were so strong that they felt almost violent. They walked the hall still kissing, bound to one another, absurdly knocking into the walls every few feet.

He unlocked the door to their room and before she even heard it click shut he was lifting her by the backs of her thighs and up onto the bed, as if she weighed nothing. He slid off her panties, and then he was down on his knees on the floor, gently spreading her legs apart.

After they made love, she did not want to go home. It seemed impossible that she should have to leave his bed. But it was after midnight, and what would she tell Henri?

Delphine stood and picked up her clothes. He lay there, watching her put them on.

"Would you go to Versailles with me?" he asked.

She laughed. "When?"

"Tomorrow."

"I don't see how I can."

"Find a way," he said. "Please. Meet me here at ten."

On the taxi ride home, she felt so light that she had to press her palm hard against her chest to keep from floating away. She tried to warn herself that he was just an American boy wanting to get the most out of a French vacation—fine wine and the Eiffel Tower and a Parisian woman naked in his hotel bed. But it had felt like more.

Henri was asleep when she came in. Her heart pounded as she slid into bed beside him. She thought the sound might actually be loud enough to wake him, but he did not stir. In the morning, when the alarm rang at seven, she hadn't yet been to sleep. He rolled over and looked at her.

"*Quelles nouvelles?* How was it with the American?"

"Fine," she said.

"Was it that bad?"

"It was all right. I'm just not feeling well now."

"My poor dear," he said, speaking to her like a beloved child. "Do you need some of my special medicine?"

The special medicine, which she had often fetched for him after too long a lunch, was just a fine scotch that he kept in the pantry.

"No," she said. "I think I might have caught your *grippe intestinale.*"

She felt certain that he must sense her dishonesty, but then he said, "Why don't you take the day off? I'm feeling better now and I don't have any meetings today. I can mind the shop on my own."

And with that, both their destinies were set in motion.

She lay in bed listening as he prepared for his day in the other rooms of the apartment. He brought her a warm *tartine beurrée* and coffee on a tray before he left.

"Now don't start organizing the closets or anything strenuous like that," he said. "Just rest."

As soon as he was gone, she showered and dressed, taking her time with her makeup, her perfume, her lingerie. The night before, P.J. had told her that girls in New York, even the young ones, wore big, ugly cotton underpants. What had he called them? *Grandma panties*, something like that. Delphine selected a bra and thong made of delicate lace, in black and violet.

She took the Metro back to Le Crillon. As the train stopped at one station and then the next, she told herself not to hope too hard. He might not even be there. But when she arrived, P.J. stood out front, and as his eyes met hers his face broke into a wonderful smile.

In Versailles, they ate lunch at a sidewalk café, kissing at the table like teenagers. She pointed out the picturesque city hall, a palace unto itself, and the candy shops that sold perfect, tiny fruits and vegetables made of marzipan. They strolled through the village holding hands, and then up to the palace, where they kissed some more. They kissed in the Hall of Mirrors, and in the gardens, in the shade of Marie Antoinette's oak tree, which, according to a plaque, the queen had saved from uprooting in 1790, not long before she was beheaded.

"Down this road is the Cimetière des Gonards," she told him as they walked back to the train that afternoon. "Edith Wharton is buried there."

He stared blankly.

"The author," she said.

"Oh!" He looked embarrassed. "I don't know much about French writers."

"Edith Wharton," she repeated, trying to pronounce it the way an American would, assuming that her accent had him confused. "She was from New York."

He shook his head. "Oh. Right."

Back in Paris, they went to his hotel, a boutique property tucked away on a side street. He told her it had once been a convent. He undressed her in front of a narrow window, its wooden shutters flung open onto an alleyway. As he led her to the bed, she could hear pigeons flapping their wings, and laughter from the elderly matinee patrons smoking outside the art house cinema across the road. Then there was nothing but the sound of her own breath, mixed in with his.

They lay in bed afterward, and he fell asleep with his head on her bare chest. Delphine couldn't sleep. She looked around the room, and there was the Stradivarius, upright on a chair in the corner. She had the sudden urge to tell Henri that P.J. had just left it out like that, not locked away in the hotel safe. It seemed irresponsible, and yet there was something thrilling about it.

She should go home. Henri would be back at seven.

"I've got to leave," she whispered, feeling exposed now, wishing she were tucked away safe in the country with her husband reading Zola or the latest Jean Echenoz in the next room.

"Not yet," P.J. protested, but she was already on her feet.

When Henri walked through the door that night, she was lying on the couch in her nightgown, pretending to be asleep.

P.J. called her cell around midnight. She had been waiting, clutching the phone in her hand, her whole body flooded with anticipation. At the first vibration, she ran to the bathroom off the hall to answer.

"I need to see you again," he said. "Can you come now?"

She laughed. "No!"

"Well, tomorrow then. Please."

The shop was closed from noon to three every day. They agreed to meet at Brasserie Élise at twelve-thirty.

Her husband only nodded when she told him she had a lunch date with an old friend of her father's, in town from Toulouse.

"I have to go all the way back toward home," she said. "He's staying near the rue Cler."

She had planned these words, in case any of the neighbors should see her and somehow end up mentioning it to Henri. She thought she sounded stiff and rehearsed, but Henri replied, "You should take the car. I've got plenty of paperwork to keep me busy here."

"All right."

The brasserie was four blocks from her apartment. When Delphine saw P.J. waiting there, she took him wordlessly by the hand and led him home. Every mundane detail of her life was suddenly electrified—pushing open the heavy door to the courtyard, turning her key in the lock, stepping into the elevator and pulling the grate closed, his lips on hers as they rose up one flight and then the next. After they made love, she stood in the kitchen and watched him as he sat shirtless at the table, flipping through the pages of yesterday's *Le Monde*. He looked like he belonged here. She could imagine years ahead, the two of them sitting in this same room in just this way.

The next day was Friday. As usual, she and Henri were scheduled to go to their country house that evening. She had told herself there was no way out of it, and maybe this was good—she needed to take a breath, to shake herself out of this silly affair. She had never had sex like this before, not with Henri or anyone. But she must remember that P.J. was a performer, and a good one at that. He did a very convincing job of making love to her as if he really were in love, but that didn't make it so. She had made that mistake all too often in the past.

Delphine had told him that she would be gone all weekend. He protested, but she reminded him that they had an entire week ahead when they might meet again. She felt proud of her resolve, but by four o'clock it had begun to weaken. By five, her stomach was twisted up at the thought of being without him. At six, as they were closing for the day, she turned to her husband and said, "I'm not myself this week. I just don't feel right."

He nodded. "The country air will do you good. I'm so excited for Monday morning. Did I tell you, Seamus O'Malley is coming from Galway?"

She felt ill. She hadn't been forceful enough.

"He's one of only four people in the world making top-quality uilleann pipes."

The words began to come out of her as if someone else were speaking them: "I wonder if you'd mind if I stayed behind this once."

He looked concerned. "I don't have to go. We can both stay in the city if that's what you prefer."

"No, no," she said. "You go. I know you've been looking forward to the chamber music on Saturday. And I hope this won't hurt your feelings, but I think it might do me good to be alone."

"Have I done something wrong?" he asked.

"Of course not. Every now and then a woman needs some time to herself, that's all."

"All right," he said. "If that's what you want."

She showed up at P.J.'s hotel, expecting him to be waiting for her. But of course, he was off seeing Paris. She went into the lobby, where a self-service bar had been set up. She poured a glass of white wine and placed a five-euro bill in the basket. Then she sat at a table and watched for close to an hour as tourists came in and out, clutching their shopping bags and street maps. She imagined the worst: that he had gone back to New York, or that he would enter the hotel with some other woman. When he finally came in and saw her there, he went right past, and had to look back twice before realizing.

"It is you!" he said, blissful. "I thought I'd imagined you sitting there. I haven't thought of anything but your face since you left me yesterday."

They walked along the Seine, past the *bouquinistes* hawking old paperbacks and posters. The tour boats glided along, their occupants waving wildly from the decks. Delphine and P.J. waved back, two *flâneurs* with no plans, no obligations. Though this was Paris, her city, it felt altogether different with him in it. Even the trees that lined the water were suddenly more alive, their branches ending in perfect green starbursts.

They stopped into a café for dinner. When they returned to the street, she was surprised to see that the sun had set. She asked him what time it was. One a.m.

Dozens of young revelers gathered on the riverbanks, singing and dancing, smashing empty wine bottles on the cobblestones. P.J. laughed, looking over the ledge from the sidewalk.

"Should we go down there?" he asked.

She started to protest, to say that she was too old for something like that, and it struck her—her life had become so stagnant, so serious, but she wasn't old at all. She kissed him, taking his hand and pulling him down the nearest set of steps to the water.

They spent the rest of the weekend in her bed, talking and making love for hours, until one or the other of them finally realized that they hadn't eaten all day. Late Saturday night, she cooked him rare steak.

On Sunday morning, she woke alone and found him in the living room. He had opened the shutters, and was looking out. Light poured in across the floor.

She took him through the bustling outdoor market beneath the elevated train tracks on the boulevard de Grenelle, where she went twice a week. A hundred stalls lined the path, each concerned with beauty and presentation as much as taste. Some sold the ripest fruit, ready to be eaten: cherries and berries and rhubarb, giant tomatoes and eggplants and artichokes, mushrooms long and thin, or wide and fat; others displayed thirty different kinds of olives in plain square bins and any herb or nut you could imagine. P.J. took a picture of the *poissonneries*, with their silvery fish heads and mussels and trout, translucent purple *poulpe* on a bed of leaves and ice. She pointed out the *fromagerie*, run by a father and daughter, with two dozen wheels of cheese, which they cut up and carefully wrapped in pale blue paper. The *charcuterie* had vats of beef bourguignon and paella, *petits poulets* rotating on a spit. The purveyor flirted with every old lady pulling her cart, his white apron smeared with blood. The flower stalls had roses and calla lilies in peak bloom. A profusion of heavenly smells hung in the atmosphere, so alive with the pleasure of good food and drink.

They strolled home along the avenue de la Motte Picquet, eating bright red *fraises*. She watched with pleasure when he took in the quiet view of the Eiffel Tower, which was hers every day.

"I don't want to leave Paris," he said.

"So don't," she said. "You are an artist. You can live anywhere."

Just then, she believed it was true. Maybe they could go on like this forever. The thought of his leaving was unimaginable.

"My life is in New York," he said. "Don't answer this now, just think about it. Would you come back there with me?"

"You know I can't," she said.

He nodded. "What I know is that it's completely inconvenient, but I've fallen in love with you."

"Don't say that," she said, even though she felt like she was falling in love too. She reminded herself to be strong— men like this made promises they never could keep.

"I've given it lots of thought," he said, "and I am positive that it's the real thing. It's not because we're here in Paris, or because you're unavailable, or even because you're beautiful. I love you. That's all."

She nodded without responding, afraid of what she might promise if she spoke.

"I would move to Paris if you wanted," he said. "But not like this. Not while you're married to another man, and we have to spend our lives sneaking around."

Delphine thought of Henri for the first time all weekend. Henri alone at the country house, where he had never been alone before. He had probably spent the weekend reading quietly and listening to music, and worrying about his strange wife, who had seemed a bit odd all week. He wouldn't have eaten much without her there to remind him. In his bachelor days, he had lived on soup from a jar.

"Are you even in love with your husband anymore?" P.J. said. "Sorry. That's not a fair question."

"I never was in love with him, not like this. But it's not just about being in love."

She saw a glimmer of hope in him then, though he did not say a word.

There was a Metro strike on Monday. She thought of him as she did the morning's paperwork and showed a young boy and his mother a collection of relatively inexpensive African instruments—a *balafon*. A double clarinet from Egypt. At noon, P.J. called to say that he would take a taxi over. She closed the shop for lunch, and they took a long walk around Montmarte while Henri gave a lecture at the Sorbonne. She showed him the apartment building she had grown up in, on a narrow street that, while modest, stood only two blocks from a grand neighborhood full of *voies privées*.

"We lived on the fifth floor," she said. "No elevator. Here in Paris, you have rich people and poor all living together in one building. The poorer you are, the smaller the apartment, and the higher up."

He laughed.

When she showed him the brick house that she had lived in until she moved in with Henri, he gasped.

"Beautiful," he said. He took a photograph. "How did your father afford it?"

"The landlady was fond of him. He gave piano lessons to her and all her friends. And he played for her whenever she wanted."

"That must have annoyed him."

"I think he thought it was a worthwhile trade," she said.

"I'd have to say he was right about that."

She felt proud of the house, and pleased that he recognized it for the jewel it was.

She took his arm and they wound their way down to the boulevard de Clichy, with its rows of seedy sex shops. Here and there, you'd see a natural foods store or a boutique mixed in, sure signs that the gentrification of Montmartre was now complete.

"This used to be much more a *quartier populaire*. A transvestite prostitute lived on our corner when I was very small," she said. "My father said this was a good sign, because it meant someone was keeping an eye out, on everything that happened."

She would have never mentioned this to Henri, but she knew P.J. would be amused, and indeed he replied, "Wow. Sure beats the neighborhood watch."

He paused, then said, "This is my favorite part of Paris, hands down."

On Tuesday, they made love in his hotel room while she claimed to be at a doctor's appointment. He would leave on Saturday night, and the knowledge of this fact saturated the air around them. On Wednesday, she couldn't get away. She thought of him constantly, his lips and his hands and every word they had exchanged in the last week.

She did not mention his offer until Thursday.

"You know that if I went away with you, I'd be giving up everything. My whole life."

"I know," he said.

"Isn't that a lot of pressure for a man your age?"

"You're the only woman for me," he said. "I know it."

"But what if that changes?"

"It won't."

"And what about poor Henri? How would I ever tell him?"

"I thought all French people had affairs and their spouses never minded," he said.

"You have seen too many movies. And besides, this isn't just an affair."

She began to cry. When he asked her why, she said she did not know, but the truth was, she had fallen in love, that was clear to her now. And she had just realized that she might consider leaving.

Delphine wished she had even one good friend to call and

ask for advice. But she had lost touch with the few girlfriends she had from university after they got married and had children. When she met Henri, she was alone in the world, and every acquaintance she had made since knew her husband at least as well as they knew her. She wanted to talk to her father, even considered visiting his grave, but what would be the use? Any answers he could give were long in the past. Delphine would have to decide for herself.

On Friday, she stayed home from work again, to think. She paced the streets of Paris, trying to be her own sensible mother, weighing all the possibilities. She could take this chance and risk everything—her marriage, her business, the only city she had ever called home. Or she could let P.J. fly away tomorrow, and return to her normal life, as dull as dishwater.

They closed the shop each August. A week from now they would leave for three weeks in the country. The house would be as still as ever. She wasn't sure she'd be able to bear her thoughts.

If she thought about it in practical terms, she simply could not abandon her husband. Besides that, it was too big a gamble to take, turning her life upside down for a man she had known for two weeks. But if she thought of herself as one speck of stardust among billions of others, when she considered that life was incredibly short and that none of this would mean anything in a hundred years' time, she could convince herself to try—why not? Her own mother had left her, and she had survived. Henri would recover.

At home, she brewed a tisane of *tilleul* and lavender, which her father had used to calm her when she got upset as a child. But she needed something stronger now, and so she switched to Henri's scotch.

By the time he arrived back from work, her suitcase was packed and she was shivering. Delphine had fixed him a

320 J. Courtney Sullivan

glass of scotch, which she handed to him as he stood in the living room, sorting through the mail. She needed to say it straightaway, before she lost her nerve. She had considered not mentioning P.J., just telling Henri she needed time apart. But when she opened her mouth, the truth spilled out: "There's something I have to tell you," she said. "And since there is no easy way, I will just put it plainly—I'm in love with someone else. *L'Américain*. The Rogue. I've been spending time with him, and he wants me to go to New York. I've told him yes. Maybe it's all a mistake, but I won't know until I try. I have to try."

Henri looked confused for a moment, as if he had walked into the wrong apartment, but then his face crumpled. He sank into the chair behind him, like his legs could no longer be relied upon to hold him up.

"I knew something had changed," he said. "I thought you were pregnant."

With that, his head dropped into his hands, and Delphine at last felt the weight of her crime.

"Forgive me," she whispered foolishly. "Please."

A dreadful hour followed, perhaps the worst of her life. Henri did not ask any questions. He did not beg her to reconsider. He just sat in his chair as she cried. Finally, Delphine kissed the top of his head and walked out the door.

As soon as the fresh air hit her face she was full of joy. She did a little turn in the street and smiled at an old man passing by. She had never before felt two such strong, divergent emotions at once. This must be selfishness at its most unforgivable, and also its most delicious. At the brasserie, P.J. waited for her. When she greeted him, he picked her up and swung her in the air.

"We're really doing this," he said.

"Yes!"

He placed her back on her feet and then, for an instant,

she thought he was falling down. But no—he was bending onto one knee.

He pulled a ring from his shirt pocket.

"It was my mother's," he said. "Will you marry me?"

She whispered yes, and they embraced. When he slipped the ring onto her finger, it clinked against her plain gold band, a reminder that this was slightly absurd: How could she stand here, promising to marry him, when she was married already?

Delphine pushed the thought away. "Do you just happen to bring your mother's engagement ring everywhere you go, in case you feel the urge to propose?" she asked.

"No," he said. "I called a friend in New York and had him send it last weekend."

"Last weekend? But I hadn't agreed to come with you last weekend."

He grinned. "I had high hopes."

Flying to JFK the next night, she felt full of something wild and thrilling. *I am marrying this handsome, vibrant man,* she thought, staring at him. *I am starting a whole new life.* She felt eager to tell someone the news, someone who loved her and would be happy. Strangely, she thought of Henri.

Eventually, she would have to ask him for a divorce. That would devastate him, she knew. She worried about how dark he could get. He was incapable of helping himself out of it. She had the urge to wrap her arms around him, to comfort him. But that wasn't hers to do any longer.

2012

After leaving Toby and Jeff behind at the inn, Kate wished she had some other errand to run, something to keep her mind off the ring. As it was, there was nothing to do but go home and keep looking.

Back at the house, her brother-in-law Josh stood in the yard throwing a football around with his boys.

"Well?" he said. "How did they take it?"

"I didn't tell them yet," she said, a bit annoyed by his curiosity.

Through the screen door, she could hear the sound of Dan singing Marvin Gaye while he washed the breakfast dishes. Her own father had been a great cook when they were growing up. His job had the most flexibility, so he was home with the girls more often than their mother and usually made dinner. Kate did all the cooking in their household now, and Dan took care of the cleaning. They were trying to have an egalitarian partnership, though parenting had made her realize how hard that truly was. When he dressed Ava, Dan might put her in two different colored socks. When he washed her hair, he used about fourteen times more shampoo than seemed necessary.

Still, she could not imagine parenting without him. Kate had a couple of friends in Brooklyn who had decided to have kids on their own, without a mate—one through adoption, the other sperm donation. She herself could never have done it.

She entered the kitchen.

"So?" he said, looking hopeful.

"I didn't tell them."

"Okay. Well, that's good. Gives us more time."

She shrugged. "I just don't understand how the ring could be there one minute, and the next it's gone. You don't think I subconsciously hid it, do you?"

Dan laughed. "Uhh, no. Did you?"

"No! But you know how I feel about diamonds."

"Yeah, and for good reason."

"Thank you." She lowered her voice. "Do you think one of the kids could have taken it?"

"Olivia?" he said.

"That's what I was thinking. How are we gonna handle that?"

"If she has it, she'll probably become riddled with guilt at some point and hand it over."

"Hope so. Hey, guess how much their rings cost."

He shrugged.

"Fourteen thousand apiece."

The look on his face made her more terrified than she had previously let herself be.

"Holy shit. We gotta find that thing."

"I know."

Suddenly every napkin and shoelace and jar of Play-Doh seemed like its only purpose might be to obscure the ring. Kate opened the junk drawer, and pulled out old screwdrivers and stamps, a box of paper clips, a few alphabet magnets that had traveled from the fridge.

"You think it's in there?" Dan said skeptically.

"I don't know."

He poured a cup of coffee. "Here, drink this," he said, kissing her neck as he handed it to her.

"You seem downright chipper compared to the guy I woke up with this morning," she said.

"Well, I'm happy for them," Dan said. "I was just thinking that marriage equality may well be the one bright spot in what's otherwise been a terrible millennium so far."

"Yeah, I suppose when the last decade's been marked by terrorism, genocide, a depression, a tsunami, hurricanes, earthquakes, war, and torture, marriage does look good in comparison."

"You forgot to mention the demise of the record store."

"Oh yeah, that too."

"Not like the nineties were so great, though," he said. "Rodney King, Columbine, Waco. The Oklahoma City bombing. O. J. Simpson."

"Yes. And all of those seem practically quaint compared to this last decade."

"True. Hey, never let it be said that we're not one cheery couple."

She grinned. "Two rays of sunshine."

The day's mail sat on the table. She sifted through it—a cell phone bill, a birthday party invitation from one of Ava's playground friends, and a few junk flyers addressed to Mrs. Daniel Westley. The fact that they weren't married never stopped anyone from calling her by Dan's last name, or referring to him as her husband. For the most part, she didn't really mind.

The first time Ava got sick as a baby, Kate rushed her to the emergency room in Brooklyn. After she filled out the requisite forms, the woman behind the desk said coldly, "Can I ask what relation you are to the child?"

"I'm her mother."

"She has two last names," the woman said. "Our system can't process that, you're going to have to pick one." As if it were 1952. As if scores of married women didn't keep their maiden names all the time, and hyphenate their children's.

It pissed her off most of all because things like that weren't supposed to happen in Brooklyn. She might have expected it in the town where May lived, a place where everyone prided themselves on the sheer throwback of it all; where a little girl whose parents had never married would probably get mocked, and all the women took their husbands' names, like the feminist movement had never happened. *It was just easier that way*, friends told her. They wanted to be family units, and in a family unit everyone was called the same thing.

She could admit that words were tricky, but that didn't mean you should dismantle your whole belief system to keep things simple. It was awkward when people struggled to figure out how they ought to refer to Dan. If forced, she'd call him her partner, but to most strangers the word conveyed that she was either a lesbian or a lawyer. She tried not to call him anything—just "Dan."

She wandered into the living room. May sat on the couch between Ava and Olivia. The girls were watching an episode of *Barney* on TV. May had her laptop turned on, but she was gazing out the window, possibly asleep with her eyes open. She liked to say that she hadn't slept through the night for the past decade, ever since Leo was born colicky and screaming.

Olivia and Ava each wore a pink plastic tiara with a medallion in the center that featured a different Disney princess. Olivia had a pink tutu on over her pajamas, and Ava wore a pink feather boa draped across her shoulders and hard plastic pink high heels on her bare feet. The shoes in particular, and all that pink in general, made Kate uneasy. She had never seen any of this stuff before. May must have brought it along. No doubt, after they left, Ava would start asking for her own cotton-candy-colored, gender-normative crap.

Kate wanted this day to be over. She wanted her family to go home and stay there, and just leave the three of them in peace.

"Hi," she said. "What's up?"

"I just saw on Facebook that my friend Rachel is pregnant again," May said.

"Oh."

"I swear to God, if she names that baby Amelia, I'll slit her throat."

Kate glanced at Ava. Her sister's choice of words seemed a tad violent for Saturday morning public television time. But Ava's attention was on the screen.

"What do you care?" Kate asked. "You're not having any more. Are you?"

"Maybe. Two girls and two boys would be nice."

She knew that it was now fashionable for couples on the Upper East Side to have four, five, six kids. A way of saying, *Look how freaking rich we are! We can afford to raise this many children at once in the most expensive city on earth.* Now apparently the trend had made its way to Jersey.

"Any updates on the ring?" May said.

Kate shook her head.

"Girls, listen to me," May's voice grew stern. "If either of you has that ring, you'd better tell us right now, or else."

Ava looked terrified—they never talked to her like that. (*Or did she look guilty?* Kate considered this.)

"Cross my heart and hope to die," Olivia said dramatically.

"Cross my heart and hope to die," Ava repeated. She cast an adoring glance at her cousin, who at the age of five qualified as an older woman, wise in the ways of the world.

On the television screen, Barney and his odd child friends were starting to sing a song about family. She hated the kids on *Barney*; they seemed like miniature cult members, their words overly cheerful and without affect.

How many in your family? Barney asked his audience, in the exaggerated, enthusiastic tone of a born-again Christian.

"How many?" May asked Olivia, sounding bored.

"Five!" Olivia said. "Ava. How many in your family?"

"Five!" Ava shouted.

Olivia crumpled her face in disappointment. "No. Three, dummy."

"Olivia!" May snapped. "Language. That's strike one."

On the screen, a kid in overalls climbed onto a picnic table and declared with effervescence, *There's a girl I know who lives with her mom, her dad lives far away. Although she sees her parents just one at a time, they both love her every day!*

"Why does she see her parents one at a time?" Olivia asked. Then, answering her own question, "They're divorced like Grandma and Grandpa."

"Probably," May said.

"My friend Lily's parents are divorced," Olivia said, sounding almost proud to know something about the topic at hand. "And also Joe and Sarah on our street, but I don't really like them. But not because their parents are divorced, just because I don't."

Kate and May were part of the first big wave of children with divorced parents. By the time she got to college, Kate knew more people whose parents had split up than stayed together. They all had awful stories—her freshman-year roommate, Taylor, had put on seven pounds the year her parents separated, because they exchanged her on Monday and Thursday nights, and on those nights they both fed her dinner. She didn't have the heart to tell them. Another girl on their hall had come home sick from a slumber party in eighth grade to find her mother having sex with a neighbor while her father was out of town on business. She had told her father right away, and then proceeded to blame herself for the divorce for the next ten years. The strangest story came from a kid named Ed, who claimed his parents were the envy of all their friends, with a beautiful home, three children, and a lake house in New Hampshire. Every night his dad came home from work at six on the nose, cheery and kind. He kissed his wife, brought the trash barrels out to the curb, and carried the toys in from the yard. Then one evening he sat down to dinner as usual. When his wife placed the food on the table, out of nowhere, he yelled, "I hate chicken." He walked out, never to return.

For Kate, it was a matter of getting dragged into every argument, of realizing at a certain point that her own mother was using her. Mona would casually ask her how much her dad had spent on his new car, or whether he was seeing anyone. Then she'd use it all against him in court.

"Where's Mom?" Kate asked now.

"She went for a walk," May said. "I think she's nervous about this reading she has to give."

"I'm not nervous," Ava said.

"Good girl!" May said.

Kate twinged at this response. There was nothing wrong with being nervous, nor was there anything inherently good about *not* being nervous. She wondered if her sister had the ability to undo three years of careful parenting in just two days.

"I'm not that excited, because there's no bride," Olivia said. "I want to see a princess!"

May patted her on the shoulder. "Last April, we woke up at four a.m. to watch the royal wedding on TV. I made scones and clotted cream, and we both wore fascinators. Olivia loved it. It ruined her for all other weddings."

"You've got to be kidding me," Kate said.

"It was a huge day. A once-in-a-lifetime. Don't you remember when we got up early to watch Diana walk down the aisle? How excited we were?"

"I was five. And anyway, look how that turned out."

May went on, "Olivia's obsessed with Kate Middleton."

As if to illustrate her mother's point, Olivia said, "She has a puppy named Lupo," without taking her eyes off the television.

May beamed, like these were the most precious words ever uttered by a child. "She draws pictures of her at school when the other kids are drawing bears or whatever."

Kate frowned. "That seems unhealthy."

"Kate, I am just trying to make conversation with you. Why do you have to make every interaction so unpleasant?"

"Sorry. You're right."

May had an uncanny way of remembering dates by whatever happened to be going on in pop culture at the moment. It was no surprise that the previous April put Kate in mind of Arab Spring while May thought of a princess in a wedding gown. Her sister wasn't a bad person, and she wasn't dumb. She just believed, like a lot of people did, that life was hard enough and there was no reason to trouble yourself with the plight of strangers. Their views of success were fundamentally different. May thought it was measured by what one could amass over a lifetime, instead of how many people one could help.

When Kate saw the news footage of Prince William's wedding to Kate Middleton, she observed the way they drove the car through the streets of London unaccompanied and made a point of letting the world know they'd invited the local pub owner and the postman. It seemed tailor-made to placate the masses, who didn't have jobs or enough food to eat but felt pleased all the same. When people were suffering, their governments would give them weddings or war as a distraction, and sometimes both.

Kate had read that same-sex weddings would generate three hundred million dollars for the State of New York in the next three years. It made her wonder if the timing of the decision didn't have something to do with money. She had run this idea by her father, and he thought it sounded a bit extreme, as he did most of her ideas. Still, he said he admired her tendency to question things. May took everything at face value, and he saw this as a failing. It was important to seek the truth, he told them, even if you only rarely came across it.

For years, he had edited the *Star-Ledger*'s letters column. Although it was entirely unethical, from time to time when he felt strongly about something he wrote letters under a fake name and published them. He had wanted to be an op-ed columnist, and at some point he realized this was as close as he would probably ever get.

Last year, after more than three decades at the paper, he was unceremoniously let go—or "offered a buyout," as they put it to soften the blow. His wife lost her job outright, since the birth of the Internet meant the death of the newsroom library she ran, which, ironically, had always been referred to as "the Morgue." Now they spent their days at home, doing crosswords and halfheartedly looking for jobs, knowing they were unlikely to find work in a dying field at their age, but still too young to retire.

"Have you talked to Dad lately?" Kate asked now.

"Yeah, we saw him and Jean last weekend," May said.

"How did he seem?"

May shrugged. "He seemed like Dad."

Kate lingered a few minutes longer, then went upstairs. She felt a guilty fluttering in her stomach as she walked into Ava's bedroom. Her niece's pink duffel bag lay open on the floor. Kate glanced over her shoulder once before going through it—she dug her fingers into every tiny satin pocket, but the ring wasn't there.

Diagnostic research revealed that the women viewed engagement as "only the beginning" of the wedding process, with the DER as "part" of that process. As a result, DER price competed against all other marriage and household preparation expenses. Women, therefore, often exerted downward pressure on the DER price.

By contrast, for men, engagement was seen as a momentous occasion, signaling a major life change. To them, the DER was viewed as the true mark of adulthood and all the responsibility that goes with it— family, home, a steady job, a lifestyle of permanence. Because men invested the DER with so much importance and meaning, it was also a source of pride that had to be sufficiently expressive of the occasion. Men were willing to spend more/make financial sacrifices to show the importance of their intent in this, the first public affirmation of their obligation to the relationship. They were, however, lacking in confidence about purchasing a diamond since they had no reference for price expectations or diamond quality.

Two months' salary is a price guideline which both respects income differences and sets an aspirational price goal.

—Internal Memo, Case History, N. W. Ayer, 1990

1988

Frances was up late, stewing. She held a cup of coffee in her hand. Most women her age avoided caffeine after noon, but she had been an insomniac all her life, and she found that it didn't make a bit of difference whether she drank coffee or not. Either way, she wouldn't sleep.

The television droned in the background. Her black Lab, Blazer, lay on the rug at her feet, his head on Frances's toes. She was working on her Christmas cards, which she had just gotten back from the printer's. They featured a photograph of the dog wearing a pair of reindeer antlers. One by one, she signed them, even though the printer said no one bothered to do that anymore. They had a typeface that looked like handwriting now, he said. The thought of this depressed her enormously.

She was thinking about Howard Davis and his very surprising proposal. Weighing whether she ought to accept.

A few days earlier, when good old Howard called to say that he and his wife were driving from Manhattan all the way to the Main Line to take her to lunch, Frances knew it must be something important. She hadn't seen Howard in eighteen years, not since her last day at Ayer. She hated to think about that day, even now. There had been no fanfare, no farewell party. She walked out alone, with a box under each arm, somehow unable to make herself switch off the lamp, as if leaving it on meant she would come back tomorrow and do it all again.

The world had changed by leaps and bounds since then; even the Philadelphia office, which had seemed somehow eternal, was gone. The first building ever constructed to house an advertising agency in America, the building she had walked into and out of five days a week for twenty-seven years, now stood empty.

Ultimately, Ayer had joined all the others in Manhattan. But the agency came to the party too late, and was now a shadow of the powerhouse it had once been. No one cared that they started it all. Advertising was about the here and now, and sometimes the future, but never the past.

When Howard and his wife, Hana, arrived in Wayne that afternoon, Frances saw that they too had aged, though they were her juniors by a decade or more. They told her their eldest son was now a writer of forty, with children of his own, and Frances felt a jolt go through her. It shouldn't be a surprise, of course, but it did shock her to remember that getting older was so inevitable. Sometimes it seemed it was only happening to her.

Frances had imagined that they would compliment her on her house, maybe spy the baby deer who had been snacking at the bird feeder all morning. She had moved in soon after she retired. The three-bedroom stone rambler stood on a hill at the end of a quiet cul-de-sac, tucked away behind a cluster of residential streets, full of pretty houses, and flowers and trees. It had dark green shutters and white trim on the garage. Towering pines stood in the front yard. She thought it was an impressive place, especially for a woman on her own.

But when she opened the door, the first thing Howard said was, "Is that gas?"

Hana pinched her nose. "It smells something awful in here, Frances!"

Apparently the damn pilot light had gone out. Somehow she hadn't noticed. It didn't seem like much to her, but they appeared deeply concerned.

"You could have been killed!" Hana said, running around, opening all the windows.

Poor Howard dropped to his stomach and started fiddling with the stove.

They reminded Frances of her younger cousins in Canada, always telling her she ought to think about selling the house and going to one of those awful retirement homes. Her glaucoma had worsened in recent years, but other than that she felt fine. She had agreed to hire a helper woman, who came in three days a week to do the bills and make sure she hadn't dropped dead.

"I've got it lit," Howard said, triumphant. He climbed to his feet. "Well now, Frances. How the hell are you?"

She was wildly embarrassed, and took them to a nice restaurant in town, where she hoped the food would make them forget about the gas. She ordered a steak and the first of the two martinis she always had with lunch.

"So what's this all about, Howard?" she asked as they handed the waiter their menus.

He laughed. "You don't beat around the bush. I forgot that about you."

"I'm seventy-three years old. There's no longer time for beating around the bush."

"Well, Lou Hagopian's the chairman at Ayer now," he started.

"Yes, I know."

"He's decided that Ayer ought to commemorate the agency's fiftieth anniversary with De Beers in a big way."

"Oh?"

She had a vivid recollection of herself snapping at Gerry Lauck after the twenty-fifth. *Where's my gold watch?* Frances felt a rush of guilt, even though Gerry had died ages ago.

"They're planning something very grand," Howard said. "A full week of celebrations in London, where the company is headquartered. There will be lunches every day, and dinners and parties each night."

"My. That does sound grand."

"The whole thing will culminate in a big, fancy dinner and a recognition of your contributions. They'll want you to give a few remarks. Talk about how you came up with the famous line."

Frances was stunned. "They want me there?"

"Yes!" Howard said. "All expenses paid. You'll be the star of the show."

There were so many things she ought to be thinking: That this was a tremendous honor. That finally she was getting her due. But the only thought she could focus on was the fact that she had nothing to wear. Her heart seized. *Seven lunches and seven dinners with the Oppenheimers?* She assumed they would not be impressed by the brown skirt suit she wore to Mass on Sundays.

"Do you feel up to it?" Howard asked.

"They'll send someone along to be your companion," his wife added. "She can help you get dressed and all. Keep an eye on you."

Now Frances realized why they had come in person. Hagopian had probably sent them to assess whether she was too old, too frail, too likely to let her cocktails go to her head and say something outlandish. She herself wasn't sure of the answer. She hadn't gone anywhere for the longest, except to church, and bridge three times a week. She hadn't been on an airplane since her aunt died twelve years earlier.

"Can I sleep on it?" she asked. "It's such a generous offer, but there's a lot to consider."

"Of course," Howard said.

Now, here she was, sleeping on it, or not sleeping, as the case may be.

Though it had been nearly twenty years since she left

Ayer, Frances still felt connected to the place. She kept up with quite a few of her old colleagues and their wives, mostly on the East Course at Merion. From what she heard, the new Ayer New York bore no resemblance to Ayer Philadelphia.

She followed what they did with De Beers. Ten years ago, she had read a story in the magazine *Ad Art Techniques* that said De Beers had become a ten-million-dollar-a-year account. And the cartel was making two billion annually.

But that was the late seventies. More recently, there had been murmurings of trouble. A few years ago, Frances clipped an article from the newspaper about a major controversy De Beers had kicked up in Australia when diamonds were discovered there—the Oppenheimers had made the move to buy them up, wanting always to control the whole world's supply. In the past, they had gotten whatever they wanted with ease, but certain people in the Australian government were pushing back, claiming that De Beers wouldn't pay fairly and that they were somehow personally responsible for apartheid.

She wondered if all three of them—Ayer, De Beers, and she herself—had simply seen their prime come and go. Perhaps that's what this week in London was supposed to be for. To remind them of better times.

Frances could say with certainty that she had completely lost touch with what the diamond-buying public was like nowadays, if the ads Ayer was running were any indication.

For the royal wedding of Princess Diana and Prince Charles a few years back, she had heard through the grapevine that De Beers paid something like half a million dollars for just a couple minutes' worth of television advertising. This baffled her, but then again, by the time television came along, it was almost too late for Frances. She was a print writer, through and through.

Even the print ads seemed awful lately. It all got so casual for a while. In *Life*, she had seen a photograph of two adults sipping a milkshake like teenyboppers, with the line: *With this diamond, we promise to always be friends.*

Could anything be less romantic? Well, yes! How about the photo of a man and woman riding a motorcycle in black leather jackets, over the following: *I know she loves rock-n-roll. So I rolled out a magnificent rock.*

They still ended every ad with her line. Sometimes she wished they wouldn't.

Just a month earlier, she had nearly thrown her *TV Guide* across the living room when she came upon a glossy page asking, *Isn't Two Months' Salary a Small Price to Pay for Something That Lasts Forever?*

The ad went on, *You have a love that money can't buy. And you'd like a diamond engagement ring that's as special as that love. But what's a realistic price for him to spend? These days, two months' salary is a good place to start.* (And there, in the bottom right corner of the page, *A Diamond Is Forever.*)

"What on earth?" she said out loud.

A week or two later, she ran into one of the creative directors, Teddy Regan, in the dining room at Merion.

"Ted!" she called out. "What's the meaning of those two-months'-salary ads?"

He laughed, coming over to her table. "You don't like them?"

"They're tacky as hell," she said.

"Tell me what you really think, Frances."

"Well, they are. You know it as well as I do. At least I hope you know it."

"It's not my account," he said. "I think the team realized that young men buying diamonds were asking their fathers how much they paid for Mom's ring and going off of that.

The cost perception just wasn't keeping up with the economy. We needed something that was attainable for every man. Two months' salary provides a guideline. And also, say the salary is on the small side. Well, the ring will reflect that. So this will encourage them to really stretch, to go as big as they can afford. Maybe even a bit bigger. Because what she's wearing on that ring finger says a lot about him."

"I still think it's unseemly," she said.

He shrugged. "I agree, but it's working."

From there, she began to notice ads along the same lines that seemed like something she might have written in the fifties.

Show her she's the reason it's never been lonely at the top.

A carat or more. When a man's achievement becomes a woman's good fortune.

It almost made her long for the ads Deanne had come up with in the hippie days, with their cartoon lions and flower children.

Howard had said that they wanted her to tell the story of her contributions. Well, first off, nowadays, everyone did the kind of stuff they had invented for De Beers—placing jewelry in movies, loaning pieces to celebrities, so they could show them off in public.

They wanted to hear how she had come to write the line. Like most of life's remarkable moments, it hadn't seemed at all remarkable until later. In 1981, when Granville Toogood passed away, she was surprised to read in his obituary in *The Philadelphia Inquirer* that *he* had written the line. Toogood was a fixture of Philadelphia's high society, a member at both the Merion golf and cricket clubs, with his own seat at the Philadelphia Orchestra. In 1930, he wrote a book called *Huntsman in the Sky*. He had been an executive on the business side at Ayer, with no hand in the affairs of the copy department, but apparently Toogood had gone through life telling his children and grandchildren that *A Diamond Is Forever* was his.

Warner Shelly, Ayer's president at the time, had called her at home to say that he was outraged. Warner made a stink and called the paper, demanding a retraction. They never printed one, and this made him even angrier. But Frances was tickled by the whole episode: this line that she had just dashed off late one night was worth stealing, and from the Great Beyond at that.

London. They wanted her to go to London.

If only the chance had come ten years sooner. She would have leapt at it then. Now she was basically an old woman. Her eyesight had gone to pot and some days she was a bit shaky on her feet. Still, it was nice to think that life could offer up the occasional surprise, even at her age.

"I think I'll go," she said. "Why not?"

It was three in the morning. The dog didn't even glance up.

As soon as it reached a respectable hour, she called Howard at home.

"Tell Mr. Hagopian I'll do it," she said.

"Oh, that's wonderful," he said. "Lou will be so pleased. He'll probably want to call you himself later in the week to talk over specifics. And someone in PR will most likely call you later today, too."

"Fine, fine."

There were sometimes entire weeks when her phone did not ring. But not twenty minutes after she hung up with Howard, it started. The kids in the Ayer public relations department were suddenly interested in who she was and what she thought. They asked questions and requested photos. Frances told them what they wanted to know about her personal background and her accounts, especially De Beers.

It was nice to have an excuse to revisit her time at Ayer. Like it or not, her life was inextricably tied to the agency.

They wanted to know what she'd been doing since retirement. She told them she kept busy playing golf and bridge at Merion, participating in various activities at Our Lady of Assumption, and caring for her dog. At the last minute she added horseback riding to the list, even though she hadn't been on a horse in fifteen years. It sounded nice.

She decided to send a current photograph of herself in a smart cardigan and pearls, no glasses. She gave instructions that it would look dandy in color, with the freckles blacked out. And she added a second picture, of herself at thirty-five or so, seated at her desk in the Ayer building. In it, she wore a short-sleeved dress with a Peter Pan collar, which she had always loved. Frances stared at the photo long and hard before slipping it into the envelope—her gray hair suddenly brown again, her wrinkles smoothed into plump white cheeks.

At one o'clock, it was time for her to pick Meg up for bridge.

Poor Ham had died of a heart attack three years back, but his wife still didn't drive and never would. Frances probably shouldn't be driving either, but she couldn't give it up.

"You'll never believe what's happened," she said when Meg slid into the passenger seat.

"What?"

"Remember I told you that Howard Davis wanted to meet with me? Well, he came yesterday and we had lunch."

"How is Howard? Ham was so fond of him."

Frances pulled the car into the road.

"He's just fine. But get a load of this. Ayer wants to send me to London for part of a big celebration with the diamond people."

Meg clapped her hands together. "Fran! How wonderful!"

They were still talking about it fifteen minutes later when they walked into the dining room. All around them, women were taking their seats and pulling out their score cards.

"Big news, everybody!" Meg said. "Frances is going to London."

They all looked up, surprised, excited to hear more.

Frances laughed. Over the years, these gals had become her family. When she first joined the bridge club in '73, she assumed she would have nothing in common with any of them, other than Meg, who had been the one to drag her into it. The team was made up of avid golfers and women who couldn't golf anymore because of bad knees or what have you, but still wanted to be social.

They were mostly the wives of prominent men. Frances was the only one among them who had never married, and one of only two who had worked past the age of twenty-five. Yet as time passed, she began to see them not as merely *the wives*, but as themselves. She had feared that they wouldn't have any interest in a woman like her, but they were fascinated by stories of her Ayer days. They seemed to afford her some level of sophistication unlike their own. Not society events and ballrooms, but pitch meetings and client dinners. They saw her as the only person who could truly answer the question *What were our husbands up to all day for all of those years?*

A lot of their husbands were gone now. In a way, it reminded Frances of the war years, when there were so few men around, and the girls banded together. They could do this without guilt or judgment, because they weren't rejecting men. They were simply waiting to be reunited with them.

"Oh Frances, you must be so excited," Ruth Elder said from her seat in front of the trophy case.

"Yes," she said. "I am. But. Well, it's silly, but to tell you the truth, I'm mostly just terrified."

"Why?" Meg asked.

"I have nothing to wear."

They got a good laugh over that.

"You've come to the right place, my dear," Ruth said. "The women in this room have heaps of clothes. And more jewelry than we know what to do with! We'll help you."

"Really?" Frances asked.

"Of course," piped up Miriam Tuttle. "I can think of five dresses I've got hanging in the closet collecting dust that would be perfect on you."

"I just bought a gorgeous blue evening gown for our cruise," said Rose Thompson. "It will look lovely with your complexion."

They arrived at her house that evening at six, twelve cars lined up along the cul-de-sac. Frances watched them come up the front stairs, their arms weighed down by gowns and brooches and shoes and furs, a fashion parade.

"Come in, come in!" she said, pushing the screen door open.

They marched to her bedroom, where she had a tray of martinis waiting on the dresser.

"Try this one first," Ruth said, handing her a long silk sheath.

Frances stepped into the bathroom and slipped it over her head.

She opened the door. "Well?"

"Gorgeous!" Meg said.

"You still have a great figure, Frances," said Marge Samuels. "You ought to dress up more often."

She laughed. "For what? To walk the dog or hang the laundry?"

Marge shrugged. "You never know. Maybe you'll meet

some dashing Brit while you're over there, and never return."

"I seriously doubt that."

She tried on the dresses one by one as her friends stood around giving their opinions—this one was too tight in the hips and that one was too short, but the third would be perfect for an evening affair.

They brought a lot of costume jewelry along, and Frances wore it all at once, just for a laugh—big ruby earrings and ten different necklaces, and half a dozen bracelets.

"It's about jewels, after all," Meg said. "Diamonds, to be specific. We owe it to you that we got these sparklers in the first place. If you need to borrow one, here." She pulled her solitaire from her finger and tossed it onto the bed as if it weren't her most precious possession.

Frances wondered if Meg had dipped a bit too far into the martinis.

"I've got another you can take," Marge said. She slid her pretty engagement ring off. "Oh, and this." Her eternity band.

"One more," Rose said. She tugged at her ring, but it wouldn't budge. "Hold on." She ran to the bathroom and held it under a stream of cold water until it dropped.

"Now!" she said, holding it out in triumph. "Here we are!"

She added it to the pile.

One by one, they took off their diamond rings. It was only a joke. They knew she wouldn't really take them. But Frances would never forget the sight of that mound of gems, glittering before her.

Part Four

1972

On the many occasions when she had thought about it, Evelyn had assumed that her son's mistress would be beautiful. But she wasn't, not in the slightest. Nicole wore platform shoes and a very short dress, though her legs were thick and unshapely. Her forehead was too high and Evelyn would swear that her stick-straight brown hair was a wig. She couldn't hold a candle to Teddy's own wife. It was just one more part of this whole ludicrous arrangement that made no sense at all.

Evelyn ushered them inside. Her inner self screamed, shouted, raged with anger. Yet all she said was, "Let me take your coats."

It amazed her how different the surface could be from what one felt beneath the skin. It made her wonder for a moment how a person could ever be certain of anyone else's true feelings. Or maybe it was just her. Another mother might have grabbed the boy by his shoulders and shaken him until he bled from the ears.

"It's a pleasure to meet you," Nicole said, her eyes roaming from the carpet to the grandfather clock, to the hat stand, to the table, as if she were a burglar assessing the value of the place. "Wow, this house is incredible! I feel like I'm in a museum."

The first time Evelyn had been to Gerald's family home, she too was overwhelmed by the level of wealth they displayed, but she had been refined enough not to act like it. So, for that matter, had Julie, who grew up on a small farm in Oregon, yet had the manners of a girl who'd been educated at Miss Porter's.

"We brought you some flowers," Teddy said, extending the soggy parcel.

Evelyn took hold of it without meeting his eye. That *we* had pierced her like an arrow. She wanted them gone. She wanted Julie and the girls here for Sunday dinner, talking and laughing while her son sat in the next room watching television with Gerald.

"Thank you, darling. Wasn't that sweet."

Her husband descended the staircase now, wearing a tweed blazer over slacks.

"Teddy!" he said in a jolly tone, shaking his son's hand and patting him on the back. He didn't seem in the least bit surprised by the woman's presence.

"This is Nicole," Teddy said.

"Nice to meet you," Gerald said.

Her husband's ease irritated her. They ought to be making this harder for Teddy. They were uncomfortable, and he should be too. She didn't like to think that way, but in this case it was for the greater good of the family. He had to be made to know that they did not approve, and never would. Not that he had ever cared what they thought.

"Why don't you two have a seat in the living room while I put these in some water," she said. "Teddy, you lead the way."

She walked toward the kitchen, with Gerald close behind.

"What is she doing here?" she whispered.

"I don't have a clue."

Sadness consumed her. He hadn't come open to changing his mind. The decision had already been made.

"These are terrible," Evelyn said, looking at the carnations. "They're practically dead. Why would he bring me these?"

"Just put them on the table, they're fine," Gerald said.

"It's not the flowers," she said. "I should have known

something was up when he said he wanted to come here to celebrate your retirement. As if he'd ever think of anyone but himself."

"It's all right."

"No it isn't. He should have warned me she was coming."

"He probably knew you'd never agree to it."

"Well, that's true. I wouldn't have. I'm not sure I can do this."

"You can."

He called out, "Kids? Cocktails?"

"I'll have a whiskey sour," Teddy called back. "And a vodka tonic for the lady."

Gerald poured the drinks, and brought them into the other room. Evelyn cut the flowers short. She placed them in a low vase, pulling off a few dead petals. She began to cry, but closed her eyes tightly to ward off the tears. *None of that now.* She took a plate of cheese balls from the icebox and carried them into the living room, setting them on the coffee table. She placed the flowers on the hope chest in the corner. It was covered in framed photographs of her granddaughters: Melody's ballet recital, and June's school play. The two of them dressed up as mermaids for Halloween. Sitting under the Christmas tree in flannel nightgowns, a sea of silver wrapping paper all around. She hoped her son would look over and feel ashamed or heartsick with longing for his children, but he wasn't paying any attention.

"How was the flight?" Gerald asked.

"Great," Teddy said. "We got champagne and orange juice and this big, amazing breakfast—fruit cocktail, and pancakes and sausage patties and scrambled eggs. Air travel is so luxurious. I never want to get off the plane once I'm on it."

"Not me," Nicole said. "It's fun, I guess, but I get restless if I'm not moving around for long."

"Nicole's a big runner," Teddy said, taking her hand.

This gesture sent a chill through Evelyn. It felt as much a betrayal as if Gerald had just kissed another woman, open-mouthed, at the dinner table.

"Oh, I wouldn't say that," Nicole said. "I just enjoy a light jog at the end of the day. It relaxes me."

Their joined hands landed in her lap, until Teddy pulled his away and began massaging the back of her neck with his fingers. Evelyn felt her chest seize up at the sight of it. How could this be allowed? She expected someone to swoop in and stop him, but who, if not she herself?

"Look for her in the Olympics one day, Dad," Teddy said. He took a cheese ball and ate it in one bite.

"Don't get me started on the Olympics," Gerald said. "This summer was our worst gold-medal showing in the history of the games."

Evelyn had often marveled at how truly worked up her husband could become about sports. When the Red Sox lost some important game early in their marriage, Gerald had locked himself in his study and (though he would never admit it) cried for fifteen minutes. She could hear him in there, sniffling like a child. She enjoyed watching sports well enough, but could never manage to feel much about the outcome. It was only a game.

"But that was in part because of the judges," Teddy said. "Stripping two men of their medals for laughing and talking on the awards podium?"

"Well now, that was a disgrace," Gerald said. "They acted like a couple of hooligans."

"Oh, come off it. If they'd been white, no one would have blinked. The whole thing now is nothing but countries fighting over ideologies in the name of sport. It's a joke. I think we ought to spread the Olympics out. Have them in several countries at once, so they'll become a less obvious target for violence."

Gerald frowned. "I don't know about that."

A month earlier, eleven members of the Israeli Olympic team had been murdered by Arab terrorists in West Germany during the games. This tragedy put her in mind of so many private sorrows, the jumble of sad surprises that had been their early days together. The time they had all gone to Lake Placid, just before Nathaniel's accident, naively thinking that it was only the beginning. Young life, cut down so soon. And then, their family temporarily parted when Gerald went off to war. He was proud to enlist and fight, but he was old for a soldier by then. She spent useless hours working in her victory garden, wondering if God would be so cruel as to take one more love away from her, even though as far as she could tell, God didn't control things like that.

"The world's gone crazy," Nicole said. "Everything is falling apart."

"Once you live long enough, you'll see that the world has always been crazy," Gerald said. "It's always falling apart, but it never completely crumbles."

"Weebles wobble, but they don't fall down," Teddy said, and he and Nicole giggled. He was acting like a teenager, not a man with a wife and children who depended on him. Evelyn knew now for certain that allowing this lunch to go on had been a mistake. She and Gerald were enabling the whole absurd thing to continue, when they ought to be putting a stop to it.

"What happened was an atrocity," Gerald said. "Certainly not what the Germans had in mind. The whole purpose of the thing was to make the world forget those horrific Nazi Olympics in 1936. And now, well—who can think of anything else?"

"Germany didn't deserve the Olympics, if you ask me," Nicole chimed in.

Evelyn closed her eyes. She agreed, actually, but she disliked talking about unpleasant topics during social gatherings. Next, they'd be onto Vietnam, or Thomas Eagleton's shock treatments, when really they were here because her son had made a horrendous mistake. She needed to get him alone. Maybe she could ask Teddy to take a walk around the property after lunch, just the two of them. The sooner they finished eating, the sooner she'd have her chance.

"Why don't you two move into the dining room?" she said abruptly. "Gerald, would you please help me in the kitchen for a minute? I need you to slice the roast."

"Already?"

"Yes."

Gerald rose from his chair. "More cocktails?"

"Sure, why not," Nicole piped up.

Evelyn looked at their empty glasses and was surprised to see that they had downed them so quickly. She believed that everything was fine, in moderation. She had lived through Prohibition, and maybe it was just a function of her age at that time but she saw more people overdoing it with drink then than at any other point in her life. But something about this girl's freeness with the liquor bothered her. Was her son to be a drunk again now, on top of everything else?

In the kitchen, Gerald said, "She seems nice, at least."

Evelyn widened her eyes. "Have you lost your mind?"

"You're not giving her a chance."

"Why should I? She's the harlot who tore our lives apart, or have you forgotten?"

"Evie! Listen to yourself."

He smiled, and reached out his arms to embrace her in an attempt at a truce. But for once she could not bring herself to do it.

"I have to fix the salads," she said, turning her back on him. "I was expecting three, not four. I'll have to make them smaller now."

"I'll set an extra place," he said, kissing her cheek.

During the first course, Nicole commented on every object at the table: She loved the water goblets and the heavy silver and the plates. She adored the crystal chandelier.

When Evelyn carried the roast in and set it down, Nicole grabbed hold of her left hand.

"Oh my goodness, look at your diamond ring!" She turned to Teddy. "Ted, that is exquisite."

As if they were staring into a jewelry case at Tiffany's. As if Evelyn's hand, Evelyn herself, had no part in the matter.

"It was my mother's," Gerald said.

Evelyn took a slice of roast beef before passing the tray of meat to Nicole. Usually, she would wait until her guests were served, but suddenly she saw no point in propriety.

"It really is the most beautiful ring," Nicole said.

She was probably imagining that one day it would be hers. The thought made Evelyn want to run outside right now and toss the ring into the pond, just to make sure that this woman would never wear it, even for a second. Evelyn thought briefly of giving it to Julie anyway, divorce or not, though no doubt she would refuse it, even if Evelyn tried to persuade her to keep it for the girls.

"My best friend just got the biggest diamond from her boyfriend—well, I guess he's her fiancé now!" Nicole smiled. "Poor guy saved up forever for that ring. He would have proposed much sooner if she hadn't had such expensive taste."

Evelyn thought it was vulgar, the obsession with diamonds nowadays. When she was young, only people from families like Gerald's wore them. No one waited years to make a major life change, in want of a piece of jewelry.

Now Nicole spotted one more thing in the room to comment on.

"That painting of the dogs on a sailboat is precious," she said.

Evelyn put a forkful of meat into her mouth so she wouldn't be compelled to speak. She smiled through pursed lips. The dogs-on-a-sailboat painting had been a point of contention, especially when her husband insisted on hanging it in the dining room, directly across from an original Antonio Jacobsen that had been in the family since 1898.

"Evie hates it," Gerald said. "I won it in a sweepstakes. Second place. The first prize was an actual sailboat."

"No!" Nicole said, humoring him like he was a doddering old fool, though Gerald didn't seem to mind. "That seems like a pretty steep drop-off."

"That's how it goes," Gerald said. "I was once the first runner-up in a sweepstakes sponsored by Rolls-Royce. The winner got a Silver Cloud, with ten thousand dollars thrown in for a chauffeur. I got a case of motor oil."

Nicole laughed. "Oh no! Bad luck!"

"But even second runner-up is a miracle," he said. "It's almost impossible to win anything when there's a big corporate sponsor involved. You take Coca-Cola's Go America Sweepstakes. They get nine million entries a year."

"Competing for Coke?" Nicole asked.

"God no, the winner gets something in the range of twenty thousand dollars, plus a couple of cars, a motorboat, camping equipment . . ."

"All of which they have to pay income tax on," Teddy said. "Some poor housewife won it a few years ago, and ended up owing the IRS more than she could ever pay."

"Well, that would never happen to your father," Nicole said. "Clearly, he could afford the tax and then some."

Evelyn felt her body tense up. She wondered if Teddy

would destroy their family, only to be taken in by a gold digger. Back in her teaching days, she most liked the scrappy boys who were dreamers and wanted something grand out of life. Her own son was happy to live off Gerald's hard-earned money and the family name.

They said you couldn't take it with you, and of course that was true. Evelyn didn't want to. But she had hoped to pass everything on to their granddaughters, and to Julie. She would be damned if it went to these two, who didn't even know right from wrong.

Nicole went on. "So what do you have to do to win one of these things? What skills does a person need?"

"No special skill. What you're talking about is a contest," Gerald said, happy as a clam with his captive audience. Her husband loved conversation, and attention even more so. She felt like he was betraying her, treating this like just another dinner party with some young couple who'd moved in down the road.

"That's really a very different thing," he continued. "A sweepstakes is determined by chance. A contest requires some talent, like maybe writing a jingle. Those have faded out of fashion a bit. I used to subscribe to *Contest Worksheet* magazine to help me with my writing, but that particular publication has changed with the times. Now it just basically lists all the sweepstakes that are out there."

Evelyn cringed, thinking of his twenty-five-word essays on cake mix, and all the failed jingles he had thought up. Even years after it was rejected, Gerald still walked around the house proudly singing, *I'm so tired! So happy to be tired! And if you really must kn-o-o-o-w, it's thanks to Goodyear Tire and Rubber Co.!*

"Isn't it really just a socially acceptable form of gambling?" Nicole asked.

"I wouldn't say so, no," Gerald said. "There's never any

purchase necessary. It's strictly aboveboard. If anything, it's just advertising. Say Skippy peanut butter runs a contest—" They had, with the top prize being a four-week world tour for two by jet. He hadn't won. "Well, they get to set up displays in every grocery store. You've got to go there to get the entry forms, you see. And since you're standing in front of this giant display, maybe you'll just go ahead and grab a jar of Skippy while you're at it."

"And do you?" Nicole asked.

"Do I what?"

"Buy the Skippy."

In truth, her husband had never set foot in a grocery store. He asked Evelyn to pick up the entry forms while she was there, or just sent his secretary to do it.

She had once forced him to turn down a prize. It was a contest sponsored by a dog food company, and Gerald won a Scottie dog, which they were supposed to pick up in Edinburgh, all expenses paid. When Evelyn pointed out that he had never once expressed interest in having a dog, he acted as deflated as a child might be by her decision; he moped around for days, telling tales of the sweet Scottie his great-grandmother had had when he was a boy.

This was what she disliked most about Gerald's hobby; the contests made you think you needed something that, left to your own devices, you wouldn't even want.

"Have you caught any of the new *Price Is Right* on television?" Gerald asked now. "You guess the prices on everyday items, like appliances and canned corn. I think I'd be quite good at it. Sometimes I quiz myself with whatever I find in the kitchen cabinets. I'm studying up!"

Evelyn buried her head in her hands, picturing Gerald on daytime TV.

"I won't do it, Evie. Don't worry."

He turned to Nicole. "My wife's the serious type. A

really smart, quality person. Doomed to go through life with a goofball for a husband."

Evelyn rolled her eyes. "Don't be dramatic. I'm not that serious."

Gerald raised a finger in the air. "Notice she didn't say I'm not a goofball."

"How did you two meet?" Nicole asked.

"In college," Evelyn said in a clipped tone. She would happily tell the longer story to many people, but Nicole was not one of them.

Nicole made a sad face and nodded, causing Evelyn to wonder if Teddy had already told her.

"How about you?" Gerald asked, perhaps forgetting to whom he was speaking.

Evelyn sent him a withering look, and he seemed to realize that he had gone too far. But it was too late. She held her breath.

"We met at a bar," Nicole said happily. "At the hotel he was staying in for business. An old girlfriend of mine was staying there too, and I met her for a drink. This guy at the next table caught my eye because in the midst of a crowded bar, he was reading that boring travel magazine—you know, the one with the yellow cover and all the pictures of naked women in Africa. So I leaned over and said, 'Excuse me, but I think my grandfather is the only other man I've ever seen reading that in public.'"

Evelyn squeezed the top of her thigh until it hurt. The next day there would be a bruise the color of a plum. She remembered last Christmas, when Julie was trying to think up an idea for a present for him. Evelyn told her she planned to get Gerald a subscription to *National Geographic*, and why didn't Julie do the same for Teddy? Perhaps it would inspire their men to take them on a trip around the world.

She hated the fact that in life you could only connect the

pieces after they'd been put in motion. If she hadn't suggested the magazine, perhaps Nicole never would have noticed him.

Nicole went on. "The three of us got to talking. And eventually"—this she said with a knowing laugh—"my friend finally got a clue and made her exit. And then it was just the two of us."

Evelyn pictured them in some dim, smoky lounge, music playing in the background, flirting and laughing and drinking, as fifteen hundred miles away Julie fixed dinner for the children and helped them finish their homework and tucked them into bed. How afterward, before turning in for the night, she had tried to call Teddy at the hotel and been told that there was no answer in his room.

"I showed him the beach, and we took a long walk," Nicole went on.

"Do you live quite close to the beach?" Gerald asked wearily, and Evelyn could see that he was struggling now. It had been too much, even for him.

"It's just a few minutes from our apartment," she said. "You'll have to come for a visit soon."

So they were living together. Evelyn didn't know why she should be surprised, but she was. Teddy had never said where he lived, and she had simply hoped for the best. In recent years, on a few occasions, she had run into an unmarried former student of hers, with a boyfriend or girlfriend she didn't know. And though none of them would be so rude as to say it out loud, over the course of the conversation she would come to understand that these unmarried children shared a bed and a home, something that gave her a start every time. She had been so relieved when Teddy and Julie had the good sense to wait until after they were married, but now she supposed that the good sense had been Julie's alone.

"Excuse me," Evelyn said softly, as she rose from her chair. She walked off without waiting for a response, down the hallway, through the kitchen, and straight out into the backyard.

She could hear footsteps behind her, and assumed they belonged to Gerald. But when she looked back, Teddy stood there, his arms crossed.

"Are you okay?" he asked.

She could feel angry tears forming in her eyes. "No, I'm not okay," she said. "How could you do this, Teddy? What were you thinking?"

He actually looked surprised. It floored her.

"Look, I didn't go to Florida expecting to fall in love. It just happened," he said. "What could I do about it?"

She closed her eyes tightly and without opening them said, "You could have walked away. You could have come home to your wife. You never should have let yourself be in that position in the first place."

"I know that," he said, his tone a bit more gentle than before. "But now that it's happened——"

"It isn't too late," she said. "Truly. I know Julie has it in her heart to forgive you. And the girls need their father back. Please."

"Mom," he said, giving her a pitying smile. "Nicole and I are in it for the long haul. I'm going to ask her to marry me."

Evelyn stiffened. "That girl is . . . she's——"

"Oh, don't be a snob," he said. "You don't know how hard it is for a normal person to walk in on all this."

As if he were a man of the people. He was the only one in the family who had never held down a real job.

"Julie gave you everything," she said. "She gave you your children."

"I never even wanted kids," he said. "I'm sorry if that sounds harsh, but it's true. No one asked me. You get married and suddenly there are all these expectations, and you're just supposed to accept them. Now I have another chance. We want to travel, go have adventures."

She turned and walked away from him, toward the pond. She could hear his boots crunching in the leaves, and she quickened her pace.

"Go back inside," she shouted. "Just get away from me. You've lost your mind."

He grabbed her elbow, and twisted her around so she was facing him once again.

He looked so much like Gerald had at that age. Once, Evelyn had imagined that Julie would be to Teddy what she herself had been to Gerald—she would bring out the best parts, and file away the ragged, childish edges. But now she saw that even back when Gerald was a young goofball, as he put it, he still had goodness at his core. Teddy was nothing like him, really.

"You made a vow," she said. "'Til death do you part. You can't turn your back on that."

"Times are changing. Vows like that made a lot more sense when the average life expectancy was thirty-five." He smiled. He was trying to make a joke.

"Julie and I had problems even before Florida. She's a very judgmental person, if you want to know the truth."

"What sort of problems?"

"I got in a little over my head with gambling. Nothing I couldn't get my way out of. But she made such a thing of it."

Evelyn thought of the money he had borrowed from Gerald just before he left. A new business venture, he had said.

"Nothing your father couldn't get you out of, you mean," she said. "Oh Teddy, will you ever grow up?"

"I'm grown, Mother."

She knew it was the awful truth, yet still she said firmly, "You're not getting a divorce," like he was seven again and she was telling him why he must never steal candy from the store.

"Yes I am," he said. "I met with my lawyer this morning and we've set the court date. It's done."

Evelyn felt the wind knocked out of her chest. "I see."

"I'm sorry to disappoint you," he said.

"Are you?"

"Yes! I married Julie in the first place because I knew she was exactly the girl you'd want me to be with."

"Oh, come off it."

"It's true. You don't think I realized how much you loved her? She's the second coming of you. Look, she's a great person, but it was never right between us. Nicole is my other half. She might not be as pure and perfect as Julie, but neither am I. That's what I'm trying to tell you."

"You are doing something so deeply wrong," she said. "If you go through with this, I swear, you will never have peace in your life."

"Sorry, but I don't buy that."

"Julie is devastated. Do you understand?"

"You love her more than you love me," he said. "Admit it."

"Fine. I love her more than I love you."

As soon as Evelyn said it, she felt regret. Not because she hadn't meant what she said, but because she had. If she could choose only one of them, it would be Julie. But Julie didn't want to be chosen, not by her, not after everything Teddy had done.

"We're leaving," he said. He began to walk back toward the house.

"I think that's for the best," she said, standing in place, watching him go.

2012

Ava, May, and Olivia were having their hair done at a salon called Gabriella's. Mona and Kate waited their turn in a pair of plastic chairs in the middle of the room. They were well into their second hour of pampering, having already gotten manicures. May had arranged the entire thing. When she'd asked Kate if she knew of any good places in the area, Kate had drawn a blank. She hadn't gotten a manicure since her senior prom. So May looked online, and found this country beauty parlor, where Frank Sinatra played over the loudspeaker and a big-haired woman and her two daughters worked side by side, their high heels clicking on the yellow linoleum. One of the daughters, Lulu, was six months pregnant. Kate felt bad making her stay on her feet all afternoon, but Lulu said she felt fine.

Kate watched Ava, swimming in a robe that was about seven sizes too big, in a chair that left her shoes dangling three feet from the ground. Her daughter was in heaven, as Gabriella twisted what little hair she had into a braid. No one but Kate had ever cut Ava's hair. The first time she trimmed it she had cried, watching the brown wisps fall to the floor.

"Ready for more spray?" Gabriella asked.

"Yes please," Ava said, in a tone that made it seem like she was getting away with something, like the woman had just asked if she'd like a can of whipped cream pumped directly into her mouth.

Kate closed her eyes and tried to pretend this wasn't happening.

Since their arrival at the salon, the lone topic worth discussing was weddings. The five of them were the only customers in the place, and the mirrored room had become like a repository of all things matrimonial.

It started when they walked in the door and Gabriella's second daughter, the oddly named Rue, asked, "What's the occasion?"

"It's our cousin's wedding," May said quickly.

"Wow! They sure did get a gorgeous day for it. Must be meant to be!"

"I'm the flower girl," Ava said proudly.

"The flower girl? Well then, we'd better do something extra special for you."

Kate took note of the jealousy on her niece's face. She felt a bit bad for Olivia.

Now Lulu said, "So how did the happy couple meet? I met my husband on Match.com. Do you know one out of every five married couples meets online these days? I tried eHarmony too, but on that one I just met a lot of strange Christian men who still lived with their mothers."

"Lulu!" Gabriella said. "I'm sorry. She never knows when to stop talking."

"Well, it's true. Match worked better for me. I had the boys winking at me from dawn 'til dusk! That's what they call it, *winking*. You basically click a button and it tells someone you've winked. I never responded to any of those. A monkey can press a button. A real man takes the time to write you an email if he's interested, which my Robby did. A really sweet, funny one, but not too over the top. It's the worst when they just jump right in and start telling you their life stories. We got married six months after we met. It's my second marriage, which frankly I think usually turns out better than the first." She raised a hand up. "Maybe I shouldn't say that if you ladies are still with your O-Hs."

"O-Hs?" Kate said.

"Original Husbands."

Kate opened her mouth to respond, but May said, "We are, but you know, in general I think you're right. Our father, for instance, is much better off with frumpy old Jean than he ever was with Mom. No offense, Mom."

Mona shrugged. "None taken."

Was Jean frumpy? Kate had never thought so.

"There were no kids in my first marriage, thank God," Lulu said. "I was twenty-three and it only lasted a year. They call it a starter marriage. They're very in these days. Really, I think the Internet is the best thing to ever happen to single girls. Of course it's not as good for married people, what with all the porn and the Facebook affairs. I know more women than you can shake a stick at whose husbands got a friend request from an old high school girlfriend and the next thing you know, the guy's on a business trip and then he's asking for a divorce." She said "business trip" in finger quotes. "If you think about it, this is probably the first time in history that the individuals in a couple each have a private world that their spouse knows nothing about. Everyone has a cell phone, an email account. It's easier than ever to cheat."

Kate thought it was an interesting observation, but Gabriella looked troubled by her daughter's ramblings.

"So why didn't the bride come along with you?" she asked, changing the subject. "Who's doing her hair?"

"No bride," Kate said. "Two grooms."

"Ahh," Gabriella said, taking this in. She seemed to be searching for words, and eventually landed on, "Where did they register?"

"Crate & Barrel, and Sur La Table," May said. "They have great taste. Their page on the Knot is just beyond."

Kate hadn't seen it, but she remembered the night, a few years back, when her college friend Caroline had called her, breathless.

I just stumbled across Evan's Knot.com registry, she said.

Evan had been Caroline's boyfriend at UVM, six years earlier.

This cow he's marrying asked for Spode. What is she, a hundred years old? And oh my God, zebra-print sheets. Are they putting together a house or a brothel?

Now May said, "I got married at twenty-six. None of my friends had any money yet. I got the worst gifts."

"May!" Mona said. "You sound awful, talking that way."

"Well, it's true! If you only knew how much I've shelled out for people smart enough to wait and get married in their thirties. I just bought Liz a KitchenAid mixer, for goodness' sake. And the bach parties now!"

"Please don't say *bach*, it activates my gag reflex," Kate said.

"Fine. *Bachelorette* parties," May said. "Marlena's seven bridesmaids took her to Turks and Caicos for a week! I got one night in the Poconos."

"If these people want to be married so bad, why do they need all that hoopla?" Kate said. "Shouldn't we save the presents and the trips for when our friends really need them? Like, say, someone just lost her job or her dog died."

May stared at her in disbelief, saying nothing.

"That's another thing about second marriages," Lulu said. "The weddings are just better. The first time around you have to do what everybody else wants. The second time, they've given up on you, so it's all yours."

Rue's cell phone vibrated on the counter in front of her station. "Do you mind if I get this?" she asked May, and then scurried outside through the screen door before she could respond.

"I'm so sorry," Gabriella said. "That was incredibly unprofessional."

"It's no problem," May said, but Kate could tell that she was thinking that something like that would never happen at the trendy salon she went to in New Jersey.

Lulu pointed in the direction her sister had gone. "Now that one's a sad case," she whispered loudly. "She fell in love with a murderer. She saw his story on the news and felt bad for him, so she wrote him a letter and he wrote back, and a year later, they're getting married. Only he isn't allowed to be at the wedding, so our cousin has to stand in for him at the courthouse. She just ran out there to answer her one call of the day. It's pathetic."

"Enough!" Gabriella said.

"They've never touched!" Lulu said fast, as if she needed to get out this one last pearl of information or she'd burst.

"Lulu!" Gabriella said.

Kate wanted to hear more. How odd. How fascinating.

May seemed to think it was only fair to give them a family secret in return. "My sister over here was supposed to bring the diamond rings to the ceremony tonight, and she's already managed to lose one."

The women gasped.

"No," Lulu said, putting her hands to her face.

"Thanks a lot," Kate said to May.

"I'm sure it will turn up," Gabriella said.

They went silent. Kate thumbed through a magazine, landing on an ad for diamond rings almost immediately.

The universe is playing a cruel, cruel trick on me, she thought.

The ad featured a leggy model in a tight black dress, beside the words

YOUR LEFT HAND SEES RED AND
THINKS ROSES. YOUR RIGHT HAND
SEES RED AND THINKS WINE. YOUR
LEFT HAND BELIEVES IN SHINING
ARMOR. YOUR RIGHT HAND THINKS
KNIGHTS ARE FOR FAIRY TALES.
YOUR LEFT HAND SAYS, "I LOVE
YOU." YOUR RIGHT HAND SAYS,
"I LOVE ME, TOO." WOMEN OF THE
WORLD, RAISE YOUR RIGHT HAND.
THE DIAMOND RIGHT HAND RING. VIEW MORE AT
ADIAMONDISFOREVER.COM

"Bleh," Kate said, closing the magazine. "Right-hand rings? So now we're supposed to think it's empowering to buy ourselves diamonds?"

"Ooh, yes," Lulu said. "That's been trendy for a while now. Of course, we still want them from our men too, am I right?"

She glanced at Kate's hand, then quickly looked away.

May said, "My sister is the last person on earth you'd want to take diamond shopping. Believe me, I speak from experience."

They had gone to look at engagement rings for May when she and Josh were dating. At twenty-two, Kate had been with her college boyfriend, Todd, for three years; May and Josh had been together only nine months. But May reminded her that she was four years older, and ready for marriage. She arrived at the jeweler's with photos in hand. Kate watched as her sister declared her wishes to the old man on the other side of the counter: "A one- to one-and-a-half-carat round diamond, ideal or at least very good cut, very few inclusions—VVS1 in a perfect world, though VS1 would be all right. And a platinum band, with maybe just a few stones running across the top. Our budget is eight thousand dollars, ten thousand max. I really don't want him spending any more than that."

Kate stared at her sister as if some alien life force had taken over her body. This was May, whose most expensive piece of jewelry was a tiny gold pendant she had received as a graduation gift. May, who bought all her clothes at Banana Republic. It was unsettling to see this hidden part of her suddenly revealed. Did most women act this way? The man behind the counter didn't seem at all fazed, in fact he seemed pleased.

"I'll see what we can do," he said. "I'll pull a few stones to show you."

He went into a back room, and they stood waiting in front of a long glass case in which hundreds of bands sat, perched on their stands, each with a gaping hole like the mouth of a child who is missing just one tooth—each waiting to be filled by a diamond. Kate had imagined that the rings would already be assembled. The whole thing seemed so impersonal.

"This reminds me of that make-your-own-pizza place in the mall," she said.

May wasn't paying attention. She gazed into the case as if her newborn baby lay on the other side of the glass.

The man returned with four small envelopes. He shook out the loose stones, and lined up a few different bands on the counter. May tried them all, asking Kate each time what she thought. Her answers ranged from *Mmm-hmm* to *Good*.

"Do you want to try one on?" May asked her.

"Me? Oh, no thanks."

"She thinks she doesn't want a diamond," May said to the man, who looked at Kate like he had just heard that she didn't want to go on living. Her whole life she had been awkward in stores. Her mother and sister made up for it by speaking to sales clerks about her as if she weren't standing right there. *(She thinks she looks bad in a bathing suit. She thinks there's something wrong with patent leather . . .)*

May turned her attention back to herself. "I do like the etchings on this band, but the hearts seem a bit much. And would a one-carat stone be too big for the setting?"

"Those are all made by hand by a pair of brothers in Cincinnati," he said. "The metal is very malleable. They could easily file those hearts right off and melt the prongs into a better shape."

May nodded. "Oh, great."

After two of the longest hours Kate had ever spent, May made her final decision. The man wrote everything down on a piece of paper and filed it under her name, with the understanding that she would then tell Josh to come in here and speak to Hank when he was ready.

"Is this really how it's done?" Kate blurted out.

"To tell you the truth," he said softly, "about half the time the man comes in alone and just picks something. I much prefer the way you girls are doing it—if you come in with your mother or a friend and decide for yourself, you end up with what you want. It's a more modern, empowered approach."

"A woman's right to choose!" Kate said.

"Exactly," the man replied.

Her sister shot her a look.

In the car, May said, "Why did you even come with me if you were going to act like that?"

"Like what?"

"You know what I mean."

"I just wasn't prepared for the intensity," Kate said. "You'd think you were making the biggest decision of your life when all you're really doing is buying a piece of jewelry."

"The ring you choose is a huge decision," May said. "The shape alone says so much about you."

"Such as?"

"Well, for example, a cushion cut says you're old-fashioned. Whereas a round stone says you're classic, yet up on the trends."

"How do you know this?"

"It's just known. I have friends who really regret choosing the wrong ring, or letting themselves get pressured into going with a ring that wasn't good enough. It's very rare to find anyone who's absolutely certain that she chose the right ring."

"I think if you replace the word 'ring' with the word 'man' in what you just said, then maybe we'll be getting somewhere."

"It's a big deal, okay? It symbolizes something important."

"Yeah, consumerism at its finest. Look, I just didn't know you'd been secretly obsessed with diamonds for the past decade, that's all."

"Knowing what you want doesn't equal obsession," May said. "Don't be so dramatic."

"Do you even know why you want it?" Kate asked.

"Yes. Because it's beautiful."

"And that's enough of a reason to—"

"To what?" May said, defiant, daring her to go on.

Kate's mood had turned dark. Really, she thought she deserved some credit for getting this far without even mentioning the obvious. But now she let loose.

"To be complicit in the rapes and murders of innocent Africans by brutal regimes so that you can wear a shiny, pretty thing for the rest of your life."

"You are such a killjoy," May said, slapping the steering

wheel for emphasis. "I should have brought Kim or Mom, or just come by myself."

"Well, why did you ask me to come, anyway?"

"Mom thought if I invited you, maybe you'd get inspired and change your mind about wanting to get married."

"Oh, Jesus Christ."

They had planned to get dinner, but instead May dropped her at the PATH train without saying goodbye.

May and Josh's wedding the following year included a blues band from Memphis, a champagne fountain, and (alongside the three-tiered cake) an ice cream sundae bar. The ice cream was served in tiny plastic baseball helmets: half of them were Marlins, to honor Josh's family in Florida, and half of them were Mets. May hired a planner named Debra, whose only job seemed to be reminding her that this was *the most important day of her life,* every time May started worrying about the expense. Although the event cost over forty thousand dollars, May kept telling everyone that the theme was "fun and low key!" She gave her bridesmaids sparkly pink zip-up sweatshirts that said I'M WITH MRS. ROSEN on the back. At the end of the night, everyone got a can of Bud Light in a Styrofoam coozie printed with the words MAY AND JOSH, SEPTEMBER 30, 2000: TO HAVE AND TO HOLD AND TO KEEP YOUR BEER COLD!

From then on, whenever Kate caught sight of her sister's diamond ring, she felt uneasy. She hated that it was supposed to symbolize love and perfection, an idea that seemed so removed from the nature of marriage itself, which even at its best was messy and mundane. She resented the whole notion that a relationship was perfect just because two people got married. When May and Josh were dating, Kate and May would discuss things between them all the time. May told her about every doubt and fear, about the time she caught Josh on the phone with his ex, and the fact that she thought he was lazy, unambitious. But those issues were never spoken of again after they got engaged, the ring and the wedding a form of hush money.

Now Kate shifted in her plastic chair. She wished they could leave the salon and go home, but she realized there was still probably an hour to go. She flipped through another magazine just for something to do.

As she came to the last page, a text message from Jeffrey arrived: *I don't think I can do this.*

He had been so calm a couple hours earlier, but Kate wasn't surprised. The moment of doubt seemed to be an inevitable part of the journey, as much as deciding what the cake ought to look like, or debating whether to go with a DJ or a band. And the doubter usually called her. Kate liked to think it was because she was a good listener, but she knew that most of the time it came down to the fact that she represented another path—the only one who didn't get married, and never would. The doubting party could say anything to her and know she wouldn't be in the least bit offended.

The men were golfing at the Fairmount. She had never known Jeff or Toby to golf, but they were wedding people now, and wedding people golfed, as sure as they registered and dieted and had second thoughts.

I'll come get you, she wrote back.

"I need to go," she told May, who was having her hair twisted into a chignon by Rue, who had since returned from her phone call.

"What?" May said. "Why?"

"Jeffrey's having cold feet."

"Ahh," said May. She had been maid of honor five times, and knew the drill. "But what about your hair?"

Kate had tried to explain to them weeks ago that she didn't need her hair done. Rather than repeat herself now, she just said, "My hair's not going to matter much if we're down one groom."

"He'll be fine," May said. "It's normal."

"I know. But still, I should go. Can you get Ava home safe?"

"Of course."

"You stay with Auntie May and Grandma, all right?" Kate asked.

"Yup," Ava said, like she did this every day.

Kate thought of how carefully she and Dan had worked at cultivating a certain kind of life for their daughter, and she was only three: fresh country air, organic fruits and vegetables, Montessori school next year, which she still didn't know how they'd pay for, and gender-neutral toys that made it clear that a girl could do anything. Yet Ava had never been so abundantly happy as she was right now, with her hot pink nails and her hairspray.

Kate shook her head and laughed as she made her way out to the car. She would worry about it another day.

When she pulled through the main gates of the Fairmount twenty minutes later, Toby stood out in front of the doors. She drove up to him and rolled down the passenger-side window.

"Thanks for coming," he said.

"Was that you who texted me?" she said. "I thought it was Jeff."

"It was me," he said. "I was trying to text you fast, so no one would notice, and I accidentally grabbed the wrong iPhone."

"Oh. Are they still golfing?"

"Yeah."

"What did you tell them when you left?"

"I said I'd just heard from the florist and there was a crisis with the cherry blossoms."

"Sounds feasible. Well, come on. Get in."

He climbed in beside her, and she smiled. Her cousin Jeff had met Toby ten years ago, right around the time that Kate got dumped by Todd. Jeff and Toby were in the process of falling in love, which under normal conditions involved selfishness, isolation, the sensation that there is no one on earth but just you two. But because she was hurting, they checked in on her all the time. They took her out for dinner on Saturday nights so she wouldn't be home alone. They set her up on dates, their only criteria being that the guy in question was straight and single. Most of the setups were colossal failures, but still she appreciated the gesture.

After four years, she met Dan, and the four of them double-dated their way through New York City. When they decided to move upstate, one of her biggest reservations was being away from Toby and Jeff. But the guys came and visited every couple of months. They came for birthdays, and the Fourth of July, and summertime picnics in the mountains. After a decade, Toby was as precious to her as Jeff was.

"I know just the place," she said.

The bar was an old log cabin dropped on the side of a country road. If you were driving fast enough, you'd never even notice it. Kate and Dan had gone there for a beer the day they drove out to see what would be their house for the first time. The bar had been nearly empty then, as it was now, besides the bartender and a couple of local guys sitting in the corner by a neon orange Bud Light sign in the shape of a cowboy hat, underscored with a neon George Strait signature. It was generally assumed that old-timers like them hated yuppies like her, who were taking over the valley.

"Two whiskeys," she told the bartender. She turned to Toby. His eyes were blurry with tears. "Honey, what's up?"

"My mother's not coming after all."

"What?"

"We knew this might happen, it's fine. She told me a few days ago that she was praying on it, and she wasn't sure it would be right for her to condone an act that she thinks will get me sent to hell. I talked to her last night, and she was going to come. But then we heard from her just after her flight should have left this morning, and she said she couldn't bring herself to get on the plane."

"I'm so sorry," Kate said.

"It's not that, really," he said. "To be honest, it will be easier without her."

"Then what's wrong?"

He spoke softly and slowly, which was entirely unlike him. "How do I say this? Okay. Well, when I first moved to New York in the late eighties, whenever someone died of AIDS, the *Times* would say he was survived by his longtime companion so-and-so. Never his husband or his partner, just 'his longtime companion.' I remember talking about that with Jeff once, not long after we met. It pissed him off. He thought it diminished reality, and they should say something more meaningful, like partner or boyfriend. Whereas I just couldn't believe that it was okay with everyone. That even if they were using euphemisms, they were admitting it right there in the newspaper and the world didn't end."

"Okay," she said.

The drinks arrived and they each took a sip.

"As a kid, I thought I was sick, and I would never be normal. I looked at my parents, my grandparents, my aunts and uncles. In high school, I saw people starting to pair off, and I knew I would be alone forever. Alone until I died, and then straight to hell. In New York, hell is a concept. Where I grew up, it's a real place. Hell with a capital H, like a state, like Connecticut. I used to lie in my bed and think about that. Sometimes I even thought of committing suicide. Kids teased me mercilessly, sensing I was different, I guess."

Kate put her arm around him.

"Our pastor was a man obsessed. Thinking back on it now, I'm pretty sure he was closeted. But he'd stand there in the pulpit and—forget war or crime or hunger or poverty—according to him, the worst thing on this earth was homosexuality. He'd talk about how all it was was the devil trying to tempt men into abhorrent behavior, wanting us to sin. He said anyone could be afflicted by these feelings, but you had to fight them off. For him, it seemed like the whole Bible came down to Sodom and Gomorrah: God hated gays, and destroyed entire cities to prove it. My father would become so enraged every time the topic came up. You'd think that the walls of our house were crawling with homos, he talked so much about it. I always thought it was funny, considering that he didn't actually know any gay men. But then I realized—he suspected me all along. He used to hit me with a belt when I was really young, and of course I'd cry. What kid wouldn't? He'd keep on hitting me until I stopped. He said it was the only way to make sure I didn't turn out a sissy."

"Jesus. What would your mother do?"

"Sometimes she'd cry herself and tell him to stop. But more often she just ignored it. Now, you have to realize that back then, I wasn't the Toby you know and love. I was a good Christian boy, and I wanted to please my parents so bad, so I hated gays too. I thought they deserved to die, even though I knew on some level that I was one. Then when I was fifteen, these two guys in town were arrested for having sex in a car one night. By the next morning, everyone knew. One of them was just passing through, but the other was the son of the local dentist, a guy who went to church with my parents. The kid was twenty years old, and they shipped him off to some reprogramming institute in Florida to fix him. He came back a year later, married some poor girl, and they had two kids."

"Holy shit," Kate said. He had never told her any of this, and neither had her cousin. "Does Jeff know all this?"

Toby nodded. "When that guy got sent away, my father really went into a tailspin. On my sixteenth birthday, he tells me he's taking me into the city for a steak dinner. I worshipped my father. So, even at sixteen years old when I probably should have thought of him as a total loser, I was so proud to have this special attention, you know?"

Kate nodded, downing her drink. She gestured to the bartender for two more. The guy was watching *Cheers* on a TV that hung overhead, which struck her as funny. She thought of pointing this out to Toby, but instead she just said, "Go on."

"I get all dressed up, and my dad takes me to this steakhouse. He ordered so much liquor—bourbon and tequila and shots of vodka, we drank it all. This was back when the legal drinking age was eighteen. I could pass, but it was still so forbidden. Out drinking with my dad! The whole time I'm thinking, *Wow, the old man finally sees me as his equal.* Toward the end of the meal, he starts in with *faggots* this and *faggots* that. I remember he said that queers should be shot on sight. I didn't think much of it, because that was my dad. After we left the restaurant, I headed for the car. But my dad said, 'No, no, we're going this way.' I had no idea where he was taking me. I could barely see straight. But I didn't put up a fight. We walked maybe fifteen, twenty blocks, until we came to this run-down apartment complex. My dad buzzes one of the units and the door opens, and he says to me, 'I'll be right back.' A few minutes later, he comes out and says, 'She's all paid for. I'll wait here.'"

Kate felt her stomach fall to the floor, like she was riding a roller-coaster, soaring free-fall down the highest hill. "Your dad ordered you a prostitute?"

He nodded.

"What did you do?"

"I was terrified. I think I was crying. I had never even kissed anyone before, and the whole thing was so confusing. Sex before marriage was a sin, too, after all. The woman was probably in her late thirties, and the look on her face when I came in was just pure shock. I'm wondering how my dad even knows this person, and she's probably wondering why the hell he sent me. Or maybe she knew."

"Did you have sex with her?" Kate said.

He nodded. "I was afraid of what would happen if I didn't. Then my father and I drove home and neither of us said a word. We never mentioned it again."

"And this was supposed to turn you straight?" she asked.

He laughed in disbelief. "Apparently. After that, I went to a Christian college for a couple years, as you know, and I dated a few girls, never for longer than a month or so. I made a point of bringing them home after just a few dates, as a way to show my parents that I was normal. But mostly, I was alone. I was the loneliest person alive. I moved to New York at nineteen, and it saved me. I really don't think that's an exaggeration. New York saved me. Oh Lord, I was so annoying. I was the full clichéd package—sleeping around, dancing all night in the gay clubs, wearing these skintight t-shirts. Letting loose in the candy store, as they used to say. It was an exaggeration, but the reason for it was that the real me had been pushed down, suffocated, for all that time. Suddenly, he was free. I've always felt that I've had two lives—before New York, and after. Two separate Tobys. But I haven't recovered from before, that's what I'm realizing now."

"I'm not sure we ever recover from our childhoods," Kate said. "We just respond to them."

"I kept telling Jeff I didn't want a big wedding, but you know how carried away he gets. And it's his day, too. I wanted him to have it. But all of this, it's almost too good. When I see those bigots on TV talking about how same-sex marriage is just a slippery slope to polygamy, or it's bad for kids, or whatever, I have the same response I used to have when the *Times* would write about the *longtime companions*. I just can't believe they're even talking about same-sex marriage on TV. That's progress!"

"Yes!" she said. "So what's the problem then, love? Isn't this all good stuff?"

"Yes. But. It's been a long time since I went to church and I really thought I was over it. But there's still this faint voice in my head saying that what I'm doing is wrong. Of course, I knew my father wouldn't be here today. And I'd prepared for the possibility that my mother wouldn't either. But somehow, getting that call from her earlier, it hit me in a different way. It mattered to me, more than I wanted to admit. There's been so much progress, but if we went to my hometown in Alabama today and walked around holding hands, we'd be killed. Can we ever really be married when so many people don't believe in it? There's this self-loathing part of me that hears people defending traditional marriage and almost agrees with them. I can't tell Jeff that because he'd just tell me I was being insane, and I know that I am, but how does that help me?"

"Toby. Today I met a woman who married a man in prison. They've never touched. He couldn't even be present at the wedding. Are you telling me that's traditional, because he has a penis and she has a vagina? More real than what you two have?"

He laughed from his belly, a deep, surprised, joyful sound that she loved. "Where the hell have you been hanging out?"

"The beauty parlor."

"Ahh. I should have known." He shook his head. "Thanks for meeting me. I feel a little better, just getting it out there."

"Of course."

"Jeff's been so obsessed with making today perfect. But when you envision the perfect flowers and the perfect food and the perfect outdoor space and the perfect weather, you forget that you can't rent the perfect family to go along with it. You're stuck with the shitty old one you've already got."

Kate took his hand. "I'm your family too, you know. And I'm letting my daughter dress up like a princess, just this once, even though it makes me want to vomit. And I have both May and Mona staying at my house for two nights. That's how much I love you."

He smiled. "I appreciate that, I do."

She could feel the whiskey dulling the hard edges of her thoughts. She had an idea, which she knew was probably a bad one, but she went with it anyway.

"Do you want me to tell you something that will take your mind off what you're thinking about?" she said.

"Yes please."

"Okay, but realize that I'm only telling you because there's no way you'll be able to think about anything else once I say this."

"Sounds juicy. Go on."

"I lost one of your wedding rings."

His eyes widened. "Of all the things I imagined you might say just then, that was definitely not one of them. You get an A plus for the element of surprise, I'll give you that. You do realize Jeff is gonna have you killed."

She felt so grateful that he was smiling. "You're not mad?"

"Nah. It will turn up, right? Have you checked your coat pocket? Did you secretly try it on or something and then forget?"

"Ha. No. I had both rings in their boxes, in the bag from the jeweler, sitting in my kitchen. When I went to check this morning, one of the boxes was gone."

"Did you dust for prints?"

"No, but I do have my suspicions."

"Olivia, right?"

"Exactly."

"I told Jeff we should have May's kids in the wedding if we were having Ava. Just to be fair. But, you know—May. He didn't want to deal with her."

"I understand completely. Are you sure you're not mad at me?"

"The rings mean a lot to Jeff," he said. "Me, not so much. I wanted to just get something on Blue Nile and be done with it."

"What's Blue Nile?"

"This website where you can buy diamonds at a deep discount. Truth be told, I didn't want to wear a diamond at all."

"Good for you."

"Not for any humane reason, just because I think they're tacky."

She laughed. "Oh."

"There's nothing special about them. Every woman at Denny's wears one."

"When's the last time you went to Denny's?"

He grinned. "Or wherever. And anyway, we're men. I've never heard of a man wearing a diamond ring. But Jeff says it's trendy. He says in five years every guy will want one."

"Hmm."

"You can get conflict-free diamonds now, you know," he said. "There are mines in Canada. The diamonds come laser printed with a microscopic polar bear or a maple leaf, or something."

"Yeah, but I've heard that even some of the Canadian mines are owned by De Beers," she said.

"Oh. Well, there are man-made diamonds, too. They make them in an oven with microwaves. There's even a company that can somehow create a diamond from a dead person's cremated ashes."

"That's the creepiest thing I have ever heard."

"I know! Jeff really had his heart set on us designing our own rings, so ultimately that's what we did. He wanted them to be unique."

Kate nodded. She wished they could change the subject.

"Are you okay?" Toby asked.

"Yes, fine. Kind of tipsy."

"No, I mean in general. I've wanted to ask you for a while. You've seemed different. At first I thought it was just an adjustment thing—moving up here and all—but now I'm not so sure."

"I love it here," she said. "And of course I love Dan and Ava. But I do feel kind of lost. I miss my job. I feel like I've turned my back on all the causes I cared about."

"Do you want to move back to Brooklyn?"

"Part of me does, but Dan's so much happier here."

She had always been surprised when people left New York. When she still lived there, her friends talked all the time about how much better life would be someplace else. She had jumped right into these conversations: *In Austin, you would never have to deal with cold weather again! You could rent a house for a dollar! In Portland, Maine, you could wake up and see the ocean every morning!*

But when someone stopped talking about leaving and actually left, it never seemed right to her. Yes, New York was a pain in the ass, but it was also New York. She suspected that visiting other places as a New Yorker was entirely different than becoming a resident of those places, and calling them home. Her former boss lived in horse country in New Jersey and commuted in each day. She had once told Kate that there would be a moment when she'd had enough. Kate waited for it. A mentally ill homeless man shoved her on the sidewalk when she was newly pregnant. She caught herself before she fell, but it was a jarring incident, and for a few days after, she wondered: *Is this it? Am I done with New York?* But then she moved on with her life, same as ever. A year before that, on a sweltering August afternoon, she had seen a teenage girl pass out onto the subway tracks and get run over by the 6 train. Kate's legs gave out beneath her. Later, at home, she cried to Dan, "I'm done. I can't take living on top of all these people and sharing all their pain." But by the next morning her tears were dry and she rode the train as usual.

Ultimately, it wasn't her moment that decided things. Dan wanted another baby. He wanted trees and meadows and space. And he wanted their life together to be easier than it was in Brooklyn. He wanted her to be less consumed by tragedy, and more by simple pleasures. Kate wanted it too, in theory, but sometimes she thought she wasn't made to be at peace. She would always seek out the strife—there would always be newspapers and websites to fill the gaps in her knowledge.

"Can't you talk to Dan about it?" Toby said now. "You two are the closest couple I know, you can say anything to him."

"It's not that," she said. She knew that she could tell Dan exactly what she wanted, and perhaps he'd even help her find a way to make it work. But it differed so much from his own desires. One of them would have to sacrifice. This was the hardest part about a marriage, or a relationship like theirs: your hopes and your fears and your happiness hinged on someone else. When you stopped thinking that they ought to, you ended up like her parents, bitter and angry and apart.

"I love Dan, but you've never been the type to let other people's expectations dictate the terms," Toby said. "Don't start now."

.   She smiled.

"It's 2012," he went on. "Can't you telecommute or go into the city a couple of days a week once Ava starts school, or something? I know how much you loved that job. Don't you think you might have given up on it a little too soon?"

Kate was startled by his words, and touched that on what was supposed to be his day, he was still thinking of her.

"You may be right," she said, and squeezed his hand.

2003

Her cell phone rang at eleven o'clock.

Delphine recognized the number.

The man's name was Paul Lloyd. He had sounded friendly when they spoke a few days earlier. He answered her online ad, telling her that he and his wife lived two hours away, in Madison, Connecticut, in a house three blocks from the ocean with half an acre of land out back. They had six-year-old twin boys who were heartsick over the loss of their basset hound, Lucky Penny, who had recently passed away at the age of fourteen.

"Your Charlie looks just like her," Paul Lloyd said, in a tone that made it clear that he too was heartsick.

The ad included a photograph of Charlie, and a brief write-up stating that he was four years old, perfectly behaved, and free to a loving home.

"Can I ask why you're not keeping him?" the man said over the phone.

"I'm very allergic," she said, and if he had any further questions, he kept them to himself.

Now, when she answered, he said he was in the car, ten minutes away. She told him to meet her at the corner of Seventy-second and Central Park West.

Delphine pulled an oversized tote bag from the hall closet and filled it with Charlie's favorite toys, his blanket and his monogrammed bowls, and what remained of the organic dog food P.J. bought for fifty dollars a bag. Then she went to the bathroom and clipped the dog's leash onto his collar.

"Come on," she said. "Time for your walk."

He looked up at her, skeptical.

"What?" she said. True, they had lived together in this apartment for a year and never taken a walk, just the two of them. It might be overstating things even to say that they lived together. Each of them lived with P.J. and ignored the other's existence.

Charlie lay there on the bathroom tile like a lump.

"Come on," she said, tugging him. He let out a groan of protest, but got to his feet after a minute and accompanied her out to the hall, into the elevator, and through the lobby, where the old Irish doorman had taken the place of the young Russian.

"Hey there, Charlie Boy," he said in a thick accent.

They walked the three blocks at a painfully slow pace, Charlie lagging behind, panting in the heat. Her heels clicked against the sidewalk. A hot breeze licked the bare skin beneath her dress.

When they reached the park, she saw an SUV with Connecticut license plates in front of the bus stop. Paul Lloyd stepped out, looking just as she had imagined he would—he had the large, chunky build of a suburban dad on a television sitcom. He wore those long shorts that all American men wore, and sneakers with white ankle socks sticking out from the tops. In France, the men she knew wanted to stay attractive after they married. Their bodies, their clothes, the way they smelled—she had taken all of this for granted. American men drank a lot of beer and got fat. Their wives didn't seem to mind. After a few months of living together, even P.J. had sprouted a belly, and she found herself fixating on it—the way he just let it hang there when she was around, and sucked it in each time he looked in the mirror or stepped onstage. When he peed in the morning, he left the bathroom door open. Delphine told him she found this habit disgusting, but he claimed it was a positive sign. He was feeling completely comfortable with her. She thought of Henri, who in six years of marriage had never once failed to close the bathroom door.

The light changed now, and she walked toward Paul Lloyd, giving him a wave.

"This must be Charlie!" he said when she reached him.

The dog looked up at him, accepting a vigorous rub behind the ears. He wagged his tail.

"Aww, look at him. Man, my boys are gonna fall in love. We haven't told them yet, since we didn't want to get their hopes up if this somehow fell through."

Delphine smiled. "I know you'll give him a wonderful life."

He turned to Charlie, bending down and speaking directly to the dog. "Stephanie's at Petco right now, getting you your very own bed and a few of the toys that Lucky Penny loved, and treats"—his voice slid into rapid-fire baby talk—"*treats treats treats treats treats*. You like treats? You love treats? Yes you do, yes you do!"

He stood up again, straightened out his t-shirt. His voice returned to normal. "I took the whole day off work. We're going to pick the boys up from school with him in the back-seat. I can't wait. I brought him some bacon. Can he have that?"

"Sure," she said. "He's your dog now."

He pulled a Ziploc bag from his pants pocket and removed half a strip of crisp bacon. "Can you sit?" he asked.

Charlie sat.

He fed Charlie the meat. "Oh what a good boy! What a good boy!"

In Paris, dogs were everywhere—lying at their owners' feet in outdoor cafés, trotting obediently behind them in the streets unleashed, walking the aisles of upscale boutiques. But French people didn't baby them the way Americans did.

They showed more respect. Here, they had playgrounds just for dogs and men who you paid to walk them in a group of ten in the afternoon. She half expected Paul Lloyd to slap a bonnet on Charlie's head and a pacifier in his mouth. And stupid Charlie, American that he was, was loving every bit of it.

She had feared a fight out of him, but when Paul Lloyd opened the car door, Charlie jumped right in.

"Oops, let's get your doggie seat belt hooked," he said, reaching into the backseat. Delphine raised an eyebrow.

Before he left, he cupped her hand in both of his.

"Thank you so much," he said. "You don't know what this means to us." As if she had just given him one of her vital organs. "Do you want a moment alone with him, to say goodbye? I could take a walk."

Delphine shook her head. "Oh no. We've said our goodbyes."

He looked confused. He was probably thinking she was a heartless French person, what could you expect?

Was it heartless of her? She knew it would hurt P.J. more than anything else she could ever do to him. But it wasn't cruel. Cruel would be strapping a brick to the dog and dumping him in the East River. Charlie was going to love living in a big house by the sea, being adored. And after what P.J. had done to her, there was no form of revenge too terrible.

She knew she could not expect sympathy. She had betrayed her husband, and now she herself had been betrayed. An outsider looking in would probably say she got just what she deserved. And yet, wasn't it human to expect that you might be the exception to that? To hope that the world might understand your reasons even when you yourself could not?

She turned back toward the building, and lit a cigarette.

A woman holding the hand of a little girl a few feet ahead was doing what all New York mothers do—teaching their children constantly, because they must be the best! Not only that, but everyone around must know it!

"What do you see, Ella?" she asked loudly.

"A ladybug."

"That's right! And what color is it?"

"Red."

"And?"

"Black."

"Very good!"

These New York children would probably never get to have a quiet, contemplative moment until they went off to college.

As Delphine passed, the woman turned to give her a poisonous look, glancing toward her cigarette. New Yorkers were so self-righteous about smoking, as if they weren't killing themselves just as hastily through their love of diet soda and cocktails and carbohydrates. Delphine gave her a tart smile.

The sight of a mother during the week was a rarity. Most of the children around here were white, with black nannies who pushed them in strollers, looking bored, talking on their cell phones. In France, they had a terrific daycare system. She had never thought about it until coming to the U.S., but it was something to be proud of.

"Be careful," the woman said, pulling her daughter to her as if Delphine were about to burn a hole in the child.

The mothers here were so afraid. *Be careful!* She heard them yelling, in the park, at the curb, as they stepped off the bus. *Careful, careful, careful!* In such a doomsday tone, as if all of life were just a disaster lying in wait.

When she reached the Wilfred she prepared for a question from the doorman, but he did not ask about Charlie. Maybe he thought she'd brought the dog to the vet or the groomers, or an SAT tutoring session, dogs in this neighborhood having almost as many social obligations as children.

She stepped into the elevator. With nothing to do but regard her own reflection, she felt surprised by the bones in her cheeks poking out, the dark half-moons beneath her eyes. She had lost twelve pounds without meaning to, and she looked sickly now.

As the numbers lit up above the doors—*third floor, fourth floor, fifth, sixth*—she imagined what P.J. would think when he came home. Would he assume at first that he'd been burgled—flatulent, overweight dogs being such a popular target among thieves these days? How long would it take him to discover the truth? He would have to piece it together with the doormen, or perhaps he would just know.

She looked down at the ring. She slid it off her finger for a moment, held it in the palm of her hand. For the first time, she evaluated it as merely a piece of jewelry. It was very pretty. She thought it might be Edwardian, or perhaps even Victorian. All together, the stones were probably three carats at least. In France, a woman wouldn't wear a diamond smaller than a carat—if you couldn't afford more, you'd simply choose a less expensive stone. A few years back, sapphires were popular. But in America, all the women wore diamonds, and they came in every size, from golf balls down to specks of dust.

She had given a lot of thought to what the best thing would be, and decided that she ought to give the ring back to its rightful owner. She thought of the Stradivarius, how perhaps it had been taken all those years ago. The two of them, the ring and the violin, were linked in her mind: both objects of great sentimental value that should not have left a family. It was really his mother's ring anyway. She had never wanted Delphine to have it.

After P.J. gave it to her, Delphine wondered why his mother was willing to part with such a stunning piece of jewelry, her own engagement ring. But she never asked P.J., and when she eventually learned the truth, she wished she didn't know.

They arrived in New York from Paris in mid-August. The heat was oppressive. Delphine had never sweated so much. It reminded her of the tropics, damp and unrelenting. P.J. said you got used to it.

He had the rest of the month off, apart from a couple of summer festival performances. They spent their time exploring the city, and taking weekend drives to Tangle-wood, where he delighted the audiences with his rendition of Bach's Violin Concerto no. 2 in E Major. One critic wrote that listening to the music he played on the Stradivarius was "such an incredibly perfect experience that no other joy in life will surpass it."

P.J.'s manager was trying to eke every last bit of press out of the Stradivarius story that she possibly could. She had him doing two or three phone interviews each day, with newspapers and music websites and National Public Radio. Delphine left the room when he did this, after once hearing him say, "The previous owner was a French collector." Henri. The knowledge pierced her heart as if she had just that instant learned the truth.

When P.J. left the apartment with the Strad in a simple backpack violin case, she would fill up with a strange mix of fear and exhilaration. Henri had treated it like a museum piece, but P.J. saw it as just a beloved instrument, meant to be played.

He came back from his travels with the funniest stories, laughing no matter what the inconvenience. A stewardess in

Germany insisted on putting the Strad in the overhead compartment; she covered it in gym bags and laptop computers. In Japan, he was forced to buy an extra seat for it.

"That's absurd!" she said, but P.J. only shrugged and said, "Violinists have it easy. A cellist always has to buy a seat for his instrument. A bass player can't even bring his, because it's so big."

"So what do they do?" she asked.

"They have to rent one in every town. Can you imagine?"

He was once detained by airport security in Poland for three hours. They said he should have brought proof that he owned the Strad. But eventually a guard came on duty who had seen him perform with the Warsaw Philharmonic the night before.

"He asked for my autograph and sent me on my way," P.J. said when he came in that afternoon. "I'd probably still be stuck in that hellhole if it wasn't for him. I guess I should carry the papers from now on."

"You should," she said. "There are so many sad examples of what happens when documentation goes missing."

"Oh yeah?"

He was flipping through the mail on the small table in the foyer.

"Do you know anything about the history of the Nazis taking violins like yours from their owners?" she asked.

Now he looked up.

"No."

She told him the story of the woman who had come into the shop, and when she was done P.J. frowned and said, "How awful." But he didn't make any connection to himself, at least as far as she could tell.

"Have you heard of Rose Valland?" she asked.

"Nope. Who's that?"

The dog was at his feet, looking for attention. P.J. dropped to the floor and began to rub his stomach.

Delphine didn't go any further. She could tell he wasn't listening.

After that, he continued to play the Stradivarius without a hint of guilt or hesitation. Delphine wondered why the whole thing bothered her so much when no one else seemed disturbed in the slightest.

In September, when his performance schedule started up again, she was alone two or three nights a week. She walked the streets, or stayed home and read a book, trying to keep busy. She reminded herself that there was so much to discover—museums and theater and SoHo boutiques. She wanted to think of New York as a brave new adventure. She had always dreamed of coming here. But she found the city bland compared to Paris.

All of Paris was a work of art. Delphine had never really appreciated that until now. The architecture, the window boxes spilling over with geraniums in June, the tall white shutters. She longed to stand before just one of the thousands of massive wooden doors painted blue or red or green, *privée* entries that disguised cobblestone courtyards, lush gardens. A treasure hidden behind every one.

In Paris, the people were unique. Here, they all wore the same shoes, and carried the same purses and read the same books and drank the same coffee. She had heard about Saks Fifth Avenue, but when she shopped there, she found it to be just like any other department store. She missed the gorgeous and grand Galeries Lafayette, with its gilded balconies and vaulted stained-glass ceiling.

The simple translations of everyday life exhausted her. When she saw a neon sign flashing the time and temperature outside a bank, she had to convert Fahrenheit to Celsius in her head. The subway maps seemed designed to confuse, and when she accidentally went uptown instead of down, there was often no easy way to get back to the train she was meant to be on. She had to go outside and cross the street, pay the fare twice. She felt a small sense of victory when she got something right, but it was usually canceled out by some other frustrating mistake within hours.

One morning, she decided to surprise P.J. with tickets to Shakespeare in the Park. She had read in the paper that they were free, and could be claimed starting at eleven a.m. She arrived at eleven-fifteen to find that all the tickets were gone.

"They all went in fifteen minutes?" she said to the man behind the counter.

"People lined up starting at seven," he said, as if queuing unnecessarily for four hours in the blistering heat made any sense at all.

The next day, she took a taxi to Greenwich Village to do some shopping. She had a long, lovely chat with the driver about his honeymoon in Nice. When she paid him the exact fare displayed on the meter rounded up to the next dollar, he grew cold. "Screw you, lady," he said, and she felt stricken. It wasn't until she told P.J. the story later that she remembered that here you were expected to tip an extra 15 or 20 percent.

It became clear quite quickly that for her, New York was only one person, and without him the city meant nothing. When P.J. was home, she felt full of life. They made love every night in a fever, with a passion she could never have imagined with Henri. While P.J. worked, she stored up tales to tell him and busied herself making the apartment perfect for him. She got manicures and pedicures and facials at a spa run by Chinese women who didn't speak a word of English. In Paris, she had gotten her hair cut and colored at the same place every few weeks for the last eighteen years, but here she could not find a salon that she liked. She tried to ration her lotions and cosmetics, knowing that when she ran out she would have a hard time replacing them. She had one bottle of Avène Hydrance Optimale, her favorite cream, which she vowed not to open for as long as she could bear it.

At first she made P.J. the meals she would have made in Paris, but when he dismissed them as too rich or too strange— they were always too *something*—she started experimenting with American cooking, the sorts of recipes his mother had prepared for him when he was a child: spaghetti Bolognese, pancakes and bacon, macaroni and cheese. She was never happy with the way any of it turned out, even though he said it was delicious. Delphine herself avoided these things and tried to continue eating as she always had: three meals a day, and that was all. For dinner, she had vegetables and a small piece of meat—simple, basic food, though she could never get it to taste the way it did in France.

"I'm missing French groceries," she said, exasperated, one night.

"Just say 'I miss French groceries,'" P.J. corrected her. "Otherwise it makes you sound like you've misplaced them."

He told her to go to Fairway if she wanted to be impressed. The store had a good enough selection, but to her mind, going to Fairway felt like going to war—the customers so pushy, the men at the deli screaming, *Next! Next! Next!* before she could gather her thoughts or find the right words.

Everything in New York moved too fast; she could feel the speed flattening her.

She thought it might be different if she had friends. She considered going to the embassy, and trying to find out if there were expatriate groups she might join. But she had never been the sort of person who joined a group. She wouldn't know what to say or how to act. It seemed desperate somehow. That left P.J.'s circle: his friends from school were young musicians, some struggling, some doing all right, but none as well as he was. They were all classically trained, but among them only P.J. was a master of interpretation. She could tell that they were jealous of him, though he denied it. One of them, a guy they called Clams, sat around smoking marijuana all day. P.J. paid him to take the dog to his place in Brooklyn when he traveled. She told him she'd be fine caring for Charlie, even though she didn't particularly want to, but P.J. said he was worried about his friend and would rather have an excuse to give Clams some cash.

Sometimes she traveled with him, but she didn't want to go to Europe, not yet. She felt uncomfortable whenever their new world overlapped with her old one. At a party after he performed with the Montreal Orchestra, the principal oboe player had approached her and said, "I'm certain we've met before." They had, at a dinner at her apartment in Paris. But Delphine only shrugged and said she couldn't place him.

In Paris, she and Henri had made something of a name for themselves, and everyone they socialized with knew them for it. But now she was merely an appendage of P.J. When they traveled together, all she ever heard was, "You must be so proud of him." When they asked, "And what do you do?" she would tell them she was in real estate, and watch their eyes fog over with disinterest.

There were a couple of female musicians she had met whose company she enjoyed. One of them, Jennifer, was about Delphine's age. She was from California, the daughter of a renowned cello player, now a renowned cellist in her own right. The other, Natasha, was a bit older, tall and lovely, born and raised in Manhattan. A flutist with the New York Philharmonic. Delphine invited them and their husbands over for dinner twice. On each occasion she prepared a traditional French meal, complete with homemade pumpkin soup, salad, meat, a cheese course, and dessert. Everyone seemed to have a wonderful time. Natasha sent flowers after the first visit, and a sweet handwritten note after the second. But the invitations were never reciprocated. Delphine told P.J. that she felt hurt by this. She wondered if she had done something wrong.

"Don't be silly," he said. "People in New York don't really entertain at home very much. I have friends I've known for ten years and I've never been inside their apartments."

She thought that was strange. What was it about Americans that made them so enthusiastic and familiar on the surface, when in reality they didn't want to share anything of themselves? She had believed that moving to America would be no harder than leaving Montmartre for Henri's *bourgeois quartier* of the Rive Gauche, but she saw now how foolish that had been.

When P.J. brought her to parties in New York, everyone talked so fast that half the time she had no idea what they were saying. For years, she had worked with Americans and prided herself on her English. But now she saw that in those interactions, both sides had agreed to go slowly, to meet in the middle. Here, they simply expected her to keep up.

At Parisian dinner parties, everyone around the table contributed to the conversation. In New York, they tended to pair off and talk to only one person, usually someone of the same gender. She found this terribly boring. The women asked her mostly about Paris. They wanted to tell her about their vacations there, and ask what she thought were the main differences between France and the U.S. They wanted to know how Parisian women stayed so thin despite the presence of tempting pastries and cheese and wine, and what brand of moisturizer she used before bed.

New York women had an obsession with French women,

even though they too were beautiful. It seemed to her that their goal was perfection: the perfect outfit, the perfect body, perfect hair. In Paris, they were far from perfect—the teeth might not be quite as straight, the makeup not applied so exact—and yet they had confidence and grace that these women lacked. But of course you couldn't tell them that!

It gave her a shock when an American she hardly knew approached her at one of these gatherings and threw herself into Delphine's arms as a greeting. She herself was naturally inclined to kiss someone on both cheeks upon meeting, but since she knew that it was not the norm here, she weighed what she ought to do on a person-by-person basis. P.J. said that New Yorkers found it charming, and so French. And that was the point, really. Here, she wore her nationality like a costume. It was the first thing people saw in her, the only trait that made her special. Nobody cared whether she was funny or sharp or a horrible angry drunk. She was French and that was all.

Through the autumn and early winter, she spent her days furnishing the apartment with a fervor that delighted P.J. Sometimes, as she hung curtains, or unpacked silver from a box, he played the violin in the next room and her heart felt heavy with love. She tried to let the feeling envelop her, using the sensation to push off any doubts. This was permanent, and it would feel that way if she could just finish decorating, get an American visa, open a bank account. For now, she still used her French credit card, and when she needed cash she had to get it from P.J. He kept a fat stack of hundred-dollar bills in his sock drawer, and told her to feel free to take what she needed, but Delphine felt odd about it sometimes. Eventually, she would get a job, perhaps as a translator. That would help some too.

In the beginning, she didn't mind his travel schedule. When they reunited, it felt exciting, and for so many years she had missed the pleasure of being alone. But as the holidays drew near, she began to feel lonesome. Delphine had grown accustomed to having Henri around, and she sometimes found herself talking to him in her head. She wondered what he would do for Christmas, whether he would stay home alone or brave the weekend in Brittany with his parents, who would no doubt baby him, filling him up with *bûche de Noël* and *lait de poule*, trying to cover his sorrows over with cream and sugar. On Christmas Eve, Henri's mother would excuse herself to cry and smoke her Gitanes, and look through old photo books of Josephine, her daughter who had died more than fifty years earlier. Henri and his father would stand by, fidgeting, awkward, unsure what to do with such unending sorrow.

The only time they had ever discussed having children, P.J. told her that he was fine without. But she knew he was young, and wondered if he would regret the choice later. She thought of Henri, who had wanted a little Josephine of his own. Would it have been better or worse if all this had happened but he had been left with a child?

Delphine had heard from him only three times, over email. The first was businesslike, asking if she knew the whereabouts of some important papers in the shop. The second had been sent at three a.m. Paris time, and in it he begged her to come home. When she didn't reply, he wrote again, this time to tell her of a wonderful performance he had attended at the Paris Opera, a message so chaste that he might have been sending it to his grandmother.

After a few months in the States, she woke one morning with a sense of dread about her father's grave.

"Nothing's going to happen to it," P.J. said. "Don't worry."

"If no one tends to his grave for long enough, they'll dig him up and move him to some anonymous crypt," she said.

"Jesus Christ, that's barbaric," he said.

She shrugged. It was just what happened.

The thought possessed her for several days, until she wrote to Henri, asking if he might visit and place some flowers on the tombstone. He said he already had, and she wanted to cover his face with grateful kisses.

Every time the phone rang, she expected it to be him, though of course he wouldn't know how to contact her. She had gotten an American cell phone shortly after she reached New York, but she had no one to give the number to. Only P.J. ever called her, to see how her day was going.

In mid-December, Delphine went to hear the Philharmonic perform with P.J. as guest soloist. When he came onstage, she leaned forward with her chin in her hands and closed her eyes to hear each note. The sound of it was heavenly. There was something intoxicating about the fact that she had heard him practicing the piece for weeks and now the world could hear what had been only hers. She wanted to tell the strangers on either side of her that she had made this man many late-night grilled cheese sandwiches after rehearsals, and sat there in her negligee as he dunked them straight into a pot of Campbell's tomato soup.

P.J. moved about the entire stage while all the other players remained stationary.

"A bit unconventional for my taste," she heard a man say to his wife as they walked out, and Delphine laughed to herself. She thought he was brilliant.

They had last left the country together to go to Montreal in early October, which meant that her passport's ninety-day allowance in America was almost up again. They spent Christmas on a beach in Mexico, drinking sweet piña coladas in a green-and-white-striped cabana. He said he didn't feel like going home anyway, he'd rather just spend his time off with her. She feared for a moment that he did not want to introduce her to his family yet, but dismissed the idea. They had planned a trip to his hometown to celebrate his father's birthday in the spring. And perhaps going home for Christmas didn't mean the same thing here as it did in France. P.J. said there were plenty of years when he had skipped the madness of family holidays to relax and recharge on his own. Delphine wondered if he had really been alone, or if he had some woman along, but this she did not ask.

On Christmas morning, he gave her an emerald bracelet from Tiffany's. He stuffed the blue box into a red felt stocking, which he hung from the corner of a dresser drawer. She had seen Christmas stockings in American movies but had never had one of her own. In France, they left their slippers beside the fireplace for Père Noël to fill with treats.

They sat by the pool and sang carols to one another—he taught her "Jingle Bells" and she laughed, recognizing the notes.

"We sing 'Vive le vent' to the same tune," she said.

"What does it mean?"

"'Long live the wind.'"

P.J. frowned. "That seems so unfestive, compared to jingling bells. Who wants the wind to go on?"

She laughed. "I know a sweeter one, which you will like."

Softly she sang "Il est né, le divin enfant." Her singing voice was nothing, but she could remember a time when she and Henri had gone to Notre Dame to hear it sung by a children's choir. Just the memory of their sweet, tender voices made her cry.

She thought of the way they had decorated the shop each Christmas, with fluffy artificial snow covering the front window.

"What's wrong?" P.J. asked.

"I'm just a little sad."

"Why?"

"I was thinking of Henri. It's silly."

Delphine had expected him to comfort her, but she could tell P.J. was uneasy. She wanted to tell him precisely how she felt—that she loved him in a way she had never known possible, but that she could not just forget her old life. She worried about what she had done to Henri, she wondered why she had ever married him in the first place, and suspected the worst of herself—he had come along soon after her father disappeared from the world, and she had replaced one with the other, as if they were interchangeable pieces instead of men made of flesh and blood. But she couldn't explain without upsetting P.J. He seemed to find the complexity of her feelings suspect.

"I was hearing this saying on television the other day," she told him. *"He loves me, he loves me not."*

" 'I heard this saying,' " he said.

"You did?"

"No. That's the right way to— Oh, never mind. What were you going to say?"

He seemed irritated, and she wondered if she should just let it drop. But Delphine continued. "In France, the saying is different: little girls picking the petals off of flowers say, *Il m'aime un peu, beaucoup, passionnément, à la folie, pas du tout* and then start again. The translation would be something like, *He loves me a little, a lot, passionately, madly, not at all.* Everything in America is so black and white. Do you understand?"

He made a face that communicated the fact that he did not. They ordered two more cocktails.

She had underestimated how hard it was to be in love with someone who didn't share her native tongue. She was frustrated by language all the time. Her English was strong and growing stronger with use, but there were turns of phrase that only an American could understand. She couldn't say everything she wanted to. Delphine translated each sentence in her head before saying it out loud. She sometimes went to French films alone during the day and basked in the feeling of understanding every word again. She still thought in French, and dreamed in it, sleep a sweet relief from having to think twice as hard as she ever had before. P.J. teased her for talking in her sleep. It was the only time, he said, that he got to hear her speak French very much. He thought it was sexy.

He was always correcting her. She would tell him, "Today I walked all the way up to One twenty-five Street," and he would laugh gently before saying, "It's One twenty-fifth." To a certain extent, she appreciated his help. But she sometimes grew annoyed by him, too. He had never learned to speak her language, other than a few simple words and phrases. He spent $500 at the Virgin Megastore on a set of CDs called Rosetta Stone that promised to teach him all of French in just a few months. But P.J. never even took them out of the package.

Meanwhile she worked so hard. She forced herself to read *The New York Times* in English. She attempted American novels as well, even though she suspected that she was missing certain parts. She knew it was unfair to compare, since he had such a busy and full professional life, while she had to search for ways to fill her time.

The sex never slowed down or diminished, as if they both knew this was the only sure, perfect way to understand one another. When they made love, it put her at ease. He was hers, this beautiful genius. He loved her and made her laugh. Everything else would improve with time.

A week after New Year's, on an unseasonably warm Wednesday night, Delphine ventured out for a walk while P.J. was in London, working. Just a few blocks from the apartment, she came across the Brasserie Montmarte. She had never noticed the place before. With warm yellow lightbulbs outlining the sign above the door, and baguettes stacked in the window, it looked like any other of the dozens of faux French bistros in New York. She never went to these places, as she suspected that they bore no stronger resemblance to real Parisian restaurants than Mr. Chan's Chinese Food on West Seventy-third did to dinner in Hong Kong. But the name made her smile, and she thought she might stop in for a glass of wine.

The room was dim. Several couples ate by candlelight in the back. Most American restaurants were so loud that you couldn't hear your own dinner companion. But here, it seemed more like Paris, soft and quiet.

A bar in front had high stools and mirrored walls, painted with an outline of the Eiffel Tower. She took a seat there and made eye contact with the bartender, a pretty blonde who looked to be in her mid-twenties.

"What can I get you?" the woman said, and Delphine realized with a slight flutter of her heart that she was actually French.

"*Un petit rouge, s'il vous plaît.*"

"We have a beautiful Côtes du Rhône tonight."

Delphine nodded with pleasure. It felt so nice to be understood.

"Have you eaten?" the woman asked. "Don't let this tacky decor fool you. The specialty of the house is a crisp *confit de canard,* as good as any you'll get at home."

Delphine smiled. "Ahh, *oui, merci.*"

"Are you visiting New York or do you live here?" the woman asked as she poured the wine. "I know I haven't seen you before."

Delphine told her she was engaged to an American, and

that she had moved to the States five months ago. It felt like so much longer.

"I've been here ten years," the bartender said.

Her name was Marie-Hélène. She came from Marseille. At thirty-one, she was older than she looked. She was not really the bartender, only covering for someone who had called in sick. She was a co-owner and the night manager, she reported, entrusted with every part of the business, since the other owners—an American couple in New Jersey—were only interested in the restaurant as an investment. She said she had put every cent she had into the place, and lived with two roommates, but so far the restaurant had done well.

"Tell me everything you hate about New York," she said after Delphine had ordered a second glass of wine.

Delphine laughed. "I don't hate it."

"Come on. We all hate it at first."

"I just have so much to learn about America."

Marie-Hélène raised a finger to correct her. "New York is not America. Remember that."

Delphine nodded. She switched to French. "I hate the way they are all slaves to the gym. They're so proud of it! You hear them talking about these machines and boot camp classes like it's a religion. It seems like Americans have been brainwashed into thinking you have to do sports to survive."

"They have."

"What about just taking a walk or playing a nice game of tennis?"

"I play every Tuesday and Friday," Marie-Hélène said. "You should come along."

"I would love that," she said.

Women from the South of France were something like New Yorkers. They made fast friendships, friendships of convenience. In the North, it was harder to meet people, but Delphine thought the connections ran deeper. In Paris, she might have been turned off by Marie-Hélène's intensity, but here she felt grateful for the kindness.

"What are you missing most of home?" Marie-Hélène asked. "I like to make a game of it—finding all the French treasures here. Try me on anything."

Delphine thought it over. There were so many things. "I miss my French fashion magazines, and the tabloids. I miss *Elle* most of all. I even miss *Paris Match*."

"The Universal News at Broadway and Broome will have them," Marie-Hélène said. "And they'll let you sit and sip your coffee while you read. What else?"

Delphine felt her cheeks strain from smiling. It was such a small thing, but it felt like a gift.

"I haven't gotten a haircut in three months. I'm afraid to go anywhere. The one place I did go, I came out looking bizarre."

"You go to Serge Bertrand down in the meatpacking district," Marie-Hélène instructed. "But you must see the man himself, and those appointments can book up weeks, sometimes months, in advance. Call them tomorrow. Say you'll come whenever Serge can take you. It's not like Paris, where you can just walk in anyplace and expect it to be good."

"Like the groceries," Delphine said out loud, before realizing this wouldn't make any sense.

But to her surprise, Marie-Hélène responded, "Exactly."

"I'm missing the food," Delphine went on. "Simple things, like an *éclair au chocolat* from the pâtisserie on my street, just the texture of the chocolate in France."

Marie-Hélène shook her head. "I know. You won't find that here, not even in the specialty shops in Brooklyn, I'm sorry to say. They just don't do it right. It's the milk or something. And you won't find decent cosmetics either, even if it's the brand you'd get at home. Anything good has to come from a doctor, the pharmacies are shit. La Roche-Posay, or Avène, or Vichy—you've got to have someone bring them to you from France. I have a cousin in Paris who comes here on business three times a year. Without his deliveries, I'd die."

She thought of her one precious bottle of Hydrance Optimale. She had been wise to save it.

They talked for over an hour, the sensation a bit like going on a wonderful first date. Delphine walked home feeling light. She began showing up at the brasserie alone for dinner two or three times a week. She sat at the bar. Marie-Hélène would sit and chat with her, no matter how crowded the place got.

In France, they would probably not have been friends. They were a decade apart in age and had nothing in common, really, besides their country of origin. But here, that was enough to make a friendship. They laughed about American ways, and spoke French while everyone around them tried to guess at what they were saying.

After a month or so, Marie-Hélène invited her shopping. On Lexington Avenue between Eighty-second and Eighty-third, there was a boutique called Ludivine, run by a woman from Provence. She sold labels that Delphine had thought would be impossible to find here—Maison Michel, Denis Colomb. Delphine bought two pairs of cloud-soft jeans for $260 each, a Carven top, and boots.

They took a taxi down to Fifty-seventh Street, to L'Institut Sothys. She had no idea the spa was even there. She had been to the original on the rue du Faubourg Saint-Honoré as a gift to herself on her thirtieth birthday. The two of them got hour-long detoxifying salt scrubs and body wraps. Afterward, they went to La Grenouille, which Marie-Hélène considered the most authentically French restaurant in New York. They ordered the blanquette de veau and a Grand Marnier soufflé. The crust was as light as snow. When the waiter cracked the surface and spooned sabayon into the steaming hot opening, Delphine held her breath with delight.

"Thank you so much," she said to Marie-Hélène, feeling like she could cry. "Thank you for everything."

Over dessert, Delphine told her the story of how she and P.J. met, and how she had abandoned her husband. Marie-Hélène did not seem the least bit scandalized. She announced that she herself had given up on men, other than for sex. She had experienced enough bad romances to ward her off them for life.

"That's just how I was before I met Henri," Delphine said. "And we ended up married."

"But then not married."

Delphine laughed. "True."

She paid the check at the restaurant as she had at the spa, knowing that her new friend was, as they said here, a little cash poor.

Sometimes P.J. joined her at the brasserie. He ordered *steak frites* or a *croque monsieur* and a beer. Delphine tried to get him to try the calf liver in red wine sauce or the potatoes cooked in duck fat, but he was like a child about new foods, wanting only the familiar.

Around midnight most nights, Marie-Hélène let the staff go, and they would stay behind, laughing and talking. A cook named Erwan, a boy from Marseille, sometimes stayed too. Erwan was just twenty. It felt like they were forming a family of sorts, a tiny bit of France right here in America. Delphine felt as if her life were finally full. She was in love, and she had made a true friend for the first time in ages.

On a freezing-cold Sunday afternoon in the middle of

February, Marie-Hélène's day off, the two of them sipped wine in a bar downtown.

"*Il fait un froid de canard,*" Delphine said, shivering every time someone opened the door. What had sufficed as her winter coat in France had not lasted here through November. She had never before owned heavy gloves or a hat, but now she wore both every day.

"Look at this," Marie-Hélène said, pointing to the TV screen in the corner broadcasting CNN.

Delphine had already seen it on the news.

A day earlier, there were protests all around the world against a possible invasion of Iraq. Hundreds of thousands of people gathered in Manhattan, filling twenty city blocks. There were millions more in Rome, and one hundred thousand in Paris. Onscreen, the camera scanned the crowd outside the United Nations—ladies in fur coats and men in suits, crammed in beside college students and young parents and old women leaning on walkers. They held signs that said MAKE LOVE NOT WAR and NOT IN OUR NAME and BUSH IS MORE EVIL THAN BIN LADEN.

"Fuck George Bush," Marie-Hélène said. "He'll never get his way."

The door opened again. Another blast of frozen air.

Marie-Hélène got to her feet. She ran toward the chill, and Delphine swiveled her neck just as her friend grabbed hold of a young, handsome creature in a hooded sweatshirt.

"This is Pete," she said, pulling him toward the table. "Peter, meet Delphine."

Delphine had never seen him before, but that was no surprise. Marie-Hélène seemed to find someone new to fall in love with every Friday night. He nodded hello and mumbled something she couldn't understand.

In March, American troops were sent into Baghdad.

Other countries followed. Delphine felt proud when France refused. She felt like telling everyone who had gathered in this city that her country stood with them.

But not long after the war began, she saw a news item online one morning. It said the U.S. House of Representatives had decided to remove the word "French" from their cafeteria menus, replacing it in all cases with the word "Freedom." No more French toast, or French bread, or French fries.

"What the hell?" she said to P.J., repeating a phrase he used all the time.

P.J. shrugged. "People are pissed. They think you guys are being a bunch of pussies and leaving it to us to fix the whole mess, as usual."

She could feel her blood rising. " 'You guys'?" she repeated, looking behind her as if searching for some group she had not known she was a part of until now. " 'As usual'?"

"You know what I mean," he said quietly. "The French."

She felt struck, but pointed out a paragraph in the article that discussed how the Americans had done the same to the Germans during World War I.

"Look at this!" she said, trying to lighten the mood. "You crazy people started calling hamburgers 'Salisbury steaks.' You changed German measles to liberty measles."

She laughed, but stopped when she saw the anger on his face.

"You weren't here when the towers fell. You didn't have to live through it."

She resisted the urge to say that no, she wasn't here—she had seen it on television in France, just as he had seen it on television while working out at the New York Sports Club on West Seventy-sixth Street.

"This isn't about the towers," she said gently.

"Bullshit," he said. "Do you know how many of my

buddies from home are fighting in Iraq, protecting the free world from terrorists, just like our grandfathers did in World War II? While meanwhile the French prance around and say they won't take sides."

She had never heard him mention these buddies before, and suddenly she did not feel like being gentle with him any longer.

"Your friends will die for nothing," she said.

"Fuck you," he said, before walking into the bedroom and slamming the door.

And so she had learned that she could not talk to him about the war. He was incapable of thinking sensibly about it. They made up a few hours later, and he gave her an almost apology.

"Look, this patriotic stuff is new to me," he said. "But ever since 9/11 I just find myself so angry about what happened. I guess I had this idea of America as invincible and now that's been destroyed."

"I understand," she said. "I do. But now more lives will be lost. And for what?"

"Revenge," he said, as if it were the most obvious thing in the world. As if he were a brutal killer instead of a sensitive musician.

Things went on as usual after that. She told herself that maybe it was even a good thing that they'd fought. Maybe it was healthy. But for the first time she let herself wonder if she had only come home with P.J. for the dream of it, or if it really was about him.

The one person she could talk about the war with was Marie-Hélène, and the topic filled many of their conversations. On French TV, they were showing dead and captured American soldiers, but not in America. And if you believed the news media, all Americans now hated the French. Marie-Hélène reported that someone had stuck a bumper sticker on a stall in the women's bathroom at the restaurant that said FIRST IRAQ, THEN CHIRAC. They laughed at that, but not long after, Marie-Hélène arrived at work one evening to find that her business partners had draped an enormous American flag across the front of the building.

"It's been empty in here lately, but I didn't realize why," she said when Delphine stopped by later that night. She was drinking pastis cut with a few ice cubes, which gave Delphine a jolt—she had never seen Marie-Hélène drinking during work hours before.

"It's a boycott of all things French," Marie-Hélène said. "Apparently it's happening all over America."

"But New York isn't America!" Delphine said. "You're the one who told me that. What about those protesters we saw out in the streets?"

"They didn't want war, but now that they're at it, they need someone to hate." Marie-Hélène buried her head in her hands. "First the smoking ban, and now this. The restaurant is doomed. I'll be lucky to get a job at Au Bon Pain."

"You're being ridiculous," Delphine said, but many nights followed when they were the only ones there. She thought of how she and Henri had struggled to keep the shop alive after September 11th, how easily it might have slipped through their hands if not for the Stradivarius.

Delphine and P.J. tried to lift Marie-Hélène's spirits. They gave her tickets to the Philharmonic, and she brought along a handsome young actor she'd met at a party. When a colleague of P.J.'s had a fiftieth birthday celebration, P.J. convinced him to hold it at the Brasserie Montmartre and the place did a better business in a single night than it had in the previous two weeks.

"You were so sweet to think of it," Delphine said.

"She's been a good friend to you," he said. "She got you out of your winter doldrums."

Delphine felt touched that he had noticed how she was feeling all those months ago. With Henri, her sadness usually got eclipsed by his own, and she was forced to put on a cheery face. She had felt comfortable with this dynamic somehow; it was so similar to the way she once was with her father. But now at last, she had met a man who truly saw her.

One night, P.J. took Marie-Hélène to a Knicks game, just the two of them. Marie-Hélène loved basketball, and Delphine didn't want to go. She sat home alone reading, her two regular dates occupied with one another. If the thought of it gave her a moment's pause, it was only a moment. She felt happy that they liked each other. And when P.J. sent her a text message saying that he missed her, and was dreaming of the new black stockings she had bought, she went straight to the closet and put them on.

Two weeks later, over a hundred people from the restaurant industry gathered at Le Cirque for a press conference, urging New Yorkers to stop the boycott. The *Times* ran a photograph, and Marie-Hélène stood in the background, her face a knot of frustration.

By the middle of May, the other owners of the Brasserie Montmartre had voted to close and turn it into a Mexican restaurant. They apologized to Marie-Hélène, and said they would be thrilled if she wanted to stay on running the new place. She turned them down. Delphine told P.J. she was worried. She felt like a big sister, wondering what she could do to help.

"I feel for her, but she shouldn't have quit without having another job lined up," he said. "She should have done the Mexican place with them. What's the difference?"

Delphine tried to explain that she couldn't possibly have stayed on.

"A Mexican restaurant? She'd be humiliated. The brasserie was her dream."

"The other owners don't seem to be humiliated," he said. "Why should she?"

"The other owners aren't even French," she said. "They're coming from New Jersey."

"Just say they're from New Jersey," he said irritably.

She sighed. She couldn't understand why he was acting this way.

"Fine. They're from New Jersey. Better?"

"Yes."

When Delphine and P.J. went to visit his parents in May, they offered to let Marie-Hélène stay at their place, to give her a bit of distance from her roommates. Delphine went to Henri Bendel for lavender soap and Chanel eye cream and Diptyque candles, and set up a spa in the bathroom, in the hopes that it might rejuvenate Marie-Hélène, boost her spirits some. She pulled her one unopened bottle of precious Avène Hydrance Optimale from the linen closet and placed it on the edge of the sink.

The trip to his parents' house did not go as she had hoped. Delphine overheard P.J. and his mother arguing about her. It was clear that his mother didn't like her, didn't approve of their relationship, and Delphine feared that her opinion had taken root in him.

On the way home, as they sat in traffic on the West Side Highway, she said, "I wish you knew someone great who we could set up with Marie-Hélène. She's so depressed. She needs some distraction."

But P.J. himself was distracted. "What did you say?"

"Never mind."

One night soon after, he roused her from a dream and said, "You cried out in English!" She remembered the dream, and he was right—the whole thing had transpired in her second language as if it were her first. P.J. laughed, but when she thought back on it, that was the moment when everything changed.

The next day, he casually said over breakfast, "I hope you didn't come here just for me."

Delphine was sure she had misheard him. "Pardon?"

"To America. I hope I'm not the reason you made this drastic change in your life."

She felt something hard and heavy drop through her body. She saw that part of him was lost to her now. She wondered whether it would come back, and when.

"Of course you are," she said. "Why else would I be here, if not for you?"

"Because you love New York?"

She scoffed, more at him than at the sentiment. "New York is nothing next to Paris."

"Oh Paris, Paris, Paris," he said, in a tone that sounded like one child mocking another on the playground. "Your perfect city only got to stay so perfect because you all surrendered to the Nazis. If it wasn't for America, who would have liberated you? London is the far more honest city. They wear their principles in the busted-up architecture."

She was certain he must have heard it someplace. He wasn't smart enough to come up with something like that on his own.

"And you let your dogs shit everywhere, like you're too good to pick up after them."

Now that precious bit of wisdom, she knew, that was all him. He slept on the sofa that night, but by the following morning they were sheepish with one another, polite, like two guests at an otherwise empty hotel who had shared dinner once and felt rather fond of each other. He offered to put her clothes in the wash, and she made him a bowl of Greek yogurt with fresh blueberries and honey.

Still she could tell that things between them had not returned to normal. He seemed closed off, distracted. They usually ate their meals together at the table, but now he took his plate and sat alone in front of the television set. They had always walked the dog together after dinner, at his insistence, but now P.J. went himself. He said he needed to clear his head. Sometimes he'd be gone for an hour or even two, telling her that he was wandering the streets of New York, or the paths in Central Park, where they said no one was safe after dark. She would picture him dead in the road somewhere, and when he returned she would be so grateful that she never mentioned the alcohol in his kiss.

After the restaurant closed, Marie-Hélène came over a few days a week. She usually arrived by noon, and started drinking pastis soon after. Delphine enjoyed the company. It was summer, time to relax and slow down, something that most New Yorkers had no intention of doing. Even the drink itself reminded her of summertime. She had had a glass or two on so many weekends away in the South of France, straight over two ice cubes.

She only wished her friend could stop at one or two glasses. By late afternoon most days, Marie-Hélène was drunk, her eyelids sagging toward her chin, her anger rising high. She was sleeping with three men—a married patron of the Brasserie Montmartre, a bartender she had worked with a decade ago, who wandered in and out of her life with some frequency, and a painter who lived and worked in a one-room studio in Williamsburg. If any of them dared not to call her back fast enough, or refused to show up at her door when summoned, Marie-Hélène would scream at them, and throw things, and threaten to jump off the Brooklyn Bridge. Delphine hated listening to her cry and shout over the phone. She felt suddenly afraid of this woman she had come to call her friend. Marie-Hélène hardly seemed to like any of the men in her life, preferring the strength of her rage to happiness.

Things could be especially tense when P.J. was home. It had become clear that he and Marie-Hélène were entirely opposed when it came to politics, which led to more than a few arguments, with Delphine in the middle trying to calm them both down. The warmth between them was gone. He insisted on calling her Mary Helen, which she hated, of course. "You're in America now," he said.

After she went home at night, he'd say things like, "She's kind of a loose cannon. I think you might want to cut back on how much time you're spending with her."

Delphine thought he might be right, but Marie-Hélène needed her; she couldn't imagine turning her away. And she was alarmed by P.J.'s pigheaded patriotism. When they first met, she had appreciated the fact that he was somewhat unpolished, certainly not an intellectual. But ever since the war began, the things he said frightened her.

During the first week of August, Marie-Hélène went out to Montauk with some new man she'd met, and Delphine felt grateful for the break. P.J. was home, but spending his days practicing with the Philharmonic for an upcoming recording. All morning and afternoon, she had peace, time to sit with her thoughts, though she wasn't sure what to make of everyone's moods. Perhaps it had to do with the heat, or the fact that so much had happened all at once: Marie-Hélène's disappointment, the realization that they did not have the blessing of P.J.'s mother, and all this nonsense about Americans and their anger toward the French.

On Thursday she went to the grocery store to get the ingredients for pasta salad, and there, squeezing avocados in the produce aisle, stood Natasha, the Philharmonic's flutist, who she had had over to dinner months earlier. Delphine was surprised to see her, and said as much.

"We're off right now for a while," Natasha said. "It's heavenly. Carl is lobbying for a trip to New England, but I'd rather stay home and read. Not a bad problem to have, is it? Oh, it's so good to run into you. We've got to do dinner soon."

Delphine felt her heart seize up. P.J. had already sent her a text message about what was happening at rehearsal. He had typed an entire story: During the slow, soft part of Vieux-temps's Violin Concerto no. 5, when he was playing all by himself, someone's cell phone started ringing. The conductor flew into a rage, throwing the phone into the wings.

Maybe she had misunderstood. Perhaps the rehearsals were only for strings.

She said nothing when he came home late that night, complaining more than usual about the day's workload. The next morning, she followed him out of the building. He usually walked to Lincoln Center, but today he got on the subway heading downtown. She felt her body begin to shake. Back upstairs she went through his pockets, but found nothing out of the ordinary.

Marie-Hélène returned on the Sunday morning train. By noon she was sitting in Delphine's living room, drinking her pastis straight.

"They say there are eighty percent fewer Americans traveling to France now as compared to last summer," Marie-Hélène said. "Here they're telling everyone that the French are spitting at Americans in the streets, that you've got to wear a Canadian flag pin over there or you'll get murdered. Meanwhile, the French are dying for the business."

Delphine thought of Henri, and wondered how the store was faring. Five American tourists spent as much as a hundred Europeans. And he had never been good with the tourists to begin with.

"*C'est stupide,*" Marie-Hélène went on. "They say Saint-

Tropez isn't affected, of course. Because the rich ones aren't such idiots. Meanwhile, they're all coming around now to what the French were saying six months ago about Iraq."

P.J. joined them on the couch and switched on a baseball game on the television. He drank several beers, and Delphine grew wary. She wanted him to go away, give her time to tell her friend about how oddly he'd been behaving, and what Natasha had said. Around four, they ordered some Indian takeout and P.J. went to pick it up. She quickly gave Marie-Hélène the update.

"I wouldn't worry about it," she said. "You probably just misunderstood. Maybe the strings and the horns practice on totally different days?"

It was unusual for Marie-Hélène to come to P.J.'s defense, and Delphine noted this, thinking that it boded well for her relationship. After they ate, she walked tipsily to the corner store for more wine, telling herself that everything would be all right.

The shopkeeper had closed early, and seeing the store's lights turned down, Delphine sighed and returned home. When she entered the apartment, there they were—her best friend and her fiancé—locked in an embrace on the sofa, their lips pressed madly together.

What followed was a blur to her now, like waking from a nightmare and remembering only the faintest bits: Marie-Hélène jumping up and screaming, as if Delphine were an intruder instead of a woman walking into her own home. P.J. telling Marie-Hélène to go. And then his pathetic apologies, coming in a string of sentences that held no meaning for her. "I got scared," he said. "I just suddenly realized what I'd done, taking you away from your life," and "I panicked. I know it was wrong to be with her, but I'm an idiot, Delphine. Please forgive me."

She thought momentarily, desperately, that it was just

an indiscretion and they could recover. But then he said, "I'm caught between these two worlds. In Paris, even here in New York, this all seemed right. You were the perfect woman for me. But the look on my mother's face made me realize I'm the same old kid. I know you have to leave me, I totally understand. Just please promise that you won't hate me."

He did not want forgiveness; perhaps that was the reason he had chosen Marie-Hélène in the first place, because he wanted Delphine to be the one to end it. He reminded her of one of those cowards who commit a hideous, violent crime and force the police to shoot him, when he should have just saved everyone the heartache and killed himself at the start.

"But you despise her," she said, and then, "Are you in love with her?"

"No," he said. "I'm in love with the fact that she doesn't want to be loved. We're both empty shells. We deserve each other."

She knew this was a lie, at least where he was concerned. He was brimming with romantic feelings and love; he had only decided that she would no longer be its object.

"How long has it been going on?" she asked. "Since the two of you went to that basketball game in the winter?"

"No," he said. "Just since we came back from my parents' place a few weeks ago."

"You slept with her?"

He closed his eyes tightly as if he too were just receiving the news.

"And all last week. You were with her?"

"I'm sorry."

Delphine began to cry, lightly at first, but soon enough there were heaving sobs that made her entire body quake. She went around the apartment, shoving her belongings into the suitcase she had brought from Paris so many months earlier. As she pulled her dresses down from their hangers, she thought of how he had insisted on walking the dog alone each night. She let out another scream.

He begged her to stay—not to be with him, but just to remain in the apartment. He could go stay with a friend, he said. *A friend*. Of course.

Finally, she paused for a moment and looked him in the eye. "You've ruined me."

He reached out, as if to embrace her. "I can't live with you hating me. You have to say you'll find a way to be my friend."

At the height of her obsession with getting the apartment just so, Delphine had allowed herself to be seduced into buying a block of top-of-the-line kitchen knives from a store in Greenwich Village. These knives, the salesman told her, were only for those truly committed to culinary perfection. They were difficult. They needed to be sharpened every three months, and could not be kept in an overly warm room. ("Oh, you mean like a kitchen?" P.J. had said. "That's fine. We were planning to store them beside our bed.")

The biggest, sharpest knife in the block had never been used, to her knowledge. She pulled it out now and went to the living room, where she plunged it into each of the plush gray couch cushions, pulling the white cotton stuffing out with her free hand, imagining that she was pulling out P.J.'s heart and leaving it on the ground to rot. She began to cry, as if something were coming out of her, too.

It was noon; time for her to go. He would be home soon. She needed to tend to a few small things before she left.

She stopped up the kitchen sink and the bathtub, turning the taps as high as they would go. With any luck, it would flood the whole place by the time he returned. She went out into the hall and threw his car keys down the garbage chute. His laptop sat open on the coffee table. This she quietly closed and slipped into the tub.

In the corner of the living room, the Stradivarius stood in its stand, regal, ever more perfect set against the mess she had made. It resembled a tiny body, with all the delicate curves of a woman. She would most likely never hear him play it again.

Delphine found the case in the hall closet and laid the violin inside. She left the door to the apartment flung open. Violin in one hand, suitcase in the other, she rode the elevator down, walked through the marble lobby for the last time, and stepped out into the humid afternoon air. The doorman never even looked up from his newspaper.

She had called Helena Kaufman's office in Brussels two days earlier, pretending to be his manager, Marcy. She said she had some exciting news. P.J. had decided to donate the Salisbury Stradivarius to the International Jewish Congress. They agreed that she would bring the instrument to the organization's New York office at twelve-thirty. They would make the announcement at four o'clock, issuing a press release and photographs. With any luck, they would get a story on the following weekend's episode of *60 Minutes*.

P.J.'s quotes in the press release were impassioned, and rather damning of anyone who didn't happen to agree that the rightful owners of such instruments were the descendants of those who had possessed them to start with.

By the time he learned what happened, he would never have the guts to say it was anything other than what he had planned. And by then, she would be flying overhead, high in the sky, gone.

1987

Maurice didn't get his cheeseburger until one o'clock. James ordered the roast beef special.

They had only eaten a few bites when they were called out again, this time to 364 Rindge Tower.

There was always some kind of chaos in the towers. The two huge, ugly buildings on Rindge Avenue housed over two thousand families, many of them immigrants. If you asked James, it was a stupid policy to have that many poor people crammed together in one place.

Twice a month, when they got their WIC allotments—butter, flour, milk—it was inevitable that some moron was going to take a bag of flour and drop it down the building's incinerator shaft, hoping to create an explosion that might blow off an apartment door or two.

Depending on the day, an EMT might not step inside the building unless accompanied by a police officer holding a gun.

There were three elevators at 364 Rindge. Today, when they walked in, carrying the stretcher, the elevator furthest to the left was already open. Maurice, in front, walked toward it before quickly pushing back.

"Fuck!" he yelled.

Someone had defecated all over the goddamn elevator.

James shook his head, pressed the UP button.

If one day he just wound up dead in this hellhole, how long would Sheila mourn? Five years? Ten? He could just see Debbie trying to fix her up with divorced men from her church. *You've gotta get back out there! Jimmy was never good enough for you anyway, honey. See this as a blessing.* Parker and Danny would hate the new guy at first, but after a couple years they'd realize he wasn't all that bad, and sometime after that they'd start calling him Dad.

When the next elevator arrived, the wall panel was newly melted, the walls themselves charred. The sickening smell of burning plastic hit them as soon as the doors opened; on the floor sat a giant bag of trash that someone had lit on fire, which now smoldered as it melted onto the carpet.

Two kids came bolting through the fire door to survey their work. They took one look at James and Maurice and hightailed it back to wherever they came from.

"Aww shit, cops," James heard one of them say.

"Man, they're ambulance drivers, not cops."

Ambulance drivers. They hated when people called them that.

"Let's just take the stairs," Maurice said.

On the seventh floor, strange cooking smells wafted out from under doorways, making James's stomach turn. In Apartment 7F, a Haitian guy lay unconscious on a couch. His wife didn't speak English, but she had summoned a cousin over who knew a few words and phrases. From him, James determined that the man had turned in early the night before complaining of a headache, and rolled out of bed sometime around six a.m., never coming to after that.

"Any health issues?" James said.

The cousin shook his head and shrugged, unsure of what he was asking.

"Blood pressure?" James said.

He nodded, his eyes widening happily, like they had just solved the puzzle and now they could all go home.

"High blood pressure," the cousin said.

"Does he take medicine for it?" James asked. "Medicine?" He tried to mime taking a spoonful of something, swallowing it down. He hoped they understood. "Medicine," he said again, this time almost screaming it, as if his volume were the problem.

The guy said something to the wife, and she looked confused. James whistled, trying to disguise his frustration. He felt for the immigrant families they dealt with. Some were afraid to call 911 for fear of deportation. Maybe that's why these people had waited so long. Others came to the United States but never interacted with anyone outside of their own culture, not trusting or understanding American ways.

Language was a huge barrier—the city had been recruiting bilingual medics for a couple of years now. But even the immigrants who spoke English were different. The Irish, his own people, never wanted anyone to know their business. To be sick was a sign of weakness, so they kept it to themselves until the last possible second, and by then it was often too late.

Maurice wrapped the cuff around the patient's arm.

"Two-fifty over one-twenty," he said.

Probably a bleed in the brain.

"He will be okay?" the cousin kept asking, again and again. The woman was talking fast, gesturing at him to translate. He sighed. "She says he's got work at six."

They were only a few years older than James himself. He saw kids' drawings on the fridge, and a tiny plastic Christmas tree on a folding card table.

Even if they had some common language, he never could have told this woman the truth: if she had called right away, her husband might have made it. But she had waited too long now for there to be any hope. He would leave it to the doctors in the ER to explain. Let them earn their fat paychecks.

For the wife's sake, they made a big show of rushing him to Mass General, even though it was too late.

James realized when they got back in the truck after that he had forgotten to write down the guy's last name. Now his form sat incomplete on top of the pile as James tried to figure out how he could explain the situation to his boss. It was a stupid mistake, one that he would never have made if he weren't so exhausted. He needed to get his head on straight. He needed some sleep.

For the past few hours, his legs shook every time he stood up. Now and then his thoughts started spinning out and pulling him under. Before the Haitians, there had been a twenty-year-old who lost two fingers in a snowblower when he reached in to fix a clog without shutting off the motor first.

As he drove the kid to the hospital, for some reason James started thinking about the McGuires, who lived next door to him. Their house was a crumbling two-family. They lived in one half and rented the other side to a couple of young guys who were nice enough, though they always seemed high. *Why the hell did they have so much stuff piled up on their front porch? Rusty lawn furniture and dirty old stuffed animals, clothes and shoes and soggy newspaper. It was like the freaking Clampetts over there. He should confront Ted McGuire about it, man-to-man. That kind of shit was bad for the neighborhood. A few days earlier, there had been batteries strewn all over their lawn. Batteries!*

The truck shook violently. Somehow he had managed to drive up onto the curb.

"McKeen, slow down," came Maurice's voice from the back.

James looked at the speedometer. He was going eighty-five.

"Sorry, man."

Batteries. Now suppose one of his kids picked one up and swallowed it. Maybe that particular scenario was unlikely, but who knew.

Had Sheila gotten batteries for Parker's robot? Every year they forgot the batteries, and spent half of Christmas morning taking old pairs out of alarm clocks and smoke detectors and the VCR remote. To be a totally together person would require nothing more than having an unopened package of double-As sitting on the coffee table once the presents were unwrapped, and yet somehow they couldn't seem to manage it.

In high school, there had been this kid they called Triple-A, because he was skinny, like a triple-A battery. Stupid nickname, come to think of it. Stupid nickname for a not altogether bright kid. One gorgeous summer afternoon, a bunch of them went up to the quarries behind Cunningham Park. They were drinking beers, swimming, having a good time, when Triple-A decided to jump in. Only he did it where everyone knew you weren't supposed to—at a spot where the ledge below jutted out too far, and the water wasn't deep enough. They heard him hit the ledge before his body flopped into the water. They all stood there. Connelly, Big Boy, Sean Fallon, Mike Sheehan. If James hadn't jumped after the kid, the rest of them probably would have left him for dead. That was something to remember.

James switched his blinker on and pulled into the Beth Israel Emergency Room lot. He put the truck in park.

"McKeen! What the hell are you doing?" Maurice yelled. "We're taking him to the Brigham! Come on, man! I've got two fingers on ice back here."

Maurice rarely got annoyed, but James could tell that he was bullshit, and rightly so. He would have been too.

Now it was half past four. They hadn't had a break all afternoon. Maurice stood in a kitchen in Inman Square, in the home of a woman in her fifties who was having chest pains. A Filipino nurse helped him make a list of all the drugs she took, while a group of old people, mostly women, hovered over them as if watching a play. One of the two men in the group was younger than the rest, but he had the telltale signs of AIDS—the lesions on his skin, his collar-bone jutting out, showing just how thin he was beneath his sweater. You saw a lot of guys like this in Cambridge the past couple years.

James remembered when Rock Hudson confirmed that he had the disease right before he died in 1985. He had never imagined that Hudson might be gay. "Do you think Doris Day knew?" his mother whispered when the news broke, and James and Sheila cracked up. But ever since, people were afraid. Sheila told him to be careful around blood, knowing how they never wore gloves in the truck, or did much of anything to protect themselves. It was a whole new mentality, and it hadn't really taken hold in the EMT community. How could it, when most guys in his company saw it as a badge of honor to be walking around the hospital covered in blood? There was a saying: *He who has the most blood on him at day's end wins.* You couldn't change that mind-set overnight.

The apartment they stood in now was a big, bright pent-house with high ceilings. In a small bedroom off the hall, the nurse had half moved in, her suitcases lying open at the foot of the bed, clothes spilling out onto the carpet.

James stood with the firefighters in the larger bedroom next door, around a birdlike woman who was lying hap-pily enough in her bed, wearing a silk dress and slippers. A woman of a similar age sat by her side, stroking her hand. A row of black-and-white head shots hung on the opposite wall, all of the same pretty, black-haired girl.

"That's me, you know," the patient said. "I was an actress. You boys are all too young to remember, but it's true."

"It's true," her friend echoed. "Jinx Murray. Look her up."

"Jinx?" James asked.

"A sobriquet. Real name Angela Morris," the bird-woman said. "The studios reinvented you back then."

He couldn't tell whether or not they were full of it. Her place was nice enough that she might have been a star. Then again, she could have just married money. James made a note of her name to tell his mother later. Jinx. That should be easy enough to remember.

"I had heart surgery two weeks ago," she said. "You'll need to take me to Mass General. My cardiologist is Dr. Warner."

James eyed the meaty firefighters on the other side of the bed—they looked amusingly out of place here, among the delicate perfume bottles and pink lace curtains.

"Curley, will you help me get her on the stretcher?" he asked one of them. Curley nodded, and together they lifted her up and over. She felt like nothing, just air in James's hands. He was afraid she might shatter.

They wheeled her down the hall and through a large living room, where the biggest Christmas tree he had ever seen loomed over a grand piano. The presents scattered beneath it had been wrapped so perfectly that the whole thing looked like a photograph in a magazine. James had offered to wrap the kids' gifts this year, but Sheila had just laughed, as if tape and scissors were heavy machinery that he could never be trusted to operate.

They hadn't gotten each other Christmas gifts in years. James was painfully familiar with the television ads for women's jewelry that sprang up by the dozens at this time of year. The subtle subtext seemed to be: *If you're a real man, you'll buy her some fucking earrings*. In the past, he had wanted to, and it hurt that she knew him so well, all the worst and darkest parts of him. It was probably better back in the old days, when men handled the finances and wives didn't have a clue what the family bank account contained. He couldn't dazzle her, because no matter what he bought, when she looked into the box she'd see nothing besides the fact that he had just dug them a few hundred dollars deeper into the hole.

But this year James was determined to get her a new diamond. Connelly told him that you were supposed to spend two months' salary now, or you'd look cheap. When James focused on it, it seemed like money wasn't real, just an imaginary obstacle that he could think his way out of.

For weeks, he had weighed what he ought to do. The credit card wasn't an option—seeing the charge on the monthly statement would put her over the edge and defeat the whole purpose of the thing. He thought about opening another card, one she wouldn't know about, but that seemed deceitful. He considered crazy ideas: enrolling in medical testing trials, sperm donation (Sheila would have castrated him for even thinking about it, had she known). He listened to Dave Connelly's brother tell a story about how after the Fore River Shipyard closed and he lost his job, he'd made tons of money doing some pyramid scheme. James gave some thought to that. But in the end, he had sold his father's 1949 Ford Coupe Flathead V8.

Connelly had been giving him shit about the car for years. "This jalopy is straight out of *Happy Days*. I'm not getting in it," he'd say, but he always got in and they always had fun driving that thing around.

The guy who bought the car off him looked like he had just stepped out of the early seventies, with muttonchops and huge, dark sunglasses. He said he was a collector. While he went to the bank to get cash, James sat in the driver's seat for half an hour, breathing in deep, trying to keep some part of it for himself.

Connelly tried to make him feel better about the situation: "Hey, you know what FORD stands for? 'Fix or Repair Daily.' You know what FORD stands for? 'Found on Roadside Dead.'"

When James thought about the fact that the car was no longer his—that come spring, he would not be driving along the coast, blasting the radio with the wind rushing by—he felt an almost sickening sense of loss. But there had been no other way. If he didn't put his family ahead of himself, what sort of man was he?

By selling the car, he had guaranteed that Sheila wouldn't have to worry about them paying anyone back. She could just be happy.

When he had picked the ring up from the jewelers a few days earlier, he had gone in full of excitement, but came out feeling deflated. He had it made to the exact specifications of the original, but it looked even smaller now, like a trinket you'd get out of a gumball machine. The guy on the other side of the counter had tried to persuade him to trade up— *After this many years of marriage, a lot of men increase the size of the stone,* he said. James couldn't afford to, but after he saw the ring he wished he'd just gone ahead and done it anyway.

He wished he could bring Sheila and the boys to this penthouse, and that the four of them could move in and have it all—the nice furniture, the presents, the crackling fire.

The sick woman's friends were concerned, but they also seemed excited by the surprise turn of events. One of them threw a mink coat over her bare legs with gusto.

"We'll wait here for you!" she said. She pushed the nurse forward. "You go ahead with her."

James and Maurice wheeled the stretcher into an elevator and rode down fifteen stories, with the firefighters packed in around them like sardines.

Outside, the snow fell in sheets, making it impossible to

see anything more than a few feet away. He hoped Sheila wouldn't try to go anyplace. Her Toyota had rear-wheel drive, a nightmare in a storm. The engine squealed and rattled whenever you started it in cold weather, and kept on squealing for several minutes. You had to let it warm up, or the car wouldn't drive smoothly. But Sheila was never patient enough to wait.

Her sister Debbie drove a new Volvo these days.

"It has an actual steel cage inside of it," she had told Sheila on a recent visit. "I thought it was too expensive, but Drew said he can't put a price on my safety."

On the way to the hospital, the Filipino nurse rode up front with Maurice and cried softly. James wondered why she was crying—she had only known this woman for two weeks. Was she afraid of losing her job? Did her whole life depend on the health of the stranger in the next room? It must be an odd existence, living out your days in other people's homes.

The patient was more matter-of-fact. "Call my son in D.C. when we get there, will you?" she instructed the nurse. "Let him know what's up."

James sat beside her and asked when her chest pains had started. "I was sitting at my piano," she said. "I'd invited some friends from my acting days over for carols and eggnog. We were having a lovely time. And then, all of a sudden it was like an elephant was sitting on my chest."

"How much eggnog did you have?"

"Not a drop! Doctor's orders!"

"Did you eat anything spicy?"

"No," she said. "And I've been taking all my medication."

Maurice called the doctor for permission to give her nitro and start an IV.

"Open your mouth wide for me," James said. He slipped the tablet under her tongue.

They passed through Kenmore Square. It looked like a ghost town in the snow. James wrapped a tourniquet around her upper arm before inserting the IV, in case she required meds before they reached the hospital.

"I was a student in the Boston University drama school just up the road here," the woman said. "Faye Dunaway was a classmate of mine. We called her Done Fade-away. We all figured she'd be a flash in the pan. Looking back, I truly think a lot of us were more talented than her. She just wanted it the most."

James nodded. Maybe the same could be said for him and his music career. Maybe he hadn't wanted it enough. He considered saying this out loud, but stopped himself.

He was fairly certain that the Beatles had ruined his life. He was eleven when *Meet the Beatles* was released. His brother Bobby, four years older, bought the record the day it went on sale. James remembered sitting next to him, watching that first appearance on Ed Sullivan, feeling incredibly cool. His brother never wanted him around, and James held his breath, trying to blend into the sofa, afraid to break the spell. After "I Want to Hold Your Hand," Bobby turned to him transfixed, and said, "Holy shit. Right?"

"Right," James said, nodding, amazed. To this day, he still thought of it as a profound moment.

He saved his allowance to buy Beatles trading cards and fan magazines, a sweatshirt and an egg cup. He spent three dollars on a Beatles wig at Woolworth's, which he wore to school the next day, only to be sent home with a note from the principal.

When he was twelve years old and Bobby was sixteen, somehow their mother had gotten tickets to see the Beatles play at Boston Garden. You could barely hear the songs. Girls screamed so loud that they drowned out the sound. But that was it. James was hooked. The four of them just seemed so at ease, so happy and unassuming, like they had made this crazy dream come true and you could too.

A few years later, when he heard the news that Bobby had been drafted, James sat very still on his bed, trying to feel something. He knew it was evil, but in part he felt relieved—he imagined going through Bobby's drawers without the fear of getting caught, stealing his records and his clothes and his cigarettes. His brother liked to beat up on him, and now James would be free of that. But at supper that night, when he saw that Bobby had shaved off his long greasy hair and sideburns, James felt it all at once: a sudden jolt of seriousness, an understanding that everything was about to change. He ran up to his room and slammed the door, putting *Sgt. Pepper's* on the record player, and turning the volume up so high that the furniture shook.

No one had ever come along to replace the Beatles. Every time a new band got popular, even decades later, the highest compliment you could pay them was to call them "the next Beatles." They remained the gold standard, the best that anyone could ever be.

His son Parker was an infant when John Lennon was killed. James would never forget that night. Sheila had taken the baby to her parents'. He was watching the Pats game at home by himself, when all of a sudden Howard Cosell said, "Remember this is just a football game, no matter who wins or loses."

James could still recall the lump in his throat. If Cosell was saying that, then something huge and terrible must have occurred. But of all the tragedies he might have imagined, this he never could: "John Lennon, outside of his apartment building on the West Side of New York City, the most famous, perhaps, of all of the Beatles, shot twice in the back, rushed to Roosevelt Hospital, dead on arrival."

He had always hated Howard Cosell. But after that night,

even though the announcer had just been doing his job, James could barely stand to hear his voice. He only watched *Monday Night Football* with the volume turned down.

Sometimes when Sheila was at work, he'd take out his old guitar and play for the boys. Danny was still too young to care, but Parker loved *Help!* and *Rubber Soul* almost as much as James did. He was amazed with Parker's pitch and his memory for lyrics—the kid was only seven and could do a version of "Yesterday" that would make you sob. James had taught him some chords on the guitar, and was impressed as hell to find that a week later Parker still remembered them.

Last Tuesday had been Parker's school Christmas concert. James got a work swap for a Sunday shift to be there. Every kid had a solo—just a few words for the young ones. It was supposed to make them feel special and boost their self-esteem, though how you could feel special when everyone else got the exact same treatment, James wasn't sure. Parker's solo came at the very beginning of "Silent Night": "All is calm, all is bright." That was it. Six words, and James had felt tears pricking at the corners of his eyes. He would do whatever it took to make sure his son became someone, instead of turning into just another loser with nothing to show for his big dreams.

"We're gonna get him into music class," James whispered to Sheila before the lights even came up.

"He already takes one at school," she said.

"I'm talking about something better than that. He's really got talent. I think he has what it takes."

Sheila patted his hand. "Jimmy, calm down. He's just a kid."

The night of Christmas Eve was busier than he would have imagined in this weather. A boy had cracked his head open sledding into a tree; a young woman had swallowed a bottle of pills, which was common at this time of year. Another had gotten a Ping-Pong ball stuck in her ass while doing something sexual with her boyfriend, also fairly common.

They took the couple to Cambridge Hospital. Inside the ER, as Maurice signed off on the girl's chart, James eyed the homeless guy they had dropped off early that morning through an opening in a curtain—he was curled up on top of the sheets in a narrow bed, wearing just a cloth hospital gown. He looked like a child, and James wanted to go to him. He wondered about the guy's mother. Had he ever had a real Christmas morning, and if so did the memory of it make his life today better or worse?

"A Ping-Pong ball. Wow," Maurice said when they left the ER.

"Yeah."

They both started to laugh, and didn't stop for about ten minutes.

Every ER in the city had a "butt box," where the doctors kept various items that had once resided in someone's ass. James had seen an X-ray of a beer bottle inside one guy, and a live mouse inside another. There was a process called the anal wink, which basically meant that once an object made it past the sphincter, it got vacuumed into the body and stayed there. None of these bozos ever seemed to have heard about the phenomenon until it happened to them.

James thought he would probably rather just go ahead and die than invite paramedics in to examine his sex life up close.

Last year, Sheila had suggested that they try some role play to spice things up in the bedroom. Apparently, her girlfriend Kathy Dolan had tried it with her husband and raved.

When Sheila first mentioned the idea, James asked, "You mean, like, wear a nurse's uniform?"

"Oh yeah. That's what gets me hot, to dress up like a nurse, the way I do every day."

"Well, I don't know." He was surprised by how bashful he felt. He liked that there could still be something about Sheila that made him feel nervous, unfamiliar.

She wanted to pretend he was a car mechanic and she was a high school cheerleader stranded on the side of the road. Apparently that was her big fantasy. He went with it. They had fun. Though now he would never ever let her take the car into the shop to get fixed.

As soon as he and Maurice got back in the truck, their tone came over the radio again.

"Jesus, is there no one else working in the entire city of Cambridge?" James said as he picked it up. "Nona, you're killing me here."

"Bad accident," she said. "Car in the river off the Mass Ave Bridge. You're going with Fire."

They had to wait on the bridge while the fire department's dive team pulled the patient from the water. According to his license, his name was Liam Stone. He lived in Somerville. Eighteen years old.

His face was shattered, his legs pointing in the wrong direction, his pelvis ripped open.

To the nurse who met them in the Mass General ER, James said, "Poor kid."

She shrugged. "He was probably drunk, coming home from some Christmas party. He's lucky he didn't kill someone else."

"Or it could have been the weather," he said. "Have a nice holiday."

Even Sheila agreed that there were angelically good nurses, and there were lousy nurses, and there wasn't much in between. He hated to leave this kid in this one's hands, but he had no choice.

James was almost certain that Liam Stone wouldn't make it. He felt grateful that at least he didn't have to be there when the parents were called. He imagined what it would be like—one minute you're sitting at home toasting the holiday, waiting for your son to get back from the mall, and the next, your life as you know it is over. He wished he could go straight home and hug his kids.

He figured that now dispatch might give them a few hours' peace anyway. They went to the break room at Cambridge Hospital, where Maurice's orphaned burgers sat on the table, along with a few sandwiches, a two-liter of Coke, and a plate of homemade brownies from Cathy at the deli. She was a good kid, that one.

James took a brownie and went out to the pay phone in the hall to call home.

"Hi," he said, when Sheila answered.

"Oh. Hi." She sounded like she had been hoping for someone else. *"Parker, I said don't!"*

"How's it going?"

"They're bouncing off the walls. We went to your mom's earlier to drop off her groceries and she gave me a pound of fudge that one of her neighbors made. I think we've already eaten half of it. My sister came over with the kids to decorate some slice-and-bakes, but the snow got so bad that they had to go home before we could even get the cookies out of the oven. Which, by the way, only seems to heat up half the time you try it now. We're gonna need a new one."

What did an oven cost? He tried to conjure up a number, but he had never bought one—the oven they had had come with the house.

"Cookies!" Parker shouted in the background.

Sheila groaned. "Yes, because clearly they needed more sugar."

James could hear the tension in her voice. Not just the usual frustration with the boys, but something worse. A fight coming on. She hadn't wanted him to work the holiday, and now she was stuck with the kids at their most demonic.

"I promise I'll take care of them all day tomorrow," he said.

"Yeah right. You're like a zombie as it is," she said. "You need to sleep. How's your day going?"

He thought of telling her about Liam Stone, but there was no reason to burden her with it now. "Busy," he said. "Earlier, there was this woman who said she—"

"Danny, sit your butt in the chair, or I swear to God," she yelled. "Sorry. Go on."

He wondered how old your kids had to be before you got to have an uninterrupted conversation in their presence. When was the last time he and Sheila had talked for longer than a few minutes without the boys around?

She sniffled now.

"Are you crying?" he asked.

"No."

"Getting sick?"

"With my luck, probably," she said.

"What's wrong?" he asked.

"You'll find out when you get here."

It sounded like a threat. He pictured her belongings by the door, the kids buckled up in the backseat, ready to go.

"Jesus, Sheila, you're scaring me."

She sighed. "I promised myself I wouldn't tell you while you were working, but fine. A few minutes after my sister left, I was sitting in the living room with the boys, and we heard this crashing sound from the kitchen. So I go in there, and part of the ceiling has totally collapsed. You know where it was peeling? I mean the size of the hole, Jimmy, it's massive. You can see clear into the upstairs bathroom. Parker had been in there like thirty seconds earlier. He could have been killed."

James couldn't think straight. The boys were safe, and that was a relief, but still he felt panicked.

"But everyone's okay? The dog's okay?"

"Are you kidding me? Yes, your precious dog is fine."

"We'll get it taken care of," he said, trying to sound calm for her.

That ceiling had been about to come down for a year, and he had done nothing. He couldn't afford to. Now one of his kids might've been crushed to death because of it. He wanted to hit someone hard, or for someone to just come up from behind and beat the shit out of him until he couldn't breathe. *I felt like an elephant was sitting on my chest.* Wasn't that how the woman had put it?

"We should have moved out of this shithole a year ago," she whispered angrily. "It's dangerous, Jimmy. I've tried to tell you that. Why don't you ever listen?"

"I'll come home," he said, even though he knew he couldn't.

"You can't leave until morning," she said. "It's okay. I swept it up as best I could and the boys know the kitchen is off-limits for now. We're fine without you."

"Thanks."

She sighed. "You know what I mean."

"Maybe you should go spend the night at your parents'," he said. He imagined the whole house falling down on them, coming home to find his family destroyed.

"My dad said it's not anything dangerous. I just don't know how we're going to pay for it."

He knew now that she'd be mad about the ring anyway, even though he hadn't borrowed the money. If he was going to sell the car, she'd say, he should have used the cash for something they actually needed. That was probably true. But Sheila never got anything, and who was to say that the ring wasn't as necessary as the ceiling over their heads?

In the background, he could hear Parker talking about Santa Claus and the Rolly Robot. He wished he could be there with them, huddled under a blanket on the couch with his wife and children, parked in front of the TV, all of them laughing, making memories, hanging stockings before drifting off to sleep.

"It doesn't feel like Christmas Eve without you," she said, her voice softening.

"I'm sorry you have to deal with putting them to bed on your own tonight. Seems like a two-man job."

She laughed. "At least."

"Honey?" he said.

"Yeah?"

"I love you. I'm so sorry I wasn't there."

James started to cry. He was never home when it mattered. He was no better than his own useless father had been.

"I love you too," she said. "Don't cry. It's under control."

"Okay. Put Parker on for a sec."

He heard an excessive amount of jostling and static at the other end of the line, and then came his son's urgent voice.

"Hi Dad! Did you hear about the hole in the ceiling? I can go up in the bathroom and spy on Mom downstairs. It's so cool."

"So I heard," he said. "Now listen, bud. I know you're excited about tomorrow, but promise me you'll be good for your mom tonight, okay?"

"I will."

"Thatta boy. I'm sorry I'm not there to tuck you in. Did you already put your letter out for Santa?"

"Yup. And I wrote him a note from Danny too, because he doesn't know how to write yet."

"That was very thoughtful. You know Santa can't come until you're asleep, right?"

"Yup."

"And he totally knows if you're faking it."

"Really, Dad?"

"For sure."

Their shift was set to end at seven a.m.

At six, they hadn't had a call in over five hours, and decided that another wasn't likely. The snow had continued to fall through the night. The stores were all closed. Around town, kids rich and poor were begging their parents to get out of bed and let them open their presents. Parker and Danny had strict orders not to unwrap anything until James got home. They could empty their stockings, but that was it.

He hadn't slept, although they had been back in the break room since one. While Maurice snored on the cot across the way and a few other guys watched an old western on TV, James just lay there, thinking about the day to come. He would stop by his mother's on the way home, and then drink coffee with Sheila while the boys ripped open their gifts. At noon, they'd go to Mass, and after that to Sheila's mother's place for an early supper.

He wanted to feel happy at the thought of all this, he ought to feel happy. But instead, he only felt weighted down and exhausted. He saw now that nothing he would do today would change anything. Parker would love his robot, but in a week's time he'd be onto something else. The bigger gifts would be impossible—they would never be able to afford to send him to college, or help him buy a house. The kid was only in second grade, and for now he worshipped James. But how long would it be before Parker realized that his old man was a failure?

And Sheila. James had sold his old Ford to buy her the ring, but now he was back to zero. He was broke. They would need cash to fix the hole in the ceiling, and the oven that was on the fritz, and the car's transmission, and who the hell knew what else.

James thought of the kid who had mugged her. What had he done with the ring? Did he pawn it, or did he give it to some girl he thought he loved? James pictured the scene, as he had so many times before: his wife, trying to manage the stroller and the groceries, not even hearing the footsteps from behind. He'd like to find that kid and shoot him in the head, point-blank, right in front of his whole family on Christmas morning.

When Maurice suggested that they start cleaning the truck early to get a jump on leaving, James thought it was the best idea he'd heard in weeks. They left the hospital, drove back to base and started refreshing the stock. One by one, James checked things off the list, as he did at the end of every shift. Fifteen clean towels, a box of tissues, restraints. Suction cups, burn kit, EKG, defibrillator, Phisoderm. He was almost finished when he heard their tone come over the intercom. Forty-five minutes left in their shift, and they'd have to go out again.

When he answered, the dispatcher said Belmont.

"What the hell?"

"Mutual aid call," she said.

From time to time, if a neighboring community was over-taxed, they might be called upon to fill in. But it was unusual to go as far as Belmont. It was a ten- or fifteen-minute drive on a good day, without snow on the ground.

"You gotta be kidding me," James said.

"They've only got one ambulance on duty and it's at the scene of a fire. Sorry. Bad luck."

"We're not gonna get there fast enough," he said.

"It's a well-being check," the dispatcher replied. "No need to rush."

"If there's no need to rush, then wait until their own people can get there," Maurice said.

"The call came in, we've got to send someone."

She told them the patient was eighty years old. Her daughter-in-law in Florida had been the one to call 911. She had been trying to reach the old woman for two days and gotten no answer.

"She lives alone at home," the dispatcher said. "Apparently she's in good health, or has been until now. I guess her husband died a couple of years ago, and she's refused assisted living. Her name is Evelyn Pearsall."

James wrote it down quickly on his hand, not wanting to forget this time.

"Sounds like you got an earful," he said.

"Yeah, well, it seemed like the woman felt guilty about not being with her on Christmas."

James thought of his own mother.

"As she should," he said.

"She went out of her way to tell me that they were planning to visit her next week."

"Sounds like they'll be here sooner than that, now," he said.

Maurice jumped into the passenger seat, and twisted the siren to hi-lo. The sound seemed even more mournful than usual.

James reached across him and took the Advil from the glove compartment. He screwed off the top, and shook a couple pills into his mouth.

Maurice gave him a look. "You know that shit ain't candy, right?"

"My back's killing me."

The roads were slick, but Route 2 had been plowed now,

and was empty at this hour. James went eighty, not caring about the speed. If Maurice noticed, he didn't say anything. He wanted to get home to his family, too.

"Sheila's gonna kill me," James said. "The kids will be up by now, and they'll be wanting to open their presents."

"Tell me about it. Cindy already gave me shit about working Christmas Eve in the first place."

"Same here."

"Massive fight," Maurice continued, shaking his head as if the memory of it might be enough to do him in. James was tempted to ask for specifics. It would be so nice to peer into someone else's marriage, to figure out whether his own was normal.

"What's up with your hands?" Maurice asked.

"Huh?"

"Your hands are shaking."

James looked down. He hadn't even noticed.

"I'm worried about you, man," Maurice said. "You need a break."

"I'll get a break when I'm dead," James said.

"That's cheery."

They grew silent as they turned off at the exit, and then took a sharp left onto Pleasant Street without waiting for the light to change from red to green. The car dealerships and strip malls gave way to Victorian houses, covered in white, with tiny white Christmas lights peeping out here and there.

They had to use a map to find the address. They turned up a steep hill with tall trees lining both sides. The snow hadn't been touched, and the road was icy. James pictured them getting stuck, having to push the truck all the way there. He slowed down, inched along. There were beautiful old homes all around.

When they reached a mailbox that read number 63, Maurice said, "Holy shit."

A brick mansion stood in the distance, separated from the road by a massive front lawn. You could play a regulation game of football on that lawn. The driveway was half a mile long.

Thinking about his own dinky house, just thrown there on a busy corner, James had sometimes wondered if people ever drove by and thought, *Who the hell lives there?* They would wonder the same thing here, but for the opposite reason.

They parked in front. When they got out, it was silent.

"It even smells better out here," Maurice said.

James wished they could stay in the yard, and not go in to find whatever sad situation resided on the other side of that door. A well-being check usually meant the person had died, but there were exceptions. He could almost hear his son's sweet voice. *All is calm, all is bright.*

They rang the bell once, twice. No answer. James mentally prepared himself to break down the door, even though his back was killing him and he wasn't sure he'd have the strength. But when Maurice tried the handle, the door opened on its own.

The place seemed even bigger once you stepped inside. It felt more like a museum than someone's house. They stood in a large entryway, with high ceilings like he had only ever seen in a church, a wide mirror on the wall, and a grandfather clock in the corner stuck on eleven-thirty.

"Hello!" they called out. "Evelyn? Evelyn, we're here to help you!"

Their words echoed back at them, but there was no response. They walked quickly through the rooms, still calling out to her. James switched on a lamp in a dining room the size of the entire first floor of his house. It was pristine and decorated like something out of *Dynasty*, with a huge table, and a crystal chandelier. On one wall, there was a painting

of two dogs in a sailboat. On another, a more formal painting of a ship in a gold frame. A layer of dust covered every
surface, as if no one had entered the room for years. He ran
his finger along the tabletop, leaving behind a clean, straight
line. He walked through to the kitchen, where a bunch of
brown bananas were rotting on the counter, giving off a
sickly sweet odor that made him cover his nose.

"Evelyn?" he said, though he could tell she wasn't there.

He went into an office with a framed Harvard diploma
hanging by the door. Figured.

Still, James hoped for some great, improbable explanation, the sort of happy ending he'd tack onto a bedtime
story for his boys. *Left alone at Christmas, Evelyn Pearsall
decided to take off for Hawaii and try snorkeling for the first
time in her life!* . . . *Sometimes Evelyn Pearsall liked to go up
in the attic with a Walkman and a Stones tape, and just shut
out the world for days.* . . . *What Evelyn Pearsall's daughter-
in-law never knew was that she had a twenty-four-year-old boy
toy living on Newbury Street, and she had decided to spend the
holiday with him.*

But then Maurice called out, "I found her."

James went to the living room, where the old woman
lay on the floor, unconscious. She wore a cotton nightgown
printed with pink flowers, the same kind of thing his own
mother wore. She had probably been living in just this one
room. There were clothes folded neatly on a sofa, and the
large coffee table was strewn with newspapers and Christmas cards, tons of them. There was a chest covered in
framed family photographs. On an end table there sat a jewelry box, open to reveal all sorts of sparkling gems, thrown
in haphazardly. Beside it stood a plastic cup for her dentures,
a toothbrush with fraying bristles, a bottle of lotion, and a
stack of hardcover books.

He had seen this plenty of times, an old lady in a big old

house living in one or two rooms. Sometimes they were afraid to climb the stairs, but more often it was because they couldn't take the reminder of their dead husbands. They didn't want to sleep in bed without them, or open a closet and see their pressed suits hanging there. James thought of the way they had found the front door unlocked. She had been so vulnerable here, all alone.

"I think she's gone, man," Maurice said. "Look at the color of her skin. Hell of a way to kick off Christmas."

James crouched beside her and felt her wrist. Her skin was cold. But he thought he could detect a slow pulse.

He knew she had nothing in common with his mom. This woman was probably the stuck-up rich type who wouldn't give Mary McKeen the time of day. But even so, it was Christmas, and she was someone's mother, and she was alone. James wanted to save her. He wished he could gather up all the lost souls of the day and bring them home with him. He pictured himself arriving at his in-laws' for Christmas dinner: *Hey Tom and Linda, meet the gang— there's the crazy, racist homeless guy, the stroke victim's wife who can't understand a word you're saying, the Harvard student from India who will probably own all of us in ten years. Here are the parents of the late, great Liam Stone. And last but not least, Evelyn.*

"Let's try," James said. "I'll ride with her."

They lifted her onto the stretcher and carried her outside. Maurice started driving and called the doctor for permission, but before they could even reach him, James turned the cardiac monitor on. She was only breathing four times a minute, with a heartbeat of twenty. She was most likely about to take her last breath.

James inserted the IV. He tried sugar and Narcan to wake her, but neither worked. He struggled to get the breathing tube into her throat. It took five tries. But he finally managed and was able to start breathing for her. He felt a surge of hope, even as he knew that just this amount of packing her up and prodding her was probably more than her body could take. There was nothing more he could do but pray. He said a Hail Mary like he knew his mother would have done, and watched the monitor as Evelyn Pearsall's heartbeat fell to ten times a minute, and then sank down to a flatline.

When he knew for sure that he had lost her, he began to cry. Softly, so that Maurice wouldn't hear. James had let her down. He was a sad excuse for a medic.

"She coded," he said finally.

He heard his partner talking to dispatch: "It's a sudden."

His thoughts started to wander back to her house: the fancy furniture and the box overflowing with jewels. Her ungrateful daughter-in-law, a woman who would leave an old lady home alone on Christmas, would inherit it all.

He thought about his wife, who was as devoted to his mother as she was to her own. Sheila deserved everything and usually ended up with jack shit. How could life be so unfair? He knew it was a stupid, childish question to ask, but truly: Why did some people have to struggle while others had it so damn easy?

James sat back and tried to catch his breath, for the first time taking note of the ring she wore. It was enormous, with two huge diamonds side by side, each of them four times the size of the one he'd bought for Sheila. There were a bunch of tiny diamonds all around, in case the two giant ones weren't impressive enough. He knew what he had paid for Sheila's ring. He could probably get ten times as much for this one. It would cover the ceiling and the stove, and then some.

In the past, on occasion, he had imagined how easy it would be to steal from his patients, but then he would feel sick at the thought. He felt that way now, but not strongly enough. Who was looking out for him while he was busy trying to do right by everyone else? Some piece-of-shit kid had stolen from his wife. Mac Kelly had let him take the rap. Who was he trying to score points with, anyway?

He would think about what happened next for the rest of his life. When James looked back on it, it felt like some fundamental part of him had floated away as he reached over and pulled the ring off her finger. It was freezing out, and the band slid right off. He believed that if it had been summer and there had been so much as a touch of resistance, he would never have gone through with it.

The sign for the ER glowed up ahead.

His heart pounded. Sweat ran down his face. He shoved the ring in his pocket as they pulled into the lot.

James looked down at her bare hand, crisscrossed with veins and wrinkles like a road map. At the top of her second finger was a ghostly white stripe of flesh where the ring had been.

A Diamond Is Forever

—Mary Frances Gerety, 1947

1988

Tonight's gala promised to be a lavish affair. Two hundred people in the ballroom of a private London club, dinner and dancing, and speeches from all the bigwigs at De Beers. Frances had never met or even spoken to these men before this week, despite decades spent working for them. They were just as she had expected—polite and dignified, but slightly removed, and positively oozing wealth.

The week had gone by in a flash. There were lots of new Ayer people she hadn't met before, as well as a few of the old greats, including Warner Shelly, who was almost completely blind. He had a chaperone—as did she—who had to take him to his room each night and make sure he could find the keyhole in the door.

There was no mistaking the fact that they had all seen better days, even Ayer itself. At dinner the night before, she watched a business executive in his twenties turn to his date and say, "Mr. Young and Mr. Rubicam both came from our agency, you know."

The girl looked unimpressed.

Frances sat now in her opulent suite at the Dorchester, perched on the edge of the bed, smoking.

She sipped her martini.

She had ordered the drink and nothing else besides from room service ten minutes earlier. A handsome Brit in a neat tuxedo delivered it on a silver tray. The act felt decadent and incredibly silly. But Lou Hagopian had told her to have whatever she wanted, and at her age she was finally willing to accept such a command. It would be a rude awakening when she had to fly home to Pennsylvania tomorrow, to the dim rooms of her house, to her dog, who probably wondered where on earth she had gone. She had never left him before for even one night.

"We want you to feel like Cinderella," Hagopian said over the phone after she accepted his offer to come.

A very old and crotchety Cinderella with no hopes of meeting Prince Charming, she thought to herself, though she only replied, "Well, thank you."

She laughed now, despite her nerves. If she had had to guess two months ago, she would have said that life's big adventures were all in the past. But here she was, living like royalty. They had given her a chauffeured limousine for the week. There had been a luncheon every day, parties each night, and shopping and sightseeing in between.

She wished her father were still alive to see it. He would have been so proud. And her old pal Dorothy Dignam from the office—imagine if the two of them could have come here together! Dorothy had passed away less than a year earlier. Her obituary said she was ninety-two. As was the case with a lot of women, the first time anyone knew her real age was the day she died.

Frances thought of her that morning, as they took a tour of the De Beers headquarters.

"Look up there," said one of the PR boys when they reached the building.

Her eyesight was terrible, even with glasses, but Frances could just make out the words carved in stone above the massive doors: A DIAMOND IS FOREVER.

"You must be so proud," he said. "It's considered one of the greatest lines in advertising."

"I know it is," she said. "I'm glad that it is."

A week of the same compliment over and over, and she still hadn't come up with a better response than that. Ever since she arrived, the De Beers folks had been telling her how much her work meant to them. She felt awfully pleased to be honored, especially at this point in the game, but in a way it almost seemed like cheating. The line hadn't meant much at the time. It was a very nice line, but nobody jumped up and down. They had just needed some way to sign the ads. She shuddered to think of what might have happened if a great line had been demanded—every copywriter in the department coming up with hundreds of ideas and the best one thrown away like the Edsel.

At the end of this evening's program, they would show a short film chronicling the campaign's success, and then she would speak. Mary Frances Gerety would have the last word. At least for tonight.

The dinner was two hours away. She felt desperate for a nap. But she still hadn't worked out what she'd say onstage. Back home, she had sat down several times to write her speech, but something else always grabbed her attention. The doorbell rang or some interesting segment came on the news, and suddenly she forgot all about De Beers. Of course, this was how she had always worked. She was at her most creative when she waited until the last possible second—a mix of necessity and fear had served her well.

Maybe she would open with that. Tell them that if she hadn't been such a master procrastinator all her life, what they were here to celebrate might never have come to pass.

Frances stood up. Her whole body felt sore from all the walking she'd done. They had seen the Tower of London. Oxford Street and the British Museum and Saint Paul's Cathedral and the Palace of Westminster. Yesterday they took the train out to Bath, where the most famous and celebrated former resident was Jane Austen, though it seemed to Frances that Austen had lived there only for about three minutes.

She had been athletic all her life. While they were traipsing around the city, she was too proud to mention that these days she rarely walked farther than the distance from the front door to the end of the driveway. But now she was paying for it. And somehow she'd have to squeeze into high heels tonight. Torture devices, that's what they were. Frances had no idea how women worked and wore heels at the same time. For her, it was utterly impossible to think a clear thought while standing on the tips of her toes.

She recalled a young Marilyn Monroe predicting such a fate for old-timers. Marilyn, who never got to get old. Or never *had* to get old, depending on how you looked at it.

Frances belted it out as she made her way into the suite's yellow sitting room. "Time rolls on and youth is gone and you can't straighten up when you bend. But stiff back or stiff knees, you stand straight at Tiffany's. Diamonds are a girl's best friend."

She plopped into a chair at the mahogany desk and looked out the window at the lush green treetops of Hyde Park. She cupped her chin in her hand and placed her elbow on the desk, a position she had assumed on a thousand other occasions when she was on deadline.

De Beers had been one of the few campaigns that invented a need that didn't previously exist. She jotted this down. Usually, when you wrote an ad, you wanted to highlight that something new and exciting had come along. But with De Beers, it was the opposite: Not only were they to impress upon average women and men—especially the men!—that diamonds were now an imperative for marriage, they were to make it seem as though it had always been that way. Before they got started, diamonds were for the wealthy alone. But now everyone and their mother wore one.

They did it again years later with *Long Distance Is the Next Best Thing to Being There*. The campaign drove AT&T's

profits through the roof. Until that line, no one made long-distance calls. It was just too expensive. But the print ads grabbed people's hearts, and eventually the television spots with the line *Reach Out and Touch Someone* took the whole thing over the top, with treacly melancholy music and video of babies talking to grandfathers three thousand miles away, and lovers telling each other how much they missed being together, and the soldier calling home from the battlefield.

Be All You Can Be was another one. With that line, Ayer created a volunteer army, while making it seem like an American tradition.

Frances didn't think it was a stretch to say that De Beers was bigger than both of those in terms of inventing the thing you could not do without. Of course, that sounded like bragging. She scratched out everything she had written.

Maybe she ought to get dressed first.

She had decided to wear a blue taffeta gown with a long, full skirt, and a jeweled shawl. The ensemble hung on the back of the bathroom door. Frances went to it and ran her fingers over the fabric. Each night this week, as she put on another frock, she thought of the woman back home to whom it belonged, and imagined that friend by her side. She had saved Meg's for tonight.

Before Ham died, Meg said that someday the two of them would take the grand tour of Europe. Afterward, everyone encouraged her to do it on her own, but Meg wasn't the type.

Frances held her glass up to the dress.

"Cheers, darling," she said, draining her drink.

She thought she just might call up the butler for one more.

Seven o'clock arrived in what seemed like seconds, and Frances was being whisked off to the club in her private limousine. There was an honest-to-God telephone in the backseat, beside an ice bucket stocked with champagne. She was slightly tipsy and had the strongest urge to call someone, but who?

Instead, she placed her hands in her lap and clasped them together like they couldn't be trusted otherwise.

They got to the club, and her chauffer, Richard, rushed round to open her door. She had to lean heavily on his arm to get out. Yes, she was a clunky old thing, but still she felt like a starlet tonight. She greeted the doormen, who nodded their replies without a word. Frances wondered if someone had instructed them not to speak, like those soldiers who stood guard outside Buckingham Palace.

The dining room was magnificent, with crystal chandeliers and sprays of white orchids and roses on every table. It looked like the Academy Awards.

She found her seat, at the same table as Warner and a few others from Ayer. She tried to enjoy the cocktails and the chicken and the Yorkshire pudding, but all she could think about was the fact that soon she would take the stage and she still hadn't a clue what she'd say.

No one knew that she was going to speak. That was a secret between herself and Hagopian and a handful of others. Lou Hagopian seemed to be channeling Tony Bennett— he loved the spotlight, and he was so smooth that it seemed like his every word might be scripted. If only whoever had written his lines could have done hers too.

After dessert, as planned, a girl from public relations came to find Frances in the crowd and ferried her backstage.

There were many lovely speeches. The chairman of De Beers paid homage to her! She was utterly overwhelmed.

Then they showed a video, a creation of Bob and Deanne Dunning, the husband-and-wife team who had left Ayer and started their own company at some point in the seventies.

It opened with a scene from *Casablanca*, Ingrid Bergman saying, "Sing it, Sam."

And then the song. "As Time Goes By." Its notes played on as dozens of Frances's ads flashed across the screen.

A voiceover announced, "The engagement of Ayer and De Beers began in 1938 with a letter postmarked Victoria Hotel, Johannesburg, South Africa."

From there, the story was told, beginning to end: Of the surveying they did in the thirties, of Gerry Lauck's plane going down the first time he traveled to South Africa. Of all the advances they had made from one decade to the next. It culminated with a silly thing that the latest creatives had made, a De Beers ad that took the form of a music video. A floppy-haired rock band looked sullen and severe, but by the end the lead singer had proposed to his girlfriend with a diamond.

As soon as the song ended, it would be her turn.

Frances had never felt so nervous in all her life. She could hear her heartbeat in her ears. For a moment, she allowed herself to picture the worst: she would go out there and fall down dead. Her one chance at recognition, dashed.

But she tried to be calm. She reminded herself that she had always done her best work under pressure.

The curtain parted, and she had no choice but to step onto the stage. When they saw her walking toward the podium and her name splashed across the screen, the crowd got to their feet. The sound of applause filled the room as Frances choked out the first of many words she would speak that night.

"Thank you," she began.

Part Five

1972

After they left, Evelyn took to her bed. She had been there now for thirty minutes. She once read that Edith Wharton wrote her novels tucked in under the covers, with her dogs all around. It seemed a somewhat depressing way to spend one's days. Bed was for sleep or sickness or, occasionally, sadness.

She could not guess how long it would be before she saw her son again. She knew now that he really would go through with the divorce, and when she pictured what this meant, she wanted to fall into a deep sleep: Julie would go, taking the girls from her. On holidays, she and Gerald would eat alone at their long dining table that could seat sixteen. Her granddaughters would grow up without a father. They could send money if Teddy refused to, but no amount could make up for his absence.

When she heard Gerald coming up the stairs, she held her breath. As soon as Teddy left, she had pushed past her husband toward the bedroom. It was a move so uncharacteristic that Gerald had laughed. This had proven a grave mistake, which she could tell he realized as soon as their eyes met and he saw her expression. Now that half an hour had passed, she felt embarrassed about how she had acted. It was a tad dramatic, to be sure. But she was truly livid with him. This was one of the few times she could remember in life, and certainly the most consequential, when Gerald's response to something was so utterly different from her own. If he hadn't talked her into having Teddy over for lunch. If he had flown to Florida right away after Teddy first met Nicole. *If if if.*

He came in now with a mug in his hand, and set it down on the nightstand.

"Made you some tea."

She couldn't remember him ever doing this before, other than when she was down with the flu.

"Thank you," she said.

"I gather you're still mad at me," he said.

"Yes."

She felt like an actress in a play. In four decades, they had had very little practice at fighting. They were both lousy at it.

"I'll only say this once more," she said. "And I'll try to be as clear as I can. I don't think I'll ever understand why you didn't try to change his mind when you had the chance."

"That's not for me to do, Evie."

"But why?"

"No one has the right to comment on the way anyone else falls in love."

She felt like she was talking to a stranger.

"Please!" she said. "That's a fine philosophy in the abstract, but we are talking about our son. You know he's in the wrong, Gerald. Why wouldn't you tell him so?"

He shook his head. "I have my reasons, leave it at that."

"No, I will not leave it at that."

"I never told you this, because I didn't want to upset you," he began, and she felt her breath catch in her chest. She wasn't certain she could live with more secrets.

"What?"

"My parents were dead set against me marrying you."

Though they had both been gone more than twenty years, Evelyn felt hurt and indignant on behalf of her younger self. "They didn't like me?" she asked, and then smiled at how childish she sounded.

"They loved you," he said. "They thought you were dynamite. Everyone does. They didn't want me to marry you because they thought it was wrong. They said you couldn't possibly love me—that you were just trying to keep Nathaniel alive and so was I."

"But that's not true," she said.

"And over time, they came to realize it. At least I hope they did. That's my point. No one can ever know the inner parts of anyone else's marriage. It's a strange business."

"You can't possibly equate what Teddy's doing to what we did."

"Why not? I married my best friend's girl. In most people's playbooks, it doesn't get much more rotten than that."

She was startled by his words. Perhaps it was surprising that she and Gerald should have come together the way they did, but ever since, theirs had been the most ordinary of marriages. Maybe the way they met was still the most interesting thing about them, but it had happened so long ago. Since then, Gerald had fought in a war and returned home unscathed to become one of the top men in his firm. She had taught hundreds of students. Their son had come into being, and both their grandchildren.

From time to time, she had imagined what her life would have been like had Nathaniel lived. They would have been happy. They might have struggled with money, something she and Gerald never had to think about. They would have talked about books, and watched less television than Gerald did. Perhaps she would have had more children, though she wasn't quite sure how all that worked, whether it was decided by the mother's biology or the father's, or just Divine Providence.

But when she let her mind wander down this path, she pictured her Gerald—alone, or married to the wrong woman, someone who would only see the surface of him. And there, her imaginings would stop, for the thought of either one of them without the other simply could not be.

"It breaks my heart to think of you carrying that around all these years," she said. "Darling, you have to know you didn't do anything wrong."

"On the one hand, you're right," he said. "But on the other, I've occasionally wondered what he'll say when we meet on the other side. Will he be angry? Will he hold a grudge for all eternity?"

"I don't think there are grudges on the other side," she said.

"Perhaps not."

"What will we ever do about Teddy?"

"We've been asking each other that question for thirty years now. Teddy is a forty-year-old man. I don't think there's much we can do about him."

"But we're his parents."

Gerald said nothing.

"That woman, Nicole. I couldn't stand the way she looked at this place. Like she was just waiting for us to die so it could all be hers. She's awful."

When Gerald didn't reply, Evelyn added, "She's tacky."

"So's he," Gerald said.

Evelyn laughed. Her husband had always been able to make her laugh, even when it seemed impossible.

"I'll bet she doesn't last a year," Gerald said.

"But it's not about her, anyway. A year from now, whatever happens, the damage will be done. I can't part with the girls," Evelyn said. "What if Julie really does take them away?"

"Then you'll write letters. We'll visit them, and they'll come see us. You're their grandmother. Nothing Teddy does or doesn't do can ever change that."

She wondered if he was right. She hoped he was.

"It will all work out, you'll see," he said. "Why don't we

take a drive down to the Cape tomorrow? I know you love the ocean in the fall. What do you say?"

"All right," she said weakly. She couldn't quite bring herself to feel excited, but she was grateful that he was there to try to cheer her, and this, at least, was something.

"Perk up, kiddo," Gerald said. He extended his hand, and she took it.

"Come on, Evie. Let's take a walk outside before it gets too late."

2003

The taxi ride to JFK never looked the same twice. Delphine had made it five times in the past year with P.J., and each time she had spent a few minutes wondering if perhaps they were about to be kidnapped. Neither of them could ever say where they were.

Today was no different. The driver was African. He had the windows rolled down, the air-conditioning turned off. He talked into his cell phone in some foreign language, yelling at the person at the other end of the line.

Her own cell phone lit up. P.J. was calling. She ignored it.

"What airline?" the driver asked.

"Air France."

When Delphine discovered the truth about P.J., she went straight to a hotel. She could not stand the thought of spending one more night in his apartment. For two weeks, she lay in bed, never eating or speaking to a soul, feeling herself coming unglued. She was a middle-aged woman, but somehow she felt like a child, as if at any moment she could yell out for her father and be saved.

Her phone rang again now, and once again she ignored it.

The taxi slowed down at a red light. They were in an ethnic neighborhood she didn't recognize, packed with low apartment buildings and storefront churches. The fire hydrants had been turned on. Children splashed around in the spray.

Her phone vibrated in her lap. A text message: *What did you do to my apartment? WHERE IS CHARLIE, you crazy bitch??*

She switched the phone off, and tucked it into the pocket of her suitcase.

Inside the airport a few minutes later, Delphine passed a Muslim woman in a headscarf and smiled. She thought of how many Americans must hate or distrust her on sight, and wanted to tell her, *They hate me too, as soon as I open my mouth.*

She got her ticket from the machine and took her place in the security line. Most of the other travelers wore sweats or pajama pants. Delphine smoothed the front of her blue dress.

A man in a uniform was shouting, "Remove all shoes, jewelry, belts. Remove all shoes, jewelry, belts." Over and over again. He seemed to be getting a lot of satisfaction from telling them what to do.

Delphine took off her watch. Drawing her hand away from her wrist, she realized with a sickening sensation that the ring was gone.

She stepped out of line, then retraced her steps to the door, with her eyes on the ground. Nothing. She sat down on a bench outside and unzipped her suitcase, even though she knew it couldn't be there. She searched the entire thing and shoved her fingers into the pocket where she had put her phone. She felt cool metal, and with it came a rush of relief, but when she pulled the object out it was only a penny.

Delphine felt frantic, searching the floor a second time, getting down on her knees at the ticket machine.

Maybe the ring wasn't in the airport at all. Maybe she had lost it even earlier.

She tried to remember the last time she saw it. It had probably been hours. Had it gone down the garbage chute? Into the fireplace? Her fingers had gotten so thin that it might have slipped off anywhere. She let herself ponder insane scenarios, in which everyone was suspicious. *The doorman had been overly friendly. Perhaps the alleged father from Connecticut was actually a pickpocket and had slid it off her hand as they exchanged Charlie's leash.*

"I've lost my ring," she said to a woman now pressing buttons on the machine, but the woman didn't even turn around.

In Delphine's version of justice, all innocent parties would leave this situation with what they brought: the Jews would keep the violin, and his family would get their ring back. Now she had lost it, and what was theirs would be gone. Delphine felt sorry for P.J.'s mother, but worst of all for his father, who had saved up to buy it all those years ago.

While visiting P.J.'s parents in Ohio a few weeks earlier, the trip that had set their demise in motion, she had learned more about him in two days than she might have otherwise learned in a year. His parents, James and Sheila, were perfectly kind people, but Delphine had little in common with them. They had no books in their house. They kept the television on at all times, the voices of conservative news pundits and sports announcers a constant backdrop to every conversation. They drank too much diet soda, and ate chips straight from the bag. They had voted for George W. Bush.

She didn't want to be a snob, but their decor was incredibly tacky: bric-a-brac on every stationary surface, porcelain figures in the shape of frogs and flowers and children covered in snow and, of course, basset hounds. The walls had borders of stenciled tulips and balloons.

Sheila was a large woman who appeared to have given up on her looks. Her shoulder-length brown hair was run through with streaks of gray, like the fat that marbles a steak. She wore it pulled back with a plastic clip. She had given birth to five boys in fourteen years, always holding out hope for a girl. She was done with childbearing now, but her stomach would never return to its original shape.

Her arms were wide and fleshy. She wore baggy jeans and a Red Sox sweatshirt around the house. You could tell she had once been very pretty. She had big blue eyes and a warm smile. But she worked forty hours a week as a nurse, and still had three children living under her roof, ages ten, thirteen, and sixteen. The boys were loud and wild. The screen porch through which they entered the house was full of hockey equipment and smelled of sweat and mold.

Her husband, James, was a slim man, much shorter than P.J. He did something with ambulances, working as a dispatcher for a fleet of medics in the city. He didn't have a college degree. No one in the family did, other than P.J. and some uncle whom they all seemed to hate.

James's mother, a frail woman in her eighties, lived with them. For most of the weekend, she sat on the sunporch alone watching religious programs on television.

"How's Nana?" P.J. whispered to Sheila, looking at his grandmother through the open door.

Sheila shrugged. "Same old. Every morning when she wakes up, she has six months to live."

Delphine wasn't sure what she meant. It sounded serious, but Sheila laughed as she said it.

On Friday night before dinner, they sat in the formal living room. Sheila set down a tray of tiny hot dogs wrapped in pastry.

"I've got some mini quiches in the freezer too if you want," she said. "They just take five minutes to heat up."

"We're good," P.J. said.

The room was like a shrine to him. There was a big table crammed with snow globes he had sent from all over the world. Framed posters highlighting his accomplishments crowded the walls: the classical charts from the times his albums went straight to number one, a solo performance in Dublin with the words *Limited Engagement: SOLD OUT*

472 *J. Courtney Sullivan*

printed in red, and newspaper reviews with the most complimentary sentences highlighted in bright yellow marker. "McKeen drew everything from his instrument that a human being is capable of drawing. His playing was masterful, brilliant, otherworldly."—*The New York Times*. "Tonight McKeen was not only a master fiddler but also a full chorus of singers, from an operatic soprano to a honky-tonk belter. An outrageous talent."—*The Dallas Morning News*.

Sheila asked P.J. dozens of questions about his work, which Delphine could tell made him uncomfortable. James remained strangely silent through most of the night, as if he too were hoping for a subject change.

P.J. had told her his parents didn't get that though his fame was an exciting topic to be bragged about for them, for him it had become just a job. He said they didn't see him the way they used to, as their son. Now he was an idea to them, not a person. He was the thing they had done right, the promise they had built their world around, and he resented them for it.

Delphine wondered if they knew how much money he made. He was generous with them—for Christmas, he had sent Sheila a pair of sapphire earrings and James a big-screen TV. She thought he had probably helped them buy the house. P.J. had mentioned once that they were deeply in debt, like everyone else in America, but to her knowledge he had never tried to get them out of it.

Clearly he was their pride and joy. Their only other grown son, Danny, was a plumber living in Columbus. He made a decent salary, but he couldn't compare to P.J.

They called him by his full first name, Parker. Apparently the initials were something he had adopted in middle school, when the kids at a summer music camp made fun of him for having a fake preppy name. "What, did your mother hear that on a soap opera?" some brat had asked, and by the time school started up again, Parker had become P.J.

When they first met, Delphine rather liked his name, but over time she had come to regard it as childish. She thought he ought to go back to Parker. She sometimes wondered if he was trading on his youth too much. Every time he got written up in a newspaper, the writer would remark on the fact that he was "just twenty-four." Twenty-four was hardly young as far as musical prodigies went. But they had been writing that about him since he was only seventeen, only eighteen, only nineteen. When would he reach an age where his talents would stand on their own?

She had once been taken in by what she saw as his rawness, his honesty, and the way these traits seeped into his music. But she no longer thought he was as talented as everyone said. Nor was he raw. Everything he did was cultivated— from the odd charity concert that he'd give only if he was guaranteed coverage in the press, to the way he had built a wall between his family and himself.

James and Sheila lived in a suburb of Cleveland, in a house with a big backyard, in which an aboveground pool took up more space than seemed reasonable. The house was a good size, but too small for six people, with only four bedrooms. Delphine and P.J. would sleep on a pull-out sofa in the den.

Over dinner, James asked her, "So what's it like living in France?"

Could she sum that up in a word, or a sentence? What would he say if she asked him about living in America?

He continued, "Is everyone over there really as crazy as they say about Jerry Lewis?"

"Dad, shut up," P.J. said lightly, though he seemed embarrassed. "You know that's just a dumb stereotype, right?"

"It was a joke," James said.

"It's all right," Delphine said. "Most of my knowledge of America came from watching *I Love Lucy* on television."

They laughed, everyone easing up a bit.

Sheila said, "The ring looks pretty on you. You have such long, skinny fingers."

Delphine looked down at it, feeling self-conscious. It was Sheila's ring, really.

"Do you snag it on things a lot?" Sheila asked. "I had to stop wearing it because it was always getting caught on stuff."

"Yes!" Delphine said. "I'm a left-hand writer, so I use that hand quite a bit."

"We say 'lefty,' " P.J. said.

James smiled and shook his head, like she was an adorable yet stupid child. " 'Left-hand writer,' " he repeated.

They all drank a lot. The wine was dreadful, but she gulped it down as if it were the best she'd ever had.

Sheila cleared the plates and P.J. rose to help her. Delphine wasn't sure if she should also help. She stood up, but Sheila said, "You're a guest! Sit!"

Delphine did as she said, still wondering what was really expected as she watched them carry the dishes into the kitchen. Americans so often said one thing when they wanted another.

James was telling her that his dog, Frank, had been listless all week. "Even for a basset hound," he said with a laugh. "I may have to bring him to the vet tomorrow."

Delphine nodded, but her ear was trained on what was being said in the next room. She could hear the heat in their voices, but not the words. And then suddenly their volume increased just enough so that she could make out Sheila saying, "I gave you that ring for Shannon. Not some foreigner who you'd only known for five minutes. Suppose she goes back to her husband and takes it out of the country."

"You gave it to me to give to the woman I wanted to marry, and that's Delphine," he said. "What are you so upset about, anyway? You never even liked that ring."

"It's not that. It's not just the ring."

"What, then?"

"It's the fact that she has this husband," his mother hissed. "I don't want you to have to go through the rest of your life knowing you broke up a marriage. You're just a kid. You don't understand what it means."

A moment later, she came through the swinging door with a big smile on her face, and offered Delphine a slice of ice cream cake.

When they got into bed that night, she said, "Why did you tell your mother I was married?"

"I don't know. Because you were. Or are. It was probably dumb of me to think she would be cool with it."

"You never told me that your mother gave you the ring for someone else."

"So? I gave it to you."

"Well, why doesn't she wear it herself? I don't understand."

"My father gave her that ring to prove something to himself. It was a stupid thing for him to spend money on when they had none, my mother always thought so. He traded in this old car to buy it. She wore it because she thought it would do something for him—make him feel like more of a man. When they were just kids, he gave her a flat ring that cost nothing, so she could wear it to work at the hospital. That was the ring she loved, not this. This ring is for a totally different kind of woman. Someone like you."

She realized that he felt fine giving her a ring that was

meant for someone else because he saw it as just an object. It was the same reason he could buy the Stradivarius and never wonder whether the Nazis had killed for it.

They lay in bed without touching. Delphine couldn't sleep. She stared at a photo on the wall, in a frame with the words HOME SWEET HOME running around the border. The picture was of a tiny, gray house on the corner of a crowded street. In the background, you could make out a car on cement blocks sitting on the next-door neighbor's lawn.

Sometime after two a.m. she got up for a glass of water. James was watching television in the darkened living room. When she saw him there, she turned to go, but he had seen her too, and said, "Come in."

There were five empty beer bottles lined up like tin soldiers at the base of his chair. He held another in his hand.

P.J. had told her that for as long as he could remember, his father had been a drinker. Not quite a drunk, he said. But close.

"Sit down," James said.

She sat on the sofa, looked toward the TV.

"*Frasier,*" he said. "That's the name of the show. It's set in Seattle. Ever been?"

"No," she said.

"Me neither. They say it's the best place on earth to have a heart attack. CPR is a public high school graduation requirement there."

"Oh."

"That or a casino," he said. "In the casinos, you're on camera and someone's watching you every second. You collapse, somebody's going to notice."

"Huh."

"Sorry, it's just boring paramedic stuff," he said.

"It's not boring."

"I was part of the first generation. It turns out now that

a lot of the things we did back then were wrong. We'd
intubate a cardiac arrest patient. Now they say that's the
worst thing you can do. CPR was completely different then.
There were a lot more ventilations. In some cases, we were
hyperventilating people. It kind of haunts you to think
about it. All the patients you thought you were saving, but
you weren't."

"You must have seen so many awful things," she said.
"Did they have some way of helping you cope?"

"Nowadays we have therapists on staff to talk to the
guys. But when I was in the truck, you coped by going to
the bar at the Ground Round after your shift was over and
sticking your head under the tap."

They sat in silence for a few minutes, until a commercial
for denture cream came on.

"Let's hope this isn't the year I start needing that stuff,"
he said.

"Pardon?"

"It's my birthday."

"Oh, that's right, it's past midnight!" she said. "Happy
birthday."

He waved her off, as if he hadn't been the one to bring
it up.

"I hate birthdays," he said. "Fifty years old. Christ."

Delphine was shocked to hear his age. He was six years
younger than Henri.

There was a newspaper on the coffee table, and he pointed
his beer bottle at it.

"I saved that for you," he said. "There's an article about
him in the Arts section. Ran a couple of months ago. They
called us up for a quote."

"You must be very proud," she said. The same thing people always said to her.

He swallowed hard, nodded.

"Do you have kids?" he asked, and though it wasn't impossible, the question struck her as odd.

"No."

"You want your kids to do better than you did," he said. "That's what the American Dream is all about. But it's hard when they outgrow you. It hurts like hell."

Delphine wasn't sure what to say.

"P.J. loves you very much," she said.

"Of course he does," James said. "No one said anything about love. Love's the easy part. It's just that he can't stand being around us."

"No!" she protested.

"We haven't seen him in a year."

"He's so busy," she said. "I live with him and we barely see each other."

James nodded, but seemed unconvinced.

"When the older boys were little, I used to take them to redeem cans up at this garage. This was back when we lived in Massachusetts. They loved it. The two of them got to split whatever measly amount of money they made. Parker started going into Boston for violin when he was eight, and about two months into it, he was too good for the cans. He'd duck down in the backseat while Danny and I went in."

She frowned. "Kids," she said.

"That was nothing. Do you know he was on Johnny Carson when he was twelve? After that it all started happening so fast. He never really wanted us around. We embarrassed him."

"I'm sure that's not true," she said.

"The worst part was that at the same time he was embarrassed of where he came from, he started using us as a story he could tell. Poor kid from a bad family made good."

"I know that's not how he thinks," she said. "If anything, it's Marcy, his manager, pushing all of that."

"Right. His manager. These big important people came in and took over. And we let them. We thought that was the best thing for him. When he was really small, I used to dream of him becoming something one day. Now that he's become something, I dream about back then, when he was just a sweet boy who adored his dad."

"Everyone has to grow up," she said.

"Sure. But let me ask you: What do you say to your kid after he has performed for the emperor of Japan and you've never even been to California?"

He drank down what remained in the bottle, then got to his feet. "I'm sorry. I don't know why I went off like that. I shouldn't have."

"It's okay."

"Naw, it's not," he said. "This is why I hate birthdays. They get you thinking about your life in such a way. I know he had to give up a lot for his dreams, but what about us? My wife and I grew up in this town outside of Boston, all our friends are there, and Sheila's family. We uprooted our whole lives and came here so he could study in a prestigious place with a teacher who wanted him. Me in Cleveland? It's like, well—maybe it's a little like you in Cleveland."

She smiled. "Why didn't you go back to Massachusetts once he left here?"

"Life has a certain momentum. You get attached, even when you don't plan on it. The younger boys haven't ever known anyplace but this. We've got steady jobs here." He trailed off. "I'm gonna get one more beer before I turn in. Do you want anything?"

"No thank you," she said. "I think I'm ready for bed."

"All right then. See you in the morning. And hey, don't worry about Sheila. She's just protective, that's all. I'm sure you make a great couple."

Delphine finally fell asleep sometime around four. She

awoke several hours later to the sound of a commotion outside.

P.J. slowly opened his eyes.

"What the hell?" he said.

They looked out the window to investigate, last night's problems evidently behind them. In the driveway, James was swinging Sheila in the air, never mind that she probably outweighed him by fifty pounds. They stood in front of a big red car that looked straight out of an American film from the fifties.

P.J. had spoken of bitter fights between his parents, but they seemed happy together, still in love after so many years. Maybe this was why he so often spoke harshly to her—in his world, words had no weight.

"Jesus," P.J. said, looking out at them. "That looks just like the car he gave up, the one I told you about last night."

They would soon learn that it was the very same car. Sheila had somehow tracked it down and bought it back for her husband as a birthday present. P.J. had mentioned his parents' credit card debt. Delphine wondered if they could even afford the car, but she thought better than to ask.

"It's so romantic," was all she said while they discussed it over breakfast.

James kissed his wife on the cheek, looking young and happy. "It's the best gift I've ever heard of in my life."

On the way back to New York, Delphine made the mistake of telling P.J. what his father had said the night before.

"We should try to see them more," she said. "I think they miss you a lot."

P.J. scoffed. "That's what he said, huh? Funny, it didn't seem to be a problem for them when I bought them that house."

"Calm down," she said.

She had been thinking as much about her own father as

James. There was this distance between him and P.J. that it seemed both had decided to just accept. But as long as they were alive, there was still a chance. Why squander it?

"My earliest memories are of my dad singing to me," he said. "He tried to get me to play guitar. Then he saw some TV show about kids who had learned violin through the Suzuki Method and decided I should try it. Turned out I was really good. I could read music right away. In the States, everybody starts off with the Suzuki Method, you learn everything by rote, you listen to a recording and you try to repeat. A good teacher makes you read the music and the notes. The first class I ever went to, we were told to look at the music. In the next class a week later, I had it memorized. The teacher saw that I had something. She referred me to this class in Boston that my parents couldn't afford. But they sent me anyway."

"They wanted the best for you," she said.

"I practiced five hours a day," he said. "I haven't had a normal life since I was eight years old. Do you get that? I couldn't relate to the kids in my neighborhood anymore, and I sure as hell wasn't like the music kids I knew. Most of them were the sons and daughters of Asian MIT professors, or famous musicians. My dad drove an ambulance. He sent me away when I was twelve. I moved out here to study with George Sennett, and as far as I'm concerned he was more of a father to me than my own father ever was. By the time they finally decided to move here, two years after I did, I didn't need them anymore."

Delphine waited until the last possible minute to go through the security line, as if waiting might somehow make the ring appear. Once she boarded that plane, the possibility of finding it would be gone forever.

But eventually the time came, and she went.

On the plane, she thought of the options she had not considered. She was alone again, and could do anything—move out west and open a Parisian spa, go to Africa and teach in some remote village. But nothing so bold had crossed her mind in any serious way. The only thing she could fathom was going back to Henri, and closing her heart to this year, as if it had never passed. Part of her wanted to return—to the shop, to their simple routines, to the city she loved, to the man who loved her.

The gold band he had given her on their wedding day was still in her purse, and had been since she left France. Delphine fished it out somewhere over the Atlantic Ocean, and slipped it onto her finger.

She had never asked him for a divorce. At first, it had seemed that she would have to do so right away. P.J. was so intent on marriage. But he soon stopped mentioning it, and Delphine felt oddly glad of that. They were engaged, that was enough. Looking back now, she wondered at what point he had known they would not last.

Had she initiated a divorce, had lawyers been hired and property divided, she couldn't say how Henri would have reacted when she called him that night from her hotel room to say that she was coming home.

As it was, he sounded relieved and not quite surprised to hear her voice. He told her he would meet her at the airport when she arrived.

Outside Charles de Gaulle, Henri's Mercedes idled at the curb. She noted that he did not come inside to help her with her bag, nor did he get out of the car when he saw her. He opened the trunk automatically, and she placed her suitcase in it. Sliding into the passenger seat, she reached for his hand. Without looking at her, he accepted her touch, even closed his fingers tightly around hers. He started to drive.

"You look thin," she said.

When he didn't reply, she asked, "How is the shop?"

"As bad as before. The Americans aren't traveling. The dollar is plunging, they're afraid to fly, and they think the French are in business with Saddam Hussein. I'm sure I would have lost the place if not for my savings."

They grew silent, both thinking, she assumed, of where the savings had come from. When they got home, he went to sleep in the guest bedroom without further conversation. Delphine woke alone the next morning to the sound of his alarm through the wall.

She found him in the kitchen a few minutes later, preparing the *tartines* and café au lait.

"We should talk," she said gently.

"There's so much to do today," he replied.

He had just reopened the store after three weeks away in the country.

Henri opened the newspaper and began to speak of the headlines, in particular the recent *canicule,* a massive heat wave which had killed thirteen thousand French people in their homes in the month of August. There had been highs between 99 and 104 degrees Fahrenheit since June, leading to forest fires and a drought that would prove disastrous to farmers. Worst of all were the stories of the thousands of people who had gone off on vacation, leaving their elderly relatives at home, which was the French way. With no air-conditioning in private homes and institutions for the elderly, many old people perished.

President Chirac gave a rare public address to the nation that morning, conceding that weaknesses in France's health system had led to the deaths. This after his return from a three-week holiday, during which he had remained silent.

"How do these people live with themselves, just leaving their weak, old relatives behind?" Henri demanded when the story came on the radio.

"It's awful," she said.

It felt good to criticize France, after a year when she had only been able to defend it. She realized that maybe he was speaking about her as much as anyone. But she had done something hideous—it was only reasonable to expect that he would find ways of letting her know he remembered.

The heat made front-page news for days. The morgues were full, so bodies were being stored in delivery trucks or buried in anonymous graves. The director general of health had resigned, and the people were calling for more resignations.

One morning, Delphine took note of a smaller story, one that no one would call a catastrophe: a 325-year-old tree at Versailles, known as Marie Antoinette's oak, had died in the drought, according to the palace gardener. Delphine wondered what happened to something as important as that once it was gone, if they would bury the tree or burn it, or chop it into mulch to feed the roses. Maybe there would be a plaque where it had stood, or maybe the land would just remain bare, with a faint scar marring the earth. Perhaps over time, something else would grow in its place.

The heat passed for good in September, and with it all the outrage and the speculation about who was to blame, and what the country ought to learn from its collective moral failure.

Delphine too escaped penalty. After three weeks of sleeping apart, Henri returned to their bed. He wrapped his arms around her. The next morning, he asked her, *"Quelles nouvelles?"* and she smiled, and ran her palm over his cheek.

Life went back to the way it had always been. Sometimes she wondered if New York was a dream.

On occasion, she thought about the ring. More than once, she dreamed that she had found it and woke up feeling hugely relieved, only to realize the truth. Delphine hoped that she had simply dropped the ring somewhere in the apartment, and that one morning P.J. might find it right there on the carpet.

For a time, she received emails and phone calls from him, all of which she ignored. She changed her email address and her phone number, and even the number at the store, which had not changed since François Dubray installed a telephone line in 1972. Her husband never mentioned the changes, or *l'Américain*, or the year they had spent apart.

Eleven months after she arrived home, Delphine gave birth to their only child, a daughter named Josephine.

1987

James steered the car onto Morrissey Boulevard. He turned the radio up and spun the dial, but every station was playing Christmas carols and he wasn't in the mood. He listened to a few verses of "Feliz Navidad" before pushing in whatever tape was already in the deck.

It was the Ides of March. "Vehicle" blared from the speakers, that opening horn solo that made you feel ten times more powerful than you would ever actually be.

He noticed the cruiser in his rearview mirror before the officer hit the siren. When the blue lights flared, his heart began to thump. There were no other cars anywhere nearby.

"Fuck fuck fuck fuck fuck," he said under his breath. So that was it, then. He pictured Sheila getting the call from the cops. He was a thief now, and he'd been dumb enough to steal from a patient, which meant that in addition to being a criminal, he would also be out of a job again.

James pulled to the right. He thought he might vomit when he had to roll down the window and act like everything was normal. The cruiser picked up speed, getting closer and closer before zooming past him.

He exhaled. Unclenched.

He was still exhausted, but he felt artificially hopped up. The ring was like a living thing in his pocket. He could swear it had a pulse.

James felt disgusted by the whole episode now. How had it even happened? Maybe he ought to mail the ring back in a plain white envelope. But mail it back to who? If he pawned it, he'd get the money, and no one would ever be the wiser. If he mailed it back, they might somehow trace it to him.

By the time he arrived at his mother's place, it was close to eight. James tested the front door, and was grateful to find it locked. He knocked, and waited, listening for her footsteps.

She came to the door in her housecoat.

"Merry Christmas!" she said. "Come in out of the cold. Take off your boots! I've already had a call from your brother."

"That's weird. It's like five in the morning out there."

"They get up early, I guess."

A stupid phone call meant so much to her, and yet his asshole brother could only manage it on her birthday and Christmas. James could hear the radio in the next room. He half wanted to stay, feeling now, as he sometimes did, the pull between his old family and his current one.

"I'm late getting home to the boys," he said. "I should get a move on. Do you want to come over and watch them open their presents?"

"Now?" she asked. "Oh no, my hair's a mess. Besides, that's something you four should do on your own."

He felt relieved. "Okay, if you're sure."

James picked up something wrapped in foil from the coffee table. It weighed a holy ton. He wondered if maybe Doris Mulcahey had stopped by after seeing him. It was only twenty-four hours earlier that he'd met her in her driveway, and yet it felt like months.

"The Oriental girl across the street brought that over," his mother said. "Wasn't that nice?"

James set the package down. "What is it? A cinder block?"

"Fruitcake, I think."

"Ahh." He kissed her cheek before heading back outside. "I'll be back at eleven forty-five to pick you up for Mass."

"Make it eleven-thirty," she said. "I want to get a seat up front."

"Okay. Merry Christmas, Ma."

She stood in the doorway and watched as he quickly shoveled the steps and the path. His back felt like it might snap in two, but he was pure adrenaline, and the rhythm of the shoveling calmed him some. When he got in the car for home, he told himself to relax. He couldn't have Sheila wondering what was up when this was supposed to be her day. He would pawn the ring first thing tomorrow, and explain the extra cash by telling her that he won some major sports pool at work. She'd be pissed that he was gambling again, but hopefully so happy about the money that she wouldn't care.

By the time he got home, Connelly had already been by and plowed the driveway. As James pulled in, he could see Parker jumping up and down through the window. He laughed.

The ring he had gotten Sheila sat in its black velvet box in the glove compartment. He pulled it out, just as he had pictured himself doing a hundred times. But now he paused. Suppose he pawned this one instead. He could give her the beautiful ring. Finally, something she deserved.

Later, he would worry that she'd be even more unsafe now, wearing that ring around town. But at that moment, he removed the flat band from the box and switched it with Evelyn Pearsall's.

He climbed the back porch steps, shaking. The dog greeted him at the door, and James patted him behind the ears.

"Merry Christmas, bud," he said.

Sheila had placed a barrier of dining room chairs under the hole in the kitchen ceiling. James looked up and could see the toilet and the sink upstairs.

"Christ," he said.

The house smelled of coffee and cinnamon buns, and when he went to the living room, the three of them were there, his family. Sheila sat on the couch in her bathrobe and slippers. The boys lay on the floor by the tree, wearing their pajamas, shaking boxes to try to figure out what they contained.

She didn't mention the fact that he was late. She just stood and hugged him and said, "Merry Christmas. I'll get you some coffee. You must be wrecked."

"Now, Dad?" Parker said, forgoing any actual greeting. "Please?"

"Just one minute." He went to the hall closet and pulled out the video camera. His show-off brother-in-law had recently gone down to Circuit City and bought an eight-hundred-dollar camcorder with a VHS tape built right in. James had the cheap kind, with the little tapes that he hadn't yet figured out how to watch. But some quiet day, he would.

Sheila returned with two fresh cups of coffee, and they sat side by side on the couch. There was nowhere in the world he would rather be.

"Okay, now," he said.

"What does your hand say, Dad?" Parker asked.

James looked down. *Evelyn Pearsall*. He had written her name on his hand. Fine fucking thief he was.

"It was the name of a patient of mine that I didn't want to forget," he said. "So what time did everyone wake up?"

"Four," Sheila and Parker said in unison, she with a tone of despair, and he with pride.

James pointed at a familiar package.

"This one looks good. Why don't you open it first, Parker?"

Sheila gave him a look, like maybe they should have started with the socks and worked their way up to the robot, but James felt like there was no good reason to wait. This would probably be his son's last year as a believer, when he had the type of faith that nothing could topple. There was something so goddamn special about that. James wished he could experience the feeling himself again.

Parker tore back the red paper slowly, making a big production of it.

"Could it be?" *A tiny rip.* "Maybe it's?" *Rip, rip.* "Oh my gosh, Mom, it's the Rolly Robot!"

And now he was dancing around the room, shaking the box over his head. Danny laughed in confusion.

"I knew it!" Parker said with glee.

"Oh you did, did you?" James said.

Sheila tapped his shoulder and whispered, "Did we forget batteries?"

Parker came over and sat at his feet. "Hey Dad, could you tell me about the drive-in movie theater again?"

It had been summertime when he first told Parker the story. They had driven by one of the old screens on the side of the road in Braintree. The theater itself had closed down years before, but no one had ever bothered to remove the screen.

"What is that big white square?" Parker asked at the time, and James had felt about a thousand years old.

"What made you think of that?" he asked now.

"I told Danny about it as a bedtime story last night," Parker said. "But I couldn't remember how your cousins got out of the trunk."

James laughed. "Well, me, Uncle Bobby, and our cousins Brian and Jon went to the drive-in. I can't remember what the movie was, but I know Jon was driving your grandma's car for some reason. You had to pay per person, and we didn't want to spend the money, so we made Brian and Jon get in the trunk outside the gates. Anyway, as soon as Bobby closes the trunk he turns to me and says, 'Let's go.' I say, 'Okay, give me the keys.' And he says—"

Parker interrupted, excited. "He said he didn't have them either! Then you realized your cousin Jon did!"

"That's right," James said. "We had to call a mechanic to get them out. It cost us fifty bucks."

"And Jon was crying in the trunk," Parker said. This was his favorite part.

"Yup."

"I won't put Danny in the trunk," Parker said in a serious tone that made James wonder if he'd been considering it.

"Good idea. Don't."

A half hour later, the kids collapsed, asleep in a heap of wrapping paper and Scotch tape.

Sheila laughed, leaning in to kiss him. "That was a great Christmas."

"Yeah."

"You'll never guess what John Travolta gave my sister," she said. "She called before you got home."

"What was it?" he asked.

"A car phone."

"What?" He had never heard of a real person having a car phone. It was the kind of thing you saw on *Lifestyles of the Rich and Famous.*

"That's stupid," he said.

"I know."

"Hey, I think we can do better than that."

"Huh?"

"There's one more present."

She scanned the floor. "There is? Where? Oh, the PEZ dispensers? I put those in their stockings."

He placed a hand on hers. "Not the PEZ dispensers." He reached into his pocket and pulled out the box. "This."

Sheila gasped. "James McKeen, what did you do?"

She took it from him and opened it tentatively, as if there were something inside that might bite her. When she saw the ring, she said sternly, "We can't afford this."

"I sold the Ford Coupe," he said.

"What?"

"I sold my dad's car and bought this, and there's money left over, too."

He wasn't sure if he should have added that last bit. Did she know how much the car was worth, and what a ring like this might go for? But Sheila only seemed stunned.

"But you can't sell the car, you love the car."

She began to cry, rubbing the tears from her cheeks.

"It's sold," he said. "So? Do you like it?"

She nodded. "Of course I do. Look at it. It looks like something a movie star would wear."

"Put it on," he said.

She slipped it onto her finger, and they both stared. The diamonds caught the glow of the lamp behind her, and sparkles of light spread out across the wall. It was the ring he should have given her in the first place, fourteen years ago.

"Will you marry me again?" he asked.

Sheila laughed. "Yes, James, I'll marry you."

For a long time, he wondered if anyone would ever come after him, wanting the ring back. But eventually, after they moved away, he stopped thinking much about it. He felt tremendous guilt, of course, but that was to be expected. He could live with it. He had done what he had to do.

It was two years later, around the same time, Christmas of '89, when he saw the brick house again. This time it was in a segment on the evening news. He recognized the place right away, and thought about that morning, thought about Maurice, who had since moved on to a management position in Providence.

It turned out Evelyn Pearsall had not left her fortune to

her son and daughter-in-law, but to her two granddaughters, who lived on the West Coast. They had visited her every summer of their lives for a month at a stretch. They were tall and blond, maybe in their mid-twenties. One of them said they had both become teachers, just like their grandmother had been. They described her as one of the most generous women who ever lived, the type who had changed the lives of so many young people for the better.

James felt tears stream down his face.

Evelyn had requested in her will that a good portion of her money go toward building a community center for troubled girls and boys in Boston. For the rest of his life, whenever he got an extra bit of cash, even ten or fifteen bucks, James would send it straight to Evelyn's House. Sheila once asked him why, and he told her that Evelyn Pearsall was a patient of his. She seemed like a nice lady. He said that maybe if he'd had someone like her in his life as a kid, he might have made something of himself.

He knew it wasn't the whole truth, but still somehow it was true.

2012

From every corner, the house was blaring. In the downstairs bathroom, May ran the blow-dryer at full blast. Her two sons sat on the staircase, fighting. In the shower, Dan sang a song from an old cartoon he once saw on *Pee-wee's Playhouse*, which he sang whenever anyone got married. It was cloying and catchy, and it always stayed in her head for days: *Everybody's getting! Ready for the wedding!*

The worst of the noise sprang from Kate's own daughter, who had been screaming for fifteen minutes straight. They were due at the ceremony location in ninety minutes and Ava had selected this moment to have the biggest fit of her life. Kate blamed May for giving her Pop-Tarts and, on the way home from the beauty parlor, Chicken McNuggets from McDonald's with a strawberry shake.

Now her daughter was writhing on her bedroom floor in just a pair of star-printed underpants, refusing the dress, which was laid out flat on the bed, with the matching shoes on the rug directly below, as if whoever had been wearing the outfit had simply melted away.

"I don't want to be the flower girl," she said through tears.

"But you've been excited about it for weeks," Kate said. "And you're going to look so pretty in the dress."

"I don't want to!" Ava screamed. She rubbed her head violently against the carpet. Strands of her braid fanned out around her scalp so that she resembled a tiny Medusa.

Despite the fact that she was an aunt three times over by the time Ava was born, Kate had been surprised about so many aspects of motherhood, the parts you could learn only by experiencing them for yourself. The hardest of these was the crying, the hysterical sobs. When Ava was an infant, Kate would sometimes cry along with her, even as she tried to calm her down. She was scared the baby would suffocate if she didn't take a breath, scared of so many things.

It had gotten easier now that Ava was a fully formed person, with words and the ability to reason. But at the moment, Kate didn't know what to do. She had never seen her daughter quite so upset.

The effects of the whiskey she had shared with Toby earlier had worn off, leaving behind a slight headache. She wished she could take a nap.

Ava lay on her back, kicking her, practically foaming at the mouth. "I won't be the flower girl! I won't!"

Kate's mother passed by in the hall, dressed in an eggplant skirt suit and heels, a cell phone pressed to her ear. She looked at Kate with the most judgmental eyes, as if Ava were having a tantrum in Mona's office during a board meeting, instead of in her own room.

Kate stuck her tongue out, which made Ava pause. "Mama, did you just stick your tongue out at Grandma?"

"Yes, I did."

Kate pulled Ava into her lap before she had a chance to start up again. Her daughter's cheeks were red and hot from crying, and Kate pressed her cool fingers against them.

"Lovey, why don't you want to be the flower girl?"

Kate imagined she might say something profound: *I don't like the idea that girls have to wear puffy pink dresses, Mama.* Or *I've decided that weddings just aren't my thing.*

But Ava sniffled, and said sadly, "Olivia said that's for babies."

"Oh. I see."

Kate had the urge to grab her niece, yank her up the stairs, and demand an apology. This was something that she'd never do to a child, though her sister May would, in a second. She took a deep breath, trying to feel calm.

"Olivia's just jealous, sweetheart. I think she wanted to be the flower girl."

Ava looked suspicious. "She did?"

"You can do whatever you want tonight, you don't have to wear the dress. But I know Uncle Jeff was really excited, and if you cancel on him, you might hurt his feelings."

She could tell she had her daughter's attention now. Kate walked to the dresser and pulled out Ava's favorite overalls. They were made of bright green corduroy, and Ava had torn a hole in the left knee, which Kate had patched over with a swatch of fabric covered in butterflies.

"You can just wear these if you want," she said. "What do you think?"

Ava shook her head. She went to the bed, and picked up her flower girl dress. "I want to wear this."

Kate took a deep breath. Crisis averted. Of course, there was still the business of the ring. She felt more certain than ever that Olivia had taken it. Was her niece trying to punish her? Would she put it back at the last minute? Or had she already done something crazy—swallowed it, or chucked it out into the woods?

Kate's mother popped her head into the room. "I just spoke to Carmen, and she said we'll find the ring at the schoolhouse."

"Who's Carmen?"

"My psychic in Newark," her mother responded, as if it should be obvious.

"What schoolhouse?" Kate said.

"I don't know. Ava's, I assume."

The only school Ava attended was a Mommy and Me class that met two mornings a week in the basement of a Mason hall.

"Oh, well, if Carmen said so, then let me just run right over there and have them open the place on Saturday night."

"Don't mock, she's usually very accurate," Mona said. "Is that what you're wearing?"

Kate looked down at her jeans and t-shirt. "Yes, I'm wearing jeans to the wedding."

"Well, you better get going!"

"It takes me five minutes to get ready."

"Hmm."

That *hmm* conveyed so much. It said, *Yes, it takes you five minutes to get ready, and it shows.* Kate remembered watching her mother put on her makeup as a child—standing in front of the bathroom mirror, or sitting in traffic, carefully applying layer upon layer, on top of her perfectly fine skin. The whole routine lasted thirty minutes or so. She couldn't imagine taking that much time every day to add something you were only going to rinse off eight hours later.

Kate helped Ava into her dress, and gently combed her curls, which looked prettier natural than they had in that stupid hairstyle anyway. Ava's hair felt stiff in places where the spray had made it clump together. Kate couldn't wait to give her a bath and watch it all swirl down the drain.

"Do you want a magnolia to tuck behind your ear?" she asked.

Ava nodded. Kate took her by the hand.

"The tree out back is blooming," she said. "Come on."

On the way, they passed the boys, still fighting on the staircase, wearing their dark suits.

"Give it to me!" Leo shouted.

"No, it's mine!" Max said.

"Fart head!"

"Puss face."

"Be careful, you two, don't fall," she said.

Boys were trouble. She'd been so lucky with what she

got. She hoped Dan could hear them too, so that he might be cured of his desire for another child.

Olivia sat out on the deck in a floral party dress, playing with her Barbies. Despite what she had said to Ava, Kate felt sorry for her. Maybe she should have asked Jeff if they could have two flower girls. She was a mother; she ought to be more thoughtful. It would break her heart if Ava were the one to feel left out.

Kate sat down beside her niece on the wooden slats, and Ava plunked down too.

"What are these?" Ava said.

Olivia looked aghast at her ignorance. "Barbies!" she said.

Ava picked one up, and stroked its plastic hair.

"Will I get Barbies when I'm bigger?" she asked.

"You can borrow Olivia's whenever she comes over," Kate said, in lieu of *Hell no, you will never have a Barbie as long as I breathe air.*

It wasn't just Olivia, she realized. Soon enough, Ava would be in school with all sorts of kids whose parents let them do and say and eat all sorts of things. The time Kate had left to shelter her was slipping away. Sometimes she wished she could put her daughter back in the womb, protect her from every bit of harm.

Kate had been scared of pregnancy, but hers was easy, as those things went. She opted for a home birth with a doula, after watching a documentary about the corporatization of hospital births. The midwife brought in an inflatable pool, which she filled with water and wedged between the TV and the sofa. Kate didn't like the sensation of her belly floating there, so they moved her to the bed.

Sixteen hours later, just after sunrise, as she stared out her bedroom window at the familiar brownstones and the blue awning of the bar across the street, Ava came into the world. Yes, it was painful, but afterward there was this rush of joy that they said you never got with an epidural. The doula placed Kate's daughter on her bare chest, and Kate felt overcome with gratitude. It was the same bed where Ava had been conceived, and something about this felt profound. Kate had discussed it with plenty of her friends in Brooklyn, and they all understood. Her sister and mother thought she was nuts.

"Giving birth at home with no drugs is like rubbing two sticks together every night so you can boil water for dinner, while meanwhile there's a Viking range in the next room," said May, who had gone three for three on the C-sections.

"Hey Olivia," Kate said now. "Speaking of borrowing stuff, I was wondering if you might have borrowed the ring from the windowsill in the kitchen. It's fine if you did. I'd just like it back for the wedding."

"I didn't take it!" Olivia said, indignant. Clearly, she had already been questioned by May, and possibly Mona, too.

"Okay," Kate said, lifting her hand. "I believe you."

There was only one possibility she could fathom at this point.

"Hold on, girls, I'll be back."

She went inside and found the jeweler's card at the bottom of the red bag. Kate was almost positive she hadn't left the ring at the store, but she figured a phone call couldn't hurt. What if it was all as simple as that—he'd pick up and say that yes, he was holding it for her, come on out and get it.

When he answered, Kate introduced herself.

"I met you a few days ago," she said. "Jeff and Toby's cousin."

She wished now that she had been more friendly at the time, but he seemed happy enough to hear from her.

"What can I do for ya?" he said.

"One of the rings isn't here," she said.

"It wasn't in the box?"

"No. I mean, the box isn't here either."

"But you had two boxes when you left."

"Did I? Okay. So I guess it's lost then."

He paused. She could picture him debating whether she was a thief or just crazy.

"I'm sorry to hear that," he said. "Isn't the wedding tonight?"

"Yes."

"I hope it turns up," he said. "It's kind of strange, actually. That ring's been lost before."

"What do you mean?"

"Well. Everything in my store is an estate piece. I collect from estate sales and private collections, sometimes police auctions. Your cousin's ring came from one of those."

Kate had no idea why he was telling her this.

"Don't worry," he continued. "I don't buy anything that comes from a horrible crime scene or anything. That one just got left in a cab and was never claimed. On second thought, don't be telling your cousin I said that. It might ruin the magic."

She wondered if he had Jeff mixed up with someone else.

"You made their rings," she said, trying to jog his memory.

"Right."

Kate shook her head. "Thanks anyway. Have a good weekend."

Back out on the porch, the girls were whispering.

"What are you talking about?" Kate asked.

"I might know where the ring is," Olivia said in a low voice. "But don't tell my mom, because it's a secret."

Kate's chest tightened. So she did have it. *No sudden moves,* she thought, as if Olivia were heavily armed.

"Where is it?" Kate asked, in a casual, just-making-conversation tone.

"I don't know."

Kate squeezed her eyes shut and counted to ten. "Please," she said.

She was now begging a five-year-old.

"I'm telling the truth, I didn't take it," Olivia said. She looked back down at her dolls.

Kate considered her options. Clearly she needed to call in the big guns. But she couldn't bear how harshly her sister treated her kids when they misbehaved. She hated witnessing it.

From inside the house, there came a crash that seemed to go on forever, followed by the sound of Max's cry.

In the bathroom, the blow-dryer stopped. Kate braced herself as she heard the door swing open, and May screamed, "What the hell was that? Leo!"

Her sister stomped toward the boys. Kate's whole body tensed up, as if she were the one in trouble. She went inside, and the girls followed. At the foot of the staircase, Leo and Max lay tangled in a heap.

Mona appeared at the top of the stairs.

"What on earth?" she said.

"Did you guys fall?" Kate asked.

"He pushed me!" Max said.

"Leo!" May pulled him up roughly by his shirt. "Go sit in the car until it's time for us to go to the wedding!"

Leo started crying now too.

"Max pulled me down," he said. "I pushed him, so he grabbed my leg and pulled me down after him."

"Are we supposed to feel sorry for you?" May snapped. "I would have pulled you down, too, if you pushed me. Why did you push him? You're the oldest. You're supposed to set an example."

502 *J. Courtney Sullivan*

Leo stamped his foot. Kate's heart raced. Her sister was lousy at defusing tension. She only managed to rile them up even more. May was average height, and, like Kate, weighed all of 118 pounds. But her children were terrified of her, even Leo, who would probably tower over her in a couple years.

"I wanted to try the Mongolian finger trap once, and he wouldn't let me."

"What the freak is a Mongolian finger trap?" May said.

"Show it," Leo commanded.

"No!" Max said. He looked at May with the sweetest eyes and said innocently, "It's just in my imagination."

"Liar!" Leo shouted. He turned to his sister. "Olivia, do you know what a Mongolian finger trap is?"

She nodded, somber. "Max almost broke my finger in it this morning." She held up her left index finger, which looked perfectly fine.

May glanced up at the ceiling. "All right, give it to me. Give it to me right now, or all three of you will have no TV for a month."

"No!" Olivia said, and she began to cry. Ava joined in, for good measure.

Max sighed. "I'm sitting on it."

"Then get up!" May said, exasperated.

He did. There on the floor was the velvet jewelry box. Kate felt her chest expand, filling almost to the breaking point with relief. She ran toward her nephew, and scooped up the box as if it might otherwise disappear.

May gasped. "Max Rosen!" she said. "You are in so much trouble. You are in more trouble than you've ever been in your life. Josh! Get out here!"

Mona descended the staircase, snapping her fingers in the air halfway down. "Carmen was right! The ring was with the children, in the house. Essentially, in a school-house."

Kate rolled her eyes.

May put a hand to her forehead. "Do you realize that we have been searching for that ring all day? Do you? You are going to be grounded until college, do you hear me? This is theft, Max. You could go to jail for this."

"I was gonna give it back," he said softly.

"You apologize to your aunt right now."

"Sorry, Aunt Kate."

"It's okay," she said. She knew she should probably be angry, but instead she felt giddy.

"You're lucky we don't call the police," May said.

Kate sighed. Her sister never missed an opportunity to blow things wildly out of proportion.

"How did it work, anyway?" Kate asked him.

Max approached her cautiously and took the box from her hands. He opened the lid. The ring was propped up a bit higher than she remembered.

"You go up to someone and you ask them, 'Hey, why don't you slip your finger into this ring?' " He spoke quickly, probably out of the knowledge that May might explode again at any second. "Then when they do, *whammo!*" With this he snapped the box shut. "Your finger is mine!"

Kate laughed, even though she knew she shouldn't. It was actually very creative. From now on, she decided, she would refer to all engagement rings as Mongolian finger traps.

May took the box from her son's hand, and said, "I need a drink. Aunt Kate and I are going out back for a while, and no one better bother us. If you want something, ask your dads."

For once, Kate agreed with her sister.

They brought a bottle of wine from the fridge, and two

glasses. May sank into an Adirondack chair, and placed the velvet box on the side table along with her drink. Their mother followed behind, and sat between them.

"Do you want me to get you a glass, Mom?" May asked.

"No, if I want one, I'll get it."

"I'm so sorry about that," May said. "Boys are seriously the devil. You have no idea."

"It's fine," Kate said. "I feel guilty now for suspecting Olivia."

"Oh, I think we all suspected Olivia," May said.

"All's well that ends well, I guess," Kate said. "I can't believe Jeff's getting married tonight."

"I can't believe he's getting married before you," May said. "There's something I couldn't have imagined ten years ago."

Kate groaned.

"Marriage is different now, you know," May said. "You can't judge it on those terms."

"What terms?"

May shrugged. She picked up the velvet box again, and lifted the lid.

"Hmm. Pretty gay design, but that's a honking stone."

"Is it?" Kate asked.

Her sister made a familiar face that took her a moment to place—it was the same one Olivia had made when Ava asked what Barbies were.

"I think Jeff said each is a little over a carat," Kate said.

May looked down at her own ring. "I'm gonna need an upgrade soon. A lot of the women in our neighborhood do it on their tenth anniversaries. The original stone becomes a baguette, and then they add a much bigger one in the middle, and a second, smaller stone on the other side."

"That's clever," Mona said.

"I'd love to do my wedding over again," May said. "I'd do it all differently now. But I don't envy them that first year of marriage. The first year is the hardest."

"Really?" Kate asked. She had never heard anyone say so before.

"Oh yeah. It's scary to realize that you've just committed yourself to a lifetime with another person," May said. "I wonder if Jeff and Toby have a prenup."

"Of course they don't!" Mona said.

"Don't be so old-fashioned, Mom," May said. "A lot of couples get them now. If you make good money and stand to make even more down the line, it's a smart idea. Divorce is messy. You know that."

"Let's not talk about their divorce on their wedding day," Mona said.

Kate looked up at the blue sky, and took a long sip of wine.

They arrived at the Fairmount at six forty-five. Jeff and Toby stood in an open-air pavilion adjacent to the ceremony garden. Jeff's parents hovered nearby. While the rest of the family took their seats, Kate and Ava went to join the guys.

They looked as handsome as ever, standing side by side in their suits, holding hands.

"Ava!" they shouted in unison, when they saw her in the dress.

They were going to make wonderful parents, Kate thought. And when they had children, perhaps she'd feel less foreign in this new way of life.

"You look like a princess!" Jeff said. He looked at Kate, anticipating disapproval. "I'm sorry, but she does."

Ava got called off by her adoring great-aunt, and skipped across the yard to gather up more praise.

Kate gave Toby and Jeff each a hug. "How's it going?" she said, feeling excited in spite of herself.

"Everything's great," Toby said.

"He's lying," Jeff whispered. "You heard his bitch mother isn't coming? She was supposed to walk him down the aisle and now we don't know what to do."

"Honey!" Toby sighed. He turned to Kate. "We had planned it so that Jeff's parents would walk him down the aisle, and my mother would walk me. But it's fine. I'm going to walk by myself. I like that better anyway. It's like here I am, this independent person, about to be joined with another independent person. It's more mature."

"Bullshit," Kate said. "I'm walking you."

Both men widened their eyes.

"You? The marriage conscientious objector?" Jeff said, but he was smiling. "You're not going to turn this into a runaway-bride situation, are you?"

Toby squeezed her hand. "Thank you."

"It's an honor," Kate said.

"All right, enough of this lovefest," Jeff said. "Hand over the rings, so I can give them to the minister."

She pulled both boxes from the red bag. Toby looked at her in surprise, but didn't say a word.

A short while later, they lined up for the procession. Kate linked her arm through Toby's and he whispered, "Thank God you found it. So was it Olivia?"

"Nope. Max."

He raised an eyebrow. "You don't know how happy it makes me to hear that one of May's sons has a taste for jewelry."

"It's not like that," she said.

"Oh. Darn. Thanks for doing this," he said. "And for earlier. You're a lifesaver."

Before she had time to respond, the music started, and they were down the aisle, with Ava leading the charge, sprinkling pink rose petals wherever she walked.

The cocktail hour that followed was more elaborate than any black-tie charity fundraiser Kate had ever attended. In a field surrounded by mountains stood a beautiful three-peaked sailcloth tent, the sort of thing you'd see in an old-fashioned circus. There were tiny lightbulbs strung around the perimeter, and white Japanese lanterns inside. She knew from one of her many conversations with Jeff that the lanterns were on a dimmer switch, which would be utilized throughout the hour to create various moods.

Kate stood with her sister and brother-in-law, and Dan, who held Ava on his hip. Waiters in tuxedos drifted by them, as if on roller skates, offering trays of champagne, crab cakes, dumplings, chicken skewers, and what seemed like a hundred other things.

As darkness began to fall, she saw Jeff a short distance away and met his eye. He smiled.

"I'll be right back," she said, kissing Dan on the cheek.

Kate moved through the crowd. She could hear snatches of conversation, which sounded funny without context: *Gluten free is the new vegan, but if you ask me they're all just a way of covering up your eating disorder. . . . But even FDR wasn't FDR. The New Deal didn't save the economy, war did. And our days of war manufacturing are over. So what now? . . . She was deferred from the early admission pool, so we have to wait two more months like every othe schlub. . . .*

When she reached her cousin, they embraced. They walked a ways outside of the tent to hear each other better.

"You did it," she said.

"Yes."

Jeffrey stretched out his left hand, like it offered the only proof.

"Did I ever tell you how our rings were made?" he asked.

"No."

She wondered how long they would wait to tell him that his ring had been missing all day. It would probably only take a couple more drinks.

"We were looking for two separate men's rings at that jewelry shop we sent you to in Stockbridge," he said. "But I ended up falling in love with a woman's ring. It was unusual, because it had two big diamonds, equal in shape and size, as well as a bunch of smaller stones all around. I think it was supposed to look like a bumblebee or something. Anyway, I just fell in love with the idea of each of us wearing part of the whole. So the jeweler melted it down, separated the two stones, and made them into two identical rings. Cool, huh?"

She nodded.

"This diamond is probably over a hundred years old. Can you believe that? Look how it still sparkles. Sometimes I wonder who wore it before me. Toby and I even debated whether maybe a used ring would have some bad juju, you know—what if the other couple, or couples, who bought this thing ended up hating each other? What if their marriages were shit?"

She thought of what the jeweler had said about the ring being found in the back of a taxi. She would never tell Jeff.

It was his wedding day and she loved him, so Kate replied, "I think their marriages were good ones. I think this ring will bring you love from the ages."

He kissed her forehead. "Me too," he said.

Kate stared into the stone. She wondered for a moment where it had come from, further back than Jeffrey would let his imagination roam. Where had it been pulled up out of the earth, and by whom? How many fingers had it decorated over the last century? Most of its owners were likely gone now, their loves as impermanent as any. She sent a silent prayer out that they truly had been happy, as happy as anyone ever got to be. She took her cousin by the hand and they turned back to the party. A full moon hung over the garden, illuminating the night.

Author's Note

In 1995, De Beers Consolidated Mines broke ties with N. W. Ayer after fifty-seven years, taking their business to the J. Walter Thompson agency. Ayer was unsuccessful in its subsequent attempts to trademark the terms "4 Cs," "diamond anniversary ring," and "A Diamond Is Forever." The agency closed its doors in 2002.

Mary Frances Gerety died on April 11, 1999, at the age of eighty-three. Two weeks before her death, *Advertising Age* magazine named "A Diamond Is Forever" the slogan of the century. It is still in use around the world today.

Acknowledgments

I must start by thanking two incredible women whom I am fortunate to have in my life: My editor, Jenny Jackson, and my agent, Brettne Bloom. Both read several versions of this book with the kind of insight and generosity that is the stuff of writers' dreams.

I set out to write a novel about worlds unknown to me—the world of paramedics, the world of classical music, the world of advertising in the nineteen forties, and so on. To get them right, I conducted dozens of interviews. Throughout the process, I felt overwhelmed with gratitude for the many people who were kind enough to share their stories and expertise.

The relationship between De Beers and N. W. Ayer and Son made its way into this book after I read a remarkable 1982 *Atlantic Monthly* article by Edward Jay Epstein, entitled, "Have You Ever Tried to Sell a Diamond?"

I first heard the name Frances Gerety in Tom Zoellner's brilliant book *The Heartless Stone*. Tom was generous with his time and knowledge. Portions of his book also informed the story of the work Kate and her colleagues do on African diamond mines and the Kimberley Process.

Many people helped me create a portrait of Frances Gerety. I am grateful to her former Ayer coworkers who shared their recollections of both the woman and the agency. Thank you to Howard and Hana Davis, Deanne Dunning, Peter Elder, Jeff Odiorne, Margaret Sanders, Tricia Kenney, and Mary Lou Quinlan. And to Ted Regan and Chet Harrington, who invited me to Merion Golf Club so I could see where Frances spent so much of her free time. Wherever possible, I used the real names of Ayer employees, with their permission.

Some of Frances's words here came from an interview she did with Howard Davis. A recording and transcript of this interview are available at the Smithsonian Institution, along with other official documents about Ayer and De Beers, and full color copies of every De Beers ad from 1938 onward. The Dorothy Dignam Collection at the Schlesinger Library at the Radcliffe Institute for Advanced Study was full of fascinating personal and professional information, including the original copies of Dorothy's daily questions from men, all her letters home, and articles she wrote under the byline "Diamond Dot Dignam." The book *The History of an Advertising Agency* by Ralph Hower and the DVD, *Celebrating 50 Years of Ayer & De Beers,* created by Robert and Deanne Dunning for the 1988 London celebration, provided further illumination.

Phil Trachtman gave me background on Frances Gerety's time at the Charles Morris Price School. And Richard DiNatale helped me figure out how to gain access to vital records when I got stuck.

Just as I was completing the final draft, a gift fell into my lap, courtesy of Susan Christoffersen, who bought Frances Gerety's home in Wayne when she moved out. For two years, I had searched for the annual reports and memorandums that Ayer created for De Beers. If only I had thought to look in Susan's garage sooner! This lucky discovery enhanced the story at the last minute, and I will be forever grateful. Susan also provided me with Frances's family photographs and a tour of her house. Leslie Post, Frances's longtime next-door neighbor, joined us for tea and cookies, and shared her memories too.

I am indebted to the great violin soloist Anne Akiko Mey-

ers, who spent so much of her precious time answering my questions. Her beautiful music served as a daily inspiration while I wrote.

When it came to writing about paramedics, I had the help of several experts. Thank you to Chris Kerley and everyone at Pro EMS in Cambridge, Massachusetts, for welcoming me in and teaching me about how you train. To Adam Shanahan and Nick Navarrett, for letting me ride along. To Sara Stankiewicz Pitman, Linda Stankiewicz, and Justin Pitman for pointing me in the right direction, and providing lots of important information along the way. And thanks especially to Will Tollefsen and Bill Mergendahl, who saved me from myself more times than I'd like to admit.

The former mayor of Cambridge, Michael Sullivan; chief of the Cambridge Fire Department, Gerry Reardon; and Cambridge city manager, Robert Healy, taught me a lot about the way their city has changed over the years. Richie Sullivan gave me additional details about one-way streets and the roast beef special at Elsie's.

I received insight into the lives of French women in Paris and New York from my French editor, Marie Barbier, as well as Sandrine Cullinane, Pascale and Ludovic Blachez, Nina Sovich, and Marie Delecourt, whose blog *Paris in New York* was also a terrific resource. Brad Newfield, a guide for a company called Paris Walks, spent many hours with me, covering the city on foot, and helping me create Delphine's personal history—from the exact location of her childhood home in Montmartre, to Henri's inherited apartment, to the Jeu de Paume. After I returned to New York, I found that I had more questions, and Brad answered them all.

Thank you to David and Brenda Troy for the wisdom about Boston, to Charlie McCarthy for the lesson in Quincy geography, and to Delia Cabe, who so generously went t' the Belmont Historical Society on my behalf.

Maggie Mertens, researcher extraordinaire, took the assignment "Do research on each decade starting in 1910" and ran with it, rather than running away. A hundred years' worth of handpicked newspaper articles helped me create the lives of every character.

Marriage, a History, by Stephanie Coontz taught me a great deal about the institution and how it has changed through the centuries. And the 1970 PTA pamphlet "How to Tell if Your Child Is a Potential Hippie and What You Can Do About It" by Jacqueline Himelstein was a welcome addition to Evelyn's story.

To my second batch of early readers, who each improved the book in ways big and small, thank you to Kevin Johannesen, Hilary Black, Jennifer Kurdyla, and my parents, Joyce and Eugene Sullivan.

I am grateful to Kathryn Beaumont Murphy and Ike Williams for all the guidance, to Dana Murphy for the research assistance, to Danny Baror and Heather Baror-Shapiro for bringing *The Engagements* to countries around the world, to Josie Freedman at ICM for handling the film rights, and to everyone at Knopf and Vintage, especially Abby Weintraub, Sara Eagle, Kate Runde, Alex Houstoun, Jenna Meulemans, Maria Massey, and Andrea Robinson.

Finally, thank you to my officemate, Landon Sullivan Johannesen, who curls up under my desk each day, and never protests when I read lousy drafts aloud.